ELLE GRAY | K.S. GRAY

OLIVIA KNIGHT
FBI MYSTERY THRILLER

NEW GIRL
IN TOWN

PROLOGUE

"WAKE UP, WAKE UP, SLEEPYHEAD!"
She opened her eyes and glared at me as I popped a can of Spaghetti-O's and poured it into a bowl in front of her. After throwing the can away, I reached into my bag and fished out a loaf of bread. Humming to myself, I pulled a couple of slices of Wonder out of the bag and set them down on the edge of the bowl. Then I gave her a napkin and a spoon.

"What do you want from me?" she said.

"I want you to eat, silly," I replied.

"I'm not hungry."

"Of course, you are," I said. "What kind of monster would I be if I didn't know when my baby girl was hungry and made sure you had something to eat?"

"Please," she said weakly. "I want to go home."

I laughed and favored her with a wide smile. "But baby, you are home."

She shook her head as tears spilled down her cheeks. "This isn't my home—"

"Eat up, my little lollipop," I said. "I know you're hungry."

I got to my feet and walked to the other side of the room and turned on the radio. A sugary, bubble gum pop song came on. Personally, I thought it was horrible. I'd always hated my little girl's music but tonight was special and I wanted her to be happy. I wanted everything to be perfect for my Lauren.

"You always loved this song," I said. "Remember? You used to dance around to this song like a lunatic."

"I've never loved this song," she said.

"Of course, you did," I said with a laugh. "You used to play it over and over and over again. It used to drive me out of my mind. But I know how much you love it so I'll play it as much as you want tonight. This is your night, my little lollipop."

"Don't call me that," she snapped. "Why do you keep calling me that?"

I cocked my head and looked at her. "Because that's always been my nickname for you. Ever since you were a little girl. You used to love that name."

She shook her head almost violently. "I've never heard that name before. I don't know who you are," she screamed. "I've never seen you before in my life!"

I sighed and turned the music off, plunging the cabin into silence once more. I stood where I was, looking at her. She stared at me defiantly, her jaw clenched, her eyes burning with rage. She's always been a little stubborn and had a temper on her. But never like this. She's never looked at me with such unadulterated rage before. I suppose because she's a teenager now I should have expected the sort of defiance I see in her eyes. Fifteen can be a difficult year for any girl. So much pressure. So many expectations. And so much uncertainty at that age. I remember it all too well. I've always tried to make that easier on my baby girl. To let her know that I'm always here for her.

"What's wrong, Lauren?" I asked. "Why are you so upset tonight?"

"My name is not Lauren!" she shouted.

"Of course, it is," I said. "I think I know the name of my own daughter."

"I'm not your daughter! My name is Megan," she shouted. "I have no idea who you are! Why are you doing this to me?"

I shook my head. "Baby, I just want to reconnect with you. It feels like we've drifted apart and I just want to make things good between us again," I said. "I've missed you."

"Please, let me go," she said.

"Lauren—"

"My name is not Lauren!" she screamed so loud it practically shook the walls around me.

A flash of anger surged through me, and I did my best to tamp it down. I didn't want to give into my anger. I didn't want to ruin the night. But she was making it really hard to keep my own temper in check—she got her temper from somewhere, after all. I took a deep breath and let it out slowly, trying to diffuse my emotions.

"Lauren," I said. "Tonight, is supposed to be—"

"Stop it! Let me go! Let me go!"

She shook her arms, glaring at the ropes that held her in place. She's always been a willful girl and I needed to make sure she didn't run off. I didn't want her to ruin our reunion. She kicked at the table, sending the bowl of Spaghetti-O's toppling to the floor. It hit with a loud crash and sprayed the chunky red goo all over the floor. It oozed like a spreading pool of blood and all I could do was shake my head as I felt my anger rising.

"Let me go home!" she shouted again.

"I don't know why you're behaving like this, Lauren—"

"Because my name is not Lauren, you freak! Now cut me loose! Let me go!"

With a heavy sigh, I turned and walked out of the cabin and

slammed the door behind me. I stood out on the porch and looked at the darkness of the woods beyond. The moon was fat and full and rained down on the clearing around me, casting it in a silvery light. A cool breeze rustled the leaves in the clearing, making a dry, scratchy sound.

I took a couple of moments to calm myself. To get my head back on straight. I needed minute to clear my mind and focus. When I got upset, my thoughts grew fuzzy and it was hard to think. I didn't like getting upset because I valued my ability to think clearly and never lose my head in tense, emotional situations.

When I felt calm enough, I turned and walked back inside. I looked at the girl tied to the chair and frowned.

"You're wrong. You're all wrong," I said.

"What are you talking about?" she asked.

"You're not my Lauren. You could never be my Lauren," I said. "My Lauren was good. She was kind. And she didn't behave like a little monster. Like you're doing right now."

"I told you I'm not Lauren," she snapped. "My name is Megan."

I nodded. "You're wrong," I said. "And this isn't going to work."

She looked at me with wide eyes and a stricken look on her face. "Wh—what? What do you mean?"

I took a step toward the girl, my frown deepening. "No, this isn't going to work at all. You're wrong," I said. "You're not my Lauren."

Her scream shattered the stillness of the night outside, echoing through the forest until it eventually faded away.

CHAPTER ONE

O LIVIA KNIGHT SANK INTO THE SOFT CHAIR IN HER NEW office with a sigh, relishing the chance to finally have a moment to herself. Her recent move to Belle Grove, Virginia had been a stressful one, but now that she was finally settled in, she could let herself relax a little. Olivia had arranged her study just how she liked it, complete with the comfy chair, a mahogany desk to stack her books and her laptop on, a large bookshelf covering an entire wall of the room, and a slightly droopy plant in the corner. This room was the perfect place for much-needed time to relax and unwind. And she needed a quiet space given how stressful her job as an agent of the Federal Bureau of Investigation could sometimes be.

She took a sip of the coffee she'd brought into the room with her. It was late, after eleven at night, but Olivia was happy to guzzle down caffeine at all hours of the day. It didn't seem to affect her. Besides, she didn't tend to sleep much, anyway. There was always something to keep her wide awake, no matter how much of the black stuff she poured down her throat. Her own constantly racing thoughts, whether it was about work or otherwise, were enough to make her feel alert at all hours of the day with or without coffee.

Already knowing that she wouldn't be getting to sleep anytime soon, Olivia decided to get lost in one of her favorite books for a few hours. Perhaps because her brain was always firing and she was always thinking—often overthinking—everything, fiction was her refuge. It was one of the few ways in which she could escape the real world for a while. In fact, reading was basically the one time-tested thing that let her wind down to sleep. She seemed able to let her guard down when she was reading. Getting immersed in a book helped Olivia let her defenses recede until they were low enough that sleep was able to claim her.

She reached for the desk and snagged her favorite book: a well-thumbed copy of *Jane Eyre*. She settled back in the chair and slid easily back into the pages. Olivia hadn't used a bookmark when she last put down the book, but the book opened itself up to the exact page like an old friend welcoming her back. She sighed contentedly to herself and slid her reading glasses on. The big frames took up half of her small, pretty face and magnified her already big, green eyes. The glasses weren't the most flattering accessory she owned, but she'd already shed her contact lenses a few hours ago, glad to be rid of them for the day.

Not that having her glasses on mattered anyway. She was home alone; no one was going to see her like that. Visitors, expected or otherwise, hadn't been an issue for her. Since moving to Belle Grove, Olivia hadn't had a single person stop by. She knew it was mostly because she didn't know anyone in town well enough yet. Her friends from the Bureau, Sam and Emily, had promised to visit soon, but Olivia knew that life in the city kept them busy—which was the exact reason she'd moved out to Belle Grove in the first place. Her adopted hometown was an hour away from headquarters in DC and out here in a more rural community, she was able to have some peace and quiet. Olivia didn't mind being on her own out there one bit.

She allowed herself to get lost in her book for a while, drifting away from the grisly world of crime and murder she lived in every day. Working for the FBI had taken a toll on her over the years. She'd seen horrific things; things that other people only saw in their nightmares. Olivia knew the things she'd seen had changed her. Had made her different than most people. The scars she bore because of her job, both inside and out, set her apart from other people. Made her different than civilians.

Other agents understood, of course. Most of them bore the same kind of scars. Most had the same kind of nightmares. It sometimes made her feel isolated and cut off from the world. The loneliness she often felt was a part of the job that wasn't talked about very often. Agents learned to keep themselves to themselves and compartmentalize their emotions. They learned to suppress their fears and pack away the bad memories they collected. If they couldn't do that, their jobs would be impossible. Functioning in civilized society would be impossible. It wasn't that they were unemotional robots—it was just a part of the job to make sure those emotions stayed in check.

That was why Olivia loved *Jane Eyre* so much. It was a tale about a headstrong young woman who faced every challenge that life threw at her. She was abused, lost her best friend, discovered that the man she loved was married to another, and was generally handed a bad deal in life. But she persevered and got her happily-ever-after ending. Olivia smiled as she found herself approaching the end of the book for the fifth time. If Jane was given such luck, Olivia was sure that she was due for some happiness soon. One of these days.

As she finished the book and placed it back on the desk, however, she felt the slow dread of her problems returning to her. In many ways, she considered herself very lucky. She was smart, resourceful, and pretty enough. She'd had a good upbringing, attended good schools, and then trained at the FBI Academy, soon earning a sterling reputation. She'd made a name for herself in a way most of her academy's classmates hadn't. Olivia would never have to worry about money, for which she was thankful. But she had some unique issues—aside from her job—she knew not many could relate to. Olivia closed her eyes and saw her sister's face in her mind's eye. Her chest tightened as she saw Veronica's face. A tear spilled from the corner of Olivia's as she remembered her elder sibling—her *only* sibling. More tears followed the first knowing Veronica was gone.

Olivia opened her eyes quickly, forcing the thoughts of Veronica to the back of her mind and silently berated herself. The worst thing she could do was to start thinking of her dead sister before bed—unless she wanted to guarantee a long, sleepless night. She hoisted herself out of the chair, taking off her glasses and rubbed her nose where the frames had dug into her skin. She wasn't overly tired but decided to try to get some shut-eye anyway.

She walked through her new home slowly, putting off the inevitability of going to bed. The cabin creaked beneath her feet. It was a strange little place where she lived, so unlike her modern apartment back in DC. While her home there had been airy and light, this cabin was almost always cast in darkness. It was set in the mouth of the forest, deep enough to be concealed by the trees, but not so far in as to be cut off entirely from the rest of the town. One of the townspeople had told her the cabin used to belong to a forest ranger, but he'd abandoned ship several years before, allowing the forest to reclaim most of the property. Every morning when Olivia made her way to the car, she told herself she needed to clear some of the foliage, but she hadn't gotten around to it yet. Her schedule was busy enough with a two-hour round trip into headquarters every day, and often working insanely long hours. She had zero desire to spend the few but precious hours she had off attacking the forest when it clearly had a mind of its own and had decided her land was its land.

When Olivia had first announced that she was moving to Belle Grove, her friends thought she'd gone crazy. Not just because of the long commute, but because it was in the middle of nowhere. They also thought FBI agents signed up for a life of action, which to them, meant living the hectic life in the city. But Olivia had already seen her fair share of action. She could retire right then, not yet even thirty, having seen enough violence and death for a hundred lifetimes. No, this new calmer, more sedate lifestyle would suit her well. She just knew it.

Olivia made her way into the kitchen, the kitchen tiles on the floor icy cold against her feet. She poured herself a glass of water, the pipes creaking loudly with the effort of the task. The tap screeched and Olivia jumped in shock. The FBI had taught her to be paranoid and alert, and she'd heard enough screams in her day to make an unwanted connection between the two sounds. Olivia shuddered and took a breath. She definitely needed to get some sleep.

But as she made her way to the stairs, her skin tingled, and a chill ran up her spine. She was sure she'd heard something unusual. The cabin itself was noisy. It was, always creaking and moaning day and night, but the forest outside generally remained silent. Almost eerily so.

When she first moved into the cabin, Olivia had envisioned being able to hear animals in the night, or at least birds sometimes. It was something she'd looked forward to. But now that she was here, it was like the forest had been deserted. That was why it stood out so starkly when she heard it: the unmistakable sound of footsteps outside.

Her body humming with a nervous tension, Olivia tried to tamp down the fear. It was the middle of the night. There was no way anyone from the town would be stumbling around out there in the dark. Not in the overgrown, dangerous forest that surrounded her home. As she stood there listening, Olivia's heart hammered in her chest.

The sudden weight of just how alone she was out there settled deep in her stomach. If there was someone out there, someone dangerous, there was no one around to help. She took a breath and reminded herself that as an expert in hand-to-hand combat, she was far better equipped for a fight than some common criminal. She preferred it didn't come to a fistfight though. Olivia quietly crept up the stairs, trying to remain calm as she grabbed her pistol from the top of her dresser. She ejected the clip and ensured it was loaded before slamming it back home and chambering a round. Olivia didn't want to have to use it, but she would if she needed to. She really didn't want to need to.

Olivia crept down the stairs again, her hands solid on her weapon even though her heartbeat was far from steady. The sound of the footsteps was getting closer, more insistent; definitely not just a figment of her imagination. Her heart leapt into her throat when the sound of leaves crunching beneath somebody's feet sounded. She couldn't tell if it was a man or an animal out there. Whatever was out there though, was moving fast. Moving erratically. She took a deep breath and tried to convince herself it was just an animal.

"It's just a deer," she murmured. "Nothing but a deer."

The animals out in the woods were wild, unused to the presence of humans. They didn't come around when people were around, usually only coming out of the woods at night. So, it made sense there was one running around outside the cabin. She was just about to write it off as such when she heard a whimper. The blood in her veins turned to ice. The whimper had sounded like anything but an animal. It sounded human. And whoever it was, they sounded scared. Olivia's heart skipped a beat. Whoever was out there was scared. They might be hurt and they might need help. But what was the person running from?

Olivia jumped and wheeled around, weapon raised when something slammed against the front window of the cabin. She quickly lowered her weapon though, feeling a surge of adrenaline coursing through her when she saw the face of a young girl pressed up against the glass. Her eyes were wide, her cheeks stained by tears, her mouth was open as though she was silently screaming, and her face was etched with fear.

Olivia quickly pushed her own emotions down and sprang into

action. Heedless of the danger that could be lurking in the darkness beyond she ran to the front door and unlocked it. Her gun poised and at the ready, she threw the door open and scanned the darkness for any sign of trouble. If there was anybody or anything out there, Olivia had to protect the young girl. But all she could hear was the girl's quiet whimpering. She cut a glance left and right but found no sign that she was being chased—by a human or anything else. The night behind the girl was completely still.

"Are you alright? Are you being followed?" Olivia asked quickly, her weapon still at the ready as she scanned the forest around her.

But the girl just stared at her wide-eyed, trembling, seeming to be unable to answer. She dropped to her knees on the porch, sobbing loudly, her tears spilling down her cheeks. Olivia stared at her in horror. The girl was in a bad way. She couldn't have been older than fifteen, possibly younger. Her blonde hair was limp and greasy strings of it hung across her face. She was covered in dirt, her tears cutting tracks through the grime on her cheeks. She was wearing pajamas, but they were ragged and filthy, as if she'd been wearing them for weeks. She smelled as if she hadn't washed in a long time and her feet were covered in scratches from the brambles in the forest. Her face was gaunt and her body so slim that she was clearly malnourished, her bones seeming to be straining against her thin skin.

Her wrists were the worst part. They were angry red marks encircling her wrists. They were raw and there were deep grooves etched into her pale skin. Olivia immediately knew exactly what those marks were and it made her sick to her stomach—somebody had kept this girl bound by her wrists. She had been taken and held captive somewhere. Olivia swung around again, looking for signs of the person who'd been holding her. But there was nothing. No one could have been making their way through the darkened forest without making any noise. For now, at least, the girl was safe from harm.

"It's all right, it's okay," Olivia whispered gently.

She knelt down beside the girl, trying hard to keep from spooking her even more. Olivia knew they couldn't stay out there on the porch. She needed to get the girl inside to safety.

"You're okay, no one is going to hurt you now," Olivia said. "I'm going to get you home, okay? Let's get you inside…"

The girl seemed unresponsive to her. She was sitting on her back side, her knees tucked up to her chest, her arms wrapped around then, and her forehead pressed to them. The girl rocked back and forth, whimpering quietly, a sure sign of shock.

Olivia reached for her phone, ready to call for an ambulance —then cursed herself. It was still inside on the table. Her heart pounded in her chest and she forced herself to remain calm. Dealing with sit-uations like this was all part of the job, but it never got any easier seeing someone in pain.

Taking a look around her one more time, she decided there was nobody around and the girl would be all right for just a few seconds. Olivia laid her hand on the girl's knee and immediately removed it when she flinched.

"Honey, I'm going to run inside for just a second. I need to get my phone," Olivia said.

The girl looked at her with wide eyes filled with fear.

"I'll be two seconds." Olivia said. "I swear it."

Without waiting for the girl to reply, Olivia got up and dashed inside. She snatched her phone off the table then ran back out to the porch. The girl was still as she left her and when Olivia scanned the forest around her, nothing had changed. Still holding her gun in one hand, she dialed with the other then pressed the phone to her ear. It was picked up before the first ring had even ended.

"9-1-1, what is your emergency and location?"

Olivia quickly rattled off her name and address to the dispatcher. "I'm FBI Special Agent Olivia Knight have a young girl, identity un-known, who just showed up on my porch. She's in a bad way, she needs medical treatment. I think she was being held hostage."

The dispatcher fell silent for a moment. When he finally spoke, he seemed rattled. "I—I understand, ma'am," he said. "We're sending an ambulance right away."

The voice on the other end of the line was young, clearly nervous. Olivia understood how he felt. Not many people could say they knew someone who'd been kidnapped, held hostage, or put in a seriously dangerous situation. But Olivia knew from experience that situations like those weren't as uncommon as people might have thought. It was unfortunate, but she dealt with cases like this girl's all the time.

"What's the ETA on the ambulance?" Olivia asked.

"Ten minutes, ma'am."

"Great, thank you," she said.

Olivia disconnected the call and they waited for the ambulance. She was reluctant to leave her again but the girl was trembling and in shock. So, Olivia ran inside to grab a couple of blankets from the sofa. She brought them back out and wrapped them around the girl's narrow shoulders. Olivia spoke softly, trying to coax some response from her, asking her simple questions, but the girl didn't respond to a single one. She just kept herself locked in her own embrace, rocking backward and forward.

Olivia's heart broke for her. A girl so young shouldn't know such trauma. No one deserved what she'd been through but it somehow seemed even more wrong for somebody so young to have known such violence. She did her best to make the girl feel safe, talking soothingly to her as they waited for the ambulance. All the while though, Olivia kept her ears open and listened intently for anybody trying to sneak up on them from behind.

The downside of living out in the country was that it took forever for emergency services to arrive. When the flashing lights finally lit up the end of the block and the sirens filled the air, it was well past midnight. The EMT's jumped out of the ambulance and rushed over to where Olivia sat with the girl. She stood up and moved a couple of paces away. Olivia let them attend to the girl, though she felt too protective to leave her entirely.

13

"She's in shock," Olivia told them. "She's had quite the night."

"Don't worry," one of the women said kindly. "She's in good hands. Would you like to ride with her to the hospital? It might help her if you stick around. I imagine she doesn't want to be taken away by a bunch of strangers."

"All right. That's a good idea," Olivia said with a nod.

It wasn't just because she felt inclined to take care of the girl that she agreed to accompany the girl to the hospital. It was also because she suspected that this wouldn't be the last she heard of the girl's case and Olivia thought gathering whatever intel she could would be beneficial. Crime in Belle Grove was minimal—bar fights, fender benders, and small time deals like that. The local police weren't prepared to deal with kidnapping cases. Once they identified who the girl was, they might be able to connect her to a missing persons case. If Olivia knew who she was, she thought they could help the girl back to her family. And get her some justice.

The girl resisted the EMT's, kicking and moaning as the paramedics tried to get her onto the gurney. She looked to Olivia for help, her eyes wide, her face filled with fear. Olivia spoke soothingly to her, trying to keep her calm.

"It's all right, these people want to help you," she insisted gently, putting a hand on the girl's shoulders. "They need to make sure you're not seriously hurt. They need to treat your wounds. You'll be safe with them. And don't worry, I'm not going to leave you alone. I'll be with you the whole time."

The girl's eyes softened and an expression of relief crossed her face. Olivia nodded to the paramedics, who tried again to help the girl onto the gurney. She didn't resist the second time. As the paramedics wheeled it toward the ambulance, Olivia quickly locked up the house and tried to avoid the curious gazes of her neighbors who'd all come out to see what the commotion was all about.

Olivia followed the others into the back of the ambulance. She took the girl's hand tightly in her own, and gave her a small, encouraging smile. As they began the journey to the hospital, she wondered how what had been a perfectly ordinary night had turned so dark, so quickly.

As the ambulance rocketed along, Olivia let her mind wander. Someone sinister was still out there. Someone sick enough to tie a young girl up and keep her somewhere long enough that she was near starvation. Who would do something like that? Who would harm such an innocent young person?

A monster, she concluded. That was the only explanation.

CHAPTER TWO

AFTER THREE HOURS OF WAITING IN THE UNCOMFORTABLE chair in the corner of the hospital room watching the girl sleep. Olivia still hadn't slept a wink. Her eyes felt grainy and her body was sore from sitting in that chair for so long. Olivia knew she probably should have gone home a while ago and come back during visiting hours. She felt that she couldn't, even though the girl was finally safe and in good hands. She was being treated for her injuries. At least the ones on the outside. Olivia knew it was the wounds on the inside that were going to need a lot more care though. Whatever the girl had gone through was going to leave lasting scars. Those wouldn't be easy to treat.

In any other scenario, Olivia would take charge and start investigating. But at the moment, there was simply nothing she could do other than sit around wait for the local authorities to do their jobs. All she could do was try to be patient and be there when the girl woke up. The least she could do was offer her a familiar face until someone could track her family down. Olivia just hoped it wasn't her family who'd kept her captive in the first place. She shuddered and thought the fact it was a possibility that even needed to be looked into was tragic.

Despite everything she'd seen in her career, she still didn't want to imagine that parents could abuse their child that way. She'd been held captive. Those marks on her wrists proved as much. There didn't seem to be any doubt the girl had been held in terrible conditions for an extended period of time. She was lucky to have escaped and found Olivia when she did. She probably couldn't have gone much longer without food and water.

Olivia looked down at the girl for the hundredth time that night. She was attached to a drip that was slowly feeding her fluids. A tray of food lay untouched beside her bed. The girl had been sleeping ever since she arrived. Now that she'd been cleaned up and tended to, her injuries were even more obvious now. There was no sign that she'd been physically abused—they'd found no broken bones or internal injuries. But her frail, nearly emaciated body was enough evidence that she was being abused in other ways.

The scratches and bruises on her body from running through the forest would heal soon enough, but the other abuses she'd survived wouldn't be so easy. That was likely something she'd be dealing with for the rest of her life. For the short time she'd been awake, she'd been in shock and unable to speak at all. She hadn't been able to explain what had happened to her. Olivia had heard of cases where that sort of trauma could render a person mute. Or suffer from some form of permanent amnesia. She feared they might never be able to find out.

Olivia couldn't imagine what she'd been through. The girl looked even younger now that she was asleep. More frail and delicate. When Olivia thought about her own life at the girl's age, she knew she would never have been able to comprehend what the girl had endured. She'd lived in a safe little bubble with a happy family and good memories. At that age, she didn't have to worry about kidnappings and murders and all the awful things the world had to offer. She knew she'd grown up sheltered and naïve. For a time anyway.

For the second time that night, Olivia's thoughts turned to her sister. She squeezed her eyes shut and tried to shut those thoughts away. But this time, her efforts did nothing to rid her mind of Veronica. Sweet, innocent Veronica. She hadn't deserved what happened to her. No one deserved a fate like hers, Veronica least of all.

Olivia's enigmatic older sister had her whole life laid out in front of her. She had attended college in Seattle to study journalism then dove straight into a promising career working for the *Seattle Post-Intelligencer*. She wasn't afraid to chase down a story, no matter how controversial it was, and she was even starting to make a name for herself as a true-crime podcaster, bringing attention to long-forgotten cases. She was unstoppable. And when she wasn't working, she was building a beautiful home and marriage with the man of her dreams. She'd married none other than billionaire Paxton Arrington, heir to the Archton Media empire.

A wry smile twisted her lips. When Veronica had started dating Paxton, Olivia had come down hard against him. She just couldn't see what her sister saw in that arrogant, egotistical jerk. But the years softened his edges. Thanks to Veronica, Paxton gave up his life of wealth and privilege to instead dedicate himself to serving his community. That was the kind of person Veronica was. Her fire and drive truly changed people. She always had the ability to look deep into someone's soul and inspire them to change for the better.

Those years she'd spent with Paxton were spent in perfect domestic bliss. She was happy. Until...

Olivia tried to take a calming breath and banish those thoughts again, but once that train of thought started, it became nearly impossible to stop. When she thought of her sister, it was difficult to keep her emotions from getting out of control. How could she ever stay calm when such a horrific tragedy had happened to her only sister?

How could she accept that her sister had died in such a senseless and horrific way?

Tears stung Olivia's eyes; she wiped them away. She couldn't bear the thought of her sister's body lying broken and shattered behind the wheel of the car, unable to cry out for help, knowing she was dying. Did Veronica feel her life slipping away from her as the blood left her body? Did she have regrets? Things she wished she'd done? What were her last thoughts of? Paxton? Did her sister think of her? Did she wish she'd spent more time with Olivia when they were younger?

Olivia knew how long it could take someone to bleed out. It was an excruciating and horrifying way to go. There would be so much pain, so much blood... Paxton never believed the official story that she hit a patch of black ice while driving one night and careened into a ditch. He'd spent the last several years trying to prove that there was some foul play or conspiracy behind Veronica's. But as far as Olivia knew, the Seattle Police Department closed the case as simply an accident.

Olivia's eyes snapped open. Despite the terrible thoughts Vernonica's memory brought, she somehow felt calmer. Even though her sister was always on Olivia's mind, it was easier when her eyes were open. Her sister's memory didn't haunt her quite the same when she was alert and awake. It had been five long years without her. To tell the truth, Olivia and Veronica were never truly that close. They'd been on friendly terms, and they'd always get along well at family events, but they weren't best pals like some siblings often are. They didn't call each other once a week for a catch-up or feel the need to tell each other all their deepest, darkest secrets. They'd just never had that kind of relationship.

In some ways, that made it even harder that she was gone. If Olivia had known that she'd lose Veronica when they were both still so young, maybe she would have made more time for her. Because now that she was gone, Olivia could see how much light her sister had brought to the world. And maybe to a lesser extent, to her world too. After what happened, life had never been the same for her, or for her family. She knew it never would be again. Things in their family fell apart pretty quickly after Veronica died. Especially for their mother...

The door to the hospital room opened and pulled Olivia out of her head and back to the present. A heavy-set nurse entered the room with a clipboard and offered Olivia a kind smile.

"You don't need to stay, you know," he said politely, not looking at her as he checked over the girl. "She's going to be fine. She's in good hands here."

"I don't doubt it," Olivia replied. "You've all been wonderful. I just....it doesn't feel right leaving her until someone she knows arrives. I want there to be a familiar face around when she wakes up."

"I'm sure she'll appreciate that. Has anyone checked up on you? What you saw must have been pretty scary. Has anyone made sure you're doing okay?"

Olivia offered the nurse a tight smile. "I'm okay. It sounds awful, but I'm kind of used to it. I work for the FBI. Horror is kind of in the job description."

The nurse's eyes widened. Olivia was used to that kind of response when she told people about her job. They were either impressed or dismayed. She thought most people leaned toward the latter.

"FBI, huh? You must have seen some stuff," the nurse said.

"You can say that again," Olivia muttered with a weary sigh. Her sister flashed through her thoughts again, but she blinked hard and Veronica disappeared once more. "Do you guys have a coffee machine? I get the feeling this is going to be a long night."

"Sure thing. It's just down the hall. I'll be here for a few more minutes, so you don't have to worry about her being on her own."

"Thank you."

Olivia rose from the chair, feeling the weariness in every corner of her body. It weighed her down and made her feel completely wrung out. She headed down the hall and found the coffee machine and as if it could sense it, her body immediately out for caffeine. Strangely, she hadn't really felt tired until she'd started thinking about Veronica. It was almost as though her sister could sap all the energy from her body, even from the great beyond. A chill slid up Olivia's spine at the thought. She didn't believe in ghosts or anything like that, but sometimes, she could still sometimes feel Veronica's presence. It was like her sister was still somehow keeping an eye on her. It was disconcerting but sometimes comforting.

With a styrofoam cup of sludgy coffee in hand, she walked back to the girl's room. The nurse was finishing up his checks and nodded to Olivia as she stepped through the door.

"She's doing just fine. She's underfed and she was pretty dehydrated, but we can handle all of that," he said. "She'll probably need to be here for a few weeks while she gets her strength back. But it looks like she'll be okay."

Olivia sighed in relief. "That's good to know. Thank you for your help."

"That's all right. Try to rest. She'll probably be asleep for quite some time."

Olivia checked her watch. It was nearly four in the morning. She shrugged with a helpless smile.

"I'll be all right. I'll probably need to go down to the station in a few hours anyway. Coffee will get me through."

The nurse gave her a pitying smile. Olivia guessed that his profession meant he'd seen plenty of insomniacs in denial before. But he left her there without another word. She stood in the middle of the room, holding her cup of coffee in both hands and stared at the young girl in the bed before her. The girl's gaunt face would probably linger in her mind forever. That was just another perk of the job: having more ghosts than a graveyard in her mind.

Olivia's job was usually to solve a problem after it had already happened. She was there to clean up the mess then find a way to keep it from happening again. She couldn't stop the bodies from piling up. It was her job to catch the culprits, not stop them from doing bad things in the first place. She sighed. She loved her job, but sometimes, it overwhelmed her entirely.

But she'd done something good that night. She'd made sure a young girl made it out of whatever terrible circumstance she'd been caught in alive. She might not have been able to save victims before their murders or save her sister from her fate.... but for once, she was responsible for somebody getting to live. That made her feel good. Made her feel it was worth having all those hellish memories stored in her head.

It was the silver linings like that one she got from time to time, that kept her going.

CHAPTER THREE

O LIVIA MUST HAVE FALLEN ASLEEP AT SOME POINT BECAUSE she was suddenly jolted back to consciousness. She'd been dreaming about her sister. In the dream, Veronica was alive and well, laughing and joking around with someone. It felt so real. Felt as if the last four years without her hadn't even happened. The details of the dream were hazy, but Veronica had come to her clear as day. It felt more real to Olivia than real life. Then she felt a sensation like she was falling from some great height and she was suddenly awake, her neck aching from dozing on the rock-hard chair, her mouth dry.

The sun slanted in through the half-open blinds and Olivia groaned as she checked her watch. It was almost seven. She glanced over at the bed and found that the young girl was still asleep. She clearly hadn't moved at all, which made Olivia feel a little less guilty for falling asleep. She felt like a faithful guard dog, set on protecting the girl when no one else could. She knew that was ridiculous when the girl was surrounded by a team of doctors and nurses who were keeping her safe and tending to her physical wounds, but Olivia couldn't help but feel some responsibility for her. On some level she thought maybe she was trying to make up for not protecting her sister. Olivia knew that thought was silly. That wasn't how it worked. But the thought persisted anyway.

She stretched and stood up to get another coffee from the machine down the hall before returning to her perch on the hard, uncomfortable chair. Keeping a watchful eye on the girl and doing her best to keep from disturbing her—God knew she needed the rest—Olivia tried to piece together what happened the previous night. A girl running through the night, away from horrors unknown, was not a terribly unusual case. Not these days. But how did the girl escape from where she was being held in the first place? How long had she been there? Had she been taken from her home? Or had she been abducted from somewhere else before being taken to where she was imprisoned? Or was it someone in her family that did this to her?

And then there was the question of where the girl had come from. Olivia thought she probably couldn't have come from far away. In her weakened condition, she couldn't come from too far off. Not on foot. If Olivia's cabin was the first place she'd stumbled upon to look for help, she must have come through the woods. Not from somewhere in town. The cuts and bruises on her feet and legs seemed to back up that assertion. That was significant, Olivia was sure. It might give investigators some clue as to where to start looking for her captor.

But as far as Olivia knew, those woods stretched for miles and miles. Searching the hundreds of square miles of the forest for where the girl was held would be no picnic. It might even prove impossible. It was possible the person who held the girl captive knew that and relied on the fact that the forest was so vast that searching for his hideaway would be an exercise in futility.

That made her think they were dealing with a cold, calculating personality. It also made her think they were dealing with somebody who was familiar with the area. Olivia knew it would be a much simpler case if the culprit was a random, impulsive type who acted rashly. Those types were prone to mistakes making them easier to catch. But given the facts in hand, sparse as they were, she thought that seemed unlikely.

Though the girl's escape seemed like an accident. A mistake. But what if it wasn't? What if she'd been let go? But if so, to what end? Why hold a girl to the point of starvation only to just… let her go?

Olivia shook her head, trying to push out all the thoughts for now. There were too many questions without answers and she was too sleep-deprived to get her head around it all. She needed someone to bounce some ideas off. Needed somebody who could help her narrow the focus of her thoughts. Olivia hadn't expected to deal with such a terrible case so close to her new home. She'd moved to Belle Grove because she wanted a quiet life. She wanted a safe place where she could find some peace. A respite from the horrors she saw every single day.

But this case shattered the illusion that sequestering herself away in a small town would keep her hidden. Destroyed her belief that strange and terrible things wouldn't occur around her. It felt like horror followed her and she couldn't escape it. Olivia got the sinking feeling that trouble would always follow her wherever she went. She shook her head as another more disturbing thought floated through her mind. Maybe the town wasn't quite as idyllic as she had first thought.

Olivia pinched the bridge of her nose, suddenly wishing she had someone she could call. Just to talk. She didn't even want to talk about the case. She wanted to talk about something mundane. Something completely random and silly. Just something to feel normal for a moment. Normal was something she hadn't known since she started working for the Bureau and as much as she loved her job, she missed it.

She didn't often feel the need to call people up just to make idle chit-chat. But she knew hearing a friendly voice and not talking about the horrors of her world would be soothing at that moment. The trouble was, there were precious few people with whom she was close enough to call out of the blue just to talk. Her father wouldn't pick up the call. His life in the military was demanding; he was often unreachable for weeks on end. In fact, in the years since Veronica had died and Olivia's mother had gone MIA, he'd only traveled further off the grid. He was the only person left in her family she felt she could call just to talk. But it had been a long time since they'd spoken and she knew it was a stretch to think he'd be there for her now.

She supposed she could call her friends. Sam and Emily would likely both be up and starting their day at the Bureau by then. Maybe they'd pick up. But they'd want to know about the case, about what had happened. They'd want to weigh in on the investigation and pose theories. And that was the complete opposite of what Olivia wanted right then. She was craving a more tender conversation. She wanted to tell someone how overwhelmed she felt without having to say why. What she really wanted was someone she could rely on, someone in whom she could confide.

But ever since she'd moved from the city, she felt more alone than ever. She felt completely isolated and knew there was nobody she could talk to. She moved out there because she wanted a little peace and quiet but, in that moment, she regretted it. So, Olivia did what she always did—bury her feelings. She stuffed them down deep inside into that box inside her that was already bulging at the seams with as much as she'd put into it.

The door opened gently, and a police officer entered the room. The woman was soft-faced, with round features and pink cheeks that brought out the bright blue of her eyes. Her brown hair was pulled back into a tight bun—far too tight to be comfortable. Olivia almost had a headache just looking at her hair pulled back so tautly. But the woman was friendly enough. She must have come to see the young girl, but she didn't have the air of someone dealing with a potential kidnapping case.

"Morning," she started, with a nod to Olivia. "I'm here to get some fingerprints and a couple of pictures of the girl. We want to see if we can track down her family as soon as possible."

Olivia stood to shake the woman's hand then flashed her credentials. "Hi. I'm Olivia Knight with the FBI."

The woman let out a low whistle. "Didn't realize the Feds were already on this one."

Olivia shook her head. "No, I'm not here in that capacity. I'm actually the one who found the girl. But I'd like to be of use to you if I can."

"Maggie Stone, Belle Grove PD. Yes, I've heard of you, Olivia. New to town, ain't you? Not many people can sneak in and out of this town unnoticed… Everyone in town has been talking about you."

The thought made Olivia feel uneasy. She had hoped to blend into the background for once and not put herself right in the spotlight. But in a little town like Belle Grove, she was probably the most exciting news they'd had in some time. An FBI agent in their midst— some probably thought it exciting. Or at least intriguing. But this case was sure to overtake her arrival as the biggest thing to happen in recent memory.

"Well, all good things, I hope," Olivia broke the silence with an uncomfortable laugh. "As far as what happened here, I'd like to help. Make sure we find this girl's family. If she can tell us anything at all, we might be able to track down who did this to her and make sure it doesn't happen again."

"'Again'? You think whoever held her hostage might have others?"

"I mean, it's possible. The girl clearly isn't from town or somebody would have recognized her, I'd think. So, maybe others have been taken from further afield and kept under the same conditions. That's the worst-case scenario, of course. I'm just theorizing."

"Well, let's not get ahead of ourselves. I know you Feds are all doom and gloom, but things like this don't happen often around here," Maggie said with authority, puffing her chest out a little. "We're a good town, a *safe* town. We'll get fingerprints from the girl and see if we can get her to talk. We can start there."

"I'm not sure she'll be able to give a statement today. She was in a severe state of shock, and she hasn't so much as stirred since she arrived here. She needs to rest."

"Hmm... all right. Well, the fingerprints are still a must. We need to try and figure out who she is and where she came from ASAP."

"Agreed," Olivia said.

Maggie pulled an electronic fingerprinting device out of her bag and started to scan the girl's fingers. Olivia stood close the side of the girl's bed as Maggie carefully took her fingerprints. When the older woman straightened back up, she gestured towards the door.

"Comin' with? I'm sure your insights could be useful at the station," Maggie said. "And given that you found the girl, maybe you can talk to the parents when we find 'em."

Olivia glanced back at the young girl, who was still out cold. Her blonde hair fanned across the pillow and her features looked a little more peaceful. She didn't want to leave the girl on her own, but she also wanted to make sure that her family could get to her as soon as possible. She nodded to Maggie.

"Okay. I'm game."

"Good. Let's get moving. No time to waste."

Olivia quickly informed one of the nurses to contact her if the girl woke up, and then followed Maggie out to her car. Maggie sighed as she settled in behind the wheel.

"Let's get this over with," she muttered. "If I never have to deal with a case like this again, I'll die happy. Like I said, things like this just don't happen in Belle Grove"

Olivia knew how she felt. Her job could be horrific at times but seeing children hurt or in danger was always ten times worse than anything else. When vulnerable young people became victims, it just seemed incomprehensible and wrong on every level. Who would *want* to hurt a child? To make her suffer and see her crying? In Olivia's mind, it was like stepping on a puppy's tail just for the fun of it. A person who could do something like that was beyond disturbed. It made her sick to her stomach but it also made her feel determined to catch him and put him away for a very long time. Forever if possible.

They drove through the town in silence. Olivia watched the world passing by outside her window. The town really was beautiful, especially so early in the day when the sun was only just beginning to rise. Just past the hospital were neat rows of big, lavish houses. The town was starting to wake up around them. People were leaving their homes for work, taking their children to school, or fetching their morning papers from the front porch. Friendly grins were plastered on the faces of these people who were now her neighbors as they greeted each other and a new day. They were completely oblivious to the awful things that had happened in their hometown overnight. She could see the blissful ignorance on their faces.

She envied them a little.

The patrol car cruised down the hill toward the town center, just off the Potomac coastline. From atop the hill, Olivia could see the cold, black river beneath dark clouds. The view fit her mood more than the smiling rich suburbanites at the top of the hill. It was as if the further they sank into the town, the further into darkness they went. After all, the sun always shone on the wealthy.

Olivia rolled her eyes to herself. She was being too judgmental of people she didn't even know. She reminded herself that she knew all too well that life was unpredictable. Anyone could be struck by tragedy at any time, and some people hid their struggles behind their smiles. Olivia settled back into her seat and told herself to keep her mind on the case.

It was starting to drizzle as Olivia and Maggie got out of the car and headed into the station. Maggie greeted the receptionist warmly, but she seemed hurried, and Olivia couldn't blame her. The sooner they got answers, the better. Maggie hooked her digital print reader to the computer and put the wheels in motion to check the girl's fingerprints in the system…

"Hopefully this'll help. If she's a missing person, they'll ideally have uploaded her fingerprints to the database already. If she's escaped an abusive family member…. well, that's a whole other can of worms."

Olivia nodded. "We can only hope that we've found someone whose parents are missing her dearly. But at least she's safe. Whatever happened to her, we'll hopefully start getting some answers."

As the system ran the prints, they waited with bated breath. Olivia could feel her heart pounding hard in her chest. She so desperately wanted good news that she even turned to a silent prayer, though she'd given up on prayer and religion a long time ago. It hadn't worked for Veronica, or her mother, or anything else, so far. But she prayed nonetheless. She prayed that the girl would have a safe home to return to. She prayed there would be a happy ending to this tale.

"Nothing so far, Maggie," called one of the techs. "We've already searched the county and statewide missing persons databases."

"Try the federal database," Olivia offered. "Here. Can I borrow your terminal for a moment?"

The man got up and she sat down, pulled up the appropriate site then typed in her access code to grant her access to the federal database. When it popped up, she stood up again.

"And…. who is this?" asked the tech with a concerned frown on his face.

"Fed," Maggie chirped. "And she's got better toys than we do." Maggie's tech sat down again and Olivia gestured to the tech to resume searching. He nodded, a look somewhere between respect and intimidation playing across his face. No sooner did he upload the fingerprints than the computer system finally dinged.

"We've got a match!" he announced.

Maggie and Olivia shared a wide grin, then both leaned in to read the screen. The picture of the girl on the database, looking happy and healthy, was almost entirely unlike the girl in the hospital room. But it was definitely her. Beside her photograph was her name.

"Amelia Barnes," Olivia read aloud. "Missing person from Seattle, Washington. Fourteen years old…"

"Seattle?" Maggie raised an eyebrow. "Then what the hell is she doing out here?"

"Beats me," replied Olivia, but already her mind was racing with thoughts of the worst.

Trafficking.

Maggie puffed out air. "Fourteen….so young. It says that she was taken from her bed in the middle of the night three weeks ago. Whoever took her managed to get inside without leaving any sign of forced entry. He or she also ensured that there was no evidence left behind. The parents had no idea she was gone until the following morning…"

Olivia had to take a deep breath to process the information. No sign of forced entry, no hard evidence left behind. It seemed clear to her that they were dealing with a professional though she would not yet rule out somebody who knew Amelia. A family member or friend of the family—somebody with a plausible reason for having access to the house.

"It sounds as if it was premeditated. The kidnapper had to have had some sort of plan, right? He or she must have gone in fully suited up. Gloves, a face mask… maybe even a hairnet. It's nearly impossible to break into a home and leave no evidence behind," Maggie said.

"It's odd and it definitely sounds like whoever took Amelia had a plan and prepared for it," Olivia agreed. "But let's not get too focused on one theory just yet. There are other possibilities."

"Such as?"

"Such as somebody living in the home already," Olivia said. "Or somebody like a family friend who had plausible reasons for being in the house. There might be DNA evidence—hair or skin—from the abductor in the house now. But DNA left by somebody who had a reason to be in that house in the first place."

Maggie nodded, her expression telling Olivia she hadn't considered that possibility. As a small-town cop, Maggie probably wouldn't have much experience with something like this so Olivia wasn't going to judge her for it. From what she was seeing on the screen though, the Seattle PD had nothing to go on. They were stumped. But then a thought floated through her mind. Veronica and Paxton lived in Seattle, neither of them had an exactly stellar opinion of the Seattle Police Department—Paxton's opinion arising from the fact that he was with the Seattle PD until recently. Even though he didn't work for them anymore, maybe he could shed some light on this case.

"It could also be that maybe Amelia left the house of her own accord, then ran into trouble along the way," Maggie mused. "You know what kids are like at that age. Always actin' out, wanting to stay out late and all. But to end up nearly three thousand miles away? That's a new one for me."

"Yeah, maybe," she admitted. "In any case, the parents must be worried sick. She's already been gone for three weeks. We need to reach out to them. Let them know we have Amelia. They might want to fly out."

Maggie nodded. "Yeah, that's good thinking," she said then turned to the tech. "Spencer, send the parents' contact information to my phone and just in case, start looking into the next available flights from Seattle."

"On it," he nodded.

"Would you mind if I called the family?" Olivia asked. "I'd like to get a sense of them."

"Sure," Maggie said. "Be my guest.

"Thank you."

Maggie rested a hand on Olivia's back. "This is good. Don't look so worried, okay? She's going to make it home safe and sound and this whole ordeal can be put to rest."

Olivia nodded again, not feeling nearly so sure. Something still felt off. The whole case seemed different now that they'd seen the girl's file. It bothered her that the kidnapper would meticulously plan the abduction of a young girl away in the middle of the night and transport her all the way across the country then be so careless as to allow her to get free?

It was possible that if the girl was a trafficking victim that whoever she was sold to was sloppy and let her get away. Not the abductor. But she didn't think somebody who spent a lot of money on a young girl like Amelia would be so careless either. There was just something off about it and Olivia couldn't put her finger on what it was.

But Olivia didn't have time to stand there and theorize. She needed to call the family. Olivia pulled out her phone and Maggie gave her the number. The first ring hadn't even finished when the call was connected.

"Hello, yes?" a woman asked, her tone tinged with desperation. Olivia pressed her phone tightly to her ear. "Am I speaking to Mrs. Barnes?"

"Yes. Yes, who is this?"

"My name is Olivia Knight," she replied. "I'm a special agent with the FBI and—"

"Oh, God," gasped the voice on the other line as if holding back tears. "Yes, this is Evelyn Barnes. Do you have any information about my daughter?"

"Yes, ma'am. We have found your daughter, and she is alive and well. She is currently in the hospital in Belle Grove, Virginia," Olivia said. "She's dehydrated, needs some food, and has some superficial wounds. But she has no major injuries. She's going to be okay."

"Oh my God!" screamed the woman tearfully in big, gasping sobs of relief. "Gabe, they found her!"

A male voice came in on the other line as the parents rejoiced and wept together. Olivia fell silent to give them their moment.

"How—how did you find her?" asked the woman.

"Late last night your daughter showed up on my doorstep. It was as if she was running from something in the woods," Olivia told her. "We got her to the hospital and ran her fingerprints through the system and they're a match."

"How did she end up in Virginia?"

Olivia sighed. This part of the job never got any easier. She gripped her phone a little tighter and looked away, trying to hide the emotions playing across her face.

"Honestly, I'm not sure, ma'am. She's been resting and trying to recover since we brought her in," she said. "We believe she was being held hostage but we haven't been able to question her just yet. As of now, she's still asleep."

The sound of the woman breaking down on the other end of the line was heart wrenching to hear. Her sobs sounded raw and painful. But at the same time, she heard the relief in the woman's voice. It wasn't often Olivia got to call with good news so she took a moment to enjoy it. But there was still a mystery to be solved.

"Oh, thank you, thank you. You don't know what this means to us. Our baby.... our baby..."

Olivia smiled as the woman took a moment to compose herself. She sniffed loudly on the other end of the line and Olivia could hear the man murmuring to her excitedly in the background. Even over the telephone line some three thousand miles away, she heard the relief in both their voices. She cut a glance at Maggie who was smiling back at her.

"I'm so sorry..." the woman said.

"It's understandable for you to be feeling emotional, Mrs. Barnes. Being overwhelmed right now is perfectly natural, it's okay," Olivia said. "I'd like to advise you to head to the airport as soon as possible. We are already arranging a flight for you and will send you that information shortly. We'll get you on the next available flight from Seattle to DC. You'll need to rent a car and take it to Belle Grove."

"I'm sorry, can you repeat the name of the town?" she asked.

"Yes, it's Belle Grove. We're about an hour south of Washington, DC," she told her. "I'm going to head back to the hospital now to keep an eye on Amelia until you're able to get here. But trust that she's in good hands and is getting excellent care."

"We can't thank you enough, agent. We're heading out to the airport right now. You're a saint. Thank you. *Thank you.*"

The call ended before Olivia could say goodbye, but she didn't mind. She was pleased the family would be reunited with their daughter. Slowly, her emotions turned to anger. There was somebody out there with the nerve to steal children away from their homes in the middle of the night. Somebody cruel enough to inflict untold mental and physical suffering on young girls like Amelia. Somebody possibly cruel enough to do even worse.

Possibly even commit murder.

CHAPTER FOUR

OLIVIA EXITED THE SEATTLE AIRPORT WITH A HEADACHE resting just behind her eyes. It had been a long flight, straight from the hospital, where Amelia and her parents had been reunited just hours ago. Olivia was there to see the moment they found each other, which admittedly brought a tear to her eye. Amelia's parents were overwhelmed, crying and hugging their daughter, who seemed comforted but oddly detached. She wrote it off to the trauma of everything she'd been through the past few weeks. What was important to Olivia was that it seemed obvious they loved their daughter. Olivia felt comfortable leaving knowing Amelia

Given that Amelia had been transported across state lines, the kidnapping was now a matter of federal jurisdiction. It was her day off, technically, and since Amelia had been recovered, there was no good reason for her to do any follow up on the case. She hadn't been assigned to it but there was still a kidnapper out there along with a pile of unanswered questions. Olivia wasn't comfortable with leaving things unfinished and unanswered. She wanted to know more. Wanted to actually close the case.

Olivia left instructions with Maggie to keep the family in town for a few days and try to get whatever information out of them she could. After that, she headed to the scene of the crime. She hopped a plane to Seattle where she planned to meet up with her brother-in-law, Paxton Arrington, to see what he knew about the case. He wasn't with the Seattle PD anymore, but she knew he had extensive contacts in the department still as well as being a resourceful man in his own right.

Paxton had agreed to meet her in a cafe in downtown Seattle, so after a difficult half-hour of trying to find somewhere to park her rental car, she half-walked, half-ran to the place they'd agreed to meet, using her phone for directions and getting turned around a few times. By the time she walked through the doors of the cafe, she was flustered. Paxton saw her and had an amused grin on his face as he stood up to greet her.

"Long night?" he asked, in his typically cocky way.

Olivia ran a hand over her hair self-consciously. "That obvious, huh?"

"No, you look *great* today," he said, his tone dripping with sarcasm.

That made Olivia smile a little. Pax always knew how to lighten a situation. He gave her a quick hug and then sat down again as she took a seat. They stared at each other for a long moment, letting the shared reason that they hadn't seen each other in a while go unsaid.

"I ordered you a coffee," he finally said. "I figured you'd need it."

"Thanks. At this point, I'm pretty sure my blood is ninety percent coffee," Olivia replied.

"Did you stay up all night?"

"I managed to get a few hours of sleep," she told him. "But to be honest, I haven't been sleeping well for a while."

"That seems like it's going around," Pax replied with a sad smile.

"I'll be fine," she insisted. She hadn't flown all the way to Seattle for a pity party. "I'm just glad Amelia Barnes is okay. You should've seen her face the night she turned up on my doorstep, Pax. I don't know that I've seen terror like that before. She was like a deer in headlights. I think she really thought her life was in danger."

"But she definitely wasn't followed?"

"I don't think so. My cabin is in the middle of the wilderness," she said, shaking her head.

"I would've heard if there was someone else in the woods."

"Hmm. Has she said anything yet? Amelia?"

"She hadn't when I left. She was in shock and still totally non-verbal. She fell asleep when we arrived at the hospital and didn't wake up until her parents arrived. I felt like I should probably give them a little time and space. They've been through a lot. Besides, I kind of figured I'd get more intel from checking things out up here."

"Let me guess," Paxton started, "Seattle PD botched the case?"

"So intuitive."

"That's why I'm so good at what I do. Knowing SPD like I do, I also figured they'd dropped the ball," he said with that cocky grin of his. "So, I had a friend who's a pretty solid journalist whose got her ear to the ground dig up some info for you. I had her look into the family as well. The parents check out. Nothing out of the ordinary came up. They're the picture of a distressed couple trying to find their only daughter. They offered a cash reward for anyone who could find her."

"How big are we talking?"

"Fifty grand. You'll be able to buy yourself something nice, Olivia."

Olivia rolled her eyes. "I obviously won't be taking a single dollar from them, Paxton," she said. "That's a lot of money for a working-class family though."

"They're not rich but they do well enough. Gabriel Barnes is a lawyer—not a big-shot or anything, but he makes good money. They've got a nice house in a nice neighborhood. I also know they've got a security system in place. And yet, someone managed to get inside without triggering any alarms."

He reached down into a bag by his feet and pulled out a file folder, which he slid across the table to her. Olivia opened it and started flipping through the pages.

"It's pretty much everything I could find about the case, the investigation so far, and the family. I got it from some of my usual sources."

"Do I want to know?"

"Definitely not," he replied with a grin.

Olivia took a sip of her coffee, hoping the buzz of caffeine would help her gather her thoughts as she flipped through the documents and photos in the file he'd given her. She skimmed the police reports, figuring she'd read them more in-depth later.

"So. Someone got into their house without triggering the alarms or leaving any trace evidence behind," she said. "Neat trick. How many entrances does the house have?"

"A front door and a back door, both of which were locked. There were no fingerprints on either of the doors, except those of the family."

"It doesn't make sense…"

"People were throwing all sorts of crazy theories around," Paxton offered, leaning forward with a mischievous glint in his eyes like he was about to impart some juicy bit of gossip. "Some people seem to think it was an inside job—as in, the parents gave their daughter to somebody to make her disappear."

"Why would they do that?"

Paxton shrugged. "Why do psychopaths do anything? Anyway, we obviously ruled that out pretty quickly. They seem like good people with good reputations and no history of domestic issues," he said. "Then people began questioning motives. Why Amelia? Did someone have a vendetta against the family? Did Amelia do something to get herself in trouble? You'll be shocked to learn the SPD ran into a dead end with that line of questioning. All in all, the Barnes' seem like a pretty normal family. Nothing popped."

"Maybe the kidnapper was in it for the money?" Olivia mused. "Maybe he or she knew there would be a big reward for finding Amelia…"

"If that were true, why did the kidnapper never call with a ransom demand?" he asked. "Or why did he not cash in the ticket to the reward money by 'finding her,'" Paxton said, making a good point.

Olivia leaned back in her chair, her brow furrowed. "Too many questions, not enough answers, too little sleep," she said. "I'm not even really sure where to start."

"You're going to get roped into it, you know. Your SAC won't be able to resist putting you on it," he pointed out. "You're directly involved with the case. You found the girl—"

"More like she found me—"

"It doesn't matter. You might have moved out of the city to enjoy a quiet life, but the trouble has literally landed on your doorstep," he said. "You're going to be lead on this case. I can just about guar-antee it."

Olivia didn't know how to feel about that. Sure, she was curious about the case. She wanted to understand what happened. She'd become invested the moment she'd met Amelia. But officially taking on the case was something else entirely. The only two leads she had were on very opposite ends of the country and neither one looked very promising. She knew if the whole thing were laid on her shoulders, it was going to get hectic."

"If anyone can figure this out, it's you, Olivia," Paxton continued, reading her mind. "I know you, Olivia. You're sharp as a knife. Just like… Veronica… was."

The pain darkened his features and she could see how much of an open wound it still was for him. There wasn't much common ground between she and Paxton but that would always be the one thing they shared. Olivia lost a sister and Paxton lost the love of his life. And some wounds are so deep they never really heal.

"Look, I know you've pulled back a little at the job since… everything," he said. "But you don't need to take a back seat anymore. You shouldn't. You're the best of the best. That was something Victoria always told me. And she'd want you to get back to helping make the world a safer, better place."

Olivia chewed the inside of her cheek, a nervous tic she'd developed since her sister's death. The inside of her mouth felt as raw as her emotions.

"I'm not opposed to the idea. It just feels like a heavy case to take on alone," she said. "I think I need another set of eyes if for no other reason than to double check my work."

"Well, if you ever need a second opinion, you know I'm around. Or I can hook you up with Blake. She's a friend of mine who works here in the Seattle field office," Paxton told her. "Honestly, you two are a lot alike. You'd get along."

"She sounds a heck of a lot more pleasant to deal with than you already," Olivia cracked with a weary smile.

"Hey, I'm not all bad," Paxton protested. "I'm starting to settle down in my old age."

Olivia laughed, but as she did, she felt her phone vibrating in her pocket and sighed. It sometimes felt like she was never even allowed a second to relax. Not even on her supposed days off. But, that was the job. She fished her phone out of her pocket and looked at the caller ID, a frown touching the corners of her lips. Paxton looked at her with a smug expression on his face she did her best to ignore.

"Would that be the big boss calling?" he asked, his tone matching his expression.

Olivia nodded. She took a deep breath and answered the phone.

"Agent Knight here."

"Morning, Knight," Olivia's boss replied.

Special Agent in Charge Jonathan James had always been gruff.

He was the skip the pleasantries and get straight to business type. But this time he surprised her when he paused for a moment before diving straight into the issue.

"You must have had quite the night," he said. "We're all indebted to you for finding the girl."

"Thank you, sir, but I really didn't do anything. She just showed up outside my home."

"You returned her to her parents in one piece. As far as the Bureau—and her family—are concerned, you're a hero."

"I did what anyone else would have done."

"Well, we appreciate it, nevertheless. But we're not comfortable closing the case just yet. There are still a lot of unanswered questions, not to mention a kidnapper still running around out there, I'm sure you already know."

"Yes, sir. I've been doing a little digging already," she told him. "I actually flew out to Seattle this morning to look around the scene a bit. I wanted to get a lay of the land."

"Well, it's good that you've familiarized yourself with the details, because I'm assigning this case to you, effective immediately, he said. "I need somebody I can count on, Knight. We have little evidence to go on, and our victim hasn't said a word yet. I've got a team already looking into possible trafficking networks or other cases that might be connected to Amelia."

Olivia nodded, even though he couldn't see her. He sighed on the other end of the line, sounding as tired as she felt.

"To put it plainly, we're not convinced Amelia is a one-off. We think there are more he's taken or will be taking," he said. "The kidnapper might have slipped up and let Amelia get away. But that doesn't mean he'll be so clumsy next time."

"Don't worry, sir. I'm on it."

"That's good, Knight. Hunt this man down before he takes somebody else's daughter," Jonathan said bluntly.

"I will, sir."

"Good. That's good," he replied. "I don't expect you to carry this case alone, of course. Belle Grove is now the center of this investigation. We believe, as I'm sure you do, that given the remote location, the girl was probably held somewhere relatively close to your cabin."

"That was my thought, sir."

"That forest is a lot of area to cover," he said. "I'm sending somebody out to assist you.

Olivia felt a little relieved to know she wasn't going to be handling the case alone. Paxton was right about her pulling back after Veronica's death. At the time, she didn't feel mentally focused enough to do her job. She was still feeling a little shaky, which was why she was glad she was getting some help.

"That's good news, sir," she said. "Anyone I know?"

"I don't think you've met Agent Brock Tanner, have you?"

"I don't think so, sir."

"He's a fine agent who does some good work. Very intuitive and observant," he replied. "He comes highly recommended for this type of case. He's sharp and I think you'll work well together."

"I'm sure we will," Olivia said, though she wasn't really sure about that.

Olivia wasn't thrilled with the prospect She didn't really feel up to trying to get to know a stranger while working the case. But at the end of the day, she couldn't afford to be picky. If her boss thought that this guy would be good for the investigation, then she trusted his judgment. Not that she really had any say in the matter, anyway. But the truth was, Olivia was self-aware enough to know she needed all the help she could get.

"He'll be arriving in Belle Grove tomorrow morning. In the meantime, see what else you can dig up out there this afternoon then get back here ASAP and talk to them. I'm sure the family is desperate to get home with their daughter. They've already spoken to local LEOs several times, but anything new you can glean from them might help your investigation."

"Understood, sir," she replied. "I'll get on it."

"Thank you, Knight. And congratulations again on finding the girl."

He hung up before she could protest that she hadn't really done anything. She glanced up at Paxton, who was still smiling and looking very pleased with himself.

"Looks like I was right," he grinned.

"You don't have to look so smug about it," she said with a grin.

"You're right, I don't," he replied. "I should be used to it by now."

Olivia laughed despite herself. "Come on. Show me the sights."

They stood up and walked out of the café. Olivia wanted to go by the Barnes home since she felt that was the epicenter of the investigation and not Belle Grove, as SAC James asserted. Seattle is where it all began and where she felt she'd start finding some answers.

CHAPTER FIVE

AFTER CATCHING A RED-EYE BACK TO VIRGINIA, OLIVIA waited nervously outside her cabin for her new partner to arrive. Brock Tanner had texted her first thing that morning, telling her that he was looking forward to working with her and that he'd drive up to her house to pick her up. It struck her as presumptuous that he'd assume she was comfortable coming to her home. And in her experience, presumptuous people were oft en arrogant—two things she did not like.

Somehow, that made Olivia feel even more uneasy about meeting him. Aside from presumptuous and arrogant, he seemed cocksure; something else Olivia was not. She had a problem with her own confi dence at times—something that both Veronica and Paxton had talked to her about in the past. She hadn't been able to conquer that particular demon and because she sometimes had a problem with strong personalities like Brock seemed to be, she wasn't convinced that they'd be compatible working together. But, it wasn't like she really had a choice. Whether she liked it or not, Brock was going to be around for as long as it took them to close out Amelia Barnes' case.

It was early afternoon and Olivia was already exhausted. Other than a couple of fitful hours on the plane, she still hadn't had much time to sleep. Still, she'd made considerable effort to look presentable, washing her hair and letting it fall in waves down to her shoulders. She'd finally replaced her huge glasses with contact lenses although her eyes were itchy and sore from lack of sleep. She'd also covered up the dark bags under her eyes with a little makeup and changed into clean, simple dress shirt and no-nonsense slacks, her typical outfit when she was working a case. She preferred practicality over fashion when she was on the job, after all.

It still didn't make her feel prepared for meeting Brock, though. She had a feeling that he was going to be a handful. She knew she shouldn't judge a man she'd never met just because of a few texts. And the fact that he offered to come pick her up may have simply been a thoughtful gesture rather than an arrogant presumption. He probably knew she'd taken the red-eye back from Seattle and was trying to be kind. Olivia thought she was being too harshly judgmental and thought she should give him the benefit of the doubt.

But when she saw his car pulling up the slope into her makeshift driveway, she knew her first instinct had been correct. Though the windows were up, she could hear the hard rock music playing every bit as clearly as if the windows had been down. The music cut off when he stopped the engine and the door flew open. Brock Tanner stepped out of his Jeep and removed his aviator shades, flashing her a toothy grin and Olivia felt her heart sink.

Brock was a handsome man. He had Hollywood leading man good looks and Olivia knew those kinds of guys tended to be the most dangerous. He was tall, at least six-foot-three, with a square jaw and was wearing a short-sleeved shirt that showed off his athletic build and muscular arms. She took note of his eyes the second he took his

46

sunglasses off. They were honey-brown and full of mischief. Once again, trouble had landed right on Olivia's doorstep.

"You must be Agent Knight," he waved, his grin expanding.

Olivia swallowed down her trepidation and smiled as she stepped forward to shake his hand. His grip was firm, but his hands were surprisingly soft. She realized she'd held his hand a moment too long and quickly pulled hers away. He seemed to notice though and a mischievous grin crossed his face.

"Olivia is fine," she said.

"Well, in that case, I'm Brock." He grinned again. "It's good to meet you. The boss really bigged you up, Olivia. I feel like I'm working with a rock star or something."

Olivia had to resist the urge to roll her eyes. She knew he was just winding her up. He really was going to be a handful. She tightened her lips and pushed away the irritation that flashed through her.

"We should get going," she said. "We want to catch the family at the hospital. I need to ask them some questions."

"Sounds like a plan. I'll drive."

Olivia chuckled. "Of course, you will."

Brock moved around to the passenger side to open the door for Olivia, and she regained a smidgen of respect for him. Maybe he had gentlemanly manners and wouldn't be so bad after all. But the second Brock got into the driver's seat and started the car, the rock music nearly bursting her eardrums, Olivia lost all hope again. Without bothering to turn it down, Brock backed his way down the driveway faster than Olivia would've liked and sped off through town toward the hospital, following directions on his phone.

"Where are you staying while you're in town?" Olivia called out over the loud music.

She at least wanted to make some polite conversation with the man she'd be working with. Though, she thought screaming at him wasn't what she would call polite conversation. He tilted his head closer to her.

"What? I can't hear you," he called back.

Frustrated, Olivia reached out and turned the music down, which made Brock smile to himself. He was definitely winding her up.

"I asked where you're staying in town," she said in a more reasonable tone.

"Ah. There's a little B&B on the outskirts of town, I don't know if you know it? It's lovely. It kind of feels like I'm staying in a little British cottage," he said. "When I was dropping off my bags, I half expected the Queen to show up with a plate of cucumber sandwiches."

"Those are some very basic stereotypes…"

"Oh, I assure you, they're not stereotypes," he interrupted. "If British people don't have a cup of tea every two hours, they go into shock. More people die from lack of tea consumption than in car accidents every day over in England. Crazy, huh?"

Olivia felt the corners of her mouth twitch with the urge to smile at his lame jokes, but she managed to keep a straight, stoic, and totally unamused face. Brock sucked in a deep breath and grimaced.

"Wow, tough crowd," he said. "I'll let it slide though. From what I was told when I was briefed, you've had a long couple of days."

Olivia nodded. "I got a case file from a contact up in Seattle that I've been poring over. It's got some good information but nothing as far as a lead goes," she said. "And I doubt the family will tell us anything we don't already know. But from what I hear, Seattle PD hasn't been the most thorough with the case, so fingers crossed, I guess."

Brock nodded. "Well, we can be in and out of there pretty quick, and then you can get some rest. I think you need a little rest and come back to this when you're fresh."

Olivia glanced out of the window. She was definitely tired, but most of the sensation came from the feeling that there was a lot of pressure on them. She felt on edge, anticipating something bad happening the moment she let her guard down.

She hadn't always been this way. Hadn't always lacked confidence the way she did now. Her years in the FBI had taken their toll on her, of course. But it was more the chaos of her personal life that made her feel so unsettled and had stripped Olivia of her belief in herself. It was as though everything she touched turned bad. How else could anyone explain the terrible events that seemed to follow her wherever she went?

She'd never tried to express that those thoughts to anybody. She didn't want people thinking she was crazy or paranoid. She didn't want anybody thinking she was on the edge and ready to topple into an abyss of self-pity. But having Amelia show up at her house the way she had only solidified those thoughts in her mind. To put it simply, Olivia thought she was a walking bad luck charm.

As they arrived at the hospital, Olivia took some calming breaths and got out of the car. She looked away, giving herself a moment to gather her wits about her before she turned back to her new partner—temporary though he was going to be.

"This way," she told Brock, and he fell into step beside her. His strides were longer than hers and she almost had to jog to ensure that they were moving at the same speed. Brock smiled again as Olivia scurried alongside him. He was winding her up yet again. A wave of irritation rumbled up inside her. She was in no mood for his quiet smugness so she deliberately slowed her pace, forcing him to either walk beside her or go ahead on his own. He slowed down, though not without that grin she found so condescending.

When they arrived at Amelia's room, they found her parents sitting on either side of the bed, whispering gently to their daughter. Olivia glanced at Brock, and he nodded to her, silently urging her to take the lead. That smug, condescending smile was gone, as if he'd been sobered by the situation, and was all business now.

"Mr. and Mrs. Barnes," Olivia started quietly, making Amelia's parents glance up. "I don't know if you remember me, but I'm Special Agent Olivia Knight and this is Special Agent Brock Tanner. We're with the FBI and we spoke briefly after we found your daughter."

"Of course, we remember you," Mrs. Barnes replied with a smile.

"I'm sorry, Agent Knight, but we really could use some time alone with Amelia right now. You can come back to collect the money later."

Olivia blinked. "Money?"

"The reward. For finding our baby girl."

Olivia cringed. "Oh, that's not actually why I'm here. In fact, I don't want to take your money at all," she said. "I'm actually here in an official capacity. Because this case has crossed state lines, it's under FBI jurisdiction. Agent Tanner and I have been assigned to it."

"FBI?" Amelia's father asked, his forehead wrinkling a little as he raised his eyebrows. "We've spoken with the Seattle PD—not that that got us anywhere."

"I understand," Olivia said, not at all feeling thrilled about having to navigate the thorny relationship between local law enforcement and the Bureau. "As she was found here, it's fallen to me to investigate further."

"But you found her. She'll be going home with us now. She's safe," Amelia's mother said with a hitch in her voice. Olivia could tell she was still on edge. "I mean, she is, isn't she? She's safe, right? You don't think he's coming back for her, do you?"

"Your daughter is safe," Olivia insisted gently. "We're going to make sure of that. But whoever did this is still out there and we've been tasked with finding him so he doesn't do this to somebody else's daughter. I'd just like to ask you some questions. Any information you might have could really help us."

"We've spoken to the police already. More than once…"

"I understand it's frustrating, Mr. Barnes. But anything you can tell us, any detail at all, no matter how unimportant or innocuous it seems might help us catch the kidnapper and stop this from happening to anyone else."

Amelia's parents exchanged a glance with one another, and Olivia held her breath. She'd been counting on them to talk to her. They were the closest thing to a lead that she had. They seemed to be silently communicating and looked as if they'd come to a decision.

"Of course, we're happy to help you. I don't know how much help we can be, though. We've told everything to the police already. But if we can help stop this from happening to somebody else, we'd like to try," Amelia's mother said kindly. "Please, have a seat. I'm Evelyn, by the way, and this is my husband, Gabriel."

"We really appreciate your helping our baby girl," Gabriel added. "And if this can help in catching whoever did this, you can talk to us as much as you want."

Olivia grabbed a chair from the corner of the room and took a seat close to the foot of Amelia's bed. She'd dozed off again, for which Olivia was grateful. The poor girl needed the rest and it gave her a chance to speak to the parents undisturbed. Olivia glanced over at Brock to see if he was joining her, but he just gave her an encouraging smile and kept his distance. She guessed he was comfortable giving her the lead while he observed.

"So, there are definitely some things I'm curious about," Olivia started, extracting a notebook from her bag. "According to the reports I've seen, the kidnapper got into your home without triggering your alarms, forcing entry, or leaving so much as a fingerprint behind."

"That's what the police told us as well," Evelyn said. "They said they found no evidence."

"Then it seems we're dealing with somebody who's very skilled. Perhaps somebody was watching you. Getting your routines down," Olivia said. "Did you notice anybody unusual around your neighborhood? Did you see anybody who didn't belong or anybody paying any undue attention to Amelia?"

Evelyn covered her mouth with her hand, a look of fear upon her face. Gabriel's jaw clenched and his eyes narrowed. He hid his fear better than his wife.

"You think somebody was watching us?" he asked.

"It's possible, Mr. Barnes. An experienced kidnapper will usually follow a subject and learn their habits and routines," Olivia said.

"What time does Amelia usually go to bed, and what time do you both head off to sleep?"

"Amelia is always in bed by nine. We usually follow suit around eleven," Gabriel told her, his voice hard. "I got up in the night to use the bathroom and checked in on her, but she was fast asleep. That was probably around one in the morning or so, I guess."

"And when did you discover that she was missing?"

"I always get up at six," Evelyn said, her face paling a little. "I went downstairs and made breakfast. Amelia's very picky about what she'll eat. Pancakes are her favorite and one of the only things I can get her to eat, so I make them almost every morning. She usually comes down by six-thirty at the latest. She always follows a very strict routine and rarely ever deviates from it. Anyway, when she wasn't down by six-forty, I knew something was wrong."

Evelyn sniffed and Gabriel reached for her hand across the bed, squeezing it gently. Olivia offered them a compassionate smile and gave them a moment.

"I'm sorry. I understand this is hard to relive," Olivia said. "Take your time."

Evelyn nodded, taking several deep breaths. Then she set her shoulders and steeled her face, as though making a conscious choice that she was okay.

"I went upstairs to see if she was still asleep. The room was dark, and for a moment, I thought she was just tucked away under the covers. But when I switched the light on, she wasn't there."

"And what did you do when you noticed she was gone?"

"Well, I checked everywhere, of course. She wasn't in the bathroom, and she hadn't somehow snuck past me to the kitchen," she explained. "I couldn't find her anywhere, and I knew then that something had happened to my little girl."

"Did you think it was possible that she'd simply run away?"

Evelyn shook her head and frowned. "Not even for a second. Amelia is autistic and non-verbal. She gets very anxious leaving the house at any time. She would never go out alone, and she'd never go anywhere near a stranger."

"Non-verbal?" Olivia raised an eyebrow, her heart thudding.

That explained a lot. It explained why Amelia hadn't seemed able to communicate with her the night she showed up at the cabin. It also explained why she still hadn't said anything since she'd woken up. Olivia had originally put it down to shock. But now that she knew it wasn't, but was part of Amelia's condition, her heart sank a bit. She knew the girl would never be able to tell her what had happened to her.

"Yes. She's never been able to communicate anything more than a few words every now and then. She understands what you're saying when you talk to her but she never really talks back to you," Gabriel added gravely, his forehead creasing with his strain. "She would never hurt a fly. We can't understand who would want to take her away from us. Why would somebody do this to our little girl?"

"Sometimes there's no rhyme or reason to why people do these things. But the more we know, the more we might be able to piece it together and figure out who was responsible," Olivia told them, scribbling a few notes down on her notepad. "The key to this whole thing might be something that's not immediately obvious. Has Amelia ever gotten into trouble at school? Upset another kid somehow? Had anybody bully her or—"

"Definitely not," Gabriel cut her off, his tone sharp. "For one thing, she goes to a special school. She's not mixing with neurotypical kids of her own age at all, so there's no chance she's managed to somehow get into trouble with anyone. If she had, we would have heard about it immediately. Her school is very good about keeping the parents informed," he said. "And secondly, she's the sweetest kid you'll ever meet. She might not talk, but she has a good temperament. She has a good heart. Can I ask why this is relevant? You don't think some teenager at her school snatched her and dragged her three thousand miles away from home, do you?"

"I'm just exploring all avenues, Mr. Barnes. I know this is upsetting and I'm sorry. But trust me when I say the more information I can gather, the better," Olivia explained. "As far as the questions go, sometimes kids get into fights at school and the parents get way too involved. You never know. But now that you've explained Amelia's circumstances, it does seem unlikely and we can probably move on from there. How about yourselves? Does either of you have any enemies or people you might be in some sort of conflict with? Was there any bad blood between you and anybody else? A neighbor or anybody you can think of?"

Gabriel straightened up. "Well, I'm a lawyer. I guess I've had a fair share of people who don't like me much. But no one specific. And I've not received any threats."

"Evelyn?"

"I spend most of my time at home, caring for Amelia," Evelyn said. "She has needs beyond those of neurotypical children. When she's not in school, I spend all my time with her. And when she is in school, I spend a lot of time at support groups and doctor's appointments. I don't know when I'd have time in the day to make *enemies.*"

Olivia chewed her lip, the dearth of information, let alone viable leads, making her start to wonder whether they would ever get any further with the investigation. It seemed that the poor family in front of her had just been the victims of a strange, random assault. But she had to press on. She had to hope that they'd be able to tell her *something* useful. She knew most cases like these didn't usually stem from strangers. Not all the time, but a substantial portion of the time, it was somebody in their life. The whole stranger-danger thing back in the day had been blown way out of proportion.

"Okay, let's go back to how the kidnapper got inside the house. The break-in must have happened at some point between one and six that morning," Olivia said. "That's a large window of opportunity for the kidnapper to have gotten in. And speaking of windows, all of yours were closed that night?"

"And locked," Evelyn confirmed. "The whole house is child-proofed, just in case. Amelia does exhibit strange behaviors from time to time, so we have to make it as safe as possible. We check every window and door before we go to bed every night."

"Strange behaviors?" Olivia asked. "Can you explain that?"

"It's hard to explain to somebody who doesn't deal with a child on the spectrum," Evelyn explained. "But Amelia will sometimes lock herself into her room for days at a time, only coming out to use the bathroom. We have to leave food outside her door and she will only take it when we've gone back downstairs. Or sometimes, when she's feeling overstimulated or afraid, she will hide in her closet."

"Her therapist said it's a way of coping with her fear or overstimulation… she hides herself in a place she feels safe," Gabriel added, stroking Amelia's hair as she slept on the bed. "Which only worried us that much more. Whoever took her, cut her off from her one sense of comfort. I can't imagine the fear she must have felt the whole time."

"I see. And there are only two doors that could be used to enter the house?" Olivia asked.

Gabriel nodded. "We have a door that leads into the garden out back and the front door. That's all."

"Does anyone else have a key for the house?" Olivia asked. "Or do you keep a spare hidden out front? Perhaps where somebody might have found it?"

Gabriel shook his head. "Amelia's grandmother has a key, but that's it. And we don't hide a spare out front for obvious safety reasons," he explained. "We don't trust many people with things like that."

"I understand," Olivia said. "I'm just curious though, why your security system wasn't triggered that night. Did you forget to arm it? And is that something you do often? Or have you given out your code to anybody?"

Gabriel and Evelyn exchanged a look. Olivia frowned. There

was something they hadn't told her, and she had a feeling she wasn't going to like it when they did.

"What is it?" Olivia asked.

Gabriel cleared his throat. "We do have a security system, but it's... inactive. We used to arm it every night. It was part of our routine. But it went off a couple of times and after that, it triggered Amelia. She hated the noise it made when it went off and it would usually take her hours to calm down after hearing it," he said. "So, for the past few years, we just haven't bothered. We never renewed our service with the security company. We never thought it would be an issue."

Olivia nodded and jotted down a few more notes. Finally, a fact that was some bit of interest to her. If there was no active security system then someone who might have known they hadn't kept their service and was capable of picking a lock might have been able to get into the house. That meant it could have been neighbors or even somebody who worked for their former alarm company. That was casting a wide net but when she had as few facts to work with as she did, Olivia knew the wider the net the better.

"Was it widely known around your neighborhood that your service wasn't active?" she asked.

Evelyn shook her head. "No, I don't think so. That isn't something we'd bring up at the neighborhood cookout or anything."

"Right. Of course not. But that is really helpful, thank you," Olivia replied. "Just a few more questions to round this out. It interests me that the kidnapper was relatively quiet for the three weeks that your daughter was missing. From what I understand, the kidnapper never reached out to you?"

"No. We didn't hear anything," Gabriel said solemnly.

"Just to confirm, nobody ever tried to contact you regarding a ransom? Or to try and collect the reward money?"

"No. After she was taken, we waited a week and put out an appeal to see if anyone had seen her. We just kept hoping that someone would know something, but when she didn't show up, we decided to offer the reward," Evelyn explained. "We were told it wasn't a good idea. The police told us that by offering a reward and showing that we had money, it might make the kidnapper ask for more or put us all in danger. But we didn't care. We just wanted her home. We would've paid anything."

Olivia's heart ached for them. Paxton had been right about the family—they seemed to be good, ordinary people. Olivia wished that she could take them back in time and make it so that they didn't have to endure the horror and pain of the last three weeks. They'd had their worlds turned upside down, and Olivia was still no closer to figuring out why—or by whom.

She'd asked so many questions, but none of the answers satisfied her or got her any closer to the answers she was seeking. Finding the truth in this jumbled up, chaotic mess was like trying to scratch an itch that was just out of reach. She wanted to believe that she was close to something that would help crack the case wide open. That if she could just get this or that piece of information, it would reveal all the secrets. But what she felt like was that she grasped at the air and catching nothing.

"Can you think of anything else you might have forgotten? Anything you might not have mentioned to the police?" Olivia asked. "Anything at all. It might be something that seems insignificant or totally innocuous. The smallest thing might actually be of real help."

Evelyn shook her head. "I can't think of anything. Gabriel?"

"No, me either," he admitted. "I'm sorry if that wasn't very helpful but there wasn't anything odd or out of place before she was taken that I can think of."

"No, you did just fine. And I appreciate your help. I know it must be difficult," Olivia insisted. "It's just a tricky one. I'll be honest, there's a lot we still don't know, and it may take some time. But I give you my word that I'll will do everything in my power to find out what happened, who did this, and bring some peace to your family."

"You've already done enough," Evelyn said, reaching out to squeeze Olivia's hand. "You brought our little girl back to us. We'll forever be in your debt."

"Please, allow us to give you something," Gabriel said, pulling out a checkbook. "We insist on giving you the reward we offered."

"Absolutely not. I was happy to help," Olivia said, standing up and handing Evelyn her card. "But I will take your number. I'll keep you in the loop with the investigation. And if you think of anything that might help me out, please, give me a call. Day or night, I'll make sure I pick up."

Several handshakes and kind words later, Olivia was ready to leave. Brock was still leaning against the doorway, waiting for her as she filed out of the room. As they walked away, Olivia finally let herself relax, feeling her shoulders drop as some of the tension left them—though she wasn't sure why she was allowing herself to loosen up. Aside from the few small details that she'd managed to glean from the Barnes' she still felt just as clueless about the case as when she'd first entered the room.

"You did well in there," Brock commented as they walked through the hospital. "The family likes you a lot. You developed a really strong rapport in a short period of time. They trust you. I'm sure they'll call you if they remember any more details."

"I get the sense that they're a dead end though," Olivia admitted. "That must have been their third interview. I don't even know if they told us anything that wasn't already covered in the other interviews."

"Well, you asked all the right questions. No one can ask more of you," he said. "No suspects, no motive, and no evidence... it's an impossible case."

"Not impossible. Just difficult," Olivia said with determination. "I'm going to get to the bottom of it if it kills me."

"Now that's more like it!" he whooped. "I love that can-do attitude."

Olivia sighed despite his enthusiasm. "I just can't get my head around any of it. I feel like the answers we need are there but we're missing something big."

"Maybe. But we're obviously dealing with somebody smart and well prepared," Brock offered. "Don't worry though, nobody is perfect. There's a clue here somewhere to find. And we'll find it."

"Yeah, I know. It's there and we'll find it," Olivia replied firmly. "And when we do, he'll show himself. And when he does, we'll be ready for him."

CHAPTER
SIX

"EVER BEEN TO THE MOST LUXURIOUS B&B IN BELLE Grove?" Brock asked Olivia as the pair of them got back in his car.

She raised a tired eyebrow. "Gee, you move fast. I insist that you at least buy me a drink first, at least. I do have some standards."

Brock laughed raucously and even Olivia managed a small smile.

"Well, I wasn't expecting you to say that. You got me there," he said. "No, I thought you could come back to the B&B with me. We can have something to eat and look at the case notes together. Bounce some theories off each other."

Olivia checked her watch. The sun was tilting low in the sky, and she was feeling the weight of sleep deprivation from the last couple of nights pressing down on her.

"I don't know. I could really use some sleep."

She didn't add that she wasn't sure how she felt about being alone with Brock in his hotel room. She'd only just met him, after all. Olivia had never been the best at one-on-one interactions with people she didn't know well. She knew she had to work with him and not against him, but her social awkwardness paired with her tiredness made her feel like it was a terrible idea to be alone with him.

"You can take a nap in the room while I catch up on the notes. I need to get caught up on all the details," he said. "Then when you wake up, we can grab some food and talk it over. Don't worry, I won't tell anyone you're sleeping on the job."

Olivia tutted. She was finding that it was typical of Brock to turn it into some kind of joke. But she had to admit, it wasn't a half-bad idea. They had no time to lose with such an important case and she lived pretty well off the beaten track. Having him take her home only to make him turn around and come back for her seemed unnecessary and would take some time. She couldn't afford to slack off just because she was tired, but she'd feel better resting if Brock got himself caught up to speed. Then when she woke up, they could hit the ground running.

"All right, let's do it," she said.

"Good," Brock grinned, starting up the car.

The music blared through the speakers once again, but he turned it off right away. He was done messing with her, at least for the moment anyway.

"Take a nap if you want," he said. "I'll wake you up when we get to the B&B."

Olivia didn't argue with the idea, pressing her face against the cold glass of the window. Her eyes closed and she fell asleep so quickly that when she woke up again, she was jarred to discover that the world had gone completely pitch black. She was disoriented and felt lightheaded as she tried to shake off the tendrils of sleep and come back to full consciousness.

She panicked for a moment, wondering why she was still in a car and unable to see. But as her eyes adjusted to the dark, she realized that Brock had parked the car somewhere and was now sitting in the backseat of the car, reading over the case notes by the light of his phone. Olivia twisted around in her seat to look at him. His feet were propped up on the seat and he was slumped like a rebellious kid at school, his expression more serious than Olivia had seen it so far as he read the notes.

He looked up at her and grinned. "Ah, Sleeping Beauty awakes."

"Why didn't you wake me up?"

"Oh, my mistake. It's Sleepy the Dwarf."

"Brock!"

"Oops. Maybe you're Grumpy the Dwarf after all..."

"I will be in a minute if you don't tell me what I'm still doing in the car. What time is it?"

"Eleven. I didn't want to wake you up when we got here," he said. "I thought it might be dangerous, and I think maybe I was right. Not a morning person, huh?"

"It's nearly the middle of the night and I've been sleeping in a stranger's car for six hours. Yeah, I'm not in the best mood."

"Oh, come on. We're partners now. Next time, you can read case notes in the dark while I snore away," he said. "And by the way, I've never known anyone to snore quite so loud. I'm impressed, actually."

Olivia rolled her eyes, feeling completely done with Brock's jokes. She unbuckled her seatbelt and opened the car door.

"All right, let's go inside and take a look at the files together," she said.

"You sure you don't want to nap a little longer?"

"Absolutely not. That's the last time I fall asleep anywhere near you," Olivia griped.

She wanted to bite her tongue, only realizing the implications of what she was saying until it was too late. Brock smiled to himself as he stepped out of the car.

"Never say never, Olivia."

Olivia took a deep breath. Brock seemed to know exactly how to push all of her buttons. But then again, maybe it was just that she was still coming out of sleep and trying to get her bearings. She had a headache forming and her mouth was dry, but at least she was feeling a little better rested—surprisingly so given that she'd slept in a car. Olivia knew she needed to be sharp if she was going to make any headway with the case.

As she followed Brock into the building, she checked her phone. Her screen, which was usually empty of notifications, was flooded with messages. Amelia's family had sent her a text, and so had Paxton. He'd texted Olivia for details on the case and again offered his help if she needed it. She also had texts from her friends Sam and Emily, too. They must have heard about the case through the grapevine because they'd texted to wish her luck. Olivia sighed to herself, grateful for their notes in a certain way. With this case, she felt she was going to need all the luck she could get.

"You alright?" Brock asked her as they climbed the stairs inside the B&B. "Got a lot on your mind?"

"Yeah, you could say that."

"Well, don't worry. I've had plenty of time while you were sleeping to get up to speed. You're not on your own in this and I'll be as useful to you as I can."

Brock produced an old-fashioned key and inserted it into a door at the top of the staircase. Olivia found herself staring at it as it turned in the lock. She still couldn't fathom how someone broke into the Barnes family home without a key. Plenty of people made picking locks look easy in the movies. But in reality, it was a skill that not many could master. Especially not amateur kidnappers. Which was another point in favor of this being done by a professional. Which brought her back to the idea of a trafficker. If that were the case though, Olivia knew she needed to find where Amelia's path had crossed with the traffickers.

In a daze, Olivia followed Brock into his room and rubbed at her temples as she walked. She reached in her bag for an aspirin and a bottle of water to wash it down. As she stepped into his room, Olivia felt a little strange standing in Brock's bedroom. It wasn't just that she barely knew him, but it was also a pretty intimate place for them to start working together for the first time. It didn't seem pro-fessional in the least.

But she watched as Brock kicked off his shoes, undid the top button of his shirt, and collapsed onto the bed, reopening the manila folder that contained the case file and seemed to lose himself in it quickly. He was silent for several long minutes before finally sitting up and putting the file down. He turned to her with a thoughtful look on his face. Olivia sat down in a chair at the small, round table across from the bed and waited.

"All right, I guess we should start by cross-referencing everything you got from the interview with the notes in here," he said. "See if there are any recurring themes."

"Sure," I replied.

"You want some coffee? I think there's a machine in the room."

"That would be great, thank you."

Brock stood up again to make her coffee in the small pot on top of the apartment-sized refrigerator in the corner. As he did that, Olivia took up the case notes, scanning them with fresh eyes. Hopefully, now that she'd gotten multiple uninterrupted hours of sleep, she'd be able to pick up on any patterns she might have missed before. There were detailed profiles of Amelia and her family members in the file that Brock had added in while she was sleeping. But they didn't tell her much she didn't already know, other than the fact that Gabriel had recently been a lawyer for a now-convicted murderer named Phil Hutchins.

"Did you see that Gabriel was a lawyer for a murderer? He lost," I said. "That's heavy stuff and could be enough of a motive for someone close to Hutchins to target his family."

"I don't know. I thought of that too. But then I read up on the case," he said. "It seems like even Gabriel knew it was a lost cause from the start. If you read further, you'll see he tried to plead Hutchins out."

"What happened?" she asked.

"Gabriel had an idiot for a client and he rejected the plea," he said. "They went to trial, they lost, and now Hutchins is doing twenty-five to life."

"That's motive," Olivia said. "We need to look into the people closest to Hutchins."

"That's the thing. Hutchins didn't have anybody close to him. Certainly not close enough that they'd risk life in prison themselves to hurt the Barnes."

Olivia sighed and continued to flip through the pages. She felt Brock nudge her arm and accepted the coffee as he handed it to her.

"Thanks," she said as she took the cup.

"So," Brock started, sitting on the edge of the bed. "New partner. I barely know a thing about you. Care to divulge a few details?"

"Shouldn't we be looking at the case?"

"All of the best lightbulb moments happen when you stop looking so hard. And if you don't stop frowning at that case file, you're going to have permanent lines on your head."

"I'm sure there are worse things than a few wrinkles," she said... But you're annoyingly, not wrong. Focusing too hard never helps. It's just adds extra frustration when the answers don't leap off the page."

"Annoyingly, huh? I really get under your skin, don't I?"

Olivia ignored the question, thinking that might be the best way to deal with a man as pompous as Brock. Most everything he did and said seemed geared toward getting a reaction out of her. He seemed to thrive on it. But he wasn't wrong. She knew from experience that staring too long at the facts usually only left you with a headache. If they were going to be partners, she supposed there wasn't any harm in opening up... if only a little bit. It might even relax her mind enough that the answers came to her more readily.

"All right," she said. "I'll tell you three facts as long as you promise we can get back to the case right after."

"All right, it's a deal. I'll start with an easy question," he said. "Where did you grow up?"

Olivia chuckled. "You call that an easy question? Well, I grew up here, there, and everywhere, to be honest. My dad is in the military," she told him. "We moved around a lot until I was a teenager. Then my mom decided enough was enough and we settled in DC."

"A military brat, huh? Me too," Brock said with an easy smile. "Seems we have something in common, then. Did you ever live abroad?"

"No. We hopped around a few states, but we never had to go too far. How about you?"

"We did a fair amount of travel, but mostly in America," he said. "My dad was deployed to Iraq for a while, but we stayed put, of course."

"Did it bother you? Moving around so much?" she asked.

Brock shrugged. "It was hard in some ways. It was hard to make friends because I was never at a school long enough to really settle down," he said. "But luckily for me, I've got a lot of natural charm, so I did okay."

Olivia rolled her eyes and Brock flashed her a cheesy grin, draw-ing a laugh from her.

"What about you?" he asked. "Did you hate it?"
"I didn't *hate* it, but I was definitely happier once we settled in DC," she said. "It was hard because my dad would be away for months at a time, and it was always hard to reach him. Still is, to be honest. But we had a good life."

Had. That was the key word in that sentence. For Olivia, life hadn't been good since Veronica died. Now, her mother had fallen off the face of the Earth, too, and her father didn't seem interested in keeping up with her. Part of her thought that maybe if she could go back in time and relive those days when they were constantly on the road, she'd do it. It was chaotic but at least they were all together. It wasn't perfect but it was something.

"Olivia?"

She looked up and met Brock's eyes. He raised an eyebrow.

"You kind of zoned out there," he said. "I asked if your family was still in the District?"

Olivia felt her mouth grow dry. She tried to swallow, but she had trouble working up the saliva to do so. How could she explain to a near stranger that her whole world had been turned upside down and that she didn't know how to make it right again? But then she thought that was too personal and not something she should share with somebody who had been a stranger to her until a few hours ago.

"Not really," Olivia said vaguely.

Brock watched her with interest for a moment, but held back, seeming to realize he'd stumbled across a sensitive subject. His eyes drifted back to the case file. She was surprised that he had that sort of discretion and was impressed by it.

"All right, new question. What do you do when you're not doing *this?*" he asked, gesturing to the file. "Like what do you do for fun?"

Olivia sighed. "I like to read, but I don't have as much time for it as I might like. I finished *Jane Eyre* for the fifth time the other day."

"The fifth time? I couldn't even get through that book once. And that was back in like, high school," Brock replied, wrinkling his nose.

"It's a beautiful book. No one writes like the Brontës anymore. Not to mention that it's full of drama," she said. "You should try it again. If you try hard enough, you might actually find something in there that you like."

"I don't think I'll be doing that," Brock said. "But thanks for the recommendation, I guess."

Olivia felt a little sour at his response. After all, he was the one who wanted to get to know her, and all he'd done so far was make fun of her interests. She sniffed.

"Well, you asked. What do you do?" she asked. "Sit around and sneer at what makes other people happy? Open beer bottles with your toes? Crush beer cans on your forehead?"

Brock grinned. "You've really got me pegged, haven't you?"

Olivia rolled her eyes at him. "You seem pretty simple to figure out to me."

"All right, then let's switch it up. Why don't you ask me something about me?"

"I know that's your favorite subject, but I'm not sure I'm all that interested in knowing anything about you."

"Okay, ouch," he said with a laugh. "Come on, it can be anything."

Olivia chewed her lip. She didn't want to ask anything really personal, and yet she couldn't help feeling curious about what made Brock tick. Beneath his cocky exterior, she knew there was something intriguing inside of him. He was arrogant and full of bluster. But she'd also seen something more than that. It was buried deep inside, but she'd seen that he could also act like a real human being with feelings. She met his eyes, feeling a surge of confidence.

"All right," she said. "What's the case you've worked that's stuck with you the most? That you can't get away from no matter how hard you try. I know you have one. We all do."

Brock's smile faded ever so slightly and Olivia immediately realized it was the wrong question. There was a reason that FBI agents kept their business to themselves. She'd just essentially asked him to lay bare his deepest wounds and scars. No one kept a catalog of the good stories from the work they all did. But they all cataloged the bad, terrible things they experienced. It was their own internal, ever expanding horror movie. Olivia wished she hadn't said anything at all, because now Brock seemed to be stuck somewhere between telling her something horrific and staying completely silent.

"Maybe that's a story for another time," he said, his eyes not leaving hers. "We all have skeletons in our closets, right? I don't think now is the time or place to drag mine out. Maybe when this case is over and done with, we can do a show and tell."

Olivia nodded, not wanting to push the issue any further. He was a master of getting a reaction out of her. But now that she'd done the same thing to him, she felt guilty. She'd taken it too far and wanted to apologize. But when she opened her mouth to speak, nothing came out. And then, the moment to say something passed.

Brock broke the silence with a deep sigh and picked up the manila folder, opening it on his lap once again. He was acting as if the conversation hadn't even happened, but Olivia could sense the elephant in the room. His smile was long gone.

"All right, playtime's over, I think," Brock announced, pretending to study the file with particular interest. "We should get back to it."

Olivia nodded, though he wasn't looking at her now. She took a sip of some coffee just to give herself something to do, trying to swallow her guilt along with the dark brew.

"Aside from the murder conviction theory, which is flimsy at best, we still haven't come up with a single thing that could be used as a motive," Brock said thoughtfully. "We don't have enemies of the family to consider. It appears the Barnes family keeps their social circle small. So why would someone want to take Amelia? And why or how did he get her all the way from Seattle to here?"

"Jealousy?" Olivia offered, hoping to immerse herself in the work and forget the awkwardness between them. "People are covetous by nature. Everyone wants what they don't have. Perhaps he thought they were a family that had it all while he had nothing. So, he took something priceless from them just so they knew what it was like to lose something precious. And of course, be willing to give him everything."

"It's a good theory. It's like the family said, they would have paid anything to get Amelia back," he mused. "But like I said before, he does well enough but he's not some superstar bigshot lawyer. All that aside though, the kidnapper didn't try to ransom Amelia back, or even ask for the reward money. So maybe it's not about money or status. Maybe it's about humiliating or punishing the family for some personal slight?"

"But then why would he let Amelia go in that scenario? Remorse?"

"Possibly. I really don't know."

The pair of them fell silent. The truth was, they were stuck once again. Neither of them was any closer to figuring out what had happened and Olivia rubbed her temple. Her headache was seemingly becoming a permanent feature.

"We must be missing something," Brock muttered irritably, flipping the pages of the file to scan them. "There's only one other thing I can think of, and it seems... it seems too dark to be possible."

"We're used to darkness in this job, right?" Olivia said quietly. "What's on your mind?"

Brock sucked in a breath. "Maybe whoever did it knows the family. He knows how to get into the house somehow without being caught. And he knows that Amelia is non-verbal. He knows that he could take her away and do horrible things to her—or hand her off to a trafficker offering more money than the reward. She'd never be able to say a word because she's unable to articulate her experiences. And that's why he was able to let her go. Because whoever did it had already had his fun, and he showed some mercy knowing... knowing..."

"That he'd never be caught," Olivia finished.

She didn't want to admit it, but it was a good theory. She didn't want to imagine that Amelia had suffered even more than they thought, but it was entirely possible. They didn't have enough information to decide whether his theory had any merit. But if it was true, did they have any reason to believe others might be at risk?

"The hospital said there was no sign of sexual trauma," she told him. "So that's a major dent in the trafficking theory."

"That they know of," Brock countered. "We have no way of knowing what went on wherever she was captured. Maybe the trauma wasn't physical."

"But that's kind of the defining feature of traffickers," she said. "They abduct these girls and sell them for sex."

70

"It's possible her sale was in the works, but they hadn't gotten around to it yet," Brock replied.

Olivia nodded, conceding the point. There were so many questions and so few answers. She knew that one thing was for sure: if they couldn't tie the kidnapper to any other abductions or find some link to a trafficking network, they might never get answers. Was it better to never get justice for Amelia? Or find the kidnapper after he snatched somebody else? Olivia felt a low, burning anger in the pit of her stomach at the thought of someone waiting out there to do this whole thing over again to somebody else's daughter.

"We have to catch this guy before he does it again," Brock murmured.

Olivia nodded in agreement. He was right. That was the only option. The rest was unthinkable.

CHAPTER SEVEN

OLIVIA WOKE TO SUNLIGHT STREAMING IN THROUGH the window of the B&B and a foggy headache that made her groan out loud. She couldn't believe she had fallen asleep again. She was obviously more tired than she'd even realized. She sat up and noticed that she was lying on the sofa in Brock's room. A blanket was draped over her, and she knew she hadn't put it there herself. Brock must have covered her with it after she'd fallen asleep, and the thought brought a small smile to her face. It was a thoughtful gesture.

She tried to piece together the previous night in her mind, though she was still half-asleep and her thoughts fuzzy. She and Brock had spent what felt like years going around in circles, but they'd come up with nothing. The complete lack of evidence was making her feel that there must be something glaringly obvious that they'd missed. But what that might be, she had no clue.

She glanced around the room. Brock had passed out on the bed, clutching the manila folder to his chest like a child's teddy bear. He was still fully dressed, and he hadn't managed to clamber under the sheets. Olivia allowed herself a moment to be amused at how different Brock looked when he was asleep. He was peaceful, unable to dazzle her with his annoying quips and snarky comments. The fact that his mouth was hanging wide open and he was drooling on himself was an added bonus.

"Not so cool now," she murmured to herself with a giggle as she snapped a picture with her phone to use as leverage later.

Olivia stood up and folded the blanket, trying to get herself organized for the day. Her body was already crying out for coffee, but she didn't want to wake Brock up. She glanced at her watch, saw it was only six and groaned softly. She felt refreshed. Mostly because she'd gotten a few more hours of sleep than he had. But they hadn't gotten to sleep until at least two-thirty and she thought he deserved to sleep for a little longer.

Olivia didn't want to admit it, but Brock was shaping up to be a pretty good partner after all. He asked all the right questions, even if finding the answers was proving to be difficult. He kept the mood light and despite his annoying and near constant teasing, he did seem to have some sense of when to take things more seriously.

Olivia knew, at least, that she could count on him for the duration of the case, and that was all she needed from him. Even if she found his company somewhat enjoyable, she found it easier to work alone most of the time. Isolating her bad experiences in the job somehow made them easier to cope with. Knowing that she was alone in many of her experiences meant that no one would ever be able to relate. Yet strange as it was, that made her feel better about things.

Olivia's phone vibrated in her pocket and startled her. She immediately felt a sense of dread descend over her. She doubted anyone calling at six in the morning was calling with good news for her. She pulled out her phone and looked at the caller ID to see it was Maggie Stone on the line. She took a deep breath knowing she was right and this wasn't going to be good news. She picked up the call.

"Olivia Knight speaking."

"Olivia, hi. I'm glad you picked up," Maggie said, rushing to get her words out. "We've got a problem."

"What's going on?"

"We have another missing girl," she said.

Olivia thought she was ready to hear those words, but they still knocked the wind out of her. There was silence on the other end of the line for a moment, and all that Olivia could hear was her blood pounding in her ears.

"Olivia?"

"I'm here," she rasped. "Okay. Okay, we can deal with this. What do you know so far?"

"The missing person is named Sophia Edwards. Fifteen years old. She's small, petite, blonde. Her parents called a few minutes ago to say that she wasn't in her bedroom when they checked this morning," she said. "No windows or doors were unlocked, and there was no sign of a struggle. Absolutely no evidence left, either. She's just... gone."

Olivia sat down on the sofa with the phone pressed to her ear. Superficially speaking, it sounded identical to Amelia's case. It didn't take a genius to work out the similarities. The girl even fit the same description as Amelia: a teen girl with blonde hair and a petite stature who disappeared from her bed overnight. Gone, as though she'd never been there in the first place with no evidence left behind.

"Okay. I'm coming straight to the station," Olivia said. "If you can contact the parents and get them to meet us there—"

"They're already on their way. I said you'd want to talk to them."

"That's great. Thank you, Maggie."

Olivia was about to end the call when she heard a despairing sigh on the other end of the line. She knew Maggie was upset by the turn of events.

"You'd think with as long as I've been in this job nothing would surprise me anymore," she said. "Belle Grove is a safe place. Or at least it used to be. Now there's some monster in our midst who's taking these girls and holding them. Using them for his twisted games—"

"We'll get to the bottom of this. I promise you," Olivia interrupted, though fear was clawing at her heart as she said the words. "I don't care how long it takes. This isn't your fault."

The only thought running through her head was how she could find the kidnapper—before he disappeared and tightened up whatever screw up that allowed Amelia to escape and put them onto him in the first place. With thousands of square miles of forest out there, Olivia knew the odds of finding him if he went to ground were slim. But with a new girl taken, she hoped they would be able to find something, anything, that would give them a bead on him.

"Hang tight," Olivia said. "I'll be there soon."

Maggie sniffed again. I'm glad you're here, Olivia. If anyone can figure this out, I'm confident it's you."

The call ended and Olivia took a second to compose herself. This was exactly what they hadn't wanted to happen. They were trying to prevent anyone from falling victim again. But they'd been sleeping as another girl was snatched out of her bed in the middle of the night. Olivia stood up and went to shake Brock. They didn't have time to rest now. He stirred slowly beneath her hand.

"Five more minutes," he slurred sleepily.

"No more minutes. We have to go. Now," Olivia told him sharply. "Another girl was taken last night."

Brock sat up immediately, alert, and stared at Olivia in shock. It took him a moment to process what she'd said, but then he nodded and got up. There was no time for either of them to shower and get changed even though they were both wearing the same clothes they were in the night before. They headed straight down to Brock's car and climbed in. Olivia solemnly directed him to the police station.

"This one's local," Olivia explained. "Parents are already driving to the station."

"But why would this one be so close to home when the other one was all the way in Seattle?" Brock mused.

"Guess we're about to find out."

When they arrived, they headed straight inside to find Maggie talking quietly to a middle-aged couple. To Olivia's surprise, neither of them looked particularly concerned. They were strict-looking people. The woman had a severe bob that sharply ended at her chin and an expression that made her look like she'd been eating sour grapes. The man was wearing a suit and tie, looking far too pressed and polished for someone who'd woken at seven in the morning to find his child gone.

As she and Brock approached, the older couple turned and looked at them, the expressions on their faces registering immediate disapproval. The sour looks on their faces grew even more sour. Olivia looked down at herself and knew she looked disheveled and out of place. After all, she'd just turned up to work un-showered and wearing the same rumpled clothes she was wearing yesterday. Given the way she looked, Olivia probably wouldn't have trusted herself with the job of finding a missing daughter, either.

"Good morning. I'm Olivia Knight, and this is Brock Tanner. We're with the FBI," Olivia started.

The woman offered her a hand to shake, still pursing her lips, that look of disapproval sharp and cutting.

"Alice Edwards. This is my husband, Elijah," she said, her tone as severe as her appearance. "Are you going to find our daughter?"

What Olivia didn't say was that she had no idea, and she

couldn't guarantee a thing. She would have liked to say she was going to find Sophia if it killed her, but she learned long ago not to make promises like that to families. It was a promise she'd broken with the Barnes', but thankfully, that had turned out all right.

"We are going to investigate your daughter's disappearance with the full resources of the Bureau behind us," she said.

Alice at least looked somewhat impressed by how confident Olivia sounded, and her disapproving expression lightened a little.

"We're going to need to ask some questions," added Brock. "Your daughter's disappearance shares some similarities with another case we were working on. So, we'd like to see if there is any other evidence that might link the cases—"

"Don't get ahead of yourself, young man," Alice cut him off.

Olivia hadn't yet seen anyone react so negatively to Brock and his charming smile, but something about him seemed to have rubbed Alice the wrong way given the way she was staring at him.

"It's not related to whatever other case you're talking about," she snapped. "The only reason we're here is because Officer Stone insisted we come."

Olivia raised an eyebrow, surprised at her comments. She could tell from being in their presence for only a few minutes that Alice and Elijah that they were likely overly strict parents. They had a stern demeanor and what seemed like permanent scowls and expressions of disapproval on their faces. Being under the thumb of parents who were so severe might make a fifteen-year-old to run away. Perhaps even more than once.

"I have to say, your reaction isn't what I expected," Olivia said. "I take it there was some tension between you and your daughter?"

"Sophia is spoiled," Alice sniffed, cutting off Elijah's attempt to speak. "She doesn't know how lucky she is to have a good home, to have parents who *care* about her. She's been acting out this past year. She just wants to run wild with that boyfriend of hers."

"Boyfriend?" Brock asked. "Have you called him to check he's not with her?"

"I don't have that low-life's number," Alice snapped. "But I guarantee you that's where she is. He's practically twice her age. We've told her that she can't see him anymore, but she doesn't listen to us. She thinks she knows better than we do."

Olivia felt a surge inside her. It sounded as though the boyfriend might be a lead for them. If he was an older guy preying on younger girls, then he was certainly a suspect.

"Can you give us his name?" Olivia asked.

"Craig. Craig Carter," Alice said stiffly, as if it pained her to say the name. "You tell me, Agents, what business does a nineteen-year-old boy have with a fifteen-year-old? It's sick."

Olivia frowned. The age gap was only four years. This Craig Carter was hardly twice her age as Alice had indicated. The guy was practically high school age—just like their daughter. That, of course, didn't clear him of suspicion, but it certainly knocked him down the list. Olivia didn't think most nineteen-year-olds had the sort of wherewithal to get in and abduct a girl without leaving evidence, nor the means to make a trip cross country and back. She thought it was doubtful but she knew they still needed to look into him.

Aside from him being four years older than your daughter," Olivia said pointedly. "Was there some specific objection you had to your daughter's boyfriend?"

"She comes home stinking of pot after she's been with him," Alice snarled, her tone like acid. "She tells me that she doesn't smoke it, but she's a seasoned liar as far as I'm concerned. She'd do anything just to try to disappoint me. She wants me to suffer. Isn't that what all teenagers want for their mothers?"

Olivia felt a pang of sadness as she glanced at Alice's weathered face. She might have been younger than she looked but the stress seemed to have aged her. Olivia wondered how many families thought it was normal for their children to want to get away from them so badly. Olivia had certainly never had the urge to hurt her parents. The idea seemed strange to her. But then, maybe she was just more sheltered than she'd thought.

"We'll need to speak to Craig as soon as possible. But before that, is there anything else you can tell us about what happened last night that might be useful," Olivia said. "I know you said that you don't think this is connected to our other cases—"

"No, what I said was that I didn't think Sophia was abducted. I think she ran off with that lowlife boyfriend of hers," she snapped.

"All right, be that as it may, just indulge me for a moment," Brock said, obviously trying to remain patient. "Did you notice anything unusual when you woke up? Anything unusual in or around your house that made you think—"

"I don't know what I think," Alice said, again cutting off Brock mid-speech. "All I know is that she's been sneaking out more and more often lately. I used to try to stop her, but she always leaves, no matter how much I shout at her. I used to track her phone to see where she went when she left, but now she always leaves her phone behind. It's still on her nightstand. I've started just letting her go, because I figured that if I don't.... maybe eventually she'll just stop coming back. And now… now…"

The first hint of emotion finally cracked Alice's hard exterior. So, she was human after all. Elijah, who had been silent the entire time, placed a comforting hand on her knee. A tear slipped from Alice's eye, and she shook her head.

"I'm sorry," Olivia said earnestly.

As much as she thought Alice Edwards was approaching parenting completely wrong, at least she was trying her best. Alice shook her head again.

"I went into her bedroom to check on her this morning. I sometimes do when I think she's asleep. Teenagers are so much less of a nightmare when they're asleep." She forced a laugh, though no one else joined in. "But she wasn't there and I just knew she'd snuck out again. At that point, I decided that enough was enough. That I couldn't do this anymore. That I needed help. So that's when I called the police. I hadn't even heard of this other case, this—Amelia Barnes girl—until Maggie mentioned her to me."

Alice sniffed and looked away for a moment, taking a couple of moments to gather herself. Elijah whispered soothingly to her. Alice nodded then finally looked up at Olivia.

"Do you think we need to be concerned?" Alice asked. "Do you really think it's possible she was—taken?"

Olivia chewed the inside of her cheek until she tasted blood. How was she supposed to tell this woman that her daughter might be caught up in something far worse than she already feared? She swallowed hard and chose her next words carefully.

"If you say this happens a lot, then maybe it's like you said and she's just holed up with her boyfriend somewhere," Olivia said. "If we can track him down, then that'll answer at least one question. But if she's not with him or with her friends then I won't lie to you, Mrs. Edwards. There might be cause for concern."

Alice nodded, her lip quivering. "All right. All right, okay. Well, I suppose we have to cross that bridge when we come to it. You'll take care of it, won't you? You'll find her?"

"We're going to do our best, ma'am," nodded Olivia, but she was much less sure than when she'd first arrived.

She wanted to promise Alice and Elijah that their daughter was just acting up again and that they would find her at her boyfriend's house. She wanted to tell the Edwards that because it was better than the alternative. Far better. But the truth was, her gut was telling her that something darker was at play. Two blonde girls had already disappeared in the dead of the night in eerily similar circumstances. She didn't want a third to confirm the pattern. As far as Olivia was concerned, the pattern was already set.

"I just have a few more questions to ask," Brock said, stepping forward and Alice pursed her lips once more.

"All right," she said.

"Where is it that you live?" Brock asked.

Alice frowned. "We live close to the edge of town. It's a little quieter than being in the middle of town, which is why we picked it. It doesn't stop Sophia gallivanting off into the forest in the middle of the night, though."

"You know where she goes?"

Alice blushed. "Well, I suspect she goes to the same place every time. I know that I shouldn't have done it, but I followed her once because I wanted to make sure she was safe," she told them. "I heard her leave the house around midnight one night. Her deadbeat boyfriend picked her up in his truck, and I followed them. The boy is so dumb he didn't even notice he was being followed. They headed to the edge of the woods on the other side of town. They passed near the old forest ranger's cabin, and then I lost sight of them. I couldn't follow them any further without getting caught."

Olivia had to resist the urge to let out a deep sigh. The story of the Edwards family was getting wilder and wilder by the minute. Olivia wasn't sure who she felt sorrier for, Alice and her wild desperation to keep control of her daughter. Or Sophia, who was clearly digging herself a hole she might not be able to climb out of.

"We should really go and see if we can speak to Craig," Olivia said then turned to Maggie who'd stood silently off to the side. "But if he's a dead end, then I think it would be wise to set up a search party. Maybe the forest is the place to start. That's the common link between both cases."

"You think... you think she might have been kidnapped?" Alice asked anxiously.

The women looked frightened and Olivia cringed, wishing she hadn't said anything.

"I'm not ruling anything out but jumping to conclusions will get us nowhere. For all we know, Sophia is back at home now," Olivia said, trying to placate her. "We understand your concern, but trust me when I say we won't rest until we find her. You can be sure of that."

Alice nodded, her hard edges starting to soften. Maggie offered the couple a smile, though Olivia could tell her heart wasn't in it.

"Why don't you head home and see if she's come back, Alice? We'll handle the rest. If you can think of anything else that might be useful, you can touch base with us," advised Maggie.

Olivia nodded, passing Alice her card. "Brock and I will go talk to Craig. Do you know where he lives?"

Alice nodded with a guilty look in her eyes, giving Olivia a sneaking suspicion that she had followed him back there at some point. "Yes. He lives close to the gas station. He works for his father. I can write down the address for you."

Olivia took down the details of Craig's home and thanked the Edwards family before walking out of the police station, Brock on her tail. She handed the address to Brock.

"Do you think it's him?" Brock asked. "Think we're getting close?"

Olivia pressed her lips together. "I don't know. Something is telling me that this issue with Craig is a separate issue entirely. Besides, I don't necessarily buy that a nineteen-year-old kid is sophisticated enough to pull this whole thing off."

"Yeah, I don't either. Alice said he's dumb, but is he really dumb enough to kidnap another girl while he's already having so much trouble with Sophia and her family?" Brock asked. "It doesn't make a lot of sense."

Brock sighed and opened his car door. He looked as frustrated as she felt in that moment. Olivia got in on the passenger's side.

"Who knows?" he said. "You're the one who lives in this bonkers town. If your gut is telling you this doesn't make sense, then trust it."

"I just can't see how it can possibly make sense," Olivia continued as she closed the passenger side door. "There's a vague outline of a motive, but the logistics of it seem wrong. Amelia was taken from Seattle, so if he's got a thing for young blonde girls, then why would he go all the way there to find one?"

"Maybe he thought we wouldn't find the connection," Brock offered. "Maybe he has some connection to Seattle and was up there for a while and she was just a matter of convenience. That would explain the distance."

"But he'd have to know exactly where to find Amelia. And then if he wasn't aware that she was non-verbal, why even take her in the first place?" she said. "Why commit to such a high-risk operation? I don't know. I think this is wrong."

"Well, best-case scenario, we head over to talk to Craig, and we find Sophia with him. Worst-case-scenario..."

"Worst-case scenario, the kidnapper is someone else," she said. "And they took Sophia."

CHAPTER EIGHT

"**C**RAIG CARTER, THIS IS THE FBI," BROCK ANNOUNCED for the third time as he banged on the door to Carter's house. Olivia stood close behind him, her arms folded. "We just want to talk."

"I don't think he's here, Brock. There's no car in the driveway. Alice said he had a truck."

"Then he might have known we were coming. Secrets aren't really safe in a small town," Brock growled. "Great. Our first possible lead and he's already slipped away."

"We don't know that. Belle Grove isn't that big of a place. If he's around, we'll find him," Olivia insisted.

"We should search the house," Brock said.

"You know we can't do that. We need a warrant," she replied. "Do you want to get yourself suspended? Leave it and get back in the car. We can drive around and see if we can find him somewhere in town."

"Well, where the hell should we start?"

"The forest. That was their meeting spot, right? Maybe they're there hanging out," she offered. "We should at least give it a shot. Just relax. We'll figure this out as we go."

Brock's face softened a little, some of the anger draining away. "All right. You're probably right. I guess I'm just a little wound up about this whole case."

"Me, too. But we need to keep our heads. Now, more than ever."

He nodded. "You're right. You're right."

As they walked back to Brock's car, Olivia let out a sigh of relief, glad she'd managed to talk Brock down. She couldn't afford for him to start going over the edge. This case was stressful enough without one of them losing their grip. They needed to stay sharp and focused if they were going to run down this kidnapper before he struck again.

As they drove back toward the forest, to where Alice had indicated she'd followed them to, Olivia texted her to ask about Craig's car. She replied almost right away, letting her know that Craig drove an old blue Ford pickup with a crude bumper sticker on the back. When pressed further, Alice admitted the sticker depicted a naked pinup girl. Olivia announced this to Brock, and for the first time in hours, he let out a hearty laugh.

"Well, that'll be a piece of cake to find," he snorted. "I've never wanted to see a bumper sticker so bad before."

"Wow, you must be really starved for romance."

"You could cure that, you know."

"Shut up," she said with a laugh, her cheeks flushing.

They drove around town then out to the edge of the woods, looking out for Craig's truck. Brock leaned over the wheel, straining to see further as they cruised slowly.

"The trees are pretty thick. Do you think he might have driven into the forest?"

"I doubt it. Didn't Alice say that she followed him to the ranger's cabin? So, in theory, he would've parked up by my house…"

"Let's try there, then."

They continued driving, but they saw no sign of Craig or his truck. After a full circuit, they drove up Olivia's driveway and parked.

"I think we should go out into the forest on foot," Brock told her. "If Craig has any sense and is on the run, that's where he'd go, right? He'd ditch the recognizable car and go to a terrain he knows well and isn't easy to navigate. That's what I'd do, at least."

"Craig is a nineteen-year-old boy who works at a gas station," Olivia said. "I don't think he's thinking that logically."

"Well, we've driven all over town. There's no sign of the car. At this point, he's either miles out of town or he's hidden in plain sight. We should call Maggie for backup and get some volunteers to start covering the ground in the forest. Don't you think the forest is likely to have something to tell us?"

Olivia considered it for a moment. "You could be right. I just don't want to miss anything. Maybe we should split up for a little while," she said. "I could take another drive around the town while you look here?"

Brock shrugged. "All right. Are you going to be okay?"

"I'm sure I'll manage. I'm a big girl."

Brock rolled his eyes with a small smile. "All right, all right. You know where to find me if you want to join the search here later."

Olivia nodded and got out of the car. She headed into her house to grab a quick cup of coffee for the road and change into some fresh clothes. Then she grabbed her car keys and headed out for a drive. It was quiet on the road without Brock, and it made it easier for her to hear her own thoughts. But strangely enough, she found that she missed his presence in the car. It was bizarre given the fact she hadn't known him very long—and that he sometimes got under her skin.

As she pondered that, the thought occurred to her that maybe she'd miss him when he went back to DC, whenever that was going to be. It had only been a day, but the case already felt as if it was going to be endless. She had this awful feeling that the kidnapper was playing a game with them. Why else would he take a girl from right under their noses? Like Brock said, in a small town, secrets spread like wildfire. It wouldn't be a secret the Bureau was in town and was looking for Amelia's abductor.

Clearly, they were dealing with someone smarter than their only suspect so far. As she scanned the town for signs of Craig, she felt more and more sure that he wasn't involved. According to what Alice said, he was not very bright and was strange. But then again, she also said he was twice Sophia's age when the gap was a mere four years. He was nineteen and didn't seem sophisticated enough to pull off an evidence-free abduction. Two seemed to stretch the bounds of real-ity. So, why was she wasting her time even looking for him?

Olivia spent another hour trawling through town before deciding to give in and join the search party in the forest. When she drove back up to her cabin, she found that she had to squeeze past a whole bunch of other cars that were parked on the shoulder just to get into her driveway. Clearly, there had been a fair few volunteers willing to join the search for Sophia and Craig.

It took a little while for Olivia to find the rest of the search party. The wilderness was a little more trampled than it had been a few days before, where people had picked their way through the brambles and bushes. But after a while, she caught sight of a group of people crunching through the undergrowth, their voices distant as they called out for Sophia.

Maggie was a little further ahead, shouting some instructions to the volunteers. Only Brock was holding back, standing by himself beside a tall tree and scanning the land ahead of him with a frown on his face. Olivia joined him by the tree and he sighed as he noticed her.

"I'm not sure what to make of all this," he admitted. "There were a few sets of footprints, but the undergrowth was too thick to pick up the prints after a point. And since then, it's felt kind of useless. We haven't seen a single thing."

"It was always a long shot," Olivia told him. "The forest here has a mind of its own. Sometimes, living in that cabin, it seems to be swallowing me whole. If there was anybody here, it could be long gone."

"Then what do we do next?"

Olivia didn't have an answer to that question. Craig was their best shot at a lead, and they hadn't been able to track him down. The thought she'd had ran through her head once more—what were they missing?

"Hello?"

Both Olivia and Brock whipped around at the sound of an unfamiliar voice. A young boy was standing in front of them, his floppy blond hair falling in front of dull eyes. He wore ripped jeans and a camouflage jacket, and the distinct smell of marijuana wafted from him. Olivia wrinkled her nose. She immediately knew who he was.

"Craig Carter?"

He nodded, avoiding eye contact with Olivia. She took a step toward him. Her dislike for the man was immediate and overwhelming. But she knew she needed to keep a level head, even if he was a predator. Allegedly, anyway.

"Agents Knight and Tanner. FBI," she introduced them. "We've been looking for you."

"I know. I heard," he muttered awkwardly, his gaze on the ground. "I went for a drive to clear my head. I thought I did something wrong…"

"No, you think?" Brock snapped.

A look of pure anguish crossed Craig's face. "No! I didn't do anything wrong!"

"Why don't you walk us through what happened last evening, Craig?" Olivia asked stiffly.

He sniffed, letting out a long, slow shrug. "Well… I was waiting for Sophia in our usual spot in the forest," he began slowly and deliberately. "She told me not to go near her house anymore. She thought her mom would kill me if I showed my face there again. But she said she wanted to see me, so I thought, why not? I like her company. So,

I drove up here and waited. I waited for hours. I tried to call her, but she didn't answer. I thought maybe she'd ditched me…"

"For someone her own age, maybe? She's fifteen. You're almost twenty years old," Brock cut in irritably, but Olivia held up a hand to hush him.

"So, you haven't seen Sophia in the last twenty-four hours?"

Craig shook his head. He seemed to be he was close to tears. "I swear, I haven't seen her. I fell asleep in my car waiting for her, and when I went home this morning, my dad told me that Sophia was gone. Her mom had called, saying all kinds of crazy things. So, I panicked. I drove out of town for a few hours, trying to get myself together. But I didn't do anything, man! I've always been nice to Sophia. We got along."

"You can see why we're suspicious, though, right?" Olivia pressed through gritted teeth. "Like Agent Tanner said, you're almost twenty. A grown man. She was still a child. What on earth were you doing dating a child, Craig?"

Craig stared at the floor, shuffling his feet. "It's not like that. I like her company. We haven't *done* anything other than kiss a few times. I know the age gap but it's not nearly as bad as her mom makes it out to be. Besides, I'm waiting for her. When she's older, we can be together properly."

Brock snorted, and Olivia shot him a glare. This was not the time or place to be prodding and alienating their only suspect. He seemed pretty loose-lipped to her, even if he couldn't look her in the eye, and she wanted to keep him talking. She folded her arms over her chest.

"So, if we were to get a warrant and search your house, we wouldn't find anything that might lead us to Sophia?"

"I swear, I don't know where she is!" Craig cried out, his lip wobbling like a child's who's about to throw a tantrum. "If I did, I sure as hell wouldn't be here talking to you two. I'd be with her. I care about her, okay? I don't want to hurt her. I want her to be found, safe and sound, so things can go back to the way they were. You have to believe me!"

A long moment of silence descended over them, and she exchanged a glance with Brock who gave her a small shrug. Craig honestly looked like a man in total torment, and it only added to her belief that he was not their man. Now that she'd met him live and in the flesh, she knew he wasn't sophisticated enough to have pulled this off. Not with Amelia and not with Sophia. He was nothing more than a lovesick kid who was scared for his girlfriend.

"Do you know anything?" he asked. "Do you know where she is? Or who took her?"

Olivia shook her head slowly. It was almost painful to admit how in the dark they were. She watched the last of Craig's walls come crumbling down, and he groaned, covering his face with his hands.

"Why would someone do this?" he asked, a sob escaping his throat. "She's a good girl. She should be at home with her family. Or hanging out with me. Why would somebody take her?"

"Maybe she would have been if you didn't insist on taking a fifteen-year-old girl out of her house in the middle of the night," Brock pointed out, unable to hide his disdain any longer. "If you want to help, stay where we can see you and help us search."

Craig's lip quivered, but he nodded and began to walk ahead of them, trembling as he wiped his face on his sleeve. Olivia and Brock exchanged a glance.

"You believe him, don't you?" Brock whispered.

Olivia sighed. "I believe he's not our kidnapper, yes," she said. "I mean, look at him. He's an absolute mess."

"Or he's a good actor."

"I doubt it. I don't think that kid has ever been described as good at anything," she said

"Maybe he's just got you fooled. And he's not a kid, he's a nineteen-year-old man. He's old enough to vote," Brock said. "He knows exactly what he's doing, and he's running around with an actual child in the middle of the night. If he's capable of that, he's capable of more."

"Why would he come to us if he was involved? You heard him, he left town. He had no reason to come back."

"Maybe he's one of those criminals who loves talking to the cops," he said. "Gets off on injecting himself into the middle of an investigation. Keep tabs on what we know—"

"Stop. We both know he's not smart enough for that. Listen, I know we both want this to be a lead, but I think he's a dead end. No, I'm sure of it. He knows he's dead meat if Alice finds out he's done something but he came back anyway," she said. "You think this guy can break into houses in the middle of the night without being noticed? Without leaving a trace? More than that, can handle a teenage girl and get her out without making a sound? Look at him, Brock. He's shaking like a leaf. I don't buy it for a second, and you shouldn't, either."

Brock ran a hand through his hair, puffing out a lungful of air. He shook his head. "I know, I know. I just really wanted this to be it."

Olivia nodded. It would've been so easy to pin both crimes on Craig. But they both knew he didn't make sense as their suspect. He wasn't exactly a good person, but that didn't mean he was a kidnapper, either.

"We should keep looking," Olivia said. "I think there's got to be something out here. Amelia came running from the forest. If we can find some way to retrace her steps, it might tell us something about where the kidnapper is taking the girls."

The search party had moved on without them. But Brock nodded silently and the pair of them began to trudge through the undergrowth together with Craig trailing along behind them. As they walked along, Olivia scanned every inch of the forest, looking for any sign of Amelia's passage through the woods. She searched for footprints or marks in the mud, trampled ground, or broken branches. She looked for anything although she knew the search party could easily have damaged any kind of evidence like that. But she didn't stop. She looked for wisps of hair, specifically blonde ones, and she looked for blood.

The whole thing was starting to feel as though the forest was deliberately withholding any secrets it might have. Whatever was going on there, she felt like the trees were deliberately hiding any evidence that might have been out there and burying it deep beneath their roots. Olivia knew that just because she lived near the forest, it didn't mean it was her friend. That feeling grew stronger as they hit mid-afternoon with no sign of anything or anyone.

It was around two that afternoon when Maggie approached Olivia, her expression grave.

"I think we have to turn back now," she said. "If there was anything here, we would have found it by now. We've covered every opening to the forest. And we don't have the manpower to cover the entire forest. It's hundreds of square miles out there."

Olivia and Brock both nodded solemnly. She was right. As of that moment, the forest posed more questions than answers. Besides, they were going to have to turn back at night, anyway, and the volunteers were starting to grow weary. Olivia sighed.

"Call off the search," she said. "Brock and I will head back to talk to Sophia's parents."

"What are you going to tell them?" Maggie asked.

Olivia chewed her lip and thought about it for a moment. "The truth," she said. "We didn't find anything and Craig is likely a dead end."

"They're not going to want to hear that," Maggie said.

"I know," Olivia replied. "But we don't have any other choice, do we?"

Neither Maggie nor Brock said anything in response. As Olivia began to trek back toward her cabin, Brock remained completely silent at her side. She looked up at the towering trees, so tall and thick that they blocked out most of the sunlight. A feeling of hopelessness washed over her, and she tried to swallow it down. What was it about this case that was so much harder than anything she'd faced before? Why did it hit her on a level other cases didn't?

She felt so guilty for not having a lead to follow. Guilt that she was supposed to be keeping people safe and had no clue how to do it. She closed her eyes for a moment and prayed that Sophia would somehow make it home safely, just as Amelia had. The alternative was unthinkable.

"I'll drive," Olivia told Brock when they reached her cabin and unlocked her car.

He nodded quietly and got into the passenger seat without so much as a smart comment. She didn't even have the energy to try to make him feel better, so she started the engine and headed to the address Alice had given her.

"Maybe the house will give us some answers," Olivia murmured unconvincingly.

Brock didn't even bother to reply to her. Olivia's car groaned as it trundled up the hill toward the high end of town. By the time they arrived at the house, Olivia's nerves were frayed. She saw Alice waiting at the window, having spotted them the second they pulled up. She was waiting for good news, but Olivia didn't have any to offer her. She took a deep breath and headed toward the house.

Alice threw open the front door, her face lit up as though she expected her daughter to run straight into her arms. Olivia had to watch the slow realization cross her face when Sophia didn't get out of the car. The realization that her daughter was still missing left her looking crestfallen. Her eyes turned stony as she looked at Olivia.

"You didn't find her?"

"No. We didn't find... well... much of anything, to be honest," she said softly. "May we come inside?"

Alice's gaze was so cold that Olivia half expected to catch a case of frostbite just standing there. She honestly expected Alice to say no, but after a moment, she nodded and stepped aside to let them inside. Her chest felt tight as she crossed the threshold. The house felt eerie, as if the walls around her knew that such an important part of the home was missing. The heart and soul of the home had left when Sophia disappeared.

Olivia decided to do a little investigating before she spoke to Alice. She thought she would perhaps find something that might shine some light on their current issues. But then a thought occurred to her.

"You said earlier that Sophia's phone is still on her nightstand. Do you mind if we take a look?" she asked. "Maybe there's something on there that can point us in the right direction."

"You can try, but it's password protected. I wouldn't know where to start with guessing the code," Alice said with a sigh.

She gestured for Olivia and Brock to follow her, and they headed upstairs together. They veered left into Sophia's bedroom, and Olivia felt her heart stop for a moment. The room smelled of cheap perfume, the kind only teenage girls wear when they're trying to impress boys for the first time. Several posters of boy bands and celebrities were hanging on the walls. It made Olivia feel both nostalgic and sad at the same time. Did Sophia feel the need to escape from those four walls that much? Did she miss them now that she was gone?

"Let's take a look at that phone," Brock said, pulling on a pair of plastic gloves to handle the phone.

Alice pursed her lips at him. "As I said, it's got a password."

Olivia peered at the screen over Brock's shoulder, racking her mind, trying to figure out what the code could be. She watched in horror as Brock punched in a number with so much confidence that it made Olivia's heart stutter. Two-seven-two-four-four.

The screen unlocked.

"How did you know?" Olivia gaped, staring at Brock in amazement.

His smile returned for a moment. "Two-seven-two-four-four. The numbers correspond to letters on the keypad. C-R-A-I-G," he said. "Makes sense for a teenage girl to make her passcode a boy's name, right?"

"Great," Alice muttered, looking irritable. "Why didn't I think of that?"

Olivia asked herself the same question. Hadn't she done the same thing when she was Sophia's age? She held her breath as Brock began to scroll through her apps.

"There are texts here from Craig," Brock announced. "He sent her a lot of messages last night, asking where she was. A few missed calls, too. He's either covered his tracks really well, or he genuinely had no clue where she was, as he told us."

"What was your impression of him?" Alice asked Olivia, narrowing her eyes.

Olivia sighed. "He's a strange guy, but we don't think he's involved. He said he left town in fear when he found out she was gone, but he came back. If he had Sophia, he wouldn't have come back, he'd have just stayed with her wherever they were. He cares about her a lot, Mrs. Edwards. It doesn't seem to me as if he is our perp here."

Alice folded her arms. "Well, I can't pretend I'm not disappointed. I was so sure he was involved."

"I know. We're not ruling anything out, but I think we're going to have to dig deeper. Hopefully, Sophia's phone can shed some light on what's going on. Is there anything else of interest in her texts, Brock?"

"Not really. She doesn't seem to have many contacts on her phone."

"She doesn't have a lot of friends," Alice admitted quietly. "She's always been a bit of a loner. I guess that's what attracted her to Craig, or vice versa."

"She last sent a text at eleven-thirty last night," Brock said. "She told Craig she was on her way. He responded at quarter past twelve, asking where she was."

Olivia's heart raced. Finally, some useful information. That meant there were at least forty-five minutes when she was out of the house. It also told her something much more important.

"Wait....so Sophia left the house of her own accord?" Olivia whispered.

"Looks like it."

Olivia didn't know what to make of that fact. It wasn't in line with what had happened to Amelia. Had Sophia simply wandered off the way she normally did, and just get lost? Had she run away from home deliberately? Or had she gone out to meet Craig only to be snatched off the street?

"Well, should I be worried?" Alice said, her voice high and shrill. "She's never been away from home this long when she's been out before. And if she's not with that stupid boy, then where is she? She's got nowhere else to go."

"Let's try to stay calm," Olivia said gently, though the feeling of terror was already squeezing the air out of her own lungs. She couldn't imagine how Sophia's mother must be feeling. "We don't know where Sophia is, but we know she went out to meet Craig. If she didn't meet him, she might possibly be with another friend. Or, as much as I hate to admit it, it's possible she could have been taken."

"Oh God, no. No, please. No," Alice wailed, starting to lose control of her emotions.

"I know you're scared, but we really need to keep our wits about us right now. We have no reason to think that anyone has hurt her. Not yet," Olivia said. "Even if she was taken by the same person who took Amelia, Amelia was returned unharmed. We just need to look a little deeper and see if we can track her down. Okay?"

Alice managed a nod, her breathing labored. "I just want my baby girl to come home."

"I know. And we'll do everything we can to bring her home. I promise."

They didn't stay long after that. The phone had unlocked a whole new level to the mystery. Olivia was sure they'd be able to find more out if they spent some time looking through it, so she and Brock left Alice behind and headed back to their car. Brock's eyes were glued to the screen as Olivia started up the engine.

"If this isn't about Craig, then where would she go?" Brock asked. "Do you think she's got some other guy on the line?"

"I don't know," Olivia shrugged. "This wouldn't be the first time Sophia has caused trouble for her mother. Maybe she heard about Amelia and took the opportunity to scare her mom. She could just be hiding out somewhere. But alternatively, what if someone knew about her habit of going to meet Craig? And what if that person used the opportunity to snatch her up? Going inside the house is a big risk. Whoever took Amelia knew that and took precautions. But what if he knew he wouldn't even have to? What if he knew he could just bundle her into a car and go?"

Olivia's thoughts were spilling out as they occurred to her. She didn't want to believe she was right. She much preferred the narrative that a bratty teenager was trying to punish her mother. But the more she thought about it, the more it seemed to fit perfectly with what they knew about the kidnapper. It was a smart, calculated move.

"Let's hope the phone sheds some light on the situation," Brock said. "Because I don't know if I can face another dead end right now."

Olivia nodded. "That makes two of us."

CHAPTER NINE

O LIVIA WOKE UP WITH A STIFF NECK, AS SHE ALWAYS DID when she was under extreme stress. It was as though her body enjoyed giving her one more thing to worry about. She sighed and sat up, staring around her bedroom. She and Brock had headed back to her house for the evening to go through the evidence and information they had but hadn't found anything particularly useful on Sophia's phone. There was nothing more than you'd find on the average teen girl's phone. It was frustrating to know that they had almost no way of getting answers.

Olivia took a quick shower and dressed, considering what to do next. She wondered whether they'd missed anything in their interviews. Deciding they hadn't, she thought perhaps they were just talking to the wrong people. She was sure that someone in town must have some useful information. After all, rumors spread like wildfire in small towns like Belle Grove. Surely there must have been someone who knew something. Somebody with a theory or a potential lead they hadn't considered?

When Olivia headed downstairs, she found Brock on the couch with a cup of coffee. She raised her eyebrows at him.

"Make yourself at home," she said.

"I have much better coffee at home. None of this instant stuff," Brock teased, though it didn't seem as if his heart was in it.

Olivia sat on the edge of the sofa by his feet, rubbing her temples. "I've just been wondering where we go from here."

"You and me both. I'm drawing a big, fat blank right now."

Olivia didn't want to agree with him, but she did. She knew she was a good agent, having solved several high-profile cases in her career, but this one was different. For the first time, she felt lost. Clueless. If only they could mine one nugget of gold out of the slurry they had. One clue that would set them on the right path.

Brock sighed. "You know, I trained all over the place. Brazil, Kuwait, Taiwan, Thailand. I always thought that made me special. Thought I had some investigative super power. I was clearly sought after, I knew that much," he said. "But now I realize that I'm just like anyone else. I'm not some Superman. You ever feel like we're meant to be more than we are in this line of work?"

Olivia nodded. She was well aware of how everyone saw her. Agents like her were meant to be on the verge of superhuman, but not quite. They were meant to be able to switch off their feelings at any given time, to handle every case quickly and easily. They were seen as smart, emotionless beings who saved the world every other day. But they were only human.

The expectations laid on them were heavy, especially in times of crisis. It wouldn't be long until Sophia's family started getting angry about their lack of progress. It already felt as though they were running out of time.

"I think we need some sort of a miracle today," Olivia sighed wearily. "Let's go back into the forest, just you and me. I think if we try to retrace Amelia's footsteps, then we might get some answers that way. There are all kinds of trapper's cabins out there our guy might be using to hold the girls. Maybe we'll get lucky and run into it. I mean, Amelia couldn't have come from too far off. It's got to be somewhere close. What do you think?"

"I think we don't have anything else to try. Let's go."

"Do you want to take a shower before we go?"

"Are you saying I smell?"

"I'm not saying that, but I probably wouldn't be wrong if I did."

Brock gave her a small smile. "All right. I'll be quick."

Fifteen minutes later, the pair of them were ready to go. As he showered, Olivia had put together a couple of packs with water, trail mix, and some protein bars. They'd need to keep their strength up throughout the day. They stood on the back patio of the cabin looking over the forest, watching its shadows darken with the secrets it held. Brock looked to Olivia expectantly, as if waiting for instructions. She frowned as she glanced around, wondering which direction they should start. Olivia closed her eyes for a moment and thought back to the night Amelia arrived on her doorstep.

She opened her eyes and nodded to herself. "I heard movement to the left of the house.... Amelia must have come from that direction. Let's circle around the cabin and walk north from the back of it."

Olivia led the way, looking again for trampled ground. The search party hadn't extended so far as the cabin, so when she saw a pathway of broken branches and trampled leaves in the undergrowth, she felt pretty confident that it was where Amelia had passed through. Even though Amelia had already been found, safe and sound, Olivia was sure that if they were dealing with the same kidnapper, then there might be some significance to the path Amelia had taken. If they could follow it far enough, maybe it would lead them to some answers. And if they were very lucky, it would lead them to where he was keeping Sophia.

"It must have been pretty intense having Amelia show up on your doorstep the way she did," Brock commented as they carefully picked their way through the forest.

"It was. I was sure she was being followed at the time. She seemed so urgent. Whatever she ran away from had terrified her."

"Doesn't it seem strange? Two sudden disappearances linked to this area. Specifically, this forest," Brock said, "There's nothing here. And yet, strange things are happening."

"Maggie said it's always pretty quiet here normally. Maybe it's me. Sometimes I feel as though trouble follows me around," Olivia murmured.

A shot of adrenaline surged through her as Olivia realized that was the first time she'd ever given voice to that particular thought. Brock frowned but nodded as if he could somehow relate. But the one thing she didn't see on his face—the reason she'd never spoken those words out loud before—was judgment. He didn't look as though he thought she were crazy or paranoid. That was what she'd feared the most and it wasn't there.

Feeling better about having let those thoughts slip, Olivia's thoughts flashed to her poor sister, her disappeared mother, her estranged father again. She thought of how she'd isolated herself from the few friends she had left. Maybe on some level, she did it to save them. To keep them out of trouble. If she really was a bad luck charm, it was only a matter of time before she rubbed off on them. After all, look what happened to her sister.

"Well, I guess trouble is a perk of the job," Brock mused. "But you know it's not your fault, right? It's not you at the center of things just because your job drags you into hell."

Olivia didn't respond. She didn't want to admit that she did believe, on some level, that she was a problem any more than she already had. She didn't want to admit that working alone was easier for her because involving someone like Brock usually meant involving him in her problems and pulling him into her troubles as well. It was like her bad luck had a gravitational pull of its own and just sucked in everybody around her. If he knew the things that had happened to her family, perhaps he wouldn't be feeling so confident and self-assured knowing it was only a matter of time before trouble found him—because of her.

They kept walking in silence. Olivia hadn't intended to shut him out entirely, but she didn't want to get in deep with Brock. She didn't want him to know everything going on in her head. After all, he'd be gone soon, and they'd probably never see each other again. As soon as the case was wrapped up, he'd be desperate to get out of Belle Grove and away from her. She was certain of it.

It was about fifteen minutes into the walk when Olivia noticed something. In the center of a small clearing was a magnificent tree, larger and wider than any of the rest in the forest. It was massive, like a redwood and it looked old—almost ancient. Thick tendrils of it roots rose out of the ground and extended away from the trunk, looking almost like reaching fingers. Olivia stopped and stared at it in awe. The base of the tree was hollowed out and the ground there dipped low, making almost a small cave inside the tree.

"That's pretty cool," Brock remarked, standing beside Olivia to admire it, too.

"It is," Olivia agreed quietly.

She knew they should move on, but something made her take a few steps closer to the tree. She placed her hand on the trunk of the tree, feeling the rough bark beneath her fingers as the wind whipped at her hair. She could hear something rustling and she strained her ears. It didn't sound like leaves in the breeze, or simply the sound of the trees. It sounded like something more synthetic. Like plastic rustling.

"Olivia? Are we moving on?"

Olivia ignored Brock and got on her knees by the hollowed entrance to the tree. She ducked her head inside and looked up, setting off a flurry of insects scampering away from her. Several large spiders had built webs all through the inside of the cave, the sight of which sent a shudder running up her spine. But behind the cobwebs and bits of bark and leaves, there was something else, too. Something concealed inside a large, dark plastic bag tucked into the side of the tree.

Olivia pulled a pair of plastic gloves out of her pack and snapped them on as she heard Brock approaching behind her.

"Did you find something?"

"I think I did…"

She plucked the plastic bag from out of the tree, surprised to find that it was heavier than she expected. It was stuffed nearly to bursting with several large objects. She ducked out from under the tree again and held it up to the daylight. Unable to see through the plastic, she pulled it open and what she saw surprised and unsettled her. The first thing she pulled out was a large, ugly rag doll. It looked well used. One of its button eyes hung loose on a piece of thread, and it was wearing a patchwork dress.

"Do you think it belongs to one of the kids?" Brock wondered, peering at it. "Sophia or Amelia?"

"I don't know… aren't they both a little old for dolls like this?" she mused. "I think the parents would've mentioned if a beloved toy of theirs was missing."

"Wait… what is *that?*" Brock asked, pointing in disgust at something in the bottom of the bag.

Olivia's heart froze when she saw what he was looking at. It was a lock of hair. Blonde and wispy. She plucked it from the back and saw that it had been bound with a rubber band to hold it together. In her mind, Olivia tried to match the shade of blonde to Amelia or Sophia, but she wasn't sure if either was a perfect match. Amelia's hair was very light, probably too light to be the lock of hair she was holding, but Sophia's hair was more of a dark blonde, from the pic-tures she had seen.

Olivia spotted a velvet pouch in bottom of the bag, too. She reached inside to see what it was and picked it up. Casting a look at Brock who looked like he wasn't even drawing breath, she shook it gently; several objects clanked together inside. She had a sinking feeling she already knew what was in there, and when she opened it, her fears were confirmed.

Teeth.

"Okay, that's just nasty," Brock cried in disgust. "What the hell?"

Olivia swallowed hard, her eyes scanning the teeth. The more she looked at them, the less ominous they seemed. At first, her mind had raced with horrific images of someone extracting teeth from their victims, but upon inspection, these teeth were much smaller than adult teeth.

"I don't think this is what you think it is," Olivia said, quietly examining the contents of the bag again. "These are baby teeth. A lot of parents keep their children's teeth. And the hair—again, not that unusual. I think my mother kept some of my hair after I got it cut short as a kid. I went through a tomboy phase, and she wanted something of mine to keep to remind her I was in fact, a little girl."

"So, you don't think these belong to Amelia or Sophia?"

"I don't think so," Olivia replied carefully. "The hair isn't the right color, for starters. It's a different shade of blonde to that of either of the girls who went missing. And both the girls will have their adult teeth by now. Besides, Amelia still had all her teeth."

"So, what are we looking at then? Is it even relevant?" he asked. "Or are these just the childhood mementos of some hobo who lives in the woods?"

"I'm not sure. Maybe it's just some kind of time capsule," she replied.

Even as she spoke the words, they rang false in her mind. Olivia's instincts screamed at her that the bag in her hand was important in some way. She just didn't know what way that was just yet. But she couldn't stop looking at the hair. Both the girls who'd gone missing were naturally blonde. It wasn't a perfect match but it was close. Very close. Did that mean what was in the bag had some kind of connection to the case? Even if the things inside didn't belong to either of the girls, the fact that the lock of hair was so similar that it set the red flags waving in Olivia's mind. She didn't like coincidences.

"Whoever left this here… they didn't bury it. They wanted easy access to it," Olivia thought aloud. "Maybe these things don't belong to the girls, but to someone's child. The fact that it's out here in the forest, not kept at home though, just doesn't sit right with me. Why would you keep something so precious out in the forest?"

"Unless you're trying to keep it hidden," Brock added.

Olivia nodded, glad that Brock understood where she was going with this. She examined everything inside again.

"And the doll looks pretty old. I don't think it belongs to either of the girls," Olivia said. Amelia's parents didn't mention a missing toy, and I don't feel that Sophia is the sort of girl who carries around a doll…"

"So how can we say it's relevant to our case?" Brock asked.

Olivia paused. "I don't know," she admitted. "Maybe we can't. Maybe I'm just hoping this matters. But I want to send it to the lab, anyway, and have the contents analyzed. You never know. And given that we don't have anything else to go on, I'm more than willing to grab at straws at this point."

"Right. Let's get it all to the labs at Quantico. Unless you want to keep searching?"

Olivia offered up the plastic bag to Brock. "You head back. I'm going to keep looking. I know the forest better; I'll be able to find my way back," she said. "But I don't want to waste any time on this bag if it's not relevant. Let's get it checked out as soon as possible. Tell them to put a rush on it."

"Aye, aye, captain," Brock cracked, pulling on gloves of his own and taking the bag from her. "I'll send the phone, too. It's unlikely, but it might pull up some fingerprints or something. I think we've got all that we can out of the texts on there."

Olivia nodded. "Okay. I'll see you later. Text me if anything important comes up."

The two of them parted ways. Olivia stood for a little longer by the hollowed-out tree, her heart beating hard in her chest, unable to describe the way she felt. She felt as though she was right on the cusp of something, of some sort of answer. She thought of everything in the bag, and her thoughts kept circling back to her mother. The thought was so insistent, it triggered a thought of her own. Maybe the person she was looking for was a mother—or somebody who *wanted* to be a mother.

But it wasn't enough to go on. She could see the shape of it but couldn't quite connect the dots. She thought hard about the similarities between Amelia and Sophia. Both were blonde, both were from relatively affluent families, and both were around the same age. But the big disconnect was the fact that although they seemingly both disappeared in the same forest, Amelia was from Seattle and Sophia was from here. She didn't know how to explain a girl from the west coast disappearing in a forest three thousand miles from her own home.

Other than the hair she'd found, was anything else in the plastic bag even remotely relevant to the case? Did the old, dirty and ragged doll suggest that maybe the person she was looking for didn't have a lot of money and perhaps, couldn't buy new toys for a child? Was it a memento from their own childhood? What did the doll have to do with anything? Or was it irrelevant? She closed her eyes to try to help her think, but she kept drawing blanks.

Eventually, she resumed walking. She had to explore every avenue. She had to try to follow the path that Amelia had run. But when every path led to a dead end, it felt as if it were all for nothing. The phone had been a dead end. Perhaps the contents of the bag would be, too.

And then where would that leave her?

CHAPTER
TEN

AFTER THE TRACKS SHE'D BEEN FOLLOWING HIT A DEAD END and she wasn't able to pick them up again, Olivia trekked back to her cabin by mid-afternoon. She felt deflated but hoped that Brock's morning might have been more productive. She texted him to let him know she was back at the cabin, reading the case notes and adding her own thoughts to the folder, and he joined her soon aft er, lett ing himself into the cabin.

"Hey," Olivia greeted him. "Did you get everything off to the lab all right?"

Brock nodded. "I think they thought I was crazy when I told them the connections we made to the case. I guess it is a prett y long shot, but we have to try, right?"

"Right," Olivia said half-heartedly.

Whoever had leftthose items hidden in the tree had chosen a strange place to stash their things. And though she wanted it to be connected to their case, Olivia didn't think they'd Fnd any trace of the kidnapper on the items they'd found. If they did belong to the kidnapper, she couldn't see him being so sloppy. After all, they'd taken two teenage girls without leaving a single trace. She thought their best hope was to find out who the teeth and hair belonged to.

"Anything we find now, we have to try to connect to the case," Brock continued. "Honestly, I've never gotten this far into a case with *nothing* before."

Olivia nodded. "Whoever is doing this has his head screwed on tight and is thinking clearly, for sure. I don't think we're dealing with some deranged psychopath," she said. "Whoever is doing this, I get the feeling he's just a normal person. Maybe someone who has been through something traumatic. Someone who wants to make other people feel the way he's been made to feel."

Brock nodded. "Yeah. That doesn't rule many people out, though, does it? I've met a lot of people over the years who feel like they've been wronged and have revenge on their minds."

Olivia pondered on that comment for a while. After her sister had died, she'd always wanted to be the one to find out what happened to her, to close the case, and get some answers. Especially after Paxton had started pressing the theory that there was foul play involved. But she'd never thought about embarking on some kind of revenge spree. She didn't want to hurt anyone in that way. She just wanted whoever might have done it to be brought to justice. The thought of revenge made her stomach turn a little. She'd dealt with plenty of horrible cases over the years, but she'd never been able to put herself in the shoes of the criminals she dealt with in that way. She could never imagine herself brandishing a knife, no matter how many people buried knives in her back.

"But revenge like this? What does that mean? Does it mean that whoever did this had a child stolen from him or her?" Olivia wondered aloud. "Did she have a miscarriage? Or lose a custody battle?"

"I'd say those are all possibilities if we're assuming the cases are linked. Remember, our first assumption with Amelia was trafficking because of the distance," Brock pointed out. "If our suspect's home base is here, that could mean that any connection would have to be very specific for him or her to go all that way."

Olivia exhaled heavily. "I feel as if I'm going around in circles. I could really use a break here," she said.

As she did, she heard a soft knock at the door, so quiet that she thought she'd imagined it for a moment, but Brock looked at the door too, then turned back to her.

"You going to get that?"

Olivia frowned. She never got visitors. In fact, until Brock was sent to work with her, Amelia was the closest thing to a visitor she'd had. She had a sudden fear that she was about to find Sophia on her porch in a similar state. But when she opened the door, she was surprised to see Craig standing there.

"Craig," Olivia said, folding her arms over her chest. "How did you know where to find me?"

"I asked at the police station. Officer Stone sent me here," Craig mumbled, shifting from foot to foot anxiously. "She said you were the person to talk to about the case."

That pricked up Olivia's ears. Was he about to come clean about Sophia?

"Well, I think you'd better come inside."

"Actually, I wanted you to follow me," Craig said nervously, nodding toward the back of her house, to the edge of the forest. Olivia's heart started racing.

"Why?"

"There's something I want to show you. I guess I want to show you that—that I'd never hurt her," he said.

Olivia's forehead creased in confusion. She had no idea what Craig could possibly want to show her, but if she was going into the forest with him, she certainly wasn't going alone.

"You won't mind if I bring my partner along, right?" she asked.

Brock appeared behind her, towering over both she and Craig.

It seemed to make Craig more anxious than he already was, but he nodded anyway.

"Okay. Sure," he said. "Come on. I'll show you."

Olivia exchanged a glance with Brock before the pair of them began to follow Craig out into the forest. It didn't take Olivia long to realize that they were following the same path they'd walked earlier that day. It made Olivia's stomach twist, her body vibrating with a case of nerves. Somehow, she already knew exactly where Craig was leading her.

The big hollowed-out tree came into view and Olivia was hit with a sense of deja vu. She imagined that something horrible had happened at the tree—and that something equally awful was going to happen to her and Brock if they weren't careful. She casually moved her hand closer to the butt of the holstered pistol that was clipped her belt and noticed Brock was doing the same. But Craig came to a stop in front of the tree and turned around and looked at them. His eyes were red and watery and he looked close to tears.

"Me and Sophia come here a lot," he said quietly. "But it's not just us. It's kind of well-known in the town. At least, among teenagers, it is. You know how quiet it is here, Agent Knight. Kids can't get away with going to wild parties or anything like that. So, I've been coming here since I was about fourteen. It's where kids meet up to smoke, drink, make out... you know, that kind of thing. People come here because it's private, and people can do all the things they're not supposed to."

Like kidnapping? Olivia thought to herself. Craig turned a little red, probably knowing exactly what she was thinking. He cleared his throat.

"Anyway, my point is, this is where we'd come. I used to drive her here, but since her mom started getting mad about us hanging out.... well, she's walked here herself a few times."

"So, you cared that much about this underage girl that you let her wander around in the forest in the middle of the night?" Brock asked coldly.

Craig's eyes widened with fear and he shook his head. "It's not like that, sir. You've got to understand, this town is very quiet. It's not like it is in the city. Kids still play out on the streets because we barely see any cars around most of the time. Everyone knows everyone here, everyone trusts everyone. Kids play out late all the time. I didn't ever think that something would happen to her. It just doesn't happen here."

"That's bull—"

"All right," Olivia cut Brock off. "That's not important right now. What made you bring us here, Craig? What's the significance of this place?"

Craig's lip wobbled a little and he moved closer to the tree, motioning Olivia to follow him. She did so cautiously, still feeling apprehensive about the young man. But when she watched him trail his finger over the bark of the tree, she understood what she was looking at.

Two letters were carved into the tree. C and S. Craig and Sophia. Craig let out a small sob as he traced the letter S.

"I really care about her," he sniffed. "On the night she disappeared, I was waiting here for her. I kept asking where she was. I thought she'd given up on me. I thought her mom had made her stay home. I waited for her here for hours. But eventually, I gave up and left. What if—what if she made it here, but then someone took her because I wasn't here?"

Olivia sighed quietly to herself. "All right, calm down, Craig. I think it's likely that she was taken on her way here. You'd probably have been waiting here alone all night. You being here probably wouldn't have changed anything."

She didn't add that it was his fault that a fifteen-year-old girl was walking around in the middle of the night in the first place. He seemed to be carrying enough guilt as it was. A certain part of Olivia felt a little sorry for Craig. He seemed genuinely upset that Sophia was missing. It made her even more determined to find the answers. To find the girl.

"Well, at least it seems more likely that Sophia left the house of her own accord now," Brock said, refusing to look at Craig as he cried. He glanced at Olivia, his jaw clenched in irritation at the young man. "And now we know she didn't make it this far. Craig, did you see anyone else around that night? Did you see anything unusual?"

Craig shook his head, still sniffling to himself. Brock sighed.

"So along with Sophia's phone records, we now know she left the house to come and meet Craig," Brock said. "If she was headed in this direction, then she could've been taken anywhere along the road."

Olivia nodded. "Then maybe we shouldn't be searching the forest for clues. Maybe we need to look along that road. If she managed to get anywhere on foot, then she might've left some sort of evidence behind. If things got violent, there might even be blood."

"B-blood?" Craig stuttered, his eyes shimmering with tears. "You think there might be blood? You think something bad happened to her?"

Olivia had to hold back from sighing. Craig had been of some use, but she was in no mood to babysit him in the middle of an investigation.

"Thank you for your help, Craig," she told him stiffly. "You should head back home now."

"But what about Sophia? What are you going to do?"

"That's for us to figure out," Brock snapped.

Olivia shot him a look before glancing back at Craig. "If we find her, we'll let you know."

Craig sniffed and wiped his nose on his entire sleeve. The sight made Olivia wince. He really did act half his age. As he shuffled away, she turned back to Brock.

"You need to stop antagonizing him. You'll make him close up," she said. "He might have more information that he hasn't revealed to us yet. But he's not going to tell us anything if you keep going for the jugular."

"The guy gives me a bad vibe," Brock snarled. "I just don't trust him."

"This shouldn't be getting so personal. We're here to find a kidnapper, not to decide who we like and who we don't," Olivia said sharply.

She needed Brock to get his head in the game if they were going to find anything useful and crack this case. When she felt her phone buzzing in her pocket, she glared at Brock.

"We can talk about this in a moment," she said, pulling out the phone to see a call from Jonathan. "It's the boss. I have to take this."

Olivia picked up the call and Jonathan quickly cut in before she could get a word out. "Knight. I'd like you and Tanner to come and see me right now. We're reviewing the information you've provided for us so far and we'd like to discuss the case in person."

"Okay, sir, we're on our way."

He hung up before she even finished speaking and she turned to look at Brock.

"Mr. James wants us in his office."

"Great," Brock grumbled, already turning on his heel. "I'll drive."

CHAPTER ELEVEN

THE FIRST TWENTY MINUTES OF THE JOURNEY PASSED IN strained silence, making Olivia anxious. Brock didn't engage in any of his usual chatter, focusing solely on the road ahead of him. He didn't even try to poke at her with loud music or by telling jokes. That's how Olivia could tell he wasn't happy with her.

She knew she shouldn't have snapped at him, but he drove her crazy. He seemed way too keen to fly off the handle at any given opportunity. His emotions seemed to hit either end of the spectrum with no in-between. She had to admit, she much preferred annoying, chatty Brock to silent, sullen Brock. After a while, though, she saw Brock rub his jaw and let out a sigh. She turned a little in her seat so that she could see him better.

"Are you alright?" she asked.

"Yes," Brock said a little too quickly, continuing to rub at his jaw. "Well, I am, but also not really. I'm sorry I got so irritable before. I just find these cases hard. Honestly, I'd prefer anything to working on a case involving kids."

Olivia nodded in understanding. She'd always felt the same way. She could understand why the case was making him so uncomfortable when young lives were potentially at stake. All she could think of then was of the way Amelia had looked, so wild-eyed and terrified, when she showed up on her doorstep. That image had haunted her dreams ever since that night.

"You don't have to explain that to me. These kinds of cases are the worst. Give me a murder any day."

The corners of Brock's mouth twitched like he was fighting off a smile. "Well, murders suck, too, I guess. The job just sucks sometimes. But something about cases involving kids makes it suck even more."

Olivia nodded again. On days like those, she did sometimes question why she'd signed up for that life. But every time she closed a case or caught a criminal, she remembered. She'd saved so many lives since her career began that she told herself it was all worth it. She'd never forget how happy Amelia's parents were to have her back, for example. She knew that a family like hers wouldn't have survived without her. They loved her so hard that life wasn't worth it without their baby girl. Olivia stuck with the job because she wanted more moments like that. Even though her own family had fallen apart, she could still try to save others.

Brock sighed beside her. "Kid cases are ten times worse. Every time I come across one, it makes me want to walk away. But I know those kids relying on me to save them. The pressure gets to me. I'm not usually so grumpy."

Olivia chewed her lip. When she'd asked Brock to talk about his worst case, he hadn't been willing to open up about it. Did something happen to a kid while he was on a case? Was he too late to save someone? She wasn't sure, but the look on his face told her that was probably the case. She could see from the creases in his forehead and the dark circles under his eyes that he was just as exhausted as she was. But now that she knew how hard he took cases involving kids, she thought there was something more to his weariness.

"Let's hope the SAC has some good news for us," she said.

Brock rolled his eyes and finally managed a weak smile. "I thought I was the comedian here."

Olivia chuckled despite herself and turned, looking out the window again. She knew they were both doing the best they could, but she couldn't help feeling irritated with their own efforts and the lack of any substantial progress. It was frustrating to put so much hard work in and get very little out of it. She felt for the families, too. Alice was probably pacing the floors at home, waiting in frustration and fear for them to do their job better. To bring her little girl home to her. Olivia knew that, in Alice's place, she'd resent them if they never found Sophia, even thought it would be no fault of their own. That was a heavy burden to have to bear, but she understood it. She'd been through something similar herself.

She'd been angry when her sister died. So angry that she took it out on anyone and everyone around her. She'd known it was no one's fault, but somehow, she'd found ways to convince herself that Veronica died because somebody didn't do their job. She'd wanted to know why the officers investigating didn't spend every waking hour on the case. She'd wanted to know why she was finding things that the police weren't. She ignored the fact that she had insider information because she was Veronica's sister and Paxton had connections. She wanted to know why after weeks and weeks of she and Paxton badgering the Seattle Police Department, nobody had seen fit to even give them the time of day. They'd just closed the case and moved on with their lives, subtly telling Olivia to do the same.

And now that Olivia was on the other side of it, struggling to solve an impossible case, she felt bad for all those past feelings. How could she not? It was just as Brock had said before: they weren't superhuman. How were they expected to have all of the answers?

"You know... I lost my sister," Olivia found herself saying aloud. She didn't want to keep it in any longer. Didn't think she could even if she'd wanted to. Brock took his eyes off the road for a moment and glanced over at her.

"She died?"

"Car accident. She was driving late one night and hit a patch of black ice," she said. "But that official explanation has never set right with me. I think she was murdered."

"What makes you say that?"

"She was a journalist. A good one. She was always stirring up trouble for people who deserved it. People who resented her for it. Hated her for it," she explained. "Veronica called out corrupt politicians, put a spotlight on the flaws in the justice system, criticized the FBI—even when I was still training at Quantico. She had a lot of opinions. She was building a pretty successful investigative podcast going after powerful people. And she was always so careful. But she still turned up dead."

"I had no idea. I'm so sorry; that's awful," Brock said quietly and the silence hung heavy in the air for a moment. "If you think there was a coverup, don't give up on the case. You know that any good cop won't let it go. Even years after something happens, good cops don't stop theorizing. Investigating. Cold cases are a thing for a reason."

"Well, I certainly don't trust the Seattle PD's official story. They completely bungled the investigation. Just like they probably did with Amelia."

"Seattle?" Brock raised an eyebrow. "Maybe this case is hitting closer to home to you because of that connection."

"Maybe," Olivia admitted. "But that's the thing. Those cops just let it go. If I was better at my job, maybe I could've solved it myself by now. Maybe I would've solved this whole thing already..."

"Olivia, don't go down that road. Please. You and I both know that these things can sometimes be totally impossible," Brock interrupted, his voice so gentle that it shocked her completely. "You know as well as I do that it can take years to catch one killer. Even then, some loose ends just never get tied up. If your sister really was murdered and you haven't found the suspect, it's not because you didn't do a good job of searching for him. I don't want to step out of line here—I know we haven't known each other long—but I really don't think I'd be trusting your judgments so much if I thought you were terrible at your job. I trust you, Olivia. And I trust that you're going to get this thing done. And who knows? Maybe someday you'll get a shot at finding out what happened to your sister, too."

Olivia sank back in her seat. The whole conversation felt heavy to her. She hadn't expected to feel so emotional, but it had been a long time since she'd talked about her sister out loud. Veronica had never really left her mind, but she kept her thoughts about her to herself. She never even talked to Paxton about her. Veronica's memory had been locked in the past. Frozen in time. Most of the time, she and her family pretended that life had just gone on as normal, but it hadn't. The moment she learned of Veronica's death, she knew nothing would never be the same again.

Opening up to Brock about it was sort of like accepting that Veronica was gone and that even solving the case wouldn't bring her back. Olivia had to take a deep breath to stop herself from bursting into tears. She hoped she was being subtle, but Brock must have noticed, because he reached out and squeezed her hand.

"It's all right," he said gently. "You don't have to be strong when it comes to this. It's been a hard week. You don't need to be embarrassed."

Olivia turned her face to the window and sniffed quietly as big tears rolled down her cheeks. "Sometimes I'm just waiting for it to get easier, and it doesn't. It's been years since we lost her, but it feels as though it was only yesterday."

"Grief's funny that way," Brock said, though nothing was funny at all at that moment. "It just keeps piling up. Everything you lose makes you feel it more, but you never get rid of it."

Olivia nodded. She was glad someone understood what she meant. He still had her hand in his.

"We won't be there for a while yet," Brock told her. "Why don't you just close your eyes for a while? Try to calm down a little."

Olivia nodded in resignation, a little embarrassed by her outburst, but at the same time, feeling a bit lighter. Unloading her thoughts onto Brock had shifted away some of her pain. She closed her eyes and took a few deep breaths. It was going to be okay. Things were hard, but they were going to be okay.

The journey felt a lot longer than it really was, and by the time they reached the Hoover Building, Olivia had begun to suspect she was about to get more bad news. She and Brock entered the building side by side, badged themselves past security, and were greeted in the lobby by SAC Jonathan James. He was a strict-looking man with thick-rimmed glasses and a head of dark hair streaked with gray. He was only in his mid-forties, but time and stress had created cavernous lines on his face, making him look a little older. He nodded to Olivia and Brock as they entered.

"You made good time. I won't keep you long, but I thought we should do this in person."

Olivia didn't like the sound of that. Did that mean they were in trouble? She followed behind Jonathan as he headed to his office, her heart racing. Even though her job was hard at times and she some-times questioned why she wanted to keep doing it, she didn't want to lose it. It was the one passion she had, the one thing that kept her going. Without her work, what would she have left?

But Jonathan offered her a small smile as they sat down at his desk and Olivia relaxed a little, folding her hands in her lap as she waited for him to say something. He adjusted his large glasses and sat back in his seat as he looked at her.

"First of all, Knight, I'd like to congratulate you on your handling of Amelia Barnes and her family. I've heard through the grapevine that they found you very helpful and kind. It's nice to hear good things about my agents."

"It's nice to hear it, too," Olivia said, feeling her shoulders relax a little. "But I get the feeling you brought us here to give us bad news?"

"Not bad news, necessarily," Jonathan replied, peering over at some papers on his desk. "We've been reviewing the things you've found about Sophie Edwards…"

"Sophia."

"Right, Sophia. Well, I can see why you thought there might be a correlation, but from everything we've reviewed so far, although the circumstances are similar, we don't believe that the two cases are related and don't want to keep expending manpower—"

Olivia blinked several times. "Sir, I know we haven't found all that much to connect the two cases yet but give us some time. Sophia might just have run away, but we haven't found anything in particular would have triggered that behavior. She was supposed to be meeting her boyfriend, and according to him, she wouldn't just not show up."

"You might be right. But even if she was taken, it doesn't mean we're dealing with the same kidnapper," Jonathan reasoned. "I understand that you're looking for a link in the hopes that it might aid the investigation into who took Amelia Barnes. But remember, that your first priority is to find where Amelia was being held and how she got transported all the way to Belle Grove. We're shifting our focus and want to stop a possible trafficking network and as of now, we have no evidence that Sophia Edwards was abducted or trafficked. You're just wasting time with this local case that has a few similarities. We'd like you to hand the Edwards case back over to local LEOs and let them handle it."

"Sir, if I may," Brock started, leaning forward. "We feel we might be on the cusp of something. I don't know if you heard about the things we sent to the lab—"

"I did," Jonathan said slowly, cutting him off. "And if you find any prints or DNA on those things, then you can use that as a lead. But if you don't, then they're not going to prove anything. Plenty of people keep mementos such like those. The placement of them was strange, but could be indicative of a homeless person and not a kidnapper. And unless you can match the items you sent in to a person, it's a dead end no matter what."

"Well, what about the connection between the two girls? Both blonde, both from affluent families, both of similar age and looks…"

"And from two opposite ends of the country. It's not enough to go on right now," Jonathan said firmly. "You were assigned to search for the person who kidnapped Amelia Barnes. Until there's more evidence to suggest that the person who did it also took Sophia Edwards, then I'm afraid it's not relevant to you anymore. I know that the evidence for this case is lacking, but Amelia Barnes is home safe now. Seattle was a dead end, so our only hope of exposing this possible network will be finding where she was held in Belle Grove. We've sent the Barnes family back to Seattle with a security escort, so they should be fine. We'll have the field office up there call you if they find anything. Just focus on what evidence you do have here and see where you can get with it. Find where Amelia was being held and expose the network."

Olivia leaned back in her chair but said nothing. She felt defeated. Even if her boss was right, even if Sophia was just a kid on the run from teenage problems, it felt wrong that they were being told not to look for her. Olivia shook her head. This wasn't right. She needed more time and resources. She was positive they were connected and absolutely certain that she could crack the case if given the opportunity.

Brock didn't seem ready to give up yet, either. He pressed his lips together, composing himself for a moment before speaking.

"Sir, I think this is a mistake," he said. "The Edwards case could—"

"I want your focus to be on the kidnapper. On the man who took Amelia Barnes," Jonathan cut him off bluntly. "If anything changes and you find something to definitively connect the cases, then, by all means, look into Sophia's disappearance as well. But right now, I want your focus on finding the man who took Amelia Barnes. Find out where she was held and find anything that can help us expose this trafficking network."

"So, you've given up already?" Brock snapped, pressing his lips together again. Olivia knew that only a guy like Brock could get away with speaking to the boss so bluntly. "I can't believe you're telling us to give up."

"I'm not saying that at all. But unless he strikes again, unless he leaves us some clue, what do you have to go on, really? No eyewitnesses, no DNA—there is nothing that connects the Edwards case with the Barnes case. So, focus on what you can solve. I'm sorry, Tanner, but sometimes you have to know when to accept that things aren't going to go your way and salvage what you can," he said.

He might be right, but that didn't make Olivia feel any better about it. She felt that she'd failed not just Amelia, but Sophia, too. She'd failed herself. She'd failed her sister, her poor sister who would never get justice for what had happened to her.

But sometimes, that was just the way of the world.

"Fine. I guess we're done here, then," Brock said, standing up. Jonathan stood, too, and shook Brock's hand.

"Don't beat yourself up, Knight," Jonathan said as he looked into Olivia's eyes and shook her hand, too. "You're doing everything you can. Keep up the good work."

Brock was muttering to himself the whole way back to the car, but Olivia was too caught up in herself to pay much attention. She felt completely deflated. Images of Sophia, of Amelia, of Veronica, swam through her mind. All the people she couldn't save, no matter how she tried. How was she supposed to just live with that?

Back in the car, Brock sighed and started the engine.

"What now?" Olivia asked.

He sucked in a deep breath. "I guess we wait for the kidnapper to strike again."

CHAPTER TWELVE

SEVERAL DAYS PASSED, AND OLIVIA'S FRUSTRATION ONLY CON-
tinued to grow. She and Brock combed the town over and over
for any sort of clues, both becoming more and more frustrated
over the lack of eyewitnesses, the lack of evidence, and the lack of
anything. She called the Barnes family several times, but they had
nothing new to offer her, and now that their daughter was home, they
didn't seem interested in pursuing it much further.

In a fit of near desperation, Olivia even tried contacting Paxton's
friend Blake Wilder out in the Seattle field office, but she'd been unable to provide any assistance or insight into the case. Olivia also
called Alice Edwards once, but she decided against doing it again
after nearly getting her head chewed off by the distraught mother.
It was becoming rapidly clear that nobody else was going to be of
any use to her.

Brock showed his frustration in his restlessness. He was un-
willing to go back to his B&B when there was still work to be done.
He stayed at her house, drinking endless cups of instant coffee and

occasionally napping on her sofa. At night, Olivia tried to sleep if she could, but she felt more awake than ever, her insomnia rising to a whole new level.

She woke after a short sleep one night and headed downstairs to find Brock with his head in his hands. She placed a comforting hand on his back. She was starting to like Brock a lot more than when she'd first met him, now that she knew he had a human heart and wasn't just purely a jokester or somebody who didn't take things as seriously as he should. Brock hid his true feelings behind that smile of his. Deep down, he let himself get invested in his cases and took things a lot more seriously than he let on. He sighed beneath her touch.

"I'm almost wishing the kidnapper would do something now," he murmured. "I know that's sick. But if there's a third victim, we can at least try to establish patterns. SAC James would have to take it seriously then."

Olivia nodded, sitting down beside him. She understood his thought process exactly. Maybe if there was a little more panic, a little more sense of urgency, the people of the town would be more helpful, too. They all seemed to be going about their business as usual, assuming that Sophia Edwards was just a troubled girl who'd run away from home. Perhaps if another girl went missing, they'd at least be more forthcoming with anything they knew. Olivia had put out a plea to the town for information, even providing her cellphone number as a hotline, but had gotten complete silence in return.

Olivia understood why. Belle Grove was a small town and she was an outsider. She wasn't a trusted member of their community. She was the black sheep in a field of white ones. Olivia knew it wasn't personal, but she realized that being an FBI agent living in a secluded cabin in the woods was like putting a big sign on her head saying, 'back off'. It was her own fault in a way that the people of the town didn't trust her. The only person she'd made a connection with since moving there was Maggie Stone. And though she was a perfectly capable police officer in a small town, she seemed out of her depth with the case of Sophia's disappearance.

That meant the only person Olivia could rely on was Brock, and he was just as frustrated and as much in the dark as she was. She had to admit that people warmed to him much more easily, and were always willing to answer his questions, but nothing had shed any light on what they needed to know. If anyone knew anything, surely, they would've come forward and said something by now.

"I didn't think this case would take so long," Brock muttered, nursing his coffee. "I thought it would be straightforward. How wrong I was."

"We're just going to have to stick it out," Olivia sighed. "Maybe we need to let our minds relax a little. Stop thinking so hard about it. Like you said that first day we met, answers sometimes come when you're least expecting them or trying so hard to find them."

Brock offered her a small smile. "The high-maintenance queen is suggesting we take a break?"

"Yes. I think in the morning we should take a walk, clear the cobwebs out of our head a little. We can go through the forest and cover the ground we've already covered, perhaps even find some new ground. Maybe something will jump out at us."

Brock shrugged. "I guess it can't hurt to walk through the forest again. But I can tell you now, there's no chance I'm going to relax."

The corners of Olivia's mouth twitched. "Me, either. I'm not sure why I suggested it, to be honest. We're both wound pretty tight right now."

Brock chuckled and shook his head. When he looked back at her, there was a softness in his eyes that made Olivia's heart beat a little faster. Over the past few days, she'd seen that look in his eyes a lot more. They were starting to understand one another better, even if Olivia hadn't quite decided yet how she felt about him. Sometimes, he drove her up the wall, but more and more often, she found herself

125

smiling in his presence, even through the hardships of the case, and even found herself laughing at his jokes easier.

All in all, their relationship was evolving. Could they call it friendship? She wasn't sure yet. But they were definitely getting there, and with those feelings came something deeper. Something closer to a crush, though she was doing her best to fight that off.

"You alright?" Brock asked Olivia. "You just turned red all of a sudden."

Olivia suddenly realized that her face was scalding hot with a blush. She couldn't believe he'd noticed when she'd been in her own little world. She nodded fervently.

"Fine. I'm fine. I was just thinking I'd make some coffee," she stammered. "I don't think I'll get back to sleep for a while."

"You don't sleep much at all, do you?" Brock called after her as she headed into the kitchen, her cheeks still hot.

"Not so much."

"Have you tried counting sheep?" Brock teased. "Or dousing yourself in lavender oil? I've heard that's good for sleep."

"I'd need a whole field of lavender just to get me sleepy," Olivia replied, stirring her instant coffee in the mug.

"Well, what's the deal? Does something keep you up at night?"

Olivia laughed quietly to herself. "I guess. I have plenty of things to think over in the middle of the night. Past mistakes. Future mistakes. Present mistakes..."

"I don't see that you're making any mistakes right now. I think you're doing fine."

"My most recent mistake was starting this conversation."

Brock laughed heartily from the other room, and she smiled, picking up her mug and joining him on the sofa. She didn't look at him, but she could feel him studying her.

"Having caffeine after midnight probably doesn't help either," he pointed out.

"Says you. You've been drinking a bucket of coffee every night since you started crashing here," she said with a grin. "I'm going to go broke if I have to keep replacing all the coffee you're drinking."

"And it still tastes terrible. When's your birthday? Maybe I'll get you a real coffee machine."

"You just missed it," Olivia said cryptically.

She hadn't told a soul, but her birthday had only been yesterday. Her father had texted her and she'd gotten texts from her old FBI friends, too, but she'd declined their offer to visit her in Belle Grove. That had been the extent of the celebration of the occasion. While she didn't mind the idea of visiting the town's only bar and having a few drinks with her old friends, she couldn't allow herself to go out and have fun when there was still a girl missing and a case to be solved. She rubbed at her temples, feeling the buzz of caffeine feeding her almost-constant stress headache. It was starting to become a struggle to remember what normal life used to be like.

"You know what always helps me sleep?" Brock piped up after a moment, picking up the remote for Olivia's ancient TV. "Old black and white movies. They're so boring that you can't help zonking out after just a few minutes. Plus, all the static is good for white noise…"

"Old movies are the only good ones!" Olivia protested. "They were actually original, for one thing. I'm so tired of seeing all the same recycled ideas making it on the screen over and over again. I barely ever use the TV, though. I prefer to read."

"Well, reading is another thing that could easily send me to sleep," Brock grinned, "but old movies are definitely better. Maybe we should try it."

"Well, it's one thing I haven't tried. I guess we could give it a shot."

Brock flicked through the channels until he found a late-night showing of Psycho. Olivia raised her eyebrow.

"Nice choice. That's a real good bedtime story…"

"Okay, I'll admit, for a moldy oldie, this is a pretty good movie," he said. "But maybe a little spooky for this time of night."

"Leave it on," she said, resting her head on the arm of the sofa. "I want to think about something else for a while."

They fell silent, the quiet buzz of the TV the only sound in the room. Olivia found herself curled up, her feet close to Brock on the sofa. She felt a sort of electricity emanating from his body and she blushed. Staying up late to watch a movie with Brock was the closest thing she'd had to a date in a very long time. And for the first time in a long time, she felt a flicker of something like happiness.

༺

Olivia woke with a stiff neck and a dry mouth, feeling a sense of déjà vu after her night in the hospital sitting vigil at Amelia's side. She heard the rumble of snoring and looked over to see that Brock was fast asleep beside her on the sofa, his head leaned against the back of the couch. She smiled to herself, noting that she wouldn't be the only one struggling through the morning with a stiff neck.

It was still early, but late enough to give up on sleep and start the day. She took a shower and prepared to go walking through the forest again. Any peace she'd felt the night before in front of the TV with Brock had gone, but she felt a little better knowing she was spending the day with him, even if the circumstances under which they were doing so were pretty dire.

When she headed back downstairs, she found Brock in the kitchen once again, making himself some coffee. It was strange to watch him looking so at home in her house. For a long time, she'd forgotten what it was like to have time to think about romance, or think about a future with someone. She'd forgotten what it was like to imagine a life outside her work. But with a strange pang in her chest, she watched Brock and thought about how nice it would be to have him around.

"Take a picture, it lasts longer," Brock teased.

Olivia blinked. She hadn't realized he'd turned to look at her. She couldn't believe she'd been caught staring.

"Sorry. Zoned out there," she admitted, another blush spreading over her cheeks.

He raised an eyebrow at her, looking smug. "Whatever you say."

Olivia scowled. Her strange fantasy had once again been replaced with irritation. Of course, she knew her irritation was based in the embarrassment of being caught mooning over him.

"All right, go get ready," she ordered. "Daylight's burning and I'm ready to get started. You can use the shower if you want."

"All right, won't be long," he said, sipping from his mug with a glint in his eye as he left the room.

Only after he'd gone did Olivia let her guard down a little, letting out a deep sigh. Whatever her growing feelings were for Brock, she had to let them fizzle out and die. She didn't want anything getting in the way of her work. Besides, she knew deep down that they could never be together. He'd be itching to leave town as soon as their case was done with, and she guessed he wouldn't be interested in returning to Belle Grove after that. After all, what would he have to come back for?

By the time Brock had returned from his shower, Olivia had downed two more cups of coffee and was feeling more in control. She'd tried to force herself to come to her senses and push any silly, quasi-romantic feelings for him out of her head. But seeing Brock with damp hair plastered to his forehead and a crooked smile only undid all the hard work she'd put into pretending she wasn't starting to care about him.

"Ready?" he asked, shrugging on a jacket. She bit her lip. Suddenly, everything he did was attractive, even when he wasn't doing much at all. She forced herself to look away from him.

"Let's go," she said.

He stayed on her mind as they trekked through the woods once again. The familiarity of the walk faded away with the onslaught of new emotions and made it all feel brand new. Sometimes, Olivia would glance over at Brock and her heart would do a hop, skip, and jump. How long had it been since she'd felt that way about someone? Long enough at least that she'd forgotten how futile it was to resist. The impossibility of their situation made Olivia wish she'd never felt the first stab of desire in the first place. She took a deep breath and scanned the woods, looking for anything to distract her from what was going on inside her head and her heart.

"I wonder how far this forest goes on," he mused, looking into the distance.

"Oh, for miles and miles and miles. This forest is literally hundreds of square miles," she said.

He nodded. "When I drove in, it seemed to go on forever. It's beautiful but if our kidnapper is hiding out in the woods, we'll be hard-pressed to figure out where," he said. "You can probably get lost pretty easily out there."

Olivia nodded. She felt pretty lost herself, but that was more of an emotional thing at that moment. She shook it out of her head, willing herself to continue walking.

"I already checked to see if there are any residential homes in the forest, but nothing came up in my search. There are a lot of cabins off the grid out there though," she said. "That would make it even harder to find someone if they decided to camp out there, but maybe we can do an aerial search. Might be able to spot some struc-tures from the air."

"Good luck getting the resources for that," Brock grumbled. "I think we're on our own out here. But I guess it can't hurt to ask. And we can maybe venture further out on our own. Although the under-growth is pretty thick. I think we'd have a rough time getting through it on foot after a while."

Olivia was about to reply when she spotted someone in the trees. Her first thought was to feel threatened, but she calmed down when she saw that the woman walking through the forest was a hiker. She had two walking sticks and was striding confidently through the tricky terrain. Olivia got an idea.

"We should ask that woman what's out there," she said. "If she's hiked these woods before then she'll probably have more clue than we do. If she's local, that is. I know some people come in from other places just to hike the trails here."

Brock shrugged. "Can't hurt to ask."

Olivia started to jog as best she could toward the woman, who was heading deeper into the forest. The woman set a pretty grueling pace. She was obviously in pretty good shape.

"Excuse me!" Olivia called out to the woman, trying to get her attention. She didn't appear to hear her. "Excuse me!"

This time, the woman turned around, looking a little perplexed. She stopped to allow Olivia to catch up and smiled at her.

"I'm sorry. I thought I was imagining your calling out to me. I don't see many people out here," the woman said.

As the woman spoke, Olivia studied her. She had a slim figure, maybe even a little too thin. Her blonde hair was starting to gray a little, the silvery strands catching in the sliver of sunlight peeking through the trees. Olivia first thought she might be younger than she looked, but the wrinkles on her face told the story of a woman weathered by life.

"Thanks for stopping," Olivia said with a warm smile. "I was just wondering if you could tell me anything about the forest. My friend and I were wondering how far out the forest goes. And maybe whether there are buildings in the wooded area. Hunter's cabins and things like that."

The woman's eyebrow quirked up and she smiled. "You're that FBI agent, aren't you? Living in the ranger's cabin?"

Olivia nodded. She'd been hoping for an informal conversation, but she'd been found out. The fact that the woman had heard the gossip and knew she was with the Bureau though, told Olivia she was probably a local.

"Yes. We're looking into the disappearance of a young girl and to be honest, all we have to go on is that she was last seen in the forest.

We were hoping we might be able to narrow down our search if we knew more about the landscape we're dealing with," she said. "Our searches on foot have been unsuccessful. The volunteer search party didn't find anything either. Is there anything you can tell us about the forest? You seem to know it pretty well, as a hiker, and all."

The woman stared out into the trees. "Well, I've been living here a while now and I go hiking in these woods fairly often. I've never seen any buildings out there. I think your place, the ranger's cabin, is the only one. Sorry if that's not helpful."

Olivia's shoulders sagged a little. Another disappointment. "No, that was great. Thank you for your help. If you do think of anything else, please don't hesitate to get in touch," she said, pulling out her card and handing it to the woman.

She gave Olivia a warm smile. "I hope you find what you're looking for."

The woman tucked the card into the pocket of her running leggings and continued on with her hike. Olivia turned to Brock with a shrug.

"It was worth a shot."

Brock sighed. "Yeah. I guess we just keep looking."

They continued their search but had no more success than the first time they went traipsing through the woods. Olivia could feel the heaviness and pressure of time on her shoulders. If they didn't find something soon, she thought she might come undone. But one thing became clear to her then.

She didn't have time to fawn over Brock Tanner.

CHAPTER THIRTEEN

ROCK AND OLIVIA WENT THEIR SEPARATE WAYS THAT EVE-ning after another day of unsuccessful searching. After their walk in the woods, they spent another few hours desperately bouncing ideas off one another, but when they came up with nothing, Brock headed back to his B&B, leaving Olivia alone with her thoughts.

She tried anything she could to distract herself. She ran herself a bath and tried to start a new book, but she found that her eyes just kept scanning the pages without actually reading the words. She tried to cook a new dish that she'd been wanting to try for a while, but she got so distracted that she burned the food and filled her kitchen with gray smoke and acrid odor. She let out a frustrated groan and had to go through the house to open all the windows to thin out the smoke.

By the time she collapsed into bed later that evening, she was practically drowning in her anxiety. Her heart was pounding, making it feel impossible to lie still and accept sleep. And when she did eventually drift off, she dreamed of awful things. She dreamed of finding young girls dead. Of Veronica and what had happened to her. Of her mother's disappearing, and her being unable to find her again. She woke up covered in sweat and decided that she didn't want to go back to sleep, no matter how tired she was.

Padding downstairs in her pajamas, she went out to sit on her patio and listen to the utter silence of the forest around her. She still couldn't wrap her head around the size of it. It was like trying to comprehend the extent of space or the ocean. How was she supposed to search every inch of it for clues when she only had Brock to help her? Besides, it had been a week now since Amelia had been returned to her parents. Any evidence they might have been able to find early on had likely already disappeared into the wilderness.

Meanwhile, poor Sophia was alone out there somewhere, unable to tell them the crucial details they were missing. The details they needed to find her. Olivia felt certain that she didn't run away. That she was scared and wanted to be found. Not many kids of her age had the nerve to be out in the world alone for very long. If Olivia could find just one detail, one lead, she might be able to solve it. She might be able to find her. Olivia silently vowed she wouldn't rest until she'd found Sophia, but she wondered if those were just words. There was nothing and no way to find her. Olivia felt she was standing in a barren desert, waiting for a puddle of water to magically appear at her feet.

When she sat down on her back porch, Olivia had hoped that the cold air outside might shock her system. That it might make her think of something she'd overlooked before. She recalled the sight of Amelia, malnourished and injured by the wrath of the forest. How far had she walked? She wouldn't have made it much further in the state she was in, but as she stared at the sheer vastness of the forest, Olivia admitted it was possible Amelia had been walking for several days. Perhaps she'd been propelled by her will to survive and had been walking for a longer than that. As Brock had said, it was easy to get lost in those woods. It could've taken her a while to find civilization.

The thought scared her. If Amelia had walked through the forest for days, there was a strong chance that they'd never find where she'd been held. Olivia pressed the heel of her hand against her eyes, feeling like she was going crazy. How many times was she going to have to go around in circles? When was she going to accept that the case was hopeless? When was she going to admit that this was one of those cases that would never be solved?

She wished that Amelia could tell them something, *anything*. She knew that some non-verbal children were able to say a few words. But then Olivia thought, if she could, she would've said something already. But she hadn't and she wouldn't. Maybe because she couldn't or because the trauma of it all made it so she didn't want to. Either way, the kidnapper committed the perfect crime when he'd taken her.

Except he'd then let Amelia get away. And that was the conclusion Olivia had come to—he'd let her go. Amelia was meek and shy. A girl who hid in a closet when she got scared wouldn't have fought her way to freedom. She was released. But why? She couldn't understand the reasoning behind that. He'd taken Amelia with no intention of asking for ransom money or anything else, so what was the prize?

He'd transported her for nearly three thousand miles only to set her free? If Amelia was what the kidnapper wanted, then why was she let go? Did something go wrong? Did he find it too difficult to handle an autistic child? Or did he just figure out that no matter what he did to her, Amelia wouldn't ever be able to tell anyone and he just didn't care anymore?

The thought was more than sickening. She tried to imagine what it would have been like to be Amelia, trapped in her own horrific memories of what had happened and found she couldn't conjure something that awful and traumatic. Tears sprang to her eyes. Who would do something like that to an innocent child? It was an even harder question to comprehend when Olivia had no idea what the motive for her abduction even was.

The situation was growing more dire by the day. Olivia knew that if they didn't find something useful soon, the case would never be solved. They'd all be told to move on with their lives, their case-loads, and forget that it ever happened—but Olivia wasn't sure she was going to be able to do that. She'd always had trouble letting go of the past, and she knew this would be no exception.

The truth was, she needed a big win. For a long while now, Olivia had felt that she needed to atone for the things that had happened to her family, to somehow make them better by doing good deeds. Working on Amelia's case had seemed like the perfect way to make things right. Or at least try to set them right. But from the start, it was like she'd taken one step forward and then ten steps back. The case was going nowhere and she felt like her opportunity to do something good was quickly slipping through her fingers.

Olivia closed her eyes for a moment, suddenly feeling indescribably tired. Her weariness was so constant and so intense that it was becoming an emotional rather than a physical thing. She wanted it to go away, but until she got some answers, she knew it would continue to weigh her down. It made her chest feel heavy and she took several deep breaths, trying to take control of the feeling.

And that was when she heard the sound of the car approaching. Her eyes snapped open, and she rushed inside to grab her gun, just in case. Who the hell would be driving around near the forest in the middle of the night? She thought it might be the kidnapper but when she spotted Brock behind the wheel of his Jeep, she relaxed a little. The heaviness pressing down on her chest lifted slightly and the tautness in her body eased.

Brock seemed to have that effect on her now. Maybe it was because he was carrying some of the same burdens as she was and could relate to what she was feeling. Or maybe it was because he replaced her anxiety with butterflies. She watched as Brock leaned casually out of his car window and flashed her a smile.

"Couldn't sleep?" he called over with a smile. Olivia shrugged.

"I've never felt more awake."

He nodded, his eyes full of sympathy. "I thought maybe you

might like to go for a drive. We could do run through the neighborhood where Sophia went missing. I know it's not technically our case anymore, but they can't control what we do in our spare time, right?"

Olivia smiled. "I think that's a great idea. It beats sitting here staring at the forest and contemplating life."

"I'm full of good ideas. You should know that by now. Hop in, Knight."

Olivia quickly got dressed then locked up her cabin and then joined Brock in the car, noting the smell of the leather seats and Brock's musky aftershave. Brock smiled at her.

"You smell like a pine forest," he commented as he started up the engine once again. "I guess I should expect nothing less from a woman living in the middle of the woods."

Olivia's cheeks warmed. Something felt strange and exciting about his noticing the small details about her. She wondered what he thought each time he looked at her. Did he ever think about her the way she thought about him? Lately, before she went to sleep at night, she'd found herself replaying conversations they'd had. Sometimes she'd construct her own fantasies of scenarios she wanted to happen. She imagined going on long walks together, spending precious Sunday afternoons in one another's company. She imagined going to the local bar together and trying out the signature cocktails. She imagined introducing Brock to her father, and their bonding over their military backgrounds.

She realized that these fantasies weren't particularly interesting or wild, but all she'd ever wanted was a quiet life. For so long, she never thought that was attainable. She'd never found anybody she felt compatible enough with to make that a reality. But now, she could picture having that life with someone like Brock. Someone who made her feel safe and at peace, even when the world around them was crumbling and in chaos.

"You alright?" Brock asked as they drove through the town. "Lately you seem kind of.... disconnected."

Olivia sighed. She needed to stop thinking about him. They had a job to do. At home, thinking about Brock was her escape from the reality of their situation, but she needed to get her head in the game.

"I'm fine. I've just got a lot on my mind," she said. "This case is important to me."

"I know," Brock said gently.

Olivia chewed the inside of her cheek, wondering whether she should expand. Brock had proved himself to be a good listener. She thought it might be good to get a few things off her chest. Maybe clearing out that mental real estate would allow for more things to move in—things actually related to the case. Maybe it would improve her focus.

"I was thinking about Amelia before you showed up," Olivia told him honestly. "I know she's safe now but knowing someone out there who snatched her up, took her cross-country, and kept her prisoner for weeks on end, all without leaving a trace of evidence just turns my stomach. And every time we hit a dead end, I feel so damn guilty. It makes me think of my sister and the ways the police failed her. I don't want that to happen here. I don't want this to go unsolved. I want to catch the monster who did this, so I don't feel completely useless."

"Olivia, you're too hard on yourself. You're so good at what you do. The odds are stacked against us and that's not your fault. It's literally impossible to solve any case without good evidence to work with. You've done your best with what we've been given, which is very little."

"I know. Rationally, I get that," she said. "In my head, I tell myself all that. But it never quite sinks in. It drives me crazy."

Brock nodded slowly. "I get that. I do. But you can't live like this forever. On the edge, always blaming yourself for things you can't control. You'll destroy yourself from the inside out. You don't deserve that, Olivia. No one deserves that."

"So, what would you suggest?"

"You should try therapy."

She gave him an incredulous look, not sure if he was putting her on or now. He gave her a sheepish grin in return.

"Don't look at me like that," he said. "Doing what we do and seeing what we see... it's completely valid to go to therapy. It's good to go to therapy and purge. I did, once."

Olivia blinked several times. She hadn't been expecting that. "You did?"

"I still go sometimes. Every FBI agent has a story that he or she can't bear to talk about with anybody, Olivia. Not our family and not our friends. I know you know that. Our job puts a lot of pressure on us. And like you said, there's always at least one case that sticks with us, one that resonates with and shakes our souls. It makes us doubt our abilities, no matter how good we are at our jobs," he said. "It sounds like you're in the middle of yours right now. It will pass, I promise you. Even if we never manage to solve the case. And if we don't, one day, you'll learn to forgive yourself for that. You need to learn to forgive yourself. And therapy is the fastest road to recovery."

Olivia nodded. She wondered again which case had sent Brock right to the edge. It was hard to imagine him breaking down. He was strong and seemed to have a good handle on his emotions. Most of the time, anyway. She recalled how cagey he'd been when she'd asked him about his worst case and she wondered if that was the one that had driven him to therapy. The one he couldn't let go of. She also wondered if he'd trust her enough one day to tell her about it.

Brock slowed the car as they reached the street where the Edwards family lived. The neighborhood was quiet. The lights in every house were turned off, and there was nobody to be seen out on the street. He pulled to the curb, giving them a good view of the family home and Olivia leaned back in her seat.

"I hope you brought coffee and doughnuts," she commented, trying to lighten the mood. "It's not a real stakeout without them."

"Well, I wouldn't want to disappoint you, Agent Knight," Brock grinned, reaching into the back seat and producing a paper bag. "Two pink iced doughnuts coming right up."

"You're ridiculous, Agent Tanner."

"I'll admit, I wasn't going to tell you about the doughnuts," Brock teased. "But you've been so welcoming since I got here, I thought it was about time I repaid the favor."

"How kind of you," Olivia rolled her eyes with a smile.

They sat quietly for a while, eating their doughnuts and sipping coffee, their eyes scanning the street. Olivia stretched out her legs with a long groan before resting her cheek against the cold window with a sigh.

"What do you think we're going to find out here?" Olivia asked.

He shrugged. "No idea. Probably nothing, to be honest," he said. "I just wanted to get an idea what the neighborhood was like. Kind of see it the way the kidnapper saw it. Maybe something pops in our mind, maybe it doesn't. But I couldn't take staring at the walls of the B&B anymore. Had to get out for a while."

Olivia laughed quietly and nodded. She could absolutely relate to that. They lapsed into silence for a few moments before she turned to him again.

"How much trouble do you think we'd be in if Jonathan found out we're on a stakeout here?" she wondered.

Brock chuckled quietly. "Well, he should be grateful. We're working overtime for no extra pay. We're more dedicated than most. But it's hard to leave this case alone."

"Isn't it? The more unsolvable it becomes, the more I want to solve it."

Brock chuckled again. "You know, you and I are a lot alike," he said. "I didn't expect it when I met you. My impressions of you have definitely changed."

"Oh, yeah?" Olivia raised an eyebrow, sitting up a little straighter, interested in what he was going to say next. "What was your impression, then?"

"I don't think you want to hear this," Brock started.

Olivia allowed him a small smile. "Let me guess. You thought I was stuck-up and uptight. You thought that your terrible jokes were wasted on a bore like me. You thought I was going to be the worst possible person to have to work with."

"Are you psychic or something?"

Olivia threw her crumpled up napkin at Brock. It bounced off his forehead and he laughed, his eyes sparkling with mischief.

"Hey! I told you my first impressions were wrong," he said.

"Well, what are your impressions now?" she pressed.

Brock's eyes softened a little and Olivia felt her heartbeat pick up. Now that she'd asked, she wasn't sure she was ready for the answer. But she waited anyway, wondering what kind of effect she'd had on him.

"Well, I don't think you're boring now, that's for sure," he said. "I think you're one of the most dedicated agents I've ever met. You're also one of the best I've had the pleasure to work with."

"You're saying that now to make me feel better."

"I'm not," Brock insisted. "You put everything into your work. I knew when I showed up at your place that you'd be awake and up for this little mission because you can't shut your mind off when you're working a case. There aren't many people who would do the same. I don't think you realize how good you are. Which is another reason I like you."

Olivia could hear her heartbeat in her ears. *You like me?* She knew he didn't mean it in the way she wanted him to, but for so long, she'd been sure he was just tolerating her. They'd had a bumpy start, but it seemed that they were finally finding common ground, and that thought pleased her. She liked the idea that they could be friends, even if nothing further came of it.

"And it's not just that. Because I was right that you can be uptight, but for all the right reasons," he went on. "I know you're probably fun when you're not concentrating on the case. You know, when this is all over, we should do something."

"Something better than eating donuts in your car in the middle of the night?" she asked with a grin. "I don't know that it gets any better."

Brock laughed. "Yes, something better than this. And I promise you it does," he said. "Maybe you could show me all the hotspots in Belle Grove. I'm sure I'll have a few days before I'm sent back to DC…"

Olivia's heart sank a little at the reminder that Brock wasn't there to stay. At some point, he'd go back to city living and forget all about her little town. And forget about her. She didn't want to admit out loud how much she wished Brock would stay. It wasn't just because of her growing feelings for him. He was company in a town where she was always going to feel like an outsider. Sure, she wanted her life to be quiet, but sometimes, it was so quiet that she couldn't stand the silence. She needed *someone*. A friend, if nothing else. And even through the hardships of this last week, he'd been there to support her. What would she do once he left, and she was alone again?

"You know, DC isn't far," Brock commented with a smile. "You could come and visit me, too. At least in the city, there's more than one bar to choose from."

Olivia's heart soared. "You want me to come and visit you?"

"I mean, sure, if I've got nothing better to do. It might be nice to hang out with you when we're not trying to catch a criminal," he said with a sly smile. "I mean, it might not but we won't know until we try, right?"

"Just when I thought you were being nice," Olivia said, trying to play it off even as her heart thudded hard in her chest.

Brock laughed at his own joke. She'd assumed that his leaving would mean the end of whatever their friendship was. Many partnerships in the Bureau weren't built to last. They were just to get a job done as well as possible. But now she could picture driving up to DC to spend the day with him and those fantasies she'd come up with didn't seem like such a stretch anymore. She allowed herself to imagine that one day, he'd feel the same way she did. One day, he'd suddenly notice that their similarities made them a good match.

"When this case is over and done with, drinks are on me," Brock promised, nudging her arm gently. "And who knows? Maybe then you'll stop being so uptight."

"Okay, this is just character assassination now. Don't make me tell you what I thought of you the day we met because I can guarantee, my thoughts about you were much more scathing than what you thought of me."

"Well, I know that already. I could tell that I was getting under your skin and that you were a heartbeat away from shooting me just to get me to shut up," Brock replied with a grin, leaning in a little closer to her. "But my question is, what about now? Am I still getting under your skin?"

Yes... but in a very different way, Olivia wanted to say. She stared into his eyes and felt her stomach twisting with nerves. He was close enough that if she leaned in just a little, their lips would connect. She watched as his eyes searched hers, too.

"Olivia—" Brock began, but a sharp, loud noise cut him off.

Olivia jumped in her seat, trying to locate the source of the sound. It was coming from Alice's house. It was her house alarm.

"Someone broke in," Olivia whispered, her heart lurching.

She already had her gun at the ready as she leaped out of the car and ran for the house, quickly followed by Brock. They darted across the street and toward the house, the blaring alarm filling the still night air with its shrill noise. Olivia saw a figure in the doorway, looking panicked as he looked for an escape route. The figure was wearing a ski mask, and Olivia's heart stuttered in her chest. Could that be the kidnapper?

"FBI! Freeze!" Brock barked, but it was too late, the man took off.

Olivia sprinted toward the masked man, who turned tail and began to run out into the street. He was surprisingly fast, but Olivia felt her training kicking in along with her adrenaline. She was prepared to outrun any amateur. She was not about to allow the guy to get away from her. This was her one chance to maybe end the whole case.

She watched as the guy jumped a neighboring fence. Instead of following him through the garden on the other side of it, she anticipated his next move, edging around the side of the house and through to the street on the other side. She hoped that Brock would catch on to what she was doing and follow through the garden, just in case. Having Brock behind him would flush the masked man right to her.

Olivia knew she'd made the right call when she saw the man make it through to the street, and she'd gained several feet on him. He spotted her and veered out into the middle of the road. Adrenaline pumped rapidly through Olivia's veins and she felt like she was in one of those chases in nature documentaries, like a lion running down a gazelle. She resolved to be ruthless if she had to. The man was running for a reason. If it was because he was the kidnapper, then she couldn't afford to hesitate. She needed this. She needed a win.

Her legs were pumping hard, her feet slamming against the concrete as hard as her heart was slamming against her ribcage. She was getting closer and closer to the target. He seemed to be losing speed and as she gained on him and she could hear him struggling for breath. As she'd thought, she had much more stamina than he did. She knew she could afford to slow down, and still catch him with ease. But she was desperate to get her hands on him. Her anger was enough to propel her closer and closer to him.

He was almost within her reach. The man glanced over his shoulder; his eyes wide and panicked behind the ski mask. As he turned back around and tried to run faster, Olivia threw herself at him, sending them both tumbling to the ground. The man cried out in pain as he landed, and Olivia's arm scraped along the ground, sending a flash of pain through her body but she didn't stop. She had to find out who he was and what he was doing there.

The man didn't struggle much beneath her, obviously knowing the game was up. Olivia drove her knee into the man's back and cuffed his hands behind him. Only when he was secure did she turn him over and took a moment to catch her breath. Brock arrived a moment behind her, panting a little.

"Damn, he was quicker than I expected. Good job," he said to Olivia as the man squirmed.

Olivia pressed her lips together, feeling her anger taking over. If he was the man they were looking for, then she had no sympathy for him. If she'd caught him in the act, then she was going to make sure he went away for a long time for the things he'd done. In fact, she wanted him to spend the rest of his days in prison.

She grabbed his ski mask and pulled it off. Beneath her, she saw a familiar face and she blinked, not comprehending it for a moment.

"Craig?"

CHAPTER FOURTEEN

"Y OU DON'T UNDERSTAND," CRAIG PROTESTED AS OLIVIA stared down at him with a vicious gleam in her eye. "This is not what it looks like!"

"Save it," Olivia hissed. "You're going to the police station with us."

"You don't get it! This isn't about Sophia! Please, let me go, I swear we can just pretend like nothing ever happened—"

"You set off an alarm that the whole town can hear, buddy," Brock interrupted coldly. "You tried to break into the house where a child went missing last week. Now shut up and don't make me tack on a resisting arrest charge."

Olivia stood up, rubbing her arm where she'd fallen down as Brock hauled Craig to his feet. Brock glanced at her, looking concerned.

"You alright?" he asked.

She nodded, but she was far from it. It wasn't the pain in her arm that was bothering her though. It was something else. She'd been so sure that Craig had been honest with them. She'd thought she could trust his word. But now that she'd caught him trying to break into

Sophia's house, she couldn't think of a single explanation that would get him off the hook. The worst part was that Craig had managed to outsmart them for over a week. If he was in fact the perpetrator, that wasn't going to be a real good look for them.

They thought they'd been dealing with someone sophisticated and intelligent, but Craig was quite the opposite. How had he managed to evade them for so long without getting caught? Maybe he was smarter and wilier than they'd thought. Maybe he played dumb so they'd underestimate him. If that was the case, he'd been brilliant and had succeeded.

"Looks like we were in the right place at the right time," Brock muttered as they walked back toward Alice's house. "It's a good thing we were around."

Olivia nodded, her mind still reeling from the reveal. She held the limp ski mask in her hand, still shaken by her own disbelief. She'd been wrong. So far off the mark. She knew she should be relieved that they'd seemingly caught the kidnapper red-handed, but something still seemed so wrong. Nothing made sense to her at that moment.

"What the hell is going on?" Alice Edwards cried from her doorstep as Brock paraded Craig toward the car. Some of the other neighbors were nosily sticking their heads out of windows and doors, craning their necks to get a view of what was happening.

"Everything's under control, ma'am. We caught Craig trying to break into your house," Brock told her, pulling Craig along by the crook of his elbow. "We're taking him down to the station for questioning. If he has anything to do with Sophia's disappearance, we're going to find out. We'll let you know if there's anything you should know."

"You've got it wrong!" Craig cried out, feebly resisting Brock's iron grip. "Mrs. Edwards, you've got to listen to me. I didn't take your daughter! I don't know where she is!"

"How am I supposed to believe a word you say!" Alice screamed at him. "I warned you, Craig! I warned you to stay away!"

She began to run at Craig, but Olivia reacted in time to block her as she came down her driveway, a look of pure malevolence on her face.

"Enough," she barked sternly. "We need to take him to the station now. I'll call you as soon as I know more. I'll call Officer Stone and get her to send someone to search Craig's house, but we don't know anything for sure yet. Don't get yourself in trouble, Alice. Let us handle this."

Alice looked distraught as Olivia let her go and she retreated back into the house, where Elijah waited at the door. He pulled Alice in for a hug as she sobbed loudly. Olivia glared around at the neighbors.

"Show's over!" she called. "Go back inside!"

The neighbors slowly began to retreat, too, as Brock buckled Craig into the back seat of his car, behind his cuffs so he wouldn't be able to run. Then he locked the car for a moment and headed back to check on Olivia. He examined the scrapes on her arm.

"Does it hurt?" he asked.

"It's fine," she insisted, pulling her arm out of his grasp. "It's not important."

"Olivia, take a breath, okay? I know this isn't what we were expecting," he said. "But we don't have all the answers yet and we shouldn't assume anything at this point."

"How could we miss this?" Olivia asked, her voice cracking a little.

She couldn't believe they'd overlooked Craig so easily—she'd overlooked Craig so easily. She'd believed and dismissed him as a suspect and she knew that if they discovered he'd taken Sophia and had done something to her, she'd never be able to forgive herself. He'd been right under their nose the entire time. He'd been the obvious choice, the only person they had as a viable suspect. And she'd let him go. She'd believed he was sincere. Believed he loved that girl. What a fool she'd been.

"Let's not jump to conclusions, okay? Let's get to the station and speak to Maggie," Brock cut into her thoughts. "You're tired and angry. Don't let that get in the way of you keeping a clear head and your composure."

Olivia sighed. She was still angrier than she'd been in a long time, but Brock was right. For the sake of being professional, she had to calm down. "All right. I'll sit in the back with him just in case he tries anything."

"I don't think you need to worry," Brock muttered, glancing at Craig, who was trying desperately to reach up and open the door with his hands cuffed behind his back. "I doubt he'll ever have the brainpower to figure out how child-locks work."

Olivia allowed herself a small smile, but she was still seething. She didn't want to be anywhere near Craig, but she let Brock open the other passenger door for her and she climbed in next to him. She met Craig's gaze and saw that he was close to tears. Crocodile tears, she guessed. She'd underestimated him once before. She wasn't going to make that mistake again.

"Stop crying," she growled. "You're in a whole world of trouble, Craig. Not only have you put yourself back on the list of suspects in Sophia's disappearance, you put yourself at the top of that list. And now you're trying to break into her house? You really aren't that bright, are you?"

"I want a lawyer!" Craig cried. "I don't want to talk to either of you. You don't understand."

"Seriously? Playing the misunderstood teenager card?" Brock prodded as he got behind the driver's seat. "Well, guess what, Craig? You're nineteen. That won't work on us. You'd better get your story straight. I'm sure the police will be very interested in what you have to say."

The drive to the police station was silent aside from Craig's occasional sniffling. Olivia couldn't believe she'd ever had sympathy for him. Couldn't believe she'd bought his act. She wondered what the hell he was doing going back to the scene of the crime. The police hadn't found anything in Sophia's bedroom when they'd searched, so why would he risk going there? Maybe he thought he'd left something behind? But if Sophia had left the house of her own accord, then what evidence could there be left in the house? They'd already searched her phone and found nothing. And if he had managed to enter the house the night she disappeared without incident, then why couldn't he manage it this time without getting caught?

Nothing about this made any sense.

On top of that was the tree in the forest to consider. Craig had taken them right there and said that was where he'd waited for Sophia that night. He'd sounded so sincere. His pain seemed so real. But if it was a lie, he was obviously trying to mislead them. He was appealing to their emotions with his little sob story. And she'd bought it. But then, what significance, if any, was there to the things they found inside the tree? Did Craig even know about them? Had he put them there? Olivia felt further from answers than ever, even with their prime suspect in the car beside her.

Olivia quietly called Maggie to let her know what had happened, and she'd promised to meet them at the station. As they pulled up, Olivia saw Maggie standing out front in her uniform, her hair a little disheveled and her face grave but looking ready for action all the same. She shook her head like a disappointed parent as Craig was hauled out of the car.

"You should be ashamed of yourself," Maggie started in on Craig as he was taken into the station. "I'm already sending a team to your house to search it. Would you like to tell us what we're going to find before we go in?"

Craig was flustered, his face red, his eyes wide, but he said nothing. Olivia exchanged a look with Maggie and shrugged.

"All right," Maggie snapped. "Let's go on in and talk about it then."

"No!" Craig shouted at her, tears streaming from his eyes. "Please don't take me in there, I've done nothing wrong!"

Maggie said nothing, turning her back on him. The tension in the air was so thick it was practically solid as they all filed quickly to the interrogation room in the back of the precinct. Olivia didn't feel ready for what was about to happen. She felt as though she was about to walk into a room and discover all the things she'd believed were wrong and everything she'd done to that point were for nothing. If that was the case, then she was about to discover her own inadequacy; about to discover that she wasn't as good at her job as she should be. The thought made her feel sick.

She glanced at Brock and was strangely comforted to see the concern on his face, too. They'd been trusted with a huge case, and they might have blown it. Their inability to see through Craig's lies had led to another girl being taken. Olivia took it hard and felt the weight of responsibility for Sophia's disappearance. Brock had been skeptical of Craig from the start. She'd believed him and shut Brock down. Even if they discovered that this was the end of it and Craig was their kidnapper, she knew they wouldn't be able to feel the pride of solving the case themselves. It was as Brock had said: they'd been in the right place at the right time. It was dumb luck. Nothing more.

And then there was Sophia to consider. She was still out there somewhere and she worried that Craig would refuse to tell them where. Olivia pictured Sophia in some dark, cramped space. Alone. Hungry. Maybe hurt. And definitely terrified. She tried to push those images out of her mind, but they persisted. And she knew it was her fault. If she had been able to see through Craig from the start, Sophia would be where she should have been—safely at home, warm and tucked into her bed.

As Olivia entered the interrogation room and leaned against the wall across from him, content to let Maggie run the interview for now. Craig was already seated, his eyes darting everywhere, glancing around him like a caged animal trying to find an escape route. Maggie sat opposite him, looking more serious than Olivia had ever seen her. Her jolly, sweet attitude was gone and she bristled with anger. She faced off with Craig, waiting for him to speak.

"I didn't take her!" Craig finally broke the silence. "You're not going to find anything at my house because there's *nothing there.*"

"In that case, let's not even talk about Sophia," Maggie replied, her voice cold as ice. "Let's talk about tonight. We don't even have to talk about the fact that you were trying to enter the premises of your missing girlfriend. Whatever your excuse is, you were breaking and entering. You'll be charged for that; you were caught in the act. So, you might as well tell us what you were doing there."

"I'm not saying anything without a lawyer!"

"Well, that is your right, young man. But we're going to find out one way or another. It will be better for you if you decide to be honest with us," Maggie said firmly, never taking her eyes off Craig.

She hadn't seen Maggie in action before and Olivia saw for the first time how good she was at her job. She knew exactly how to walk the line between stern and understanding. Craig shifted in his seat, glancing over at Brock and Olivia with suspicious eyes.

"They're trying to get me for something I didn't do."

"Then stop telling us about what you didn't do and tell us about what you did do," Maggie pressed. "Why were you breaking into the Edwards' house tonight?

Craig shifted again. "I don't want to say."

"Why not?"

"Because—because I'm going to get in trouble."

"I hate to tell you this, Craig, but you're already in trouble. Breaking and entering is a serious offense," Maggie said. "But maybe Sophia's family will be willing to drop the charges if you explain why you were trying to get into their house."

Craig sucked in a deep breath, shaking his head fervently. "I don't know, I don't know... I feel like you're trapping me."

Maggie leaned back in her chair. "Craig. You've lived in this town all your life. We might not know each other very well, but I've seen you around," she said. "I know you sometimes get yourself into trouble. You've spent the night here a few times, haven't you? For underage drinking? But nothing as serious as what you did tonight, Craig. Nothing."

Craig nodded slowly. Maggie leaned toward him again.

"Then you know that you never get into as much trouble as you think you will. Everything seems worse in the heat of the moment," Maggie said. "I'm sure a young man as smart as you knows a little about US law. If you get convicted of a kidnapping, I'm sure that will be much worse than whatever you're trying to cover up. It'll be better for everyone involved if you tell the truth."

Maggie gestured at Brock and Olivia. "These two people—they're not out to get you. This ain't a personal attack. They're doing their best to try and find your missing girlfriend," she said. "But you understand, they are federal agents. The longer you hold back information, the longer you waste time I'm sure they'd rather be spending looking for Sophia, the worse it is for you, Craig. So, I'll ask you one more time. Why were you breaking into the Edwards' house tonight?"

Craig was shaking hard. Olivia could see his hands trembling from across the room. He took a deep breath.

"I was looking for something," he said.

The room fell utterly silent. No one dared breathe for fear of spooking Craig. Maggie finally nodded.

"Okay," she said. "What were you looking for?"

Craig swallowed. Another long silence stretched before them and then he spoke.

"I gave Sophia something. I was looking for that. I thought… I knew the cops might go looking in her house again and I didn't want you finding it."

"What did you give her?" Maggie asked.

Craig shook his head again and Olivia narrowed her eyes, feeling her irritation bubbling up inside of her. If he was withholding information, it was because what he gave her was illegal, or at least, something he didn't want her parents to find. Something he thought he'd get in big trouble for.

"What did you give her?" Maggie pressed as Craig's lip trembled. "I can't say," he said.

Maggie's phone dinged and she made a show of pulling it out to read the incoming message. She looked at Craig with an even expression.

"That's my team now. Looks like they're all set up and about to start searchin'. They're going to start at Sophia's house. And after they check out the Edwards home, I just might send them over to take a peek in yours. How do you feel about that, Craig? Think they'll find any surprises?"

Craig let out a trembling breath but said nothing in response.

"They're waitin' for my order. What'll they find, Craig?" Maggie pressed. "This is your chance to tell us before it gets bad for you. Real bad."

Craig put his head in his hands, muttering to himself as Olivia and Maggie glanced at one another. Olivia knew Maggie could feel how close they were to an answer. Craig was going to break soon and then they'd finally have some answers. He squirmed in his chair and shook so hard, Olivia thought he might just shake himself right out of it.

"Okay, okay. I'll tell you. I don't know whether she still has it there, or where she might have put it," he said. "But I gave her... I gave her a couple of joints."

Olivia's heart stopped. "You supplied marijuana to a minor?"

"She wouldn't stop asking me for it!" Craig cried out. "She gets these horrible headaches. She said she did some research and thought it would help with the pain. I didn't want to give her anything, but she wouldn't stop asking. She said she'd stop seeing me if I didn't give her some. I didn't want to lose her, so I gave in."

Olivia felt like slapping the idiotic kid sitting in front of her. It was so obvious now that he hadn't taken Sophia that she wanted to kick herself. He was just a stupid boy who had made a colossal mistake. Olivia knew that supplying a minor with marijuana in the state of Virginia was a felony conviction, carrying a mandatory minimum sentence of two years in prison. Maggie knew it, too, and she sat back in her chair, watching Craig come undone before her eyes.

"I gave her two the day before she disappeared," Craig whispered. "She said she was saving them for when she next got sick. I didn't want her keeping them in her house, but she wouldn't listen to me. When she disappeared, I forgot about it for a while. But then I remembered, and I got scared. I didn't want to get in trouble. I thought if someone had managed to get into the house unnoticed once, then I'd be able to do it too. But I didn't mean any harm, I swear. I was just trying to help. I just wanted to help stop her pain."

"Why in the world would you risk everything by breaking into her house just to take back a couple of joints, Craig?" Olivia finally asked. "Joints we never would have been able to tie to you in the first place."

He shrugged. "I didn't know that. I thought with DNA and everything that you—"

"Do you really think we'd run a couple of joints for DNA?" Olivia interrupted. "Seriously?"

Craig shrugged again. "I didn't know. I didn't want to risk it."

Olivia closed her eyes and wanted to slap him for being so stupid. She didn't know whether to feel glad he was just a moron, relieved that he hadn't kidnapped his girlfriend, or distraught that they still hadn't found the culprit. She couldn't decide between being happy that it wasn't her fault they hadn't caught their kidnapper and being anxious that she still might fail her task.

"Craig, just to confirm. You had nothing to do with Sophia's disappearance, and we won't find anything at your house that relates to her?" Olivia pressed.

"Of course not! I've been telling you people all along. I would never do something like that." Craig sank a little deeper into his seat. "I've made bad decisions and know that I'm in trouble. I messed up real bad this time. But the one good thing I've ever done is care about her. I wouldn't do anything to hurt her or her family."

Olivia rubbed her forehead. At least she knew her initial judgment about him had been right. But now she had an impossible task before her. Their one suspect had just shown his innocence. Their only lead had come to yet another dead end. Olivia knew that Maggie could handle the rest of the issue, so she excused herself from the room and walked out. As she headed out of the station, she heard Brock call her name.

"Olivia, it's okay," Brock said, running to catch up with her. "We did what we could."

"But we're right back where we started," Olivia said desperately. "I really thought we were on to something tonight. I thought we were finally going to get some answers. But... but this is impossible."

Brock put his hands on her arms, rubbing them gently. "I know. I think unless something changes, we're not going to be on this case for much longer. But it's not our fault. There's only so much we can do with what we had to work with. But hey, you never know. We might get lucky with the stuff we found in the forest. Don't give up hope just yet."

Olivia didn't even want to get her hopes up. She had lost all confidence in their leads. The kidnapper was too smart for them. It was over. She wondered whether Sophia was being kept somewhere dark, in terror, and being mistreated by the same person who took Amelia away, wondering if she was going to make it out alive. Olivia felt as though she was falling apart at the seams. As if the kidnapper was somehow slowly and deliberately unpicking the stitches holding her together.

It's over, she couldn't stop thinking. *It's over.*

CHAPTER FIFTEEN

Brock pulled up outside Olivia's house just as the morning sun was beginning to make an appearance in the sky. As she sat there staring at her house, she felt heavy with weariness and disappointment. Disappointment in the case, in their failed leads, and in herself. The way she felt about herself in that moment was the hardest thing she'd had to bear since her family had fallen apart.

"Say something," Brock told her gently.

She shook her head. "This is a real low point, Brock. I think it's going to take a while to bounce back from this."

Brock sighed. "I wish you could see this rationally. This isn't your fault. We just got dealt a rough hand. Do you know how many cases go unsolved every year? I don't know the exact number but I know it's a lot."

"I've never failed a case before," Olivia admitted quietly. "Sometimes it takes me a long time, but I get to the bottom of it eventually. But this time feels so different. It feels like I was set up to fail from the beginning."

"I know. I know the feeling well. But I wish I'd had someone telling me the first time I had an impossible case that it wasn't my fault. So now I'm telling you because you need to hear it," he said. "They could have assigned a thousand agents to this case, and they wouldn't have gotten any further with it. The important thing is that Amelia is safe. She's going to be okay, and that's because of you."

"Barely. She showed up at my door and I made sure she was okay. That was before I even knew about the case. Anyone could've done the same," Olivia said. "And Sophia is still out there somewhere. My gut is telling me that she didn't just leave. I think she would've come back by now if that had been the case. And now that we know Craig isn't involved…"

Silence fell between them in the car. Olivia knew Brock was feeling as deflated as she was, even if he wasn't showing it. She felt so angry that she could punch something. She'd prayed for the answers she needed to save Sophia. That was all she'd ever asked of the universe. To give her a sign, to help her solve the case. But she was realizing that maybe some things just weren't meant to be.

"I guess I should go in," Olivia said quietly.

Brock looked uncomfortable with the level of upset that Olivia was showing. He chewed his thumb and looked at her like he was worried about her.

"Do you want some company?" he finally asked.

Any other time, Olivia would've jumped on that offer. Having Brock beside her was the only thing that had kept her sane that week. But right then, she needed something else. Time alone to reflect and come to terms with how things had panned out. She shook her head.

"I think I'll just go to bed," she said. "Try to get some sleep."

"You should. But Olivia, I'm only a phone call away if you need anything. Don't hesitate if you want to talk to someone. I mean it," he said.

Olivia managed a small smile. "I was worried that we wouldn't work well together when I first met you, but you've been a pretty good partner. Thank you, Brock. I owe you a lot."

"You don't owe me anything," Brock said, his eyes gentle. "Except maybe a drink when I'm back in town."

Olivia's heart skipped a beat. "Back in town?"

"Yeah, well, I'm guessing I won't be here much longer now. I think they'll pull me from the case first if they think it's a dead end. And they probably will when I file my field report," he said. "Maybe they'll let you stay on a little longer, but I think they'll send me back home and assign me to another case. It makes sense."

Olivia nodded, feeling a little numb inside. She always knew that Brock would have to leave at some point. But she wasn't ready for him to go. She wasn't ready to let go. But she couldn't say any of that to him, she had to be professional. She smiled tightly at him.

"Well, if that is the case, then I'll miss you," he said. "It's been great working with someone new instead of by myself for a change."

Brock smiled back. "It was my pleasure, Olivia."

Olivia managed a half-hearted scowl to make Brock laugh. As she opened the car door to get out, she felt strange. It felt wrong to walk away from him after everything they'd shared since they'd met. Was she walking away from him for the last time? Would she ever work with him again? Or were they done now? She had no idea, but she didn't want it to end. She didn't want to say goodbye. She did, anyway.

"I'll see you around," Olivia said quietly.

Brock nodded to her, his smile not quite meeting his eyes. Olivia lingered for a moment, waiting for something to happen. She wasn't sure what she wanted to happen, just that she wanted something. But the moment passed. She walked up the steps to her house as Brock drove off. She wanted to look back, but she didn't. By the time she got inside and shut the door, she felt well and truly alone.

She didn't bother to get changed. She simply kicked off her shoes and headed upstairs to bed, clambering under the covers and tried to find some comfort in the warmth of them. With her eyes closed, she played back everything she could've said, everything she could've done. Not just in relation to Brock, but in terms of the case as well. It wasn't even ten in the morning and she'd already had one of the worst days she could remember—and she'd had a lot of those.

Even as her body begged her to fall under the veil of sleep, her anxiety wouldn't allow her to drift off. So, she just laid there for a long time, feeling the weight of her misery, wondering how everything had fallen apart so quickly.

∽

She must've fallen asleep at some point because she found herself stirring at the sound of her phone ringing. She groaned and sat up, expecting it to be Jonathan telling her that Brock would be heading back to DC. She didn't have enough time to prepare for the blow of it, so she just picked up the phone and tried to brace for the pain. Better to rip the Band Aid off and be done with it rather than let it fester.

"Knight."

"Olivia, it's Maggie. I've got something for you."

Olivia sat bolt upright, feeling alert all of a sudden. "What's going on?" she asked. "Did Craig say something?"

"No. We've got him in holding. Based on his confession, we're going to charge him with giving marijuana to Sophia. But his statement otherwise was about as useful as a screen door on a submarine," she said. "So, I thought it was all over at that point. But I just got a call this morning. Another girl has gone missing."

"Oh, my God…"

"Her name is Hayleigh Roberts. She's fifteen and blonde. She looks like the other girls. But there's something really strange about this one," Maggie said. "She went missing in the middle of a sleepover with her friends. No evidence. No sign of a break-in."

Olivia was floored by the new information. Another girl of a similar description to the others meant there was a pattern. It also made it far more likely that the cases were connected, putting Sophia's case back on her radar. But the fact that she went missing during a sleepover—that was new and seemed crazy to her. How could the kidnapper have possibly gotten away with stealing another young girl when she was surrounded by her friends?

"Okay, this is major. I need to make some calls," Olivia said. "Then I'll come down to the station and we'll get this sorted out."

Her first thought was to call Jonathan. Her second was that she needed to speak with Brock. Maybe he'd be able to stay after all. For a little while longer, at least. Maybe they would get a second chance at solving the case and finding the girls. Hopefully alive.

Until they found their bodies, there was still hope.

CHAPTER SIXTEEN

WHEN OLIVIA DROVE OVER TO THE B&B TO PICK BROCK up, she had a smile on her face. She couldn't help herself. A random bystander might consider her crazy or just wildly insensitive for looking so pleased with herself given the circumstances, but they just didn't understand. The new kidnapping had blown the case wide open. There might be witnesses for the first time. There might be some evidence left at the scene this time. There might be a second chance to save Sophia that they wouldn't have gotten otherwise.

It was all good news, even if the thought of another girl's being snatched from her home in the middle of the night was unthinkable. But sometimes things had to get worse before they got better. She'd hit rock bottom only hours before, but she was slowly climbing out of the hole she'd thrown herself into. She was going to solve the case this time. She was more determined than ever that she would.

Brock was already standing outside the B&B when she turned the corner. Olivia was pleased to see that she wasn't the only one with a huge grin on her face. Brock climbed into the car with a spring in his step and a sparkle in his eye.

"Onward, taxi driver," he declared. "We have a case to solve."

They didn't say another word to one another as they drove to the station, but they didn't need to. There was an energy between them that made Olivia feel as though she'd had one too many cups of coffee. She was a little manic with excitement and she was ready for anything. And with Brock beside her once more, she felt unstoppable.

However, when they arrived at the station, she wiped the smile from her face and got serious. They'd need to talk to Hayleigh's family, and she knew that was going to be hard. It was never easy talking to the family when they were so understandably overwrought. Still, she felt positive that someone would be able to tell them something of use. This new incident was different from the others. It was a bolder strike, but that also meant there was more room for the kidnapper to have messed up. And if he'd made even one tiny slip up, she vowed to herself that she would catch it.

She knew she would.

"Let's do this," Brock stated, getting out of the car and striding toward the station.

Olivia followed him, feeling the adrenaline surging through her veins. She was ready for this. She was going to make up for lost time. She was going to make herself proud. And she was going to return these girls to their families.

"Thank you for coming so quickly," Maggie said as they entered the police station. "The family are here and are ready to talk to you. The girls from the sleepover are going to come later and give statements once they've calmed down."

"Thanks, Maggie. We can take it from here," Olivia said. "Do you have crime scene techs at the house already?"

"As we speak. Fingers crossed that there might be some evidence this time. It was a much riskier kidnapping." She paused. "What do y'all think? Do you think that the kidnapper is losing control? Or just looking for a bigger thrill?"

"Hard to say at this point. If there's evidence left behind, I'd say he's possibly devolving. If not, it might be for a bigger thrill," Olivia acknowledged. "It was a very bold move, taking a child from a sleepover when so many other people were around. I guess we'll just need to take some statements, sift through whatever evidence there might be, and try to piece it all together."

"Good luck. I'll be around if you need anything," Maggie said.

Olivia and Brock made their way through the station to speak with Hayleigh's parents. They found a couple huddled up together, both of them crying as they waited for Olivia and Brock. Olivia offered them tissues from her pocket.

"Special Agents Olivia Knight and Brock Tanner. We're with the FBI. I'm so sorry about what you're going through," she said as Mr. and Mrs. Roberts clutched one another tightly. "We are here to find out as much as we can about what happened last night."

"We just don't understand how something like this could happen," the woman sobbed.

She was in her late forties and had bleached blonde hair. Her foundation was too orange for her pale skin, and her tears had left tracks through her makeup.

She sniffed loudly. "Our poor baby girl," she moaned.

"I know it's terrible, but the sooner we get the details, the sooner we can start searching for her," Brock told the woman. "Why don't you start by telling us your names and take us through what happened last night?"

The woman sniffed. "I'm Andrea Roberts, and this is my husband, Richard."

"I'm Hayleigh's stepdad," Richard added. "But I love Hayleigh like she's my own. What do you want to know? We'll try and give you everything that we can."

"Well, we'll start with when you noticed that your daughter was missing. When did you first realize Hayleigh wasn't there?"

"One of the girls noticed first. Cassie did. They thought she must have just gone upstairs to her bedroom. They were camping out downstairs in the living room," Richard said. "We thought there was nothing to worry about. We of course, made sure the house was locked up before we went to bed, like we do every night. But when the girls came upstairs and told us they couldn't find Hayleigh, I felt sick to my stomach. I was terrified and couldn't believe it. I'd heard about Sophia Edwards going missing. She used to spend time with Hayleigh, but she's gone off the rails a little in the past few years, so we figured that she had just run away from home."

Richard began to sob, and Andrea held him close, her face also creased with the agony of facing their reality in that moment. Olivia pushed the box of tissues on the table toward them and they thanked her graciously.

"Whenever you're ready, can tell us about what time the girls woke you up?" Olivia said.

Andrea cleared her throat, managing to compose herself first. "It was about ten past eight this morning. The girls stayed up late, so they slept in a little, I think. We were tired, too. You know how girls can get at sleepovers; they kept us up with all the noise. So, by the time they figured out that Hayleigh was gone—well who knows how long she'd been gone."

"Do you have any idea what time the girls went to sleep?" Brock asked.

"Not sure. I think it was around four this morning," Richard said. "I remember looking at the clock at around ten to four and then the next thing I knew, I was awake, and the girls were telling me Hayleigh was gone."

Olivia nodded, jotting down several notes as Brock picked up the line of questioning.

"Did you notice if anything else went missing from your house?" Olivia asked. "Do you still have her cellphone?"

"Yes, we handed it over to Maggie when we got here," Richard sniffed. "She's glued to that thing. She won't go anywhere without it. You know how teenage girls are with their phones. She's never liked the dark. She wouldn't even go into the garden at night. That's why we don't think she left the house voluntarily."

"And just to confirm—no broken locks or windows? No signs of forced entry?" Brock asked.

Andrea shook her head, her lips quivering. "No. There's nothing. We have a few people in the neighborhood with keys, but of course, we trust all of them," she said. "We also have a cleaner who has a key. But nobody else has one."

"A cleaner?" Olivia asked.

"A cleaner might know how to cover up her tracks if she accessed the house using a key," Brock pointed out, finishing Olivia's thoughts. "Can you tell us a little about the cleaner?"

"She's a lovely woman," Andrea said, sounding almost defensive. "She's worked for us for a very long time. She's like family to us and has always been a big help to us around the house. Her daughter is in some of Hayleigh's classes. There's no reason she'd have any reason to come to the house in the middle of the night."

"We just have to explore all avenues. We don't want to leave any stone unturned," Olivia explained.

Olivia felt the excitement bubbling up inside of her. She needed to up her game. She wanted every single detail that she could turn up. The kidnapper was good at covering his tracks, but he would slip up at some point. He had to. Olivia could only hope this was the time it happened.

"We can come back to the keyholders, though it would be useful if you could make a list of them for us when we're done here," Olivia said. "Now, did anyone see or hear anything during the night? Anything unusual or out of place?"

Andrea shook her head. "The girls didn't mention anything. That's why they seemed so shocked when they couldn't find Hayleigh this morning. They couldn't fathom how she'd just—disappeared. And honestly, I didn't hear anything. I was so tired by the time we got to sleep that I didn't even wake up in the night."

"Even if we'd heard someone moving around, I don't think we would've thought anything of it," Richard said miserably. "We would've assumed it was one of the girls. They stay over every few weeks and they make a lot of noise. We've just kind of become used to it."

Olivia nodded. "It's possible the kidnapper used that to his advantage. But that means it would have to be somebody familiar with your routines. Still, it was a high-risk thing to do. It's one thing to go into a child's bedroom and snatch her from her bed, but it's dangerous and highly unusual to take a girl from a group of possible eyewitnesses," she said. "This wasn't spontaneous. Whoever did it must have planned this out well in advance. Did you tell anyone about the girls coming over?"

"No. The only people who would've known were the parents of the other girls... and possibly the neighbors. I didn't tell them directly, but they know the girls come over every few weeks," Richard explained. "We've had a few noise complaints from next door a few times in the past, so I guess they're aware of the girls' coming over even when we don't mention it."

By then, Olivia had a scribbled page of notes. Once again, she was finding the details to be hazy. The kidnapper really had a knack for being elusive. She knew that the interview was crucial, though. So far, the kidnapper had managed to get away without leaving a single fingerprint, hair, or footprint behind at any of the crime scenes, so whatever Olivia and Brock could glean from the interview was going to be vital.

"All right. Do you think there's anyone in town who would have some kind of a personal vendetta against you?" Brock asked. "And

I don't know if you'd even know, but can you think of anyone who might have similar issues with Sophia or her family?"

Andrea sucked in a breath. "That's such a huge question. I mean, they're kids. I'm sure they have high school drama to deal with all the time. And I know I said that Sophia has gone off the rails, but she's a good kid," she said. "When she and Hayleigh grew apart, Hayleigh never said that Sophia had fallen out with her friends or anything. She just started hanging out with older boys, and Hayleigh wasn't ready for all that. She's still just a child."

Her expression darkening, Andrea waved her hand in front of her face as she tried to hold back a fresh wave of tears. Richard held her close, looking at Olivia, then picked up where his wife had left off.

"Hayleigh has a lot of friends at school, but she's a quiet kid. She doesn't get into all the drama and arguments most kids her age do. I can't imagine that she has a single enemy in this world. And as for us, as a family, I think we get along well with everyone in town. It's a very tight-knit community," he said. "I can't think of a single person in this neighborhood, or anywhere in town really, who would want to do something this terrible. I don't know that anybody has an issue with us. Certainly not one that we know of. I just can't understand it."

He shook his head, overcome with emotion. Andrea gripped his hand tightly and quietly cried. Richard sniffed and quickly composed himself. He looked up at Olivia, his jaw clenched.

"I just want her to be found as soon as possible," he said.

"We all do," Brock told him. "Is there anything else that you can tell us? Anything that you think might help? Did anything odd or unusual happen? Have you noticed anybody hanging around or paying undue attention to your family?"

Richard shook his head. "No, I can't think of anything that was out of place. Everything's been so normal," he said. "Nothing much happens around here. Life is pretty simple."

Andrea shrugged helplessly. "This is all a blur. We don't remember as much as we hoped. I'm sorry. I feel so useless."

"It's okay," Olivia said kindly. "Situations like these can make things hazy and I know it can be difficult to remember details. But please, give us a call if you think of anything else you might recall. You'll need to stay awhile, anyway, while the police take evidence at the house, but we'll give you some time. We'll be talking to the girls too and find out what they know."

"You should speak to our neighbor," Richard piped up. "She said she heard something last night. We were pretty shaken up as you can imagine, so she drove us here this morning. She might still be around."

"That's really helpful. Thank you both," Olivia said. "You know where to find us if you remember anything, no matter how insignificant you might think it is."

Olivia and Brock gathered their things and left the interview room. They fell into step with one another as they headed back to the reception area.

"What do you think about what they had to say?" Brock asked Olivia quietly.

"Not sure yet. Once we have the list of people who have keys, we'll look into them further. But I'm interested to hear what the neighbor has to say," Olivia replied. "If she said she heard something, that might give us a timeframe for when Hayleigh went missing."

Back in the reception area, they found Maggie talking to someone Olivia recognized. She paused for a moment and tried to recall where she knew her from. It took Olivia a minute to realize where she recognized the other woman from. And then it hit her. She was the hiker they'd spoken to in the forest. She spotted Olivia and Brock and smiled at them, though she looked tired and saddened. Olivia gathered that she must be the neighbor the Richards' mentioned.

"Hello again," the woman said pleasantly, stepping forward to shake Olivia's hand. "It's good to see you again. I'm Susan Combes. I live next door to the Richards. I've been waiting to speak with you. I'm hoping that I can be of some help."

"Well, we're taking all the help we can get," Brock replied with his charming smile. "Whatever you tell us will surely be helpful."

"Great," she said. "Is there somewhere we can go to talk?"

"I'll let you use my office," Maggie said, leading them all through. "Can I get anyone some coffee or water?"

"Some coffee would be fantastic, but I'll come with you," Olivia said.

She wasn't particularly interested in the coffee for a change, but she wanted to get Maggie alone for a moment. Brock began chatting with Susan in the office and Olivia walked with Maggie to the break room.

"What's on your mind? You look a little confused," Maggie said.

"Maybe I am, a little," Olivia admitted. "Do you know Susan well?"

"Not real well, but well enough. She hasn't lived here too long, but she's always friendly. She's the kind of person who always says hello when she sees you on the street, even if she don't know you," Maggie said. "Not many'll do that these days it seems. I like that about her."

Maggie said fondly, smiling to herself as she poured a cup of coffee for Olivia. She handed Olivia her cup and turned to her with a quizzical look on her face.

"Why do you ask?" she asked. "And why is it you seem so suspicious?"

"I don't know. She just seems very forthcoming," Olivia said. "I guess that fits with what you said about her, but I don't meet many people who are so willing to be interviewed. And I'm just curious. Hayleigh's family said that she claimed to have heard something in the night. If she did, then why didn't she report it at the time?"

Maggie shrugged. "Who knows? If she knew the girls were there, she might have just chalked it up to that. Probably didn't think anything of it until she got the context of the disappearance."

Olivia nodded, but she still felt a little uneasy. The morning's events had put her on edge and made her suspicious of everything. Of course, her job gave her a healthy dose of suspicion of everything too.

"I guess that could be true," Olivia said. "Is she known as a busy-body? I mean, does she tend to be nosy?"

"I don't know that I'd go so far as to call her a busybody—"

"What would you call her?"

Maggie shrugged. "I don't know. I guess I'd call her curious. She does ask a lot of questions around town, I guess," she said. "She's just friendly. I wouldn't say she's acting out of character by coming in today."

Olivia frowned. Her experience had taught her to be skeptical of people who seemed too friendly. Too forthcoming. But, she had to admit it might just be that she was a little jaded.

"I know what you're thinking. A lot of people who get involved in crimes like this like to get all chummy with the people investigating," Maggie said. "But that's just how she is. Maybe interview her before you jump to conclusions."

Olivia rubbed her forehead. "You're right. You're absolutely right. I'm sorry, it's been a tough few days. I guess I'm just ready to get to the bottom of this," she said. "This new abduction has given the case a boost."

"I understand," Maggie said, putting a hand on Olivia's arm. "This whole thing has been as aggravatin' as a rock but keep at it. You'll find these poor girls."

Olivia's cheeks flushed. It was one thing having Brock reassure her when he spent every day at her side watching her work. But she found a compliment from Maggie to be flattering.

"Thank you," Olivia said. "That means a lot to me."

Maggie gave her an encouraging smile. "You go in there and do your thing. I'm chasing up a few leads at the house, and hopefully I'll have something useful for you when you come out."

"Thanks, Maggie."

Olivia felt a little better as she returned to the office where Brock was sitting with Susan speaking quietly. She sipped her coffee and felt reinvigorated. She told herself not to go in on the offensive. Susan was being kind enough to help them and she needed to remember that. She needed to keep herself from going on the attack. Most people didn't react well to it.

Susan smiled warmly at Olivia as she entered the room and she couldn't help being taken by her smile. Susan looked like a kind person. There was something in her gentle gaze and her softly aged face that made Olivia want to like her, even if she'd been unsure of her at first. But Olivia really didn't want to start forming opinions so early on. She needed to stay balanced if she was going to be an asset in such an important investigation.

"Susan here was just telling me that she woke up at around four-thirty and thought she heard a noise outside," Brock told Olivia. "Would you mind telling Agent Knight what you told me?"

"Of course," Susan nodded readily. "I woke up at four-thirty. I don't sleep well at the best of times, so it's not unusual for me to be awake at the oddest of times. Anyway, I'd heard the girls giggling all night long, but it had quieted down by that time. I took it to mean they were finally asleep."

"Hayleigh's parents mentioned that you've made noise complaints before?" Olivia asked.

Susan favored them with a grandmotherly smile. "Oh no, that wasn't me. That was the neighbor on the other side of them," she said. "No, I don't mind the noise at all. I think it's nice to hear those girls having a good time. They're carefree and happy. I wouldn't dream of trying to dampen that."

"Do you know the family well?" Olivia asked.

"Well enough. We're neighborly, of course. I've babysat for Hayleigh several times when her parents have been out on dates, but she's really old enough to look after herself now," she said. "We always chat when we cross paths. They're a nice family."

"And can you tell us what kind of girl Hayleigh is?" Brock asked. "Her family don't think she'd be likely to go out in the middle of the night, but children don't always tell their parents everything."

"Oh, they certainly don't tell their parents everything. I know plenty of the kids around here sneak around at night. I sometimes hear them giggling outside on the streets when I can't sleep," Susan said. "But not Hayleigh. I'd know if she ever left in the middle of the night. I'm very sensitive to noises. I'd hear her leaving. She's a good girl. A real straight arrow, that one."

Olivia nodded to herself. "Okay. So, you woke up at four-thirty. You said the girls were quiet by then?"

"Yes. I remember waking up and thinking just how quiet it was. But then I heard a door closing somewhere. I can't be certain it was Hayleigh's house, but I don't imagine it was on the other side of me," she said. "My other next-door neighbor is elderly and barely gets out of bed. And my bedroom is on the side closest to Hayleigh's house. The door closing sounded as if it was close by."

"And you didn't think it was unusual when you heard it?" Olivia pressed. Susan shrugged.

"Not really. It wouldn't be the first time the girls went out to the garden late at night. I know a few of the other girls sometimes sneak out to smoke. I can smell it from my window whenever they do, and I hear them talking sometimes," she said. "They're fifteen, they're feeling rebellious—they're all like that at that age. I certainly was. So no, I didn't think it was particularly unusual. But when I heard this morning that Hayleigh was missing, well, of course I had to say something. I didn't want it to get overlooked in case since it might be important."

"It's good that you came to tell us," Brock told Susan. "You might have been the only one to hear anything. Did you hear anything else? Or see anything?"

"No, I was in bed, and I didn't get up. I'm usually up early to hike, but I didn't sleep well, so I went right back to sleep. Honestly, I'd forgotten all about it until this morning. Now I wish I'd just gotten up and looked out the window. Maybe then I could've been of more use."

"Believe me, Susan, this is extremely useful," Brock told her. "Another question, have you seen any unusual activity in the neighborhood lately? And is there anything you can tell us about the other missing girl? Do you know Sophia Edwards at all?"

Susan let out a long sigh. "I'll admit, I haven't noticed anything out of place in the neighborhood. Of course, people have been on edge since the Edwards girl went missing, but other than that, I can't think of anything," she said, sounding pained. "As for Sophia, I know that she's been running into trouble lately. It's funny. She and Hayleigh couldn't be more different. Hayleigh has her lovely little group of friends—I often see them hanging out together in town—but Sophia has become kind of a loner. I've seen her sometimes with her boyfriend, who I think is definitely a bad influence on her. But I think she gravitated toward him because she felt misunderstood. You know how it is to be her age, to feel that the entire world is against you. To feel you have nobody to turn to. I think I understand that young lady very well, though, even if nobody else does. She needs to be handled with care."

Olivia didn't know what to say in response to that. Susan seemed to be a woman with a lot to say. She seemed to be more than just a busybody. Even the details she was giving about her neighbors were bordering on obsessive. But then again, Olivia knew what it was like to lie awake at night with nothing better to do than just observe the world around her. Maybe if she lived in the middle of town, she'd be more observant, too. But the way Susan spoke about Sophia suggested she'd spent a lot of time getting to know her.

"What do you do for work?" Olivia asked Susan.

She blinked in surprise. "Why do you want to know that?"

"I'm just interested in how you form relationships around town. You seem to know Sophia Edwards quite well. Do you work with children?"

Susan shook her head, looking a little flustered. "No, not directly. I'm actually a volunteer at the moment I do work at the rec center. I've run into Sophia once or twice there. But it's not a big town, Olivia. You tend to pick up little details about people that you see all the time. You know, you see these young people every day as you're going about your life. You see them and you see yourself in them, you understand? We always look at our peers and we feel we're completely different from them, but when I see young people, I know their struggles. Being a teenager is a universal struggle, don't you think? At that age, you don't know what you want or how to be. It's a sickness. Sometimes we carry it over into our twenties. As you get older, you earn your sense of self, but I look at young people and I pity them at times. They just don't know who they are."

Brock exchanged a glance with Olivia. She knew what he was thinking: this interview was veering off the rails. She felt there was something that Susan was trying to say, to allude to, but she had no idea what it was or how it might be relevant to the abductions. All she'd gained from the conversation was the knowledge that Susan was an outsider. She might be known well in town, and she might be friendly with everyone, but Olivia would bet anything that she didn't have any real friends. She made a few cryptic notes, noticing that Susan's eyes were constantly being drawn to what she was writing down.

"You seem pretty observant," Brock said encouragingly after a pause. "Perhaps you can keep your eyes peeled for anything else that seems unusual. You've been a big help so far."

"I'd like to be as helpful as I can," Susan replied, smiling at them again. "These girls are precious. I want to make sure they make it home safely. I'll be sure to tell you anything else that comes to me, but I've told you everything I know."

"That's okay. You've given us a lot to think about and follow up on," Olivia said, closing her notebook.

As she slid it into her bag, she noticed that Susan was watching her. She thought it strange that Susan was paying so much attention to her but then, Olivia knew she gleaned all the information she had by paying close attention to the people around her.

"Have you spoken to the young ladies yet?" Susan inquired. "Those poor things. It must be so traumatic for them."

"Not yet, but we will," Olivia said.

"Of course, of course. Well, I'll head home now, if there's nothing else you need from me," Susan said. "Do you have a number I can call if I think of anything else?"

Olivia slid Susan her card and she took it eagerly, slipping it into her pocket. Her smile was a little too wide for someone whose neighbor had just disappeared in the middle of the night, but Olivia could tell that Susan was a people pleaser. She clearly wanted Olivia and Brock to like her. Still, something about Susan seemed a little off to Olivia.

"Thank you for all your hard work, Agents," Susan said as she put her bag on her shoulder. "I hope you find what you're looking for."

Brock and Olivia smiled until Susan had left the room, but the instant the door closed behind her, they let their expressions drop. Olivia folded her arms over her chest, slumping a little in her chair.

"That was weird," she said.

"Definitely weird," Brock concurred.

"Still, it's good that we have a timeframe now for the kidnapping," Olivia offered, thinking back to her notes.

Brock pressed his lips together. He didn't look particularly convinced. He frowned and looked down at his hands for a moment, fidgeting with them in his lap.

"What's on your mind?" Olivia asked him.

"Did you notice anything unusual about her?" Brock asked her.

She shrugged. "What wasn't unusual about her," she said. "Were you thinking of anything in particular?"

"I think she might be an alcoholic."

Olivia hadn't been expecting that assessment and she raised her eyebrow. "What makes you think that?"

"She looked flushed in the cheeks, but it's not warm in here. I remember an aunt of mine was an alcoholic, and she used to look like that. It has something to do with enlarged blood vessels in the face or something like that," he told her. "She also had a slight tremor in her hands. She tried to keep them flat on the table, did you see that? And she's very thin. My aunt lost a lot of weight when she was at her worst. She lost interest in eating. I guess you could say she had a liquid diet."

"I didn't notice. Do you think that's why she was so all over the place?"

Brock shrugged. "It's definitely possible. There was definitely something strange about her. I don't mean to judge her, but she doesn't seem completely stable, does she?"

Olivia shook her head. "What does that mean for us? Do you think her story is unreliable? If she'd been drinking, then maybe she misremembered some of the details."

"I think that could be the case. But on the other hand, we can't really afford to be picky with which details we pay attention to. She may be the only lead we've got so I think we'd better follow up on it anyway."

Olivia nodded. This really was their last chance, unless the kidnapper was bold enough to strike again. And that was not a risk she was willing to take. They needed to take any details they could get, especially if they didn't find anything at Hayleigh's house. She stood up and stretched herself out.

"We should talk to Maggie about setting up a curfew. Now that we know there's a pattern, we should be focusing on keeping the town safe. The young girls around here are going to be terrified that they'll be next. If we can get Maggie to put some police patrols on the streets, too, then we can focus on getting to the bottom of this," she said. "I say we take everything we know and run with it, no matter how unreliable it might seem. I want to ask the other neighbors on the street if any of them saw or heard anything unusual last night, particularly at the time Hayleigh supposedly went missing. We need to try to paint a picture of the entire night."

"I can go and ask around," Brock offered. "What are you going to do?"

"I think we're supposed to get the lab results for what we found in the forest back today. I'd like to go up to the lab and get more information about it," she said. "I know it might be nothing, but I've just got this feeling that it's important."

"I trust your instincts," Brock told her with a smile. "You do what you need to do. I'll see what I can get around here and speak to Maggie. I can interview the girls whenever they get here."

"Perfect," Olivia said, returning Brock's smile with her own. "I was worried SAC James was going to pull the plug on us."

"Me, too," he replied. "I think we're going to crack it this time."

"Here's hoping."

They stood awkwardly for a moment. Olivia wanted to head out and start her day, but she had this feeling that something was being left unsaid between them. It hung heavy in the air but when neither of them made an attempt to say anything else, she gave him an awkward smile.

"All right, I guess I'll head out now," she said. "We can meet up later and discuss whatever we find today."

"Sounds good," he replied. "You know I'm only a phone call away."

Olivia nodded and left the room, feeling her face flush. She felt like she'd just made an idiot of herself in front of Brock. She knew she could easily spend the rest of the day replaying the uncomfortable moment over and over in her head, scolding herself for how easily she came undone in his presence. But she didn't have time for any of that. She had to take control of the case. She had to focus.

She was not going to mess up her final chance.

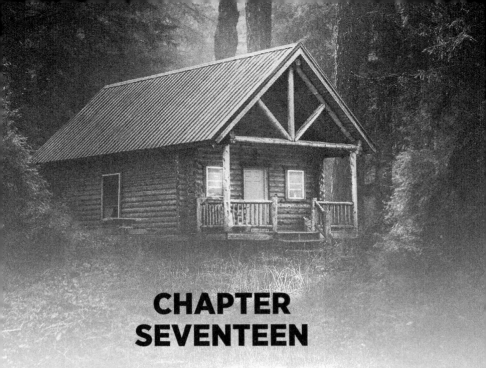

CHAPTER SEVENTEEN

OLIVIA HEADED STRAIGHT FROM THE HOSPITAL UP TO THE lab at Quantico. They had offered to send the results out to her, but she wanted to speak to the tech who ran the tests on the items. She was desperate to see if there was anything in the plastic bag they'd found in the tree that could be tied to the missing girls. There was no proof it was connected and Craig didn't seem to know anything about it, but Olivia was sure that the evidence from inside that bag would be the key to cracking the case wide open. She could feel it.

After checking in, Olivia made her way through the long hallways of the lab with a sense of purpose. She knew she had no reason for it, but she had a good feeling about what she was about to discover. When she made it to the Trace Evidence Unit, she found their resident Evidence Analyst, Joanna Chu, examining something under a microscope. Not wanting to distract her, Olivia waited off to the side until Joanna was done.

"Come in, Olivia, come in," she said without looking up.

Her long, dark hair was pulled back in a ponytail that was so tight it looked painful.

"I'll be with you in a minute," Joanna said.

Joanna finished what she was doing and jotted down a couple of notes before swiveling in her chair to face her. She gave Olivia a wide smile.

"I hope you have some good news for me," Olivia said wearily, trying not to touch anything to avoid any possible contamination.

"Well, I'm not sure what I have can be classified was good news, but I'm not familiar with the case you're working on. We'll see."

A minute of silence passed before Joanna stood up straight and crossed the room, beckoning for Olivia to follow her. She watched as Joanna changed her plastic gloves and then picked up a box that contained the items they'd found in the bag. She set it down on a workbench then turned to Olivia.

"No fingerprints anywhere, I'm afraid," Joanna started. "So, if you're looking for that, then I have to disappoint you. Sorry. But there might be a few things of interest. I'll start with the hair. I ran the DNA, but we don't have a match in our system, I can tell you that it's female. I wasn't able to extract much more information from it because there are no hair follicles to work with," she said. "So, in other words, someone cut this hair off deliberately, not at the root. But judging by the band tying the hair together, it's pretty old. The band is a little grubby, like someone has been handling it a lot. My guess is someone took it out a lot and stroked the hair. I don't know why someone would keep this to be honest. It's kind of creepy. But as I said, I wasn't able to lift a fingerprint from anything in the bag or the bag itself, so I'm just speculating."

Olivia nodded. "Okay, well, I guess that could be useful. If this belongs to the kidnapper I'm investigating, perhaps it's a keepsake from a victim."

Joanna shrugged. "Maybe. But to me, this whole bag just looks like some kind of memory box or something," she said. "What makes you think it's connected to your case?"

"I don't know that it is," Olivia admitted. "It's just a feeling."

Joanna raised one perfect, thin eyebrow as though to ask, "*You're wasting my precious time over a* feeling?" Even so, she turned back to the tray that held all the evidence, lifting the doll carefully out as though she was concerned that it might fall apart.

"I tried my best with the doll. I really thought I'd be able to get something from it, but the material is coarse, which makes it harder for me to lift any fingerprints from it. I checked for any manufacturer's tags, but it looks like it was handmade, which means there's no way to tell where it came from. About all I can tell you is that this doll is old. I'd say, fifty or sixty years old. It's obviously been well-loved. But if someone was keeping it with hair and baby teeth, it might have been passed on through several generations. I don't know, but it seems like a strange thing to keep in a tree, right?"

"I mean, anything is a strange thing to keep in a tree," Olivia pointed out. "What about the teeth?"

"The teeth were definitely the most useful thing I looked at," Joanna said, pointing at the pouch that sat in the tray. "As I'm sure you figured out, they were baby teeth, but the interesting thing is that they're pretty old. I think they're probably close to twenty years old, and there's no sign to suggest that they were extracted. That tells me they probably fell out naturally, as teeth do with any child. I was able to extract enough material for a DNA comparison and confirmed they're from the same person as the hair. So, if this is related to your case, perhaps you're looking for someone who is now somewhere around twenty-year-old. Or maybe someone who has a twenty-year-old daughter."

Olivia pondered on that for a moment. She thought about what all of the items could mean if she made the assumption they were related to the case. The items were very personal things to keep, but she knew that many killers often kept mementos from their murder victims. If the teeth were twenty years old though, then none of the three girls were old enough for the teeth to belong to them. In any case, she'd provided the lab with DNA samples for all three victims and there had been no match—meaning there was possibly a fourth victim out there. But certainly, she would have heard about it by now if another blonde teenage girl from the area had gone missing in the last few years.

So, what else might be a possibility? Did the kidnapper have a daughter? That would make a lot of sense. Perhaps the kidnapper was preying on children similar to his or her daughter. She thought about the ages of the girls. If the teeth were twenty years old, but the girls were at least five years younger, what did that tell her?

"Maybe the kidnapper lost a child," she mused aloud. "Five years ago, maybe, to account for the age gap in the teeth and the children who are going missing. He or she is searching for someone to replace a daughter, to make it seem as if the child is still there. The daughter was a teenager when she died, so the kidnapper is looking for a young girl, around fourteen or fifteen, who can pick up where the daughter left off."

Joanna wrinkled her nose. "That seems pretty dark."

"Something pretty dark has to happen to you to make you want to kidnap a child in the first place. Maybe I need to be looking for someone in the area who has lost a daughter," Olivia continued.

Joanna put the bag of teeth down and folded her arms over her chest and looked at Olivia. She frowned as if she had something to say but was biting her tongue.

"Out with it," Olivia said.

"Okay, so you've got a theory. But do you have anything to prove it? Anything to link these items to the case you're working at all?" she asked. "Because if not, I don't know how much further you can push this. There's only so far you can go on a hunch, Olivia."

Olivia didn't respond. She knew that Joanna was right, but she was getting desperate. She'd already heard from Maggie on her way to Quantico that nothing of use had been found in Craig's house or the Richards'. It was what she'd expected but it was still a disappointment. She knew the girls Brock was interviewing wouldn't be much help, as they hadn't actually witnessed anything the previous night. She'd needed a breakthrough in the lab. She'd been convinced it was the one thing that was going to save the case. But she didn't get her miracle and it wasn't looking hopeful anymore.

"I don't have anything to connect the evidence to the case yet," Olivia admitted quietly. "But I'll find something."

Joanna looked at Olivia with pity in her eyes. "Is this the hill you want to die on, Olivia? A scruffy old doll and some ancient baby teeth?" she asked. "There must be something else you can work with."

"You'd think so," Olivia said, laughing without humor. "But we're struggling. That's why I really needed some good news here. The kidnapper might not have taken these things from one of his victims, but if these things belong to the kidnapper himself, then it could tell us a lot. We might be able to build a profile of the person we're looking for."

"Look, I know how committed you guys are about your cases, but I just don't think you can catch a perp with something from this in a million years," Joanna said. "If there's no evidence, there's no evidence. It's like trying to catch a ghost. You might be best served shelving this and moving on. I'm sure there are other people who need your help."

"I'm not giving up," Olivia replied firmly. "Not yet at least. Is there anything else you can tell me? Anything at all? What about the plastic bag itself? Can you tell how long it was out in the forest?"

"I'm not a magician, Olivia," Joanna sighed impatiently. "It doesn't look very weather-worn, but it was inside a tree, for goodness' sake."

"But there must be—"

"Olivia, I like you a lot, I really do, but I'm going to have to say I'm done with this now. You can come back to me any time if you find something connected to the case, but I've spent enough time on this already," she said, her tone sharp. "I have to analyze evidence from an actual murder scene today. I've given you all I have and can't just manufacture evidence where there is none. I'm sorry but I can't help you with this anymore."

Olivia nodded, feeling as though her heart was an anchor dragging her down to unknown depths.

"I'm sorry, Olivia. I'm a little stressed today. I didn't mean to—"

"It's fine. You're not the only one," Olivia mumbled as she headed for the door. "Thanks for your help, Joanna."

She was gone before Joanna could say anything further. She couldn't believe she'd hit yet another wall. If Joanna was telling her as an outsider that her case was about to crumble, then maybe she should just believe that. But she didn't want to believe that this was it. She kept tossing her theory around in her head about the parent who'd lost a child. Did she have any evidence to back up the theory? No. Not yet. But she didn't have evidence to back up any theory at the moment. No new leads, no way to get new information. Maybe she'd just have to accept that she was going to have to work on theories instead of hard facts.

On the drive back to Belle Grove, an idea popped into her head. She decided to try calling Paxton's friend in the Seattle FBI field office, Blake Wilder again. She pulled up Blake's number and called. But Blake didn't greet her—she was met at first by the sound of chattering conversation and laughter in the background.

"Hello?" Olivia asked.

"*—what I've been saying!*"

"*I can't believe—*"

"*—oh, my God, shut up, Rick!* Wilder here."

"Hi, Blake. This is Olivia Knight, I'm with the Bureau down in rural Virginia. Paxton's, ah…" she paused, "…friend. I talked to you before about the Amelia Barnes case?"

"Hi, Olivia. Yeah, I've been looking into it, but unfortunately, I haven't found really anything to give you," Blake said. "It's kind of a big mystery, honestly."

Olivia let out a deep sigh. "We've got two more cases down here that are almost identical to the Barnes abduction. Kidnapped fifteen-year-old blonde girls with no evidence to be found. There's a lot I still don't get but I'm really struggling with understanding why the first victim was taken from Seattle."

"I really wish I could help, but your guess is as good as mine right now," Blake offered. "I searched the crime scene myself and couldn't find a thing. I've gone over all the SPD reports, interviewed the Barnes' and all the other witnesses they already spoke with. I've gotten exactly nowhere with this. I'm sorry."

"Thank you. This case is just driving me up the wall."

"Believe me, I get it," Blake said. "I've had a few of those impossible cases myself. The only advice I can really give is to trust your instincts. You made it through the Academy for a reason, you made it this far and have built the reputation you have for a reason. It may take some time, but you'll figure it out."

"Thanks, Blake."

"Anytime. Good luck on this one."

The clamor of voices called Blake back to her team, and they said quick goodbyes and hung up. Yet another dead end. With nothing else working for her, the lost-daughter theory was starting to look better and better.

As she got closer to town, she wondered what to tell Brock. She wanted to give him good news, but she wasn't sure how he'd react to her baseless theories. Still, it was better than telling him nothing at all. She decided that she'd bounce ideas off him and see if he agreed with them. They had very little else they could do without evidence, anyway.

After going back and forth for several minutes, she decided just to call him. He picked up right away and she put him on speakerphone.

"Hey, Knight."

"Brock. Did you find anything?"

"Not really. The kids from the sleepover were pretty incoherent. None of them heard Hayleigh in the night, or the sound of any doors opening or closing. In fact, they all said they slept through the whole thing."

"Great," Olivia muttered.

She suddenly felt very tired. But she couldn't allow herself to lose momentum. She chewed her lip for a moment, pondering how much to tell Brock, before deciding to dive head first into the deep end.

"I've got a theory. Some of the stuff that Joanna told me at the lab got me thinking. I was thinking I'd run it by you and get your take."

"You have a lead?"

"I didn't say I had a lead. I said I had a theory, so don't get too excited," she said. "I don't know whether I'm just grasping at straws again or if there might be something there. But I thought I'd share my thoughts with you, anyway."

"Well, I for one can't wait to hear what you've got to say. I'll meet you at that diner in town. I could use a burger."

❧

Olivia pulled into the parking lot of the one diner in town. She had yet to visit it since she moved to Belle Grove, finding that it was mostly filled to the brim with regulars and teenagers too young to go to the bar. But it was the middle of the day, and when she walked inside, the lunchtime rush had been replaced by just Brock. He was sitting at a booth alone, looking a little lost. Olivia slid into the booth opposite him.

"Not much for atmosphere here, huh?" he murmured to her, looking around him.

A waitress in a bright red apron came over to tend to them with a distressed look on her face. She'd clearly overheard him.

"It's all these disappearances," she sighed, shaking her head. "Parents are scared to let their kids out, even in broad daylight. The sooner they catch the person doing this, the sooner we can all go back to our lives."

Olivia didn't mention that *they* were the ones supposed to be catching the culprit. Brock scanned the menu, seemingly not willing to let that particular cat out of the bag either.

"Can I get a triple cheese and bacon burger with sweet potato fries?" he asked. "Actually, scrap that, can I have both types of fries? And a strawberry milkshake? Thanks."

Olivia raised an eyebrow but said nothing. She took a quick look at the menu, but she was so pumped that she could barely read the plastic sheet.

"Um… just a black coffee and some mozzarella sticks, please."

"Oh, make that two portions," Brock added, leaning back in his chair.

As the waitress left the table, Olivia stared at him and he chuckled.

"What? It's brain food," he said.

"You'll never eat all that."

"Just watch me," Brock grinned, puffing out his chest seemingly in pride. "Besides, you're the one who needs to do all the talking. I'll just stuff my face while you tell me what went down. So, let's hear it."

Olivia began to explain what she'd discovered at the lab with Joanna, trying not to miss any of the details. She paused when the waitress brought over their food to the table in record time, and then continued to relay her thoughts as Brock ate. He was halfway through the burger and fries when she finished talking.

"Let me get this straight," he managed through a mouthful of what looked like half the burger. He swallowed it and washed it down with a slurp of his milkshake. "You think that the kidnapper has lost something precious, so he or she is trying to replace it with the next best thing. That they're pretending life hasn't gone down the crapper. Pretending these girls are their daughters and that life is perfectly normal. And you got all of that from some old teeth?"

Olivia nodded anxiously. She couldn't tell whether he thought she was crazy or not. But after a moment, he smiled at her.

"I think that's genius. And I also think it's all we've got," he said. "Let's see if we can find anything to strengthen the theory. You may be on to something, Olivia."

"What if I'm not?" Olivia asked quietly.

Brock shrugged. "Well, what do we have to lose?"

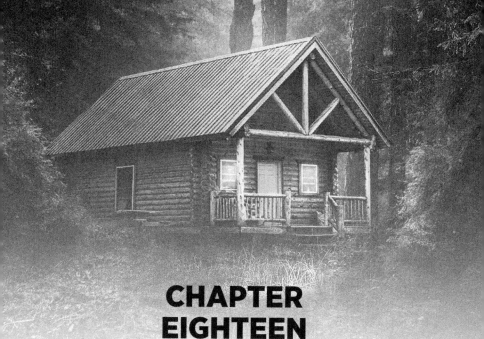

CHAPTER EIGHTEEN

OLIVIA AND BROCK WERE JUST FINISHING UP AT THE DINER when Olivia got a call from Jonathan James. Her phone buzzed on the table in front of her, his name lighting up the middle of the screen. Brock raised his eyebrow at the phone.

"Wait, wait, I have a prediction. He's going to say he wants you back on Sophia's case," Brock said. "Though I don't think he'll apologize for taking you off it in the first place."

"Not a chance," Olivia commented as she picked up the phone. "Knight."

"Knight," Jonathan started in his blunt manner. "I need you to continue looking at Sophia's case alongside Amelia's. Now that a third girl has gone missing, we can certainly establish a pattern."

"We certainly can," Olivia replied coolly, feeling a little irritated.

She understood why he'd taken them off the case—or at least, thought he'd taken them off the case—but it didn't make it any less frustrating for her.

"You and Tanner are doing a good job," James said. "Keep it up and report to me if you find anything of interest. I look forward to seeing what you come up with."

The call ended as quickly as it had started. Olivia glanced up at Brock, who was slurping up the last of his milkshake with a knowing smirk.

"Was I right?" he asked.

"Pretty spot on, actually."

Brock rolled his eyes. "I knew it. Jonathan is a nightmare. He always wants to do everything by the book and he has no imagination," he said. "Imagine if you tried to tell him the theory you've come up with today. He'd stamp all over it in no time."

"Well, imagination can be dangerous in this job," Olivia pointed out. "We're looking for hard evidence and facts, not a good story to tell ourselves. But you're right, he doesn't have an open mind. He likes things done a certain way."

"I like my steak medium-rare, but if I have a steak in front of me, I eat it no matter what. Steak is steak, theories are theories," he said. "You might be onto something with your theory, but he'll never support it because it's not done how he's used to it."

"How can you even think about steak after the meal you just ate? I'm bursting at the seams just looking at you."

"I told you, it's brain food. And now, I'm ready to solve this case. Let's go."

Brock and Olivia paid their bill and headed out to Olivia's car. She drummed her fingers on the window of the driver's side.

"I was thinking about something the other night. Amelia walked a pretty long way to get to the cabin, most likely. She was on her last legs by the time she arrived, so it looks as though she really wore herself out. Which makes sense, considering she's not from this area," she mused. "I'm wondering if we should check out the neighboring towns, see if anyone there has seen or heard anything that might be helpful? If there aren't any buildings out in the forest, it might be a good bet that she came from one of the next towns over."

"Good thinking," he said. "Let's go check it out."

Brock continued to complain about Jonathan the entire drive over to the next town over, a place called Pine Woods. She half-listened as they drove along the road connecting the two towns, the forest thick and dark the entire way. The further out of Belle Grove they got, the more the trees seemed to converge, casting shadows over everything. It seemed crazy to Olivia that Amelia had made it through on her own. The trees stretched for miles in every direction and were so wild, a grown adult could get lost in the woods forever.

"He just stopped us from doing our jobs," Brock continued to complain. "We might have gotten somewhere by this point if we'd been given free rein."

"Don't forget that we kind of took free rein on our own," she said. "We didn't really stop working the case just because SAC James told us to."

"No, and it was only because of our own initiative that we caught Craig," he said. "If we'd had our eyes peeled for the right things and had the proper resources to support us, maybe Hayleigh wouldn't have been taken."

"We don't know how things could've been different," Olivia reasoned. "We'll never know now. All we can do is move forward with what we have."

Brock smiled to himself, leaning back in his chair. "You don't like criticizing the boss? Come on, it's just you and me. You can be honest."

Olivia's lips twitched into a smile. "All right, he's kind of an ass."

"Kind of?"

"Okay, he's definitely an ass."

"Well, well, well. I never expected to hear such rudeness coming from your mouth," he said. "I must be a bad influence on you."

"Yes. Yes, you are," Olivia said, rolling her eyes. "But I'm not saying anything else about Jonathan. He means well."

"You're too nice, Olivia."

"And you're too mean. He's old and stuck in his ways—"

"Old? He's only got about ten years on us," Brock said with a laugh. "Now who's being mean?"

Olivia laughed, genuinely, and she felt some of the stress of the day melting away from her. She was beginning to feel so comfortable around Brock that she'd let her guard down a little. She couldn't remember the last time she'd done that around anyone. In a little over a week, she'd told him more personal details than she'd told her closest friends. Sure, her friends knew that her mother had disappeared, and of course they knew about what had happened to her sister, but she'd never told them how she felt about it. All they knew were the facts of the case. But she'd gone from talking about the serious stuff with Brock to laughing and joking with him. There were very few people she felt comfortable doing both with.

They made their way to the town's police station. Pine Woods was even smaller than Belle Grove, but it made Olivia even more sure that if something was amiss in the town, then they'd find out what it was. Brock and Olivia headed inside together and found a man with a thick gray mustache sitting in the reception area, watching something on the computer screen that sounded like a sports game. He looked up and saw them and quickly switched off his monitor then jumped to his feet, looking as guilty as a kid caught looking at porn.

"Can I help you?" he asked.

Olivia badged him and stepped forward to shake his hand. "I hope so. Special Agents Olivia Knight and Brock Tanner. FBI."

"FBI, huh?" the man asked, putting his hands on his large hips. "You're not here about those kidnapping cases, are you?"

"Actually, yes. We're looking to extend our search and see if we can find anything out about the neighboring towns," Olivia said. "We think that the young girl who escaped her captor might've come from one of the towns but escaped through the forest."

"You think she was held here?"

"Maybe. We're in an unusual situation. Amelia Barnes, the

surviving victim is non-verbal, and additionally, she's not even from the state. She hasn't been able to tell us anything about the case. There are no residential homes in the forest where she could've been held that we've found. And frankly, the forest is so vast and overgrown that we don't know whether she'd have been able to tell us anything about it even if she was able to speak," Brock explained. "We're just exploring other avenues. I assume people have been concerned here, too?"

"Definitely," the officer told them. "A lot of parents have been keeping their kids at home after school, not letting them go to their extracurriculars. Our town has always been very safe; the children are used to playing out on the streets and walking around in the evenings alone once they're a little older. But the teenage girls in particular have been concerned for their own safety. In fact, I think the whole thing has created some unnecessary hysteria."

"What do you mean?" Olivia asked, intrigued.

The officer sighed. "Well, for starters, there are lots of rumors are going around. We've taken a whole bunch of calls from people who are reporting seeing dark figures out on the street in the middle of the night," he said. "One young lady claimed that she saw someone standing outside her home, staring up at her window."

Olivia shuddered at the thought. It was so creepy that it didn't seem possible that it was true. And she had no doubt some of it really was just hysteria and paranoia taking hold. But she thought maybe their kidnapper was more brazen than she thought. He'd been under the radar the whole time they'd been investigating, but maybe Olivia and Brock had just been looking in the wrong place.

"It sounds like urban legends and panic to me," Brock shrugged, sounding unimpressed. "I mean, kids make up crazy ghost stories all the time. Some kid probably just heard about what's happening over in Belle Grove and thought it would be funny to wind everyone up."

"That's what I thought, too," the officer nodded. "But people are getting nervous, anyway. We've suggested that people stay home if they can, so anyone out on the street looks suspicious to everyone else. Everyone's been on edge lately."

"Interesting," Olivia said quietly. She knew that they were grasping at straws once again, hoping to make something out of nothing, but she did think it was a little strange that things were a little amiss in Pine Woods, too. It was possible that with all the heat on in Belle Grove that the kidnapper might strike there next. But the main question still remained unanswered—how was he getting inside the houses? As with the other homes, the Roberts house had shown no signs of forced entry. Even if Sophia had left the house on her own accord and been snatched, that didn't appear to be the case for Hayleigh. She was definitely taken from her home and there was no trace evidence.

"I don't think it's anything to worry about, but it's better to be safe than sorry," Brock told the officer. "Belle Grove has enforced a curfew. It might be wise to do the same here, and to increase police patrols."

"Well, I hope you manage to find some answers soon. Like I said, we're all a little on edge here, too," the officer admitted. "We have nothing concrete to go on. Like you said, kids make up things for fun all the time. It's entirely possible that no one here has seen anything real. But if there's someone out there terrorizing kids, I want to put an end to it. I want my community to be safe. I'll try to enforce a curfew by tonight. I appreciate your coming up here to talk to me. We're not used to things like this happening around these parts."

Olivia nodded and handed him her card. "Call us if you have any trouble. Anything you see or hear, we want to know. Even if it turns out not to be relevant, it's better safe than sorry."

"Will do. Thank you," he said as he took Olivia's card. "From what I've heard, this case is a real bear."

"You don't know the half of it," Brock replied with a weary smile.

As he and Olivia retreated to the car, Brock let out an overexaggerated shudder. She looked at him and laughed.

"What's that about?" she asked.

"Just these urban legends about people walking standing in the shadows or staring up at somebody's bedroom window is enough to give me the heebie-jeebies," he said with a grin. "Do you think there's any truth to it?"

"I don't know. Hopefully, if there is, the police patrols will make the kidnapper think twice," Olivia said. "But stealing a young girl in the middle of a sleepover—that was ballsy. I've said it before, but this person really seems to know what he's doing. I think the towns will feel safer with police protection, but I wouldn't put it past the kidnapper to strike again. He seems to get off on taking girls right out from under our noses. This is getting worse and worse."

"I guess we're just going to have to try to get a step ahead of this guy. I think it was the right call to come here. And I want to drive around and see if there's anything to be seen," he said. "But after that, let's head back and review what we have. We've got some new information to work with. In the morning, we can check in with Maggie and see if the police had any luck overnight."

Olivia nodded and got in the car. She felt more in control of the case now than at any time since it had started, but there was still a lot of work to do. They were still two steps behind the kidnapper and she desperately wanted to get ahead of him. They needed to stay on their toes because Olivia could guarantee that the kidnapper was on his.

CHAPTER NINETEEN

AFTER RETURNING FROM PINE WOODS, OLIVIA AND Brock cruised through Belle Grove and somehow, the town seemed different. It had turned into a ghost town literally overnight. Nobody was out walking between the little shops on the main streets. No cars were on the road. No children were playing beneath the setting sun out on the streets. Most of the driveways in town were already filled with people's cars—everybody was desperate to get home and locked away as soon as possible. A lone police car cruised through the streets, looking for trouble. Brock shook his head.

"I bet the people here never thought they'd have to live like this. It's awful."

Olivia nodded. "It's for the best, though, if it keeps them safe," she said. "Though I'm not so sure that it will given that our kidnapper can seemingly walk through walls."

"With everybody already at home and locked inside, if our unsub tries again, we'll definitely be able to get more evidence this time, right?" Brock mused. "Or at least an eyewitness. He's getting more and more reckless. That last strike was bordering on crazy. But if he tries again now, it definitely crossed the border into full on insanity."

"Maybe we need things to get a little crazier," Olivia murmured. "Sometimes, crazy actions are easier to pick up on than sane ones."

Brock didn't respond to that, but Olivia knew he agreed. That was the reason the case had been so difficult so far; she was sure of it. They were dealing with someone so level-headed that he was almost ordinary. Olivia didn't think the suspect was some crazed psycho-killer. But the kidnapper, whoever he was, was teetering on the edge of madness now, doing things that he should have thought twice about. That was a difficult thing to get used to. The case was evolving, and they needed to as well.

"I don't think I want to head back to the B&B yet," Brock admitted. "I want to feel like we're doing something. Like we're being productive. Why don't we take a shift on the patrol for a while? I'm sure they can use all the eyes they can get."

"Sure. I've got nowhere to be," Olivia shrugged.
She didn't want to admit aloud that she had no issue with spending some extra time in Brock's presence. As they drove around in silence, she felt comfortable in their quietness. Having him next to her made some of her anxiety from the day melt away. He was the only one who was going through the same thing that she was, and he was the only one who could help provide her some comfort as they went through it. Together. Having him at her side was quickly becoming the only piece of normality and happiness she could still cling to.

The windows were misting up a little as they drove around, making it harder for Olivia to keep her eyes peeled for trouble. They drove up past the Edwards home, where the lights in the house had already been extinguished. Olivia's heart ached for Alice and Elijah, trapped in their misery with no new information. She desperately wished she had something to tell them. Olivia wished more than anything that she could solve the case just so that she could give them some good news. Just so that she could bring them some peace. Brock seemed to know what she was thinking because he reached over and patted her leg.

"Soon. We'll be able to give them good news soon," he said gently.

Olivia blushed. Was she really so easy to read? Or was Brock just learning her inside and out, from front cover to back?

"Have you heard anything from the Barnes family?" Brock asked a few minutes later. "Has Amelia been okay?"

"She's recovering fast, the last I heard," Olivia told him, smiling a little. "She's managed to put some weight back on. Her parents said she's been eating a lot, and she seems to be in a good mood. Of course, she'll never forget what happened to her, and without the ability to talk about what happened to her, she'll always be alone in her experience, but her parents will take good care of her, I'm sure of it. She'll be okay."

"So, I was thinking…"

"Did it hurt?" Olivia cracked.

Brock made a face as if to pretend he was wounded and they both shared a laugh. It tapered off after a moment, leaving them in a comfortable silence again. But then Brock finished what he'd just started to tell her.

"The kidnapper let Amelia escape, right? Either she got out of there on her own and the kidnapper didn't track her down, or the kidnapper actively allowed her to leave," he said. "She was held for three weeks and then she ran off through the woods."

"Okay…"

"What if the kidnapper lets Sophia and Hayleigh go, too?" he mused. "What if two or three weeks from now, they'll make it back here, a little worse for wear, but otherwise unharmed?"

Olivia chewed her lip. "I mean, it's possible. And that would be a happy ending. But I don't think we can rely on that at all. The kidnapper has established a lot of patterns, but that might not be one of them," she said. "He might only have done that because he knew Amelia wouldn't be able to speak about what happened to her, and because she was nowhere near home. Besides, I'm hoping somehow that we'll find him before then."

"Of course, that's the hope. But I don't know, I guess I've been clinging to the idea that they might somehow come back, anyway," he said. "There have to be silver linings in a case like this, right? Even if we can't solve it, maybe things are going to be okay. Maybe those girls will be fine in the end."

Olivia felt something in her chest lift a little. Brock was right. It was a nice thought. She wanted to be the one to solve the case, to put the kidnapper away for good, but more than anything, she wanted those girls to make it home. She wanted their parents to be able to rest a little easier knowing their children were okay. She wanted to see some light at the end of the very dark tunnel they'd somehow been trapped in.

Brock's words suddenly made everything easier to process. She hoped it was accurate. She didn't know how likely it was going to be, but nevertheless, the idea made everything easier to deal with.

They turned into the road where Hayleigh had been reported missing and the heaviness returned to Olivia's chest. It was hard to believe that in an affluent neighborhood such as Hayleigh's, something so awful had happened. She knew that it was often the poorer neighborhoods that were burdened by tragedy—and the police were never as interested in getting to the bottom of the issues there.

Yet in a richer neighborhood, any kind of crime was rarer and was taken very seriously. A lot more seriously than in the poorer ones. Their kidnapper could have operated with impunity in the poorer sections of town. But he chose to hit the more affluent neighborhoods, thus drawing more attention to himself. Why?

Olivia wondered what had made the kidnapper decide to hit the richer neighborhoods. It wasn't for ransom, as his complete indifference to the Barnes' family's reward and lack of a ransom demand proved. Sophia's family were very well-off, too. Did the kidnapper want something that they had? Did he want to get a taste of the life of luxury, or steal it away from the people who had it? Or did he simply understand that while the rich felt untouchable, they were far from it, and wanted to shatter the illusion by stealing their children away? Olivia didn't know. She found it very hard to get inside the mind of a kidnapper when she'd never had the urge to overturn someone's life so completely.

"What's going on there?" Brock asked suddenly, slowing down.

Through the misted-up window, Olivia saw that they were outside the Roberts residence, but Brock wasn't looking at her house. She saw Maggie standing outside Susan Combes' house, writing something down as Susan gesticulated wildly, telling a tale that Olivia couldn't hear. She exchanged a glance with Brock and they both silently got out of the car, curious to see what was going on.

It only took Olivia a second to realize what the reason for all the fuss was. There was a huge hole where Susan's front window used to be, with only a little bit of shattered glass still clinging to the window frame. Susan seemed very distressed by it all, and her cheeks were even streaked with tears. Olivia and Brock joined Maggie on the grass and listened to Susan's overwrought, overly emotional story.

"What happened?" Olivia asked gently as she faced Susan.

The woman turned to her and took a shuddering breath, her lip quivering.

"Someone put a brick through my window!" Susan cried out. "Some little thug threw a huge brick through my window and now there's no way I can stay here. I'm not safe. Someone has it out for me. Next thing you know, I'm going to be kidnapped."

Olivia bit her lip, not wanting to tell her that she was well outside the kidnapper's age preference. Susan seemed even more manic than she'd been at the station. After Brock's assessment that she was an alcoholic, Olivia could now see the signs that he'd pointed out to her. She was shaking like a leaf, and her nose looked red and blotchy. The rest of her skin looked a little gray, like the color had been sucked out of her. Her eyes were full of angry red veins, and she looked as though she hadn't slept in weeks.

Olivia was a nurturer. That was just how she'd always been and her first instinct was to feel sorry for her. Sure, the brick through the window was probably just kids messing around, but she had a right to be upset with so much going on in her hometown. Olivia just thought that Susan was a little too overwrought by it all.

"I'm sure this was nothing personal, Susan," Brock told her gently. "What reason would someone have to target you? It's probably just a stupid kid's prank gone wrong."

"But there's a curfew," Maggie pointed out. "I doubt any kids are running wild on the streets tonight. The strange thing is that no one saw anyone in the area after it happened. It caused a commotion among the neighbors, but none of them saw who did it. It's as if whoever did it just vanished into thin air."

Olivia felt a chill run down her spine. Could this have been done by the kidnapper? Was he simply trying to play with them now? Trying to scare them by causing chaos then hiding in plain sight after such disruptive actions?

"Someone's got it out for me," Susan cried once again. "I was trying to be helpful, giving the police information about what happened to Hayleigh. But now it feels like someone is trying to send me a warning. They know what I did. They want me to suffer for getting too close to the truth. They're coming for me."

Olivia sighed. Susan's theatrics certainly weren't helping the situation, but she was too far gone in her own interpretation of the truth to bring her back to reality anytime soon. Still, she had to try.

"Susan, I need you to take a deep breath for me," she said. "I doubt anyone was watching you go to the station to give evidence. I have a feeling this is what Brock said, just a stupid kid's prank gone wrong."

"Then why me?" Susan snapped. "Why my house? It's too much of a coincidence."

"Where were you when the brick was thrown through the window?" Brock asked, trying to divert her back onto some kind of coherent, less emotional track. Susan looked at him with startling intensity.

"I was asleep upstairs. I've had a long day, so I decided to take a nap. But of course, I woke up right away when I heard the noise," Susan sniffed.

She ran her entire arm under her nose, wiping it messily. She was certainly looking a little worse for wear. It was then that Olivia noticed how untamed her hair was. As if she'd just woken up. It made the story seem credible, at least.

"I came downstairs, not sure what happened, but I ran straight outside to see the damage. I noticed the broken window and then my neighbors came outside a moment later to see if I was all right, but there was no one else around. No one who could've done this. And the person disappeared without a trace. The person who did this wants what I have."

"What is it that you think he wants? What is it you have?" Olivia asked curiously, but Susan had already moved on.

"He wants me to suffer. He doesn't want me to have nice things like everyone else," she said.

Susan slurred a little as she spoke. As she did, Olivia noted the smell of alcohol on her breath and winced a little. Her drunken mumbling wasn't going to help anyone. She looked at Maggie, who nodded and placed a hand on Susan's arm.

"Why don't you come and stay at the station overnight? We've got beds there; you might feel safer than being alone in your house. I can stay here and see if I can figure out who did this. I'll get a board for the window until you come back."

"He won't find anything in my house," Susan muttered. "I have nothing he wants. I have to get out of here. I can go stay with family. This town just isn't right anymore. It's not safe for me here. I have to leave."

"You're in no state to drive," Olivia said, trying not to point out that she was clearly steaming drunk. "It's been a rough evening. Let us take you to the station and we can get you settled in for the night."

"I don't want to be here," she said miserably and shook her head. "Not here."

"You can drive to see your family in the morning when you're feeling better," Olivia told her calmly. "I think it's for the best that we keep an eye on you, okay? Let Maggie take you to the station where they can keep you safe."

It took some time to convince Susan to abandon ship and get into Maggie's car. She was growing more and more upset, but by the time she was put in the back of the police cruiser and on the way to the station, Olivia felt a little calmer. Susan's presence had been unnerving in some ways, and she hadn't been able to think straight. After she was gone, Olivia stared at the window, peering in to see what had done the damage. The brick was the same color as the house, and she soon spotted a small pile of loose bricks on the side of the house.

"Seems as though someone was just being an opportunist," Olivia said, showing Brock the pile of bricks.

He shook his head. "But what's with the vanishing act?" he asked "How can someone do something so disruptive and then get away unnoticed by anybody?"

"My guess is that he's done it before and he knows the area," Olivia shrugged. "Doesn't it feel familiar?"

"You think it's the kidnapper?"

"Maybe. It's just the timing of it all. Susan's right. It does feel targeted," she said. "She's Hayleigh's neighbor, after all. And she did give evidence, too. She makes a good point. Maybe someone has it out for her. Perhaps this was a warning. Not just to her, but to all of us. Maybe the person who did this wants us to know that he's watching."

She glanced around, wondering if she was being watched at that moment. She felt so cold all of a sudden that it turned her stomach. If they weren't alone, then maybe they needed to tread more carefully. Maybe they needed to watch their backs, too. Or maybe they'd be the next targets and they'd get a lot more than a brick through their windows.

CHAPTER TWENTY

OLIVIA FOUND HERSELF FACING ANOTHER SLEEPLESS night. Ever since she'd seen what had happened to Susan's window, she'd been feeling oddly paranoid. If Susan was right and there was a target on her back because she'd given evidence, then what sort of grudge would the kidnapper have against someone like Olivia or Brock, the ones actually trying to solve the case?

Out in her little cabin in the woods, Olivia felt truly alone, especially since Brock was spending a rare night in his B&B. If someone wanted to come for her in the middle of the night, there would be no witnesses. No one to protect her. Even the police patrols didn't extend as far as her cabin. She was on her own out there.

Despite her paranoia, she made it to the morning without incident. She'd listened to every sound in the forest through the night and hadn't even heard so much as a crackle of leaves nearby. It was a wasted night of lost sleep. She truly was living in fear. She had to remind herself that she was a well-trained federal agent more than capable of defending herself, but just one single brick sailing through

Susan Combes' window had changed the game entirely for Olivia and left her totally rattled.

She got up and showered, feeling even more vulnerable as she stood naked in the stall. She wondered if the feeling would ever go away. It was worse when Veronica had died, but it had eased for a while. Ever since the disappearance of her mother and her sister's murder, Olivia questioned whether she'd be next. Half of her family unit was unaccounted for. Why was that? Another unsolvable case that Olivia had to live with. A case that haunted her. Despite her exhaustion though, Olivia felt determined. Something told her that they were creeping closer and closer to the truth and some kind of solution. She couldn't say why. She had no reason to feel that way but she felt it all the same.

When Olivia got out of the shower, she found she had several missed calls from Jonathan and Brock. She called her boss first, knowing that the two calls were likely related. Jonathan picked up almost right away.

"About time," he said coolly. "I don't know if you've heard from Brock yet, but you need to get up to Alexandria. There's been another kidnapping."

Olivia's blood ran cold. It seemed wrong. Had the kidnapper moved into another area, the way he'd moved from Seattle to Belle Grove? Had he decided that the risk was too high in Belle Grove now that police were crawling the streets twenty-four-seven? Her heart beat uncomfortably hard in her chest, making her feel a little nauseous.

"Are you sure we're looking at the same kidnapper?" she asked.

"You tell me once you get there," he replied curtly. "Police are still on the scene and they're currently looking for witnesses. Missing girl's name is Tasha Hart. If you can get up there and speak to everyone involved with the case, it might shed some light on everything you're doing down in Belle Grove."

"Yes, sir."

"Be quick, Olivia. It's look like our kidnapper is becoming more frenzied. So many attacks in quick succession on our watch doesn't look good for us. We need to find out what's going on before the Bureau's reputation is tarnished."

Olivia pressed her lips together. Was he really more concerned about their image than the young women being kidnapped and held captive? And besides, if this case did fall apart, it wouldn't be the Bureau's image being tarnished; it would be her own. She was the one in the middle of it all, responsible for this case. People would call her capability into question. Olivia knew the company politics would turn against her and she'd likely be reassigned to menial cases, or worse, desk duty. She knew she had one shot to make things right, and she wasn't going to waste it.

"I'll look into it, sir."

"Good," he replied. "Keep me updated."

He hung up before she could respond again. She was irritated by his attitude during the call, but she didn't have time to feel sorry for herself. She got dressed after Brock sent her a message letting her know he was already on his way to pick her up. Ten minutes later, she was in the car with damp hair and her phone in her hand, typing up a text to Maggie to let her know where they were going and to ask about any updates she might have. She got a reply moments later.

"Maggie said that Susan refused to stay at the station overnight and got a ride to her family's house in the end," Olivia reported to Brock, with a shake of her head. "She must have really been shaken up by the whole thing."

"She's paranoid," Brock insisted. "I know it's a scary time, but it's made ten times worse by her drinking and her mental state. She needs to go to therapy, or rehab, or something. She's clearly been having a hard time for a while now and she's afraid, but I guess she must feel like she's on her own."

"At least she has some family nearby she can rely on," Olivia said.

She felt a stab of pity for the woman. But after a moment, she reconsidered why she felt that way. If Susan had some family she could call upon, then she was definitely in a better situation than Olivia was. Olivia hadn't had an actual conversation with her father in a long time, and though Paxton checked in every now and then, the two didn't just call each other up for a casual chat. And they certainly didn't share their feelings with each other.

She pictured Susan going to her family's home and being welcomed with open arms. She imagined some maternal parent offering her a sobering cup of coffee and a blanket. And all of a sudden, Olivia felt so homesick that she had to wind down the window and get some air just to feel capable of breathing.

"I'm sure she'll be fine with her family, especially if they're out of town. If this hit in Alexandria is the same kidnapper, he's obviously too busy to be chasing Susan down, anyway," Brock pointed out.

Olivia shuddered. "I wonder if this will be a lead," she said. "It's so soon after Hayleigh—the attacks are getting much closer together. What's he doing with all these girls? Is he warehousing them? Killing and dumping their bodies somewhere?"

"I wish I could answer that for you."

The drive took some time and Olivia spent the majority of the journey updating her notebook. She added the details of the brick incident and the few details she knew about the kidnapping in Alexandria. She was desperate for information, silently begging and praying for any kind of direction to go in. She felt she'd been idle too long, making up theories and hoping they'd turn into fact. Now, if they found a solid piece of evidence, then maybe one of her theories would finally bear some fruit. She just hated it took for another girl being taken for that to happen.

When they arrived at the scene of the crime, Olivia immediately realized something was off. Police were milling around the property, but it looked so different from the homes of the other victims that Olivia was instantly sure that the cases couldn't be connected. She knew she was jumping to conclusions, assuming that the class of the victims was a factor in the case, but she just had a gut feeling that something wasn't right.

"This doesn't feel right," Olivia said, staring at the house.

It was by no means a flophouse. But when compared to the large, airy townhouses of the families in Belle Grove, it was clearly nowhere near as grand. In fact, it was at least half the size and twice the age of any of the other houses they'd been to. The garden looked a little overgrown, as though the people who lived there simply didn't have time on their hands to care for it. And like most of the other houses on the street, there was no car in the driveway. The paint was a little faded and there seemed to be a little less TLC given to it.

"You never know," Brock shrugged, unclipping his seatbelt. "We're assuming that the kidnapper goes for rich kids, but we don't want to overlook anything at this point. The pattern might be changing if the kidnapper is getting more desperate. We might have forced him to change his patterns. Let's go and see what we can find out."

Olivia reluctantly got out of the car, feeling that they were about to waste a colossal amount of time, but she knew he was right. They had to check for connections, and at the end of the day, this was still a young girl who had gone missing. This was still a family who needed their help. She approached one of the police officers and explained why they were there.

"I'm not sure how much we can help you right now," the officer told them. "We're dusting for fingerprints, trying to find some evidence. We've also got some muddy boot prints to take a look at in the house. We can't say for sure yet, but the parents think this might be the work of a jaded ex."

"The jaded ex of a teenage girl?" Olivia frowned.

The officer glanced at her with a confused look on his face. "Well, I wouldn't say she's a teenager. She's eighteen. Definitely old enough to have had some boyfriends in her life."

Olivia looked at Brock and shook her head. Now she knew for certain that something was wrong. Jonathan hadn't mentioned that the girl was older than the other victims. She knew that it was possible that age wasn't a factor in the other abductions, but they'd established a pattern with the other girls. All three previous victims were between the ages of fourteen and fifteen—and it was a pretty big gap to eighteen.

She shook her head. "This isn't right…"

"We still have to investigate," Brock insisted. "You know we do. If the kidnapper is as smart as we think, then maybe this whole attack is a red herring to show us that we're no closer to finding him than before. It could be an elaborate taunt."

"But there's already signs of evidence at the scene. There might even be fingerprints here. This isn't anything like the abductions we've been looking at. The muddy boot prints? That's a rookie mistake. Shoes can give a lot away. I just don't think the kidnapper is that much of an exhibitionist."

"What about the brick through the window?" Brock argued. "This might be a cry for attention. Maybe he's getting bored with the chase. Maybe he wants to be found. Or maybe he wants to rub our noses in it. Stranger things have happened, right?"

Olivia murmured under her breath, not feeling sure of anything at this point. She knew Brock was making good points, but every fiber of her being told her that they were in the completely wrong place. That this case had absolutely nothing to do with the others. What if the kidnapper targeted Belle Grove while they were out of town? What if he was relying on this misdirect to move on to his next victim? They could be wasting precious time here when something terrible could be happening back there.

But Olivia had been ordered by SAC James to look into this. And she had no choice other than to follow Brock to the police station to speak to the family. When they arrived, even the family seemed wrong to her. They didn't have the same air about them. She noted the mother's weathered hands, the father's deep frown lines, their casual clothing. They seemed comfortably middle class, but not anywhere near the socioeconomic league of the other families. And neither one of them was remotely close to blonde.

"This is Ashleigh Hart and Sam Hart," an officer introduced Brock and Olivia as they entered the interrogation room at the police station. "The parents of our missing victim, Tasha. I'll give you some time to speak to them while I make some calls."

"Thank you," Brock said, taking a seat opposite the distraught parents and shaking their hands. "We're gathering any information that might help us find your daughter. We think there's a possibility Tasha's abduction is the latest in a series of kidnappings. If this case is indeed related, then we'll need to know everything we possibly can about what happened to your daughter."

"I'm not sure how much we can help you. We're already pretty sure about what happened," Sam started, his dark eyebrows knitting together. "We've been having some trouble with Tasha's ex, Alex. He's been coming to the house late at night, banging on our door and trying to get in. We've threatened to call the police a few times and that's usually enough to make him leave, but maybe he finally snapped. The shoe prints in the house look like his size, but that's just a guess."

"Does your daughter have blonde hair?" Olivia asked.

She was sure that was a crucial detail. It was the key detail linking all the cases. Brock glared at her for changing the subject, but Sam seemed happy to answer her question.

"No. She's got dark hair like us."

"And would you describe her as having a babyface?" she pressed. "Currently, the victims in our case have been young girls, fourteen or fifteen years old. Do you think she could possibly be mistaken for a young girl?"

"I doubt it," Ashleigh said, looking anxious as she spoke. "If anything, Tasha looks older than her age, especially when she's wearing makeup. She's always had a full figure. There would be no mistaking her for a child."

"Okay. Thank you," Olivia said, feeling irritable as she jotted down some notes.

She couldn't understand for the life of her why Jonathan had thought the case might be related. Anyone with any knowledge of the case would dismiss Tasha's situation entirely. SAC James should have assigned somebody else to it. Olivia had been there for all of five minutes and knew, beyond the shadow of a doubt, that Tasha Hart's case had nothing to do with the others. And she was angry at James for wasting their time.

They stayed for a while longer, but Olivia let Brock lead the questioning, quietly seething at the fact that they'd wasted an entire day they could have been back in Belle Grove looking for Sophia and Hayleigh. Looking for the man who'd taken them. She knew the case inside out and she saw right from the start that they were looking in the wrong place.

She was so angry that she felt she was about to burst. She wished they could just get up and leave, but Brock seemed intent on carrying out the interview all the way to the end. Even though she knew it was their job to speak with the family and gather the facts, she was desperate to get back to business.

When Brock eventually stood and shook the Harts' hands, Olivia felt some of her anger slip away. But as they headed back to the car, she could sense Brock's irritation with her. It was only after they were both seated inside that he inhaled deeply, trying to calm himself, and asked her the question she knew was coming.

"What the hell was that?" he snapped. "We were trying to conduct a serious interview and you just checked out completely. What happened?"

"There was nothing for us there. We wasted our time," Olivia replied just as irritably.

Brock sighed. "You don't know that."

"Yes, I do. How many hours have we spent studying this kidnapper? I haven't slept in weeks, staying up and thinking about this case instead. We know the kidnapper has a certain type of victim, and I knew from the moment we arrived that this was wrong. I can't believe Jonathan sent us here."

"Okay, so what if it was a dead end? We have to keep exploring new avenues, you know that. Why are you so upset about this one?"

"Because every second we waste means that the kidnapper is one step closer to taking someone else!" Olivia cried out. "Every second we're looking in the wrong direction, we're letting another child down. Every second we're exploring the wrong avenue, we could be missing something crucial. I'm tired of getting nowhere, Brock. How are we supposed to ever get to the bottom of this if we're not putting all of our time and energy into the right places?"

An uneasy silence settled over the car. Brock stared at Olivia; she knew her cheeks were flushed red in anger and embarrassment. She couldn't believe she'd just blown up like that. Her emotions had been building up the whole day, but she was usually in total command of her feelings. But she was so tired of it all that she couldn't hold it back anymore and she'd exploded. She really needed something to change, but everything was standing still.

"You know what you need?" Brock finally broke the silence. "A huge burger and a coffee."

"Brock…"

"No arguing, Olivia. You're burned out. Anyone can see that. We're going to have a meal and talk things over. You need a little time off," he said. "You're no use to anyone when you're this wound up."

Olivia's mouth hung open, all her unspoken words waiting to spill out of her lips, but she stopped herself. Brock started the car and began to drive, so Olivia let him. He was right. She needed an intervention, even if she hadn't asked for one.

It was as if Brock always knew exactly what to do. Always knew how to calm her down.

CHAPTER TWENTY-ONE

ONCE AGAIN, THE DINER WAS ALMOST EMPTY AS BROCK and Olivia entered. Olivia felt reassured by the fact, knowing that she was in a safe space to talk about her little breakdown in the car. She still felt the urge to run out of there and get back to work, but she realized that her feelings were unhealthy. She'd become obsessed with the job lately, and she needed to at least take a break to eat. Brock was right, she would be of use to nobody, least of all the girls who were depending on her, if she burned out.

They slid into the same booth they'd sat in last time, and Olivia forced herself to look over the menu properly this time. She usually had a pretty healthy diet, aside from her copious amounts of coffee, but she decided that if there was ever a time to treat herself, it was now. She ordered bacon-loaded fries with coffee. The waitress brought her a mug and poured her a cup, but Olivia told her to just leave the carafe. Brock tutted.

"You and your coffee," he said. "You really are inseparable, aren't you? It's not just a casual flirtation."

"I definitely drink more coffee than water," Olivia said.

She didn't want to have to talk about everything going on in her head. She'd rather just joke around for the rest of the day and try to forget the anxiety growing inside her. But Brock was looking at her intently and she knew he was about to get back down to business. He suddenly wasn't his usual joking self and it made her feel strange, as if she was peeling back a new layer of his personality.

"All right Olivia, lay it on me. What's going on in that head of yours?" he said. "And don't say you're fine, because I can tell you're not. I can't have you falling apart when we're working, so now is the time to tell me everything."

Olivia sighed. What exactly was she supposed to tell him? She was traumatized, quite simply. She'd spent years of her life being forced to reflect on the strange things that had happened to her family, and now she had to face up to the fact that just as she'd failed them, she was failing at her case. She felt she was constantly walking on hot coals, each sharp stab of heat that seared her flesh reminding her of all her failures.

"This isn't just about today, is it?" he asked.

Olivia shook her head with a sigh.

She topped off her coffee and took a long sip, letting the scalding liquid slide down her throat. She winced, feeling as if she'd just swallowed some of those hot coals she was thinking about walking on.

"Do you ever feel that your life is just more complicated than anyone else could ever comprehend?" she said. "That you've got so many demons, you'll never be able to count them all, let alone shake them?"

Brock tentatively shook his head. "Not really."

Olivia sighed. "I guess that's a good thing. Maybe it is just me," she said. "The truth is, life has been really tough these past few years and I don't like to admit it to myself, but sometimes, it overwhelms me. I've been like this before, but I always get myself out of my rut. I just need some time. Or a win, I guess."

Brock leaned back in his seat with a frown. "Is this because of what happened to your sister? Because of course, that makes sense."

"It's not just that. My family—we've got a strange history," she said. "There's a lot I don't talk about with other people, and as much as I hate to admit it, it sometimes affects my work. This case just feels so personal to me."

"Why is that?"

Olivia pressed her lips together, unsure how much to unload on Brock. They'd grown close over the span of the case and she certainly considered him her friend. But she had a lot of internal crap and she didn't want to freak him out. Everyone who knew about her past treated her differently. They treated her like she was some delicate, fragile thing that might break in the slightest breeze. Maybe she was, but she didn't want to be seen that way. She'd joined the FBI and felt unstoppable. Now, here she was, being consumed by her own emotions.

"My mom disappeared," she whispered after a long silence. "After my sister died, Mom just vanished off the face of the Earth. Of course, we searched for her, and we got the police involved, but they never found a thing. It was just the same as with Sophia. Her phone was still on the bedside table. She didn't take anything personal with her. She couldn't have had any money with her because her debit card was untouched. She didn't use her passport to leave the country— it was really as though she was just wiped off the face of the Earth."

"You keep saying she didn't take anything with her," he said. "Do you think she went of her own accord? That she just went somewhere without telling anyone?"

Olivia chewed her lip. She hadn't even realized she'd phrased it that way. "Not exactly.... but I find it so hard to believe that she was taken. Anyone who knew my mother feels the same. She was so strong. She was a force to be reckoned with, and she wouldn't go down easily," she said. "I don't know what happened to her, but to say that she was taken or something just feels wrong. She was too smart to get caught out like that, too strong to let anyone lay hands on her. But regardless of what I think, she's gone now. No one has found a single lead to suggest where she might be. And maybe that's what makes this case so complicated for me.

I feel so desperate to solve an impossible case, to prove that it can be done. I feel that, maybe if I can do this, then I'll somehow magically find out what happened to my sister the night she died or figure out what happened to my mom. It's ridiculous, I know, but somewhere in the back of my head, I have so much hope. And it's making my life ridiculously difficult."

"But you can't give up. And honestly, Olivia, I know you won't. You've got to believe that things will get better. And you will believe that. It's how people live their lives," Brock told her with a confidence she wished she could grasp. "And after everything you've been through, you have every right to feel everything you're feeling. But keeping it all bottled up inside you isn't going to help. You need to open up a bit, Olivia. I'm your partner now. You can talk to me about anything, you know?"

Olivia didn't feel like telling him that despite the fact she'd told him her deepest, darkest secrets, she still barely knew anything about him. She held back from saying it because she knew he was only trying to help her, and she appreciated that. She sighed and topped off her coffee yet again, taking a sip and feeling the buzz of the caffeine in her throbbing head.

"I know that. I guess I just got caught up in everything. Sometimes I need to just stop for a minute and tell myself to get it together. I'm usually okay. I don't usually spin out like I did. But lately, things have just been overwhelming me more than usual. And with this case, it feels kind of like whoever is doing this is just watching us fail and is laughing at us. That's what I mean when I say it feels personal. I've spent the last five years feeling that there must be a target on my back. First my sister dies, and then my mother goes missing, so there's some part of me that believes I must be next. Is that crazy?"

Brock pursed his lips, considering his answer carefully. Then he looked her in the eye, his gaze gentle, his smile even softer.

"No. It's not crazy. I'd feel the same in your situation. That's a lot for one person to bear," he said. "I can understand why you might feel like someone has it out for you and your family."

Olivia nodded, feeling relieved that she wasn't just being some paranoid idiot. She'd known all along that her situation was hard to understand and relate to, but hearing Brock tell her that she wasn't crazy was an unexpected balm of comfort. She let out a deep sigh and felt some of her worry and anxiety lessen as she exhaled.

"This whole thing is partly why I moved to Belle Grove, you know," she continued. "It wasn't just that I was tired of living in the city. I wanted to go somewhere where nobody knew anything about my past. Somewhere that would allow me to have a fresh start. I felt my friends were walking on eggshells around me, worrying about upsetting me because I'd been through a rough time. It was suffocating," she said. "And I know it's crazy, but I somehow feel as though I'm hiding out by living here. As if I'm so off the beaten path that if someone wants to hunt me down, they'll have a hard time finding me. Which is crazy, of course. I'd blend in better in the city, for sure. But I have honestly felt a little better since coming out here. Or at least, I was feeling better until all of this started."

"And now it feels as if the past is catching up with you?"

Olivia nodded. She couldn't believe she'd been so honest with Brock. But she felt a profound sense of relief that he seemed to understand her. She had to admit that some part of her was scared that he'd pull away now that he knew about her past. She knew she had a lot of baggage, and she was used to having to lug it around on her own. But Brock didn't seem fazed. In fact, his face or temperament hadn't changed at all during the conversation.

Olivia guessed he'd had to deal with some level of the unusual with work, just as she did. But it felt good that revealing her demons to him hadn't seemed to change the way he saw her. She'd never admit it aloud, but she desperately wanted Brock to view her in a good light. She wanted him to like her. She wanted that more with each passing day.

"You know that the case isn't your fault, don't you?" he said. "You're doing everything you can and more. You are the walking embodiment of above and beyond."

She laughed slightly. "I know it's not my fault. I really do," she said. "I'm just beating myself up because I feel I should be able to do something more about it all. I mean, it's my job to figure these things out."

"But here's the thing, Olivia. You're only human and as far as I know, you're not psychic. There's only so much that you can do with the information we have. And even if you could have a direct insight into the kidnapper's mind, you still wouldn't be able to figure out what's going on in there," he said. "Not just because the human mind is complicated, but because you're not a psychopath. We can study psychology all we want, but because we're not psychopaths, we'll never fully understand why they do what they do. And let's be honest, Olivia, you might be having a tough time and your mind might be in turmoil, but you're about as far from a psychopath as a person can possibly get."

Olivia barked out a surprised laugh, somehow flattered by the comment. "Man, you really know how to make a woman feel good," she joked.

Brock burst out laughing, tilting his head back as he did. That opened the floodgates and both of them collapsed into a fit of hysterics.

"I like to think so," Brock finally managed with a twinkle in his eye.

He reached across the table and took Olivia's hand in his. She flinched at the sudden contact, surprised by the gesture, but she didn't pull away. She didn't ever want to pull away. He held her gaze firmly, his expression one of sincerity.

"You can stop beating yourself up now," Brock told her firmly. "You're one of the best agents I've ever worked with. I know Jonathan doesn't appreciate you half as much as he should—and I know some of your theories go overlooked—but I believe in your ideas. You're great at your job, and I know I would've fallen apart on this case, too, if I didn't have you alongside me."

"Because I'm falling apart enough for both of us?"

Brock smiled. "No. Because I trust you," he said. "I know that if this case is solvable, then you'll get to the bottom of it all."

"Well, it feels nice that you trust me," she replied. "I don't know if your faith is misplaced or not, but thanks for trusting me."

"Any time. Now, it's time for you to trust me. After we're done here, I'm sending you home to bed," he told her.

"But—"

"No buts, Knight. The bags under your eyes are getting bigger by the second. I know you haven't been sleeping well. You need a solid twelve hours of rest and then you can come at this case with a new energy tomorrow."

"But we've already wasted so much time today," she argued. "We could be missing something crucial—"

"Then I'll stay up. I'll sleep on the sofa for a few hours later, but I'm well-rested. I can spend time looking into all the notes we've gathered so far. I know you're finding it hard to relax right now, but you'll be much more useful once you've slept. It's non-negotiable, Olivia."

She smiled and lifted her mug to her lips, but he snatched it out of her hand and put it and the carafe on the table behind him. She started to protest but he held up a finger to forestall her argument.

"And I'm cutting you off," he said. You'll be bouncing off the walls all night."

The waitress returned with their food, and Brock rubbed his hands together in excitement. Olivia's stomach gurgled, and she suddenly realized that she hadn't eaten all day. She couldn't believe the words coming out of her mouth, but she asked the waitress for a glass of water.

Brock was right. She really needed to start taking better care of herself. Starting with eating a big meal and then getting some rest. She'd needed to give herself permission to do what was best for her, and now that she'd given herself that permission, her body was craving it all at once. But she wasn't going to neglect her needs anymore. She was going to make sure that she put herself first again.

And by helping herself out, she was going to help the missing girls by solving the case.

CHAPTER
TWENTY-TWO

O LIVIA AND BROCK HEADED BACK TO HER PLACE FROM THE diner a little after five that evening. And as soon as they got back to the cabin, Brock, as promised, poured Olivia a big glass of water and sent her off to bed. She rolled her eyes and obliged, knowing that she wouldn't be able to sleep while it was still light outside. Instead, she drew herself a bath and spent an hour in the bubbles, doing nothing but soaking with her eyes closed.

She felt a little drowsier by the time she'd put on her robe and grabbed a book from her bookshelf and laid down. She felt like she could have dropped off but her body had other ideas and she spent several hours reading before she was tired enough to get under her covers and attempt to fall asleep. Anxiety kept her awake a little longer, but by ten, she was fast asleep in the warmth and safety of her bed.

Olivia couldn't believe it when she woke up and saw sunlight. It was rare that she slept through the entire night without waking, but she'd been asleep for almost ten hours, according to her watch. She felt groggy for several minutes, so she lay where she was, trying to process the fact that she'd slept so well. She hadn't even had any of her usual nightmares.

She managed to get herself out of bed and when she did, she felt like a completely new person. She was still a little groggy and her thoughts a little fuzzy around the edges, but she was strangely refreshed. She got dressed and brushed her hair before heading downstairs to pour herself a glass of water. She was so well rested and awake, she didn't even feel like she needed coffee.

She found Brock sleeping on the sofa, his mouth hanging slightly open, and the case file sprawled open on the floor where he'd dropped it when he'd fallen asleep. Olivia smiled affectionately and picked up the file, slotting the sheets of paper that had fallen out back into place. She knew that Brock must've been up half the night, and she didn't want to disturb him. But even as she settled quietly into the chair to do some reading, he stirred and slowly opened his eyes. He sat up and ran his hands over his face.

"I fell asleep?" he muttered, his face drooping as though he was sorely disappointed in himself.

Olivia smiled. "I didn't expect you to stay up all night. You're acting like me."

Brock gave her a sleepy, lopsided smile. His cheek was red where he'd had it pressed into the sofa and she grinned.

"All right, point made," he said. "But I actually did come up with something useful last night. Well, at least, I think I did. Sleep deprivation makes things a little hazy."

"You get used to that," she told him. "What did you find?"

"Give me ten minutes. I think I'm the one who needs coffee this morning."

Olivia obliged, flipping through the case notes while Brock readied himself for the day ahead. He returned with a steaming mug of coffee, sipping it as he walked.

"Is it just me or does your terrible coffee taste slightly better than it used to?" he said, still wincing a little. "I think I've been drinking this crap so long, it's burned out my taste buds."

Olivia rolled her eyes with a smile. "Tell me what you came up with."

Brock nodded, sitting on the sofa and leaned toward her. "Okay, so I started looking at the families of the girls. I kept trying to make connections among the three of them. We know that Hayleigh and Sophia were classmates, and they spent some time together, but of course, Amelia isn't even from here. I read over the interviews again and did a little online research, looking for something that might connect them," he said. "In the newspaper articles I found, they reported on the girls and their hobbies. You know, painting the picture of their being sweet little angels to appeal to the public. But I couldn't find any similarities or connections between them all. I guess I was hoping that maybe they had a mutual connection of some sort who might be a suspect, but there was nothing I could find. So, the only thing that I could find that connected them was the obvious things that we already knew. Blonde hair, similar ages, middle-class families."

"Okay, so, what was it you found?"

"Well, I thought more about it, and there is one other thing that connects all the girls. All three of them are only children. Each of the three families is the same: a mom, a dad, and a daughter. All of the girls have parents who seem to be in healthy marriages, or at least, none of them is divorced. And that's another reason the Tasha Hart case doesn't fit—she has a younger brother."

"It's a very specific profile," Olivia agreed.

"Obviously, we already talked about the idea that the kidnapper is someone who lost a child—that's if we can connect what we found in the forest to the case, of course—but this further supports the idea that maybe the kidnapper is targeting families who replicate what he used to have. By taking away one girl from a single-child household, he's depriving the parents, the way he was deprived while at the same time, getting back what he lost."

The theory was exciting to Olivia. It made so much sense to her now that Brock had said it out loud. Perhaps it didn't give them any new suspects or evidence, but it built on the theory she'd come up with and the profile of their kidnapper was taking shape.

"Okay, this is good. This we can use. Maybe we can use this to map out where the kidnapper might strike next and further develop our profile to narrow down our suspect," she said. "We need to put together a list of single-child families with young blonde girls. Maybe we get lucky and catch the kidnapper in the act. That's really good work, Brock."

"That's what I thought. And then I also thought that we could speak to Maggie about anyone in town who might have lost a child," he said. "Obviously, it might not be someone from here, but given that all three cases have revolved around this town, and two of the missing girls are from here directly, it's starting to feel personal. It's sensitive to be looking into people who've been through something so horrible, but it's the only type of motive that we've identified so far. It's somewhere to start, at least."

"Agreed. Maggie knows everyone around here; she'll definitely be able to give some insight. Want to head over to the station and see what we can do?" she asked.

"Let's roll out!"

After they got ready, Olivia took the wheel and drove to the station. She was buzzing with excitement once again, feeling like they were inching closer to answers. She didn't want to get her hopes up again, only to be let down, but she had a good feeling that they were on the right track. She liked to believe that her theories weren't too outlandish to work, and now that Brock had made further connections to support them, she felt so much less alone.

When they arrived at the station, they found Maggie nursing a coffee in her office. She was sullen and looking a little worse for wear. Perhaps she and Brock weren't the only ones having sleepless nights over the missing girls.

"Mornin'," she said to Olivia and Brock, her voice still bright.

Olivia smiled at her. "Hey, Maggie. How are you holding up?"

Maggie sighed. "I'm not having the best time with all this, to be honest. We've never been so busy here. Not just with the missing girls, but after Craig was arrested it's just been one thing after another," she said. "But I can't complain. How can I help you kids? I'm sure you didn't come here just to chat about the weather."

Olivia felt awful moving on from the subject, wishing they had more time to catch up, but she couldn't afford to waste any more time. The kidnapper might not have struck in Alexandria, but if they continued to follow the same pattern, another child might go missing that night.

"Brock came up with some new ideas which might help the case, but we're going to need your help," Olivia told her.

Maggie frowned, threading her fingers together. "Okay. Well, I'll do everything I can to help. What do you need?"

"We're looking into an angle," Brock started carefully.

Olivia could tell that what they were about to say might be a little controversial. The people in Belle Grove were tight-knit and cared a lot about each other. Having Maggie dig into people she'd know for most of her life wasn't going to be easy and might ruffle some feathers.

Brock cleared his throat. "We think that the kidnapper is going for young, blonde girls because he might have lost a child who looks similar to the victims," he said carefully.

"Which means we need to get a list of people in town who have had a family tragedy—suffered the loss of a teenage girl specifically—possibly in recent years," Olivia added.

Maggie looked suitably shocked at the theory. "You think someone in town—from Belle Grove—is doing this?"

"My theory is that it has to be. I checked in with the Seattle field office, and it's been completely silent on their end. No matter which way you look at it, all three cases have centered around Belle Grove," Olivia said. "Then there are the reports we had from Pine Woods of

226

a figure spying on houses. It makes us think the kidnapper is local. Not to mention what happened at Susan Combes' house."

"You don't think she was just being hysterical?"

"Entirely possible. I wouldn't put it past her. But even if it's unrelated, we still have enough evidence so far to point at the kidnapper's being in Belle Grove or the surrounding area," Brock said coolly. "It's a terrible thing to have to investigate. We obviously don't want to accuse people who've lost their children of such a terrible crime, but we need to look into anybody who has."

"You have to admit it makes some kind of sense," Olivia added. "From a certain perspective, losing a child could give someone a good reason to want to take children in the middle of the night. We don't want to have to do this, but if it leads us to the kids, then it will be worth it."

Maggie took a deep breath. "All right. I don't really like it, but if you think it'll help, I'll try to put together a list of who's lost a child—a blonde, teenage girl specially."

"Okay," Maggie said with a nod. "Let me see what I can do. It'll take me some time to go through everyone in town, but I think I can cover it today. Is that all right?"

"That would be great," Olivia said. "Thank you so much, Maggie. We're sorry to add to your workload."

"Beats office paperwork any day," she waved them off with a warm smile. "The sooner we find these kids, the better. I'll get started now."

Brock and Olivia stood up and followed her out of the office, but she stopped them with a gentle hand.

"Now you two just hold on a minute. I am not about to have two federal agents tagging along behind me to ask these poor families about the circumstances of the deaths of their children."

"But we..." Olivia protested, but Maggie held out a firm hand.

"I like you, Olivia, and I know you'll do great in this town. But that don't mean you're ready for the, uh... delicate nature of Belle

Grove neighborhood chatter," she said. "Y'all make yourselves comfortable, grab some coffee in the break room. I'll take care of this and get back to you."

Olivia thanked Maggie again, and they headed over to the break room. She found it hard to relax, pacing around the room while Brock steadily downed two more cups of coffee. Eventually, he sighed.

"Please sit down, you're making me edgy," he said.

"Sorry," Olivia said, sitting down beside Brock. "There's just so much riding on this. We might finally have a lead. Or we might just be left with nothing again."

"I know, but there's not a lot we can do about that right now," he replied. "We're just going to have to face the fact that this could go either way. It's part of the job."

Olivia nodded, rubbing her temples. "I know. I know."

"You're doing great, Olivia," Brock said wearily, leaning his head back against the wall. "We just have to be patient. Believe me, I feel your frustration, but it's out of our hands. Let's just see what Maggie comes up with."

Olivia did her best to distract herself. She found a copy of a fashion magazine tucked down the side of the sofa, but the issue was several months out of date and full of winter clothes, so it did little to distract her. She wished she'd brought a book with her. She always found it easiest to escape from reality inside a book. Brock flicked through the channels on the old TV, but found nothing other than news channels and ended up switching it off again.

More than two hours passed before Maggie came to fetch them, looking even more exhausted than she had that morning. She didn't look particularly excited, either, and Olivia's heart sank. She was almost certain that meant that Maggie hadn't found anything.

"I've got a few things," Maggie told them as they headed back to her office. "Not sure if this is what you're looking for, though."

Maggie sighed deeply as she lowered herself into her chair,

sounding like a deflated balloon. Olivia's foot tapped impatiently as she waited for Maggie to tell them what she'd found.

"Okay, here goes. I found four results in town. First is the Okoro family. They lost a child three years ago, but the couple is still together, and they're African-American, so they don't fit the profile at all. Then there are the Millers. Amber Miller had a stillborn child five years ago and has now split from her husband, but of course, her child never made it to childhood. I also don't know whether the child was blonde or not."

Olivia nodded, knowing that neither of the families made sense within the case they were trying to build. She waited patiently for the next set of details. Maggie consulted her notes.

"Then there's my good friend, Jennifer Sands. She had a daughter around twenty years ago, so that fits the profile, but she was severely depressed after the birth and ended up giving the child up for adoption to a gay couple up in Pine Woods."

"That could be it," Brock cut in. "Maybe she feels she missed out on the experience and is now making up for lost time by stealing children away."

Maggie leveled him with a look. "Not a bad theory for a city slicker, but she's still in contact with her daughter and they have a good relationship," Maggie said. "She's good friends with the adoptive parents and they have a sort of three-way parentship. I don't think it's likely that she fits your profile."

Olivia took note that Maggie was biased, because they were discussing her friend, but she had to admit, based on what Maggie just said, she didn't think it was likely Jennifer was the kidnapper. She hit some of the markers in the profile but didn't fit others. To her, the net result was that because she was in the child's life and had a good relationship with her, it made it unlikely that she was involved. Olivia clasped her hands together hopefully.

"What about the last one?" she asked, trying to keep the desperation out of her voice.

Maggie sighed. "I know this isn't what you want to hear, but this might be another dead end. The only other family that I know to have lost a child is the Wainwright family," she said. "But they have three other children, and the mother lost her child during a complicated pregnancy. It's not a fit for what you're looking for, as far as I can tell. I even had Spencer look through local obituaries for the last few years, but I can't think of anyone who fits your profile."

"Of course, I don't know everything about everyone in this town. Plenty of people move here to escape a past they don't want to talk about. I think you know exactly what I mean, Olivia. Belle Grove is meant to be a safe haven for people, and plenty of them likely have secrets they'd prefer to stay buried. But as far as the information I have, I can't help you."

Olivia nodded in understanding. She knew that there was only so much that Maggie could tell them, but it didn't mean that they were looking in the wrong place. The problem was, they had no way of finding out if anyone else in town had lost a child without asking, and it wasn't the kind of information anyone would disclose to a stranger. As frustrating as it was, they'd hit another wall.

"Thank you for your help, Maggie," Brock said with a small smile that didn't meet his eyes. "You've been very helpful."

"Glad to have helped somehow," she replied. "Sorry, this didn't pan out, but we'll keep at it. I still have hope we can find them."

"Me, too," Olivia replied with a long sigh. "Maybe we'll get lucky and strike gold. We'll be in touch soon."

Olivia and Brock left the police station with the weight of the world on their shoulders. Olivia could feel her hope trickling away from her once again as she fished out her car keys. But then she felt a finger under her chin, tilting it up to meet Brock's eyes. He smiled at her.

"Head high," he murmured, the touch of his finger on her skin making her want to shudder in unexpected delight.

And with that one single touch, some of her hope returned.

CHAPTER
TWENTY-THREE

I T WAS LATER THAT DAY, WHEN BROCK AND OLIVIA WERE SEARCH-
ing for new theories in the case file, that Olivia heard a knock on
her front door. She frowned.

"I don't ever get visitors here," she said.

She stood up from the sofa, picked up her weapon, and headed
to the front door. When she opened it, she was horrified to find that
the Edwards and Roberts families were standing on her porch. Alice
Edwards stood at the front of the posse, her arms folded, her lips
pursed, and her eyes full of anger.

"May we come in?" she asked before promptly pushing her
way past Olivia and heading straight into the living area without an
answer.

Elijah looked apologetic as he followed his wife inside, leaving Andrea and Richard Roberts standing awkwardly on the porch.

"We're sorry to come to your home like this," Andrea started,
her eyes sorrowful. "But we just wanted to talk to you. We're so

worried about our baby girl. We want to know when we're going to get answers."

"I understand, Andrea, but this is my home," Olivia said. "I have to be off duty at some point, and this is my space. None of you should be here. How did you even get this address?"

"Everyone knows you're the FBI agent living in the woods," Alice snapped, appearing again from the living room. "Or *hiding* in the woods, I should say. What on Earth have you been doing this whole time while our daughters have been missing? Canoodling with your FBI boyfriend? Is that it?"

Olivia's face turned bright red. She couldn't decide if she was angrier with the accusation or embarrassed that they thought she and Brock were hooking up instead of working. She decided on anger.

"I have been working very hard trying to find your children," Olivia replied through gritted teeth.

She didn't often let anger get the better of her, but when she did, she found it almost impossible to hold back. The last thing she wanted was to fight with the families of the missing girls. But she knew that she had to stand her ground and fight. The worst thing she could do was let these people think they could walk all over her. It would set a precedent Olivia knew she wouldn't be able to walk back so she needed to nip it in the bud.

"You have no idea how much effort we're putting into this search," Olivia growled. "We barely eat and sleep. We are living this case twenty-four-seven."

"If that's the case, then why haven't you found anything yet?" Alice snarled.

Olivia had to bite the inside of her cheek to stop herself from shouting back at her. She turned to face Andrea and Richard, glad that they at least seemed calm.

"Please come inside and have a seat," she said. "Let's talk about this calmly."

As she shut the door behind Hayleigh's parents, she took several calming breaths. It was the only way she was going to get through the next few minutes without screaming. It was so typical of Alice to put all of the blame on someone else. In the short time Olivia had known her, it had become clear to her that Alice was a hothead but coming to her house to accuse her of giving up on Sophia was a bridge too far. There was no way that Olivia was going to lie down and take that kind of abuse from a woman whose child was clearly out of her control.

It was those kinds of thoughts that made Olivia realize that she was going to have to tread carefully. She didn't really think that Alice was a bad mother, just a normal one struggling with a troubled child. She didn't want to argue with her. She just wanted to be honest about the mess they had all been dragged into.

As she re-entered the living room, she found that Andrea and Richard were perched together on the chair, while Alice stood in the middle of the room, her hands on her hips. Elijah stood just behind her, looking embarrassed. Olivia took her seat beside Brock again, but realized it was a mistake as soon as she did. She could see Alice's accusing eyes boring into her, making her feel guilty just for being within inches of Brock. Plus, with Alice standing over her, she felt like a child in school about to get a lecture from a stern teacher about talking in class.

"Now, I want straight answers out of you both. What the hell are you playing at?" Alice snapped at them. "It's been ten days now since my Sophia went missing. How hard can it be to find her? And do you really think you can find her sitting on the couch enjoying a little domestic bliss like you seem to be doing?"

"First of all, Mrs. Edwards, have some respect," Brock growled. "You're the one who just came barging into someone else's home, pretending to know more about this whole thing than two trained professionals. Secondly, let me tell you, it's not easy to find a missing child in any circumstances. But this case is particularly challenging and we need you to have a little patience."

"You keep saying that over and over, but it sounds to me like you're just making excuses!" Alice cried. "There must be something!"

"You have no idea how many times we've come to a dead end here, Alice," Olivia said as calmly as she could. "It's as frustrating for us as it is for you. But that's part of the investigative process. It takes time. It takes patience. We want nothing more than to see your children make it home safely, I promise you that. I understand you're having a hard time processing this, but it's not our fault. We're doing our best."

"Your best is nowhere near good enough," Alice snapped. "There are young lives at stake here!"

"We are fully aware of how serious this is," Brock replied through gritted teeth. "Which is why we're doing everything we can. You might not think we're capable of this, but I can guarantee that we're doing more than a lot of agents ever would. Olivia here has been working day and night to get to the bottom of this. You don't see how much work she's been putting in every single day. You just think you know best, don't you, Alice?"

"I think we should go," Elijah started timidly, but Alice waved him off as though his thoughts didn't matter at all.

"I think you should, too," Brock said, standing up and walking over to Alice.

He was much taller than she was, but somehow, her presence in the room made her double in height.

"I'm not going anywhere until I get some answers. We all deserve them," Alice said, pointing at Andrea and Richard. "If you're so hard-working, then you won't mind showing us evidence of what you've been doing, will you? Because from what I hear, the two of you are too busy giggling away at the diner to be getting any work done."

Olivia felt her jaw clench. She was suddenly fully aware of how small the town was. Who had possibly been spying on them for Alice? The target that Olivia always felt on her back seemed to be getting larger by the second.

"I'm sorry, Alice, I didn't realize that dinner breaks weren't allowed in our line of work. What do you want us to do? Starve ourselves until we find your child? And what have you done to help find her, by the way?" Olivia spat. "Sat at home and waited for her to come back? Why haven't you been out searching, putting up posters, trying to help us out instead of making us feel bad for giving you our best effort?"

Alice opened her mouth to respond, but for once, she seemed to have nothing to say. She gaped like a goldfish out of water, knowing she'd shown herself up. She looked close to tears, and though she'd earned her telling off, Olivia wondered if Brock had taken things just a little too far.

Brock folded his arms over his chest. Olivia had seen him angry a few times and she expected to see irritation creasing his face, but to her surprise, there was something else in his expression. He looked as if he pitied her. He waited a moment before sighing and stepping a little closer to Alice.

"Alice, why don't you sit down with your husband, and we will tell you what we know as quickly as we can. We'll get you up to speed then we can get back to actually investigating the case. You're right, we should have kept you more in the loop. We got caught up in our work and we've been neglecting to check in with you all. That's on us. But I hope that once I show you what we've been doing you'll understand how difficult this whole thing has been for us. We're trying so hard to bring your girls home. I hope you'll see that once we're done here."

Olivia let Brock take the lead as he opened the case file and presented to the two families everything they'd found so far. There was a lump in Olivia's throat as she watched the four of them processing everything that Brock was telling them. From the lack of fingerprints and no signs of forced entry, to the absence of eyewitnesses, they were in the dark.

He explained every lead they'd explored, from the plastic bag in the woods, to the case in Alexandria, to the theories they'd followed up with Maggie. He showed them the notes he'd made and how each point they'd looked at had been a dead end. He even showed them the original case file of Amelia's disappearance from Seattle PD and how there had been nothing to go on in that case as well.

Slowly, Olivia saw the realization dawning on their faces. Even Alice's eyes began to darken as she discovered that she was in the wrong. The reality of the situation was hitting them hard, and Olivia was very glad she wasn't in their shoes at that moment. She thought that perhaps they hadn't sensed the hopelessness of it all until that moment. They had expected some easy explanation, some easy way out of it all. They'd expected to be able to pick holes in their investigation, to prove that it was Olivia's and Brock's fault their daughters were still missing. But as they saw the inner workings of their investigation, they began to understand that if the FBI couldn't figure it out, there was no chance they would, either.

"So, you see," Brock continued calmly. "We have looked into every possible route to the truth. We have tried our hardest. And I know you don't think our best is good enough, Alice, but if that's the case, it's because whoever is doing this is simply too many steps ahead of us. I'm sorry that we can't give you the comfort and relief you deserve. I'm sorry we don't have more definitive answers. And I'm sorry that we can't snap our fingers and bring your children home. But trust me when I say it's not from lack of trying. It's certainly not Olivia's fault, and it's certainly not because we're busy 'canoodling,' as you called it."

That caused Alice to cover her face with her hand but not before Olivia saw the abashed look on her face. Despite herself, Olivia found a hint of satisfaction in that.

"Whatever you think you've heard, I'm telling you it's not true. We've put everything we can into this case, and while we don't appreciate your criticism, we know it's only because you're concerned. And honestly, we're concerned, too. I'm sure you don't want to hear this, but there is a possibility we won't figure this out," Brock said.

"We're still following leads and still following up on a few theories. We're holding onto hope that the kidnapper will slip up, or new evidence will come to light—and who knows, maybe the girls will be released the way that Amelia was. But for now, we're doing the best we can with what we have."

As Brock finished speaking, the entire room fell silent. Then there was a sniff, and Olivia turned to see tears falling down Alice's cheeks. Olivia was quick to grab her box of tissues and offer them to her. Alice sniffled as she plucked one from the box, dabbing at her eyes.

"I'm sorry," she whispered, looking up at Olivia. "I'm sorry about coming here and being rude to you. I'm just—I'm terrified."

"I know," Olivia whispered.

She wished that she could give some words of advice. Wished she could say something that would provide them some bit of comfort. Then she realized that she could. She was the only other person in that room who could relate to what those parents were facing. She was the only other person who'd had a family member go missing before, after all. She leaned forward a little.

"It doesn't get easier to process. Believe me when I tell you that I know exactly what you're going through. And you'll always hold onto hope that you'll get answers if your daughters don't come back. It's impossible to face. People will tell you to have faith, to pray, all of that—but sometimes people just don't make it home," she said. "I know you don't want to hear that, and I hope you get your girls back more than anything, but if they don't come home, I promise you, it won't be because Brock and I have neglected our duties. We're in this together. We're rooting for you. And we're working as hard as we possibly can to bring your girls home."

Alice sniffed hard, nodding as she spoke. Olivia stood up, feeling a little more confident as she did so.

"Why don't I make a round of coffee?" Olivia offered.

The four unexpected guests stayed a while longer, and Olivia answered more questions for them. By the time the small group left, there had been a lot more tears and they'd all gone home without getting what they'd come for. But Olivia knew that she couldn't doubt herself anymore. She knew that only she and Brock could give those families peace. If it was possible, she'd make it happen. Time was ticking and they were all running on empty. But Olivia felt she had one last push in her to find the answers. To bring the girls home.

And Olivia vowed she would make sure she had the energy to carry on.

CHAPTER TWENTY-FOUR

ONCE AGAIN, OLIVIA COULDN'T SLEEP. IT HAD BEEN ALmost six hours since Sophia's and Hayleigh's families had left her house. They'd given her a lot to think about. She wasn't doubting herself so much anymore, but they had made her wonder whether the girls really were gone forever. Most missing persons cases were solved within forty-eight hours, and the ones that weren't often had bleak endings.

But this was different. One victim had escaped before. She wanted to believe it could happen again. But the question was, why? Why did he let Amelia go? Did the kidnapper have more of a conscience than they thought? Or did Amelia escape and get away before the kidnapper could get her back. Were they dealing with a cold-blooded psycho? Or just someone who desperately wanted something he'd never been able to have again?

Olivia tried to put herself in the kidnapper's shoes. If she was going by her own theories, then he'd lost the most precious thing in the world… his only child. She imagined the trauma of a young girl's life being snuffed out before her time. She imagined how it would feel to outlive your own child, to know that no matter what you did for the rest of your life, it would be without your child. She tried to imagine how it would feel knowing you'd miss out on all their life's milestones—graduation, marriage, children. She imagined that the man—or woman—behind the attacks was divorced, alone in the world. No family to speak of. She tried to tap into the sheer loneliness and isolation that would make them feel—and how close to the edge it might drive them to.

And suddenly, she realized that maybe she wasn't so different from the person who was terrorizing the town. She'd had everything she loved taken away from, too. Of course, she still had her father, which she considered a blessing, but she'd always felt as though he could be taken from her at any time, too. In some ways, he was already gone. Nothing felt permanent in Olivia's life. She was sure that everything good she built would soon be taken from her. Even the presence of Brock wasn't forever. As soon as the case was done, he'd be gone. She'd faced that idea once before, and she didn't like it.

So, was it possible that Olivia could've gone down a different path? Was it possible that she might've done the same sort of unspeakable things if she'd let her grief and misery take over? She considered the possibility that no one was born a villain, but that circumstances could always shape a person into someone bad. What had pushed the kidnapper over the edge? Was there something she was missing? Or was it just hard for Olivia to comprehend because she was a better person?

She closed her eyes and laid back on her pillow. She needed to sleep. She needed to be alert for the following day so she could pick up the investigation once again. She didn't have time to be questioning the origins of good and evil in the middle of the night.

Sleep was just beginning to drag her under when she heard the noise outside. She sat bolt upright, her eyes adjusting fast to the dark and her ears pricking up. She was already reaching for her gun on the bedside table, rising slowly to her feet so that she didn't make any noise. She wanted to be able to hear everything going on around her.

She heard the sound again, unmistakable this time. The sound of a twig snapping under somebody's foot outside. She felt her heart racing. All of her paranoia came rushing back. Was someone out there, waiting to kill her? Was the target on her back more than a figment of her imagination?

She listened so hard that she felt she could hear noises that weren't even possible for humans to hear. She felt sick with the sudden flood of nerves, and she wished she hadn't sent Brock back to the B&B for the night. She could use some back-up if there really was someone out there coming for her.

But all of a sudden, the night exploded with noise. She heard the scurrying of feet and two garbled screams from right outside her cabin. She hurtled down the stairs, her heart in her throat. Those screams weren't threatening to her.

They sounded young.

Young, as in teenage girls.

She threw her front door open and aimed her gun into the dark, looking for a target. She could hear the screams still echoing through the forest, but in the chaos of the moment, she was struggling to locate the source of them.

"Hello?" Olivia called into the dark. "Who's out there?"

That was when the two girls came crashing through the trees. Olivia gasped and narrowly avoided pulling the trigger. She raised the muzzle of her weapon and stared at the girls rushing her in horror. The pair of them were skinny, covered in mud, their hair scraggly, but there was no mistaking who they were.

"Sophia? Hayleigh?"

The two girls stumbled closer, clutching one another, sobbing uncontrollably. They practically fell the last few steps toward Olivia, who rushed to them and held them close. As the girls sobbed against her chest, she scanned the forest behind them, searching for the person they were running from. She held her breath for a moment, waiting, still gripping her weapon tightly. But nobody came out of the forest behind them.

"It's okay. It's okay, you're safe now," Olivia said. "You're going to be okay. I'm going to get you home, I promise. Were you followed?"

The girls shook their heads, panting hard, shaking like leaves. Olivia couldn't believe what was happening. She had the strangest feeling of déjà vû ever, and yet the situation was so unlikely that it didn't quite feel real. She bundled the girls inside, holding them gently as they sobbed. She had to get to the phone and call their parents as soon as she could, but she had to make sure they were okay first.

She took them into the living room and sat them down on the sofa, turning on the lights as she went. The pair were too hysterical to speak, still clinging to one another like a lifeline.

"Are either of you hurt?" Olivia asked them gently.

Hayleigh whimpered slightly as she held out her wrists. Olivia's heart stopped. The injuries were the same as those she'd seen on Amelia less than two weeks before. There were deep grooves in her wrists where she'd clearly been tied up. A quick check proved that Sophia had the same injuries. Both girls seemed to have lost some weight, their faces were gaunt, and their eyes were haunted as they stared at Olivia, apparently unable to believe that they'd made it out alive.

"You're going to be okay," Olivia whispered. "I'm going to call your parents. They've been so worried. They will be so glad to have you home. It's going to be okay. I swear to you."

Hayleigh and Sophia both seemed unable to speak, still holding on to one another as Olivia quickly left the room and called Alice first. Her daughter had been gone for the longest, and she knew she needed good news the most. Alice picked up after two rings.

"Hello? Yes?"

"Sophia is here," Olivia told her immediately. "Hayleigh, too. I found them outside the cabin. They're going to be okay. But they're here and they're alive."

Olivia heard Alice come undone on the other end of the phone, sobbing uncontrollably. It was a horrible sound to hear, but it filled Olivia's heart with happiness. Happiness that she could finally get the girl's home. Happiness that they were safe, and the kidnapper's reign of terror was soon going to end. She finally had eyewitnesses right from the scene who could speak. With any luck, the girls could lead her right to the kidnapper.

Minutes later, when Olivia had contacted Hayleigh's family, Maggie, and Brock, she began to fuss around the girls, making sure they were comfortable. She got out her first aid kit and gently cleaned the wounds on their wrists. She found them blankets and made them hot chocolates to warm them up after a night in the forest. She talked to them in soothing tones, explaining who she was and what had happened while they were gone. Both of them were still stunned and silent, shivering beside one another and still joined at the hip.

Olivia didn't want to think too hard about what they'd been through together and the ways that it had bonded them. But she knew they'd both been to hell and back. At least she could try to ensure that they would never suffer so horribly again, and that no one would go through the same thing at the hands of the kidnapper.

Come morning, she was going on the offensive.

❧

When everyone arrived at the cabin, all was chaos. Olivia stood back as Alice and Elijah arrived first. Alice swept Sophia up into her arms, sobbing uncontrollably while Sophia clung to her mother the way a drowning man clung to a life preserver. Elijah enveloped them both in his arms, crying silently with them.

Hayleigh looked a little lost without Sophia at her side, so Olivia sat beside her and took her hand, acting as a poor replacement just for a while. But when Hayleigh saw her parents come through the door, she sprang to her feet and ran to them, holding them tight, all of them talking at once between their sobs.

It was at that point that Maggie and Brock quietly made their entrance, observing the scene with tired smiles and tear-filled eyes. It wasn't over, but it would be soon enough, and that was enough to lift everyone's spirits. Brock crossed the room and pulled Olivia into a hug. She was shocked at first but quickly relaxed in his arms, her throat tight as she held back her unshed tears.

She didn't want to break down in front of everyone when there was so much going on, but as Brock rubbed her back, she let out a choked cry. She couldn't help it. Everything had happened so fast, but as she felt some of the tension leave her body, she knew she was experiencing one of the best nights of her life.

"I'm so glad you got the girls home," Maggie told Olivia with a proud smile, touching her arm gently. "I know how much you put into this case. You deserve one hell of a vacation after all this is over."

Olivia smiled. "Well, I might do that once I've put the kidnapper behind bars," she said. "I'm so happy the girls are home, but we can't afford to get complacent. The kidnapper is still out there and we still need to nail him."

"Don't worry. We've still got a heavy presence out on the streets. We can speak to the girls after they've had some rest. Then we'll end this once and for all," Brock told her. "And Maggie is right. You deserve a break after all of this."

Olivia closed her eyes as a smile crossed her face. She pictured herself on a beach in Fiji, reading books all day in the sunshine. But when she opened her eyes again, she knew she wouldn't be going anywhere anytime soon. Her place was in Belle Grove, trying to protect the people living there. She needed to stay on her toes and get to the bottom of the case once and for all.

"You can take the girls home," Olivia told both families. "But we need to speak to them both as soon as possible. If you bring them down to the station in the morning, maybe we can finally figure out what's happening and nail the creep responsible for this."

"We will. Thank you, Olivia. Thank you," Alice said.

She seemed like a completely new woman now, her eyes softened and a smile gracing her face. As she and the others left the cabin, the girls still shell-shocked, Olivia had a moment of peace and silence to process what had just happened. She couldn't believe that things were going to be okay. That was, as long as they managed to catch the kidnapper. With both Sophia and Hayleigh gone, either escaped or let go, Olivia had a feeling the kidnapper was going to be on the hunt for a new girl soon.

"This is it," Brock said, his eyes glinting. "We're going to finally nab this sicko for good. Once we're done, drinks are on me."

Maggie let out a loud laugh. "Oh, I'll hold you to that, mister."

Brock tipped her a wink. "My pleasure, Officer Stone."

She laughed again, clearly relieved that the girls were back home safe and sound. "Ain't no way I can sleep after all this excitement," she said. "I'm out to update the patrol on this situation. I'll see y'all later."

Maggie left, and then it was just Olivia and Brock left. Brock smiled at Olivia.

"Do you think you're going to be able to sleep?" he asked.

"Absolutely not."

"Then let me make you some coffee," he said, disappearing from the room.

Olivia sank onto the sofa, unable to believe that only a few minutes before, two kidnapping victims they had been moving heaven and earth to find had been sitting there. Soon, she'd be able to deliver justice for them. She closed her eyes for just a second, thinking that she'd stay awake, but before she knew it, the darkness claimed her and she was fast asleep.

⁓

Olivia woke to find that both she and Brock were curled up uncomfortably on the sofa. On the table, the coffee Brock had made her was stone cold. Olivia stretched. She usually felt groggy when she woke up, but her racing heart made her feel more awake than she had in a long time. It was going to be a big day.

She checked her watch and found that it was only seven-thirty, so she took a quick shower and prepped herself for the day. She triple-checked her pistol, knowing that she might well need to use it that day. She pulled on a loose-fitting top that would fit her bulletproof vest underneath it. Part of her felt fearful about what the day would hold, but she was more concerned about catching the kidnapper and wasn't going to let her fear control her. It didn't matter so much what happened to her. She just wanted justice.

Brock was ready to go by the time she got downstairs, and they silently headed out to Brock's car together. He drove them to the station, and they waited there in the quiet reception area for the families to arrive.

Hayleigh and her family arrived first. She looked a lot better than she had in the middle of the night. There was some color in her cheeks and her hair was damp from being freshly washed. She was unsteady on her feet, like a baby deer learning to walk, but she rushed over to Olivia and pulled her into a hug.

"Thank you," she whispered.

It was the first time Olivia had heard her voice, and it was huskier than she'd expected. In the light of the day and without so much fear in her eyes, she looked older than she had before. Olivia wondered how much of that was because her experience had stripped her of some of her innocence and forced her to grow up faster than she would have on her own.

"I'm so glad you made it back safely," Olivia told her gently. "We're going to ask you some questions today so we can find the person who did this to you. Is that okay? Do you feel okay talking about it?"

Hayleigh glanced back at her parents for a split second before nodding. "I want to help," she said firmly. "I don't want this to happen to anyone else."

Sophia arrived a minute later. Elijah was escorting her, looking his usual nervous self. He glanced at Olivia, unable to meet her eye fully.

"Alice isn't coming," he explained quietly. "She hasn't slept in days. I thought it was best that she stayed at home and rested."

"That's okay. We really only need the girls," Brock told him kindly. "How about you two come with us and we can get started? The sooner we talk this over, the sooner we can get out there and find who did this to you."

Both Hayleigh and Sophia nodded. They silently grabbed one another's hands, an almost subconscious gesture, and Olivia was strangely touched by the sight of it. They'd bonded for life over something they'd never forget. They might not share good memories, but they understood one another in a way no one would ever understand them in return. In some strange way, Olivia envied them. She'd never known someone who'd been through the same things as her family. She never had that kind of a bond with anybody and she wondered how things might be if she had someone to talk to about those things. Somebody who shared her experiences and knew her traumas.

But she knew she couldn't be thinking about herself right then. She had a job to do. She felt they were teetering on the very edge of something big, and it could still go either way. She had to make sure the day went well. She had to make sure the day ended with her capturing the kidnapper. Brock sat the two girls down in the interrogation room and offered them both some juice, which they took. Olivia sat down opposite them and took out her notebook.

"How are you both holding up?" she asked gently.

Hayleigh and Sophia exchanged a look as if they were speaking telepathically. Then they both looked at Olivia.

"We're glad to be home," Hayleigh said.

Sophia nodded to affirm she felt the same way, and Olivia smiled at them both sympathetically.

"Well, we're glad to have you both back," she said. "Now we need to find the person who did this to you. Is there anything you can tell us that might be useful? Would you be able to describe the kidnapper?"

Sophia shook her head. "She wore a mask the whole time, one of those ski mask things."

"She?" Brock asked, raising his eyebrow and Sophia nodded.

"She didn't speak much, but when she did, it was clear she was a woman."

"Can you describe her body type?" Olivia asked eagerly.

Finally, they were getting somewhere. She hadn't expected that the kidnapper would be a woman but she was somehow unsurprised by it.

"She was thin," Hayleigh said, twirling a strand of her hair around her finger. "We never saw her eat, and she didn't feed us much. I think she forgot to."

"I'm sorry about that, girls," Brock said gently. "I think it would really help if we could hear both of your stories from the start. Can you tell us anything about how it happened? Starting with Sophia because you disappeared first."

The girl nodded with a little uncertainty. She was nothing like the strong-willed girl that Alice had described. At least, not anymore. Something had changed in her since she'd been taken away. Something had been broken. Sophia cleared her throat quietly and couldn't meet Olivia's eyes.

"Well, I was heading out to meet my boyfriend. We usually go to the woods together at night to get away from the house. I always felt suffocated. So, I headed out on my own. Craig was going to meet me in our usual spot, to avoid my mom seeing him," she said. "I've walked that way a million times before, even before me and Craig started hanging out. Kids in this town always go out at night. If they want to have a life, that is. But as I was walking, I got this strange feeling. I felt like I was being followed."

Olivia felt a chill slither down her spine. "And did you manage to get a look at the person who was following you?"

"That's the thing. I looked around, but I couldn't see anyone, or hear anyone. The road is pretty open and I thought I'd be able to see if someone was behind me. But it's dark out that way and there aren't any lights. And that's probably how she managed to sneak up on me," she said. "I didn't see her when she came at me. Just felt a hand clamp over my mouth and then she dragged me away. I was fighting against her. I was sure that I'd be able to fight her off. She didn't feel strong. But she was determined. She kept shushing me. Almost like how a mother shushes a baby."

Olivia and Brock exchanged a look. Maybe Olivia's theory about the kidnapper being a parent didn't seem so far-fetched anymore. Olivia turned back to Sophia.

"Are you okay to keep going?" she asked softly.

She took a deep breath and nodded.

"Well, she managed to get me into the back of her car. She had child-lock on, and I wasted a few seconds trying to get out of the back door. Then I tried to attack her when she got into the driver's seat, but she pointed a gun at me, and I was so scared that I just… I just curled up on the back seat like a little kid. She told me to close my eyes, so I did. I thought she'd kill me if I didn't. But now I don't think she was ever really going to kill me."

"What makes you say that?" Brock asked curiously.

Sophia wrapped her arms around herself, slumping in her seat as a look of upset crossed her face. Hayleigh squeezed Sophia's hand and gave her an encouraging nod. That seemed to give Sophia the courage to continue.

"Because she kept referring to herself as 'Mom.'" Sophia said.

Olivia felt a flutter of nerves and excitement in her stomach. This was the sign they'd been looking for. Proof that they were on the right track. Proof that they were looking for someone specific. She began to scribble notes in her notebook.

"Where did she take you?"

"Deep into the woods," Sophia whispered. "She seemed to know where she was going. As soon as we got out of the car, she gagged me so I couldn't scream and grabbed my arm and dragged me through the wilderness. It was so dark I couldn't see anything, but she seemed to be familiar with the path she was walking, even though the trees were scratching me the whole way. I begged her to let me go. I just wanted to go home, but she just kept shushing me. I kept thinking about the gun. I didn't want to die."

"Could you describe the weapon?"

"I don't know, some kind of pistol?" Sophia responded. "I don't know much about that kind of thing."

"Okay. So, she took you somewhere. Did you get a look at the place?"

"It was some kind of run-down cabin. She had a key for the door. There was no electricity inside, and it was really cold. She tied me up with rope. It hurt, but she said she didn't want her baby to run away," Sophia said. "She left me there for days and days. I didn't see her for a long while and I couldn't understand why I was there. When she came back, she fed me a little, but I was starving. Those days I was on my own, I didn't see anyone else, drink anything, or eat anything. It was awful. I thought... I thought I was going to die out there."

Olivia winced. It was a hard conversation to hear. But Sophia was giving them useful information. Now that they knew the kidnapper had held the girls in a cabin in the woods, they could narrow down the search.

"Just to backtrack a little, how long do you think you were in the car?" Olivia asked. "Just so that we can have an idea of how far into the woods she took you."

"I'm not sure. It felt like forever. But I think maybe it was only about twenty minutes."

"Did she drive fast? Like she was in a hurry?"

"No, she was pretty calm. Weirdly calm, actually," she said. "It was like she'd done it before."

Olivia nodded. They'd have to try to use that information to pinpoint a location.

"Okay, Hayleigh," Brock said, moving the investigation forward. "You were taken in the middle of the night too. But from what we know, your situation was a little different. You were at a sleepover?"

"Yes," Hayleigh said quietly. "It sounds terrible, but I remember thinking that night that I was glad I had all my friends around me. I felt safer after Sophia went missing. I thought that being surrounded by people would make me safer. But—but I was wrong."

She sniffed and Sophia reached for her hand to give it a squeeze. Hayleigh took a deep breath, her face creased in fear as she recalled the night.

"I went to the kitchen to get a glass of water. I didn't see the person sitting at the kitchen table until I heard the scrape of a chair on the floor. By then, it was too late. I felt someone grab me, and she stuffed something in my mouth to stop me from screaming. Then she dragged me out of the back door. But there was something strange about it."

"What was it?"

"Well, she got out a key and locked the door. And that's when I realized that whoever it was had let herself in with a key."

Olivia felt her chest tighten. She hadn't been expecting that. So *that* was how the kidnapper was getting in and out of houses unnoticed. Did she have a key to Amelia's house too, all the way up in Seattle? She shook her head in disbelief. That seemed far too strange. How would the kidnapper have keys to two houses thousands of miles apart? But it did explain how she had passed in and out of the houses without forcible entry.

"Are you sure? Your memory can play tricks on you when things get a bit crazy," Olivia asked Hayleigh carefully.

She nodded. "I'm sure. I know it sounds weird, but that's why I remember it so well. It was like time slowed for a minute as I watched her do it. I thought, how is that possible?" she went on. "But after that, I don't remember a lot. She was holding me too tight. I remember feeling like I couldn't breathe. She dragged me away to a car parked outside my neighbor's house. And then it was like Sophia said. She took me away in the car. She made me walk through the woods. But when I got there, the first thing I saw was Sophia. And I remember being glad I wasn't alone."

Olivia felt a pang of sadness for the pair of them. They were only teenagers. Still children. They didn't deserve the horrors they'd had to endure.

"Can you tell us anything else about your time there?" Brock asked the girls.

They exchanged another silent glance with one another. It was like they were communicating with each other without words.

"We tried our hardest to get away," Sophia said. "We tried to help each other out of our rope ties, but it was no use. We tried screaming, but that didn't do any good either. We used all our energy on trying, and then we were just so hungry and so exhausted we just laid there on the cold floor, waiting for... *Mom*," she said it with a bitter shudder. "She'd come every few days and she'd feed us, and then sometimes, she'd just stare at us. She'd sing to us sometimes and try to remind us of what she thought was our favorite song. Sometimes she'd try to make us dance with her and when we didn't, she'd cluck her tongue like she was disappointed in us."

"Or she'd tell us we were wrong," Hayleigh added.

Brock frowned. "Wrong about what?"

"Not wrong about something. More like there was something wrong with us. Like she was looking at us and finding all our flaws."

Olivia made a note of that. If her theory was correct, maybe the kidnapper was discovering that no matter who she tried to replace her child with, no one was good enough. No one was similar enough. It would make the narrative she was building make sense.

"Okay, now one thing we really need to know. How did you get away?" Brock asked.

Sophia sucked in a deep breath, glancing at Hayleigh. "She let us go."

Brock tapped his pen against the table. Olivia knew it wasn't a complete shock to either of them. They'd thought from the start that Amelia had been let go, but that was different. She wasn't able to tell anyone about what had happened to her. Sophia and Hayleigh were able to tell them more than they'd even been able to figure out before. So *why*, was the question. Why had she let them go and put herself at risk of being exposed? Olivia couldn't understand it.

"Do you know why she let you go?" Olivia asked.

Sophia shook her head. "She changed. She was becoming more and more impatient with us. She shouted at us and told us we were wrong, over and over again. And then she lunged at us and we thought that was it. We thought she was going to hurt us. But she never tried to hit us or anything like that," she said. "And then, she started untying us. I kept thinking something terrible was going to happen. I thought she was going to kill us. But she just turned away from us and told us to go. Told us we weren't right and to get out. She seemed upset."

"She was crying," Hayleigh whispered. "I almost—well, I felt a little sorry for her for a second. But that's crazy, right? I just grabbed Sophia's hand and we ran out together. It was still light when we left, but we were really weak and we got pretty lost, especially after sunset. But we just kept moving, wanting to get away from the cabin, and then eventually, we found you."

"And I'm so glad that you did," Olivia told them gently. "Everything you've told us has been really helpful, girls. Is there anything else you think might be helpful to us? It might seem small, but any details we can get might really help us find the person."

Hayleigh took a deep breath. "There was something weird. She

253

never asked what our names were, but she kept calling us both the same name. Sometimes she'd call us her little lollipops. But most of the time, she referred to us both as Lauren."

Olivia's heart skipped a beat. That was important. They were looking for someone who'd lost a child named Lauren. That was the key to the theory they'd constructed. That was the key to finding the woman who'd taken the girls. Olivia noted down the name and underlined it, knowing they needed to find a woman who'd lost a daughter named Lauren.

"That's amazing. Thank you, girls," Brock said. "You are both really brave. Really brave."

"Are you going to go find her?" Hayleigh asked, chewing on her nail.

Olivia nodded. "Yes. Absolutely. We're going to make sure she'll never be able to do this to anyone again."

"You should be careful," Sophia said darkly. "Toward the end, she was getting more and more paranoid. I think she knew she was being chased by the police. She kept saying she was being watched."

Olivia nodded. "Okay. We'll keep that in mind."

"I don't think you should go out there," Hayleigh said, her eyes wide. "She's got a gun. She might hurt you."

"Don't you worry about all that," Brock said firmly. "We'll take it from here, girls. We're just thankful to you for how brave you both are. You did great."

Hayleigh didn't look so sure, but she nodded, anyway. Brock took a deep breath and smiled at the girls.

"I think we've got everything we need for today but we might need to interview you again," he told them and slid them a fifty across the table. "Go and get yourselves some milkshakes at the diner. Our treat. Take your parents. I think you could all use it."

For a split second, the girls giggled with glee, returning to their normal selves for just a moment as they forgot all about the horrible things they'd endured and were just teenage girls again. It tugged at

Olivia's heartstrings. She was so happy to see them home that it still felt hard to believe it was actually happening. That they'd be found alive and would be sleeping in their own beds tonight. As she stood and collected her notes, the girls joined hands once again and rushed out to join their parents.

Brock held back with Olivia, his face grave. He turned to her and all traces of the smile that had graced his lips a moment ago were gone.

"We're going in?" he asked.

Olivia nodded, the fire of determination burning through her veins. "We're going in."

CHAPTER
TWENTY-FIVE

T HE REST OF THE MORNING PASSED IN A BLUR FOR OLIVIA.
After she'd called SAC James to update him on the situation,
she and Brock prepared themselves to go after the kidnapper.
If she'd had any sense, the woman who'd taken the girls would've fled
the forest long ago, but Olivia knew well enough that paranoid people
don't often act rationally. She hoped that they'd find the mysterious
kidnapper waiting for them in the cabin. But first, they had to find it.

Based on the information the girls had given her, Olivia narrowed down the area for the search a little and then she used an
online map to quickly scan the possible sections of the forest that
matched the descriptions of clearings in the direction they had come
from. It took her an hour of clicking and scanning the area, not to
mention consultation with Maggie, as she tried to make sense of the
landscape before her.

Eventually, she found something of interest on the satellite maps.
Deep in the heart of the woods, tucked nearly two dozen miles away
from civilization, was a cabin in a small clearing. It was so small and

obscure she wouldn't have even noticed it had she not known it was there. It barely showed up as a tiny brown smudge on the map. The area was overgrown, just as the girls had said. It wasn't the clearest picture ever but she could see the cabin itself had clearly seen better days.

"Well, I can certainly believe that's the place they were held," Brock murmured. "It doesn't exactly look like a luxury cabin, does it? I'll bet it doesn't get electricity all the way out there. It's about as far off the grid as you can get."

"Agreed. I think that's the place," Olivia said. "We should send the image to the girls and get them to confirm."

"Good thinking," he replied.

The girls had given their numbers to her before they'd left the station so Olivia texted them with the picture. Hayleigh immediately texted back to confirm it was the right place. Olivia's chest was tight with anticipation. They were so close to the end that her heart was racing and her body hummed with an electric excitement. She was ready for it all to be over. She was ready to bring this woman in and send her to prison for the rest of her life.

Of course, the hardest part was yet to come. Trying to catch someone as elusive as their kidnapper wasn't going to be easy. She suspected the kidnapper would already be one step ahead. But she was prepared. She'd already donned her bulletproof vest. She was ready to go as soon as she needed to. And she wouldn't leave those woods until she had something to show for her time there.

"So, we've got our cabin," Brock said. "Are we calling for back-up?"

"No. It'll take way too long to get a SWAT team down here from Quantico," Olivia replied right away. "It's one woman we're dealing with. We don't want to give her the time to get away. Nor do we want to give her any reason to panic and start shooting. No, a one-on-one would be better, I think. I can go in on my own, with you as my back-up."

"Are you sure that's a good idea? She seems really dangerous," he countered. "Remember, this woman is capable of crossing the country and moving in and out of houses without leaving a single trace of evidence. She's not some off the rails psycho."

"I know what I'm doing," she said.

"I know you do, Olivia," he replied. "I trust your judgment one hundred percent. I just don't want you to get hurt."

Olivia looked up at Brock. His eyes were filled with what seemed to be genuine concern. She smiled at him and felt a flutter in her heart.

"It'll be okay. I'll be in and out of there without incident, I hope. From what I can tell, she's very emotional. She lost something close to her and she's been searching for a reprieve from her pain. I don't think it comes from a place of destructive malice or of sheer criminality. It's a way of her trying to capture a happiness she lost. Push comes to shove; she won't die or try to kill me for this."

"Underestimating her could get you hurt."

Olivia nodded. "I know. I'll be careful. I promise."

"You'd better be. I don't want to lose the best partner I've ever had."

Olivia felt her cheeks warming. She knew they didn't have time for such tender moments, but she wondered if maybe once it was over, they could spend a little more time together. Hadn't he promised drinks all around once they'd caught the kidnapper? She could definitely get behind that idea.

"All right," he said. "Are you ready?"

Olivia was about to respond when her phone began to ring in her pocket. She pulled it out and answered right away.

"Olivia, we have a problem," Jonathan started as soon as she picked up.

Her heart leaped into her throat. What could possibly be wrong now?"

"What's happened?" she asked.

"We've had a report of a missing woman in Baltimore. She seems to have gone missing in the middle of the night, as many of our victims have."

"Okay…"

"She's blonde, twenty-one years old, from a broken home—I know it doesn't fit your profile and I might be wrong, but it might be related to your case," he said. "Her mother is out of the picture. I'm concerned that she's the kidnapper."

Olivia leaned back in her chair, taking a second to process the information. "Okay. What's the name of the missing woman?"

"Her name is Lauren Best."

"Lauren? The girls said that the kidnapper referred to them as Lauren," Olivia breathed. "Okay, this changes things. If the kidnapper has just taken her own daughter, then obviously, her daughter wasn't dead after all. She just had her daughter taken out of her reach."

"According to Lauren's father, his ex-wife Sandra has been unstable for some time. She had a troubled childhood, which led to alcoholic tendencies," he said. "The pair of them had a difficult marriage and divorced not long after they bought a home together. She lost custody of the child because the court deemed her an unfit parent."

Olivia sighed. She'd been right about a lot of parts of the case, but she'd gotten a lot of it wrong, too. If the kidnapper finally had her daughter back in her grasp, then she must have finally come undone. She'd gotten what she wanted, but what would the cost be?

"But here's the most pertinent issue," Jonathan continued. "That home they bought before the divorce? It's the same house in Seattle that Amelia Barnes lives in now."

That sent a lance of shock straight into Olivia's heart. Suddenly the connections made sense. All this time, she had been putting together a puzzle without seeing the picture on the box, and now it appeared right before her. She took a deep breath and nodded.

"Okay, Jonathan, thank you. We're going to go back to the cabin where the kidnapper—Sandra, possibly—held the girls. If she's gone into a manic state, she might still return there. We have to hope she will, because it's the first real lead we've had this whole time."

"Good luck, Olivia."

"Thank you, sir."

He disconnected the call and Brock waited for Olivia to explain what had been said.

"Well?" he asked.

"I think we're looking for a woman named Sandra Best," she said quietly. "Lauren Best just went missing from Baltimore. She's older than the other girls, but she fits our theory. We were wrong. Her daughter didn't die. She was denied contact with her in the divorce proceedings. And get this—before the divorce, she lived with her daughter in the same house in Seattle that the Barnes family now lives in."

"Oh, my God," Brock gasped. "That's it! That's the connection!"

Olivia nodded. "She has been trying desperately to get her back, but it hasn't been enough. Now, she's taken her real daughter—and hopefully, she's still going to be hiding out in the forest."

"Well, we can hope, at least. Let's go," he said. "We don't want to give her any opportunity to run again."

Olivia and Brock rushed out to his car. Olivia checked her gun and pressed her hand to her bulletproof vest anxiously. This was it. They had to get it right. There wouldn't be any second chances.

"This changes everything," Brock said as he began to drive. "If she's got another hostage, then we need to be even more careful than before. There's more at stake now. And I don't think she's going to just let her daughter—her real daughter—go like she did with the others."

"I'm trained in hostage negotiation," Olivia said firmly. "I think it's still best if I go alone."

Olivia could see the concern in Brock's eyes. She could tell he wanted to dissuade her from her plan. But she also knew he trusted her. He took a deep breath, his lips pressed firmly together and nodded.

"You're only going to get one shot at this. Make it count."

"I plan on it."

~

Brock parked up at the very edge of the forest and Olivia got out of the car as quickly as she could. They'd only been driving for twenty minutes, but it was enough time to make her feel nervous about what she had to do. There was a lot of pressure, but Olivia knew she could do it. She knew that she could avenge the girls for all they'd suffered.

"Are we in the right place?" she asked Brock.

He nodded. "I used the coordinates we came up with from the map. If we head straight through the forest from here for a few miles, we should reach the cabin. The only issue is that it's pretty wild out there. Hard to get to on foot."

Olivia stared out into the thick trees. He was right. The ground was a tangle of brambles and overgrown vegetation. She knew it would be a difficult walk, and it would be easy for them to get off track. Worse still, the sun was beginning to set, so they'd have to do it in the dark. She had a flashlight to guide her, but she wasn't sure how much use it would be in the complete darkness of the woods. But she thought of Lauren, out there with her crazed, drunk of a mother, probably scared out of her mind, and Olivia knew she would face whatever the forest had in store for her just to save the young woman.

"Let's get this over with," Olivia said, trying to move as quickly as possible as she picked her way through the forest.

As they stumbled through the obstacle course of wilderness, Olivia felt thorns snagging her legs and tree roots threatening to trip her up. She usually appreciated nature in all of its glory, but right at that moment, she wished she could bulldoze the forest just to get to her goal.

She'd been thrown many challenges in this case, more than any other case she'd worked, but this somehow felt like the hardest. She was so close to the end of it all that she didn't want this final hurdle to be what felled her. She couldn't fail. She couldn't allow another case to go unsolved. She held her sister and her mom close to her heart as she soldiered on, Brock close on her heels.

The sky darkened to the point where it was impossible to see without the flashlight. Olivia used it to scan the path ahead of her, but it was getting harder and harder to proceed. The trees around her were tall and the leaves knitted together to form a huge green blanket above their heads. She couldn't even see the moon through the thick canopy of leaves. Feeling her heart pounding hard in her chest, she told herself to just keep moving. She ignored the sharp jabs of tree branches that seemed to be warning her to stay back, to keep her nose out of business that wasn't hers. But Olivia wouldn't stop until Lauren was safe and Sandra was locked away and couldn't hurt anyone else.

Olivia had lost all track of time. It was too dark to see her watch, but she suspected they'd been walking for about two hours, and still, there was no sign of the cabin. At least the darkness of the forest would give her some bit of cover when she finally made it to Sandra's hideaway. Every minute that passed out there made her feel more and more anxious. So much could go wrong. She could end up with a bullet through her head and she'd never see it coming. She was walking into the situation not really knowing who she was dealing with.

But Olivia thought maybe she could deal with it if she was the one who got hurt. She'd put so much into the case that she was willing to die to get those girls the justice they deserved. She wanted to prove that she was good through and through. She wanted to prove that she had it in her to be brave and to do whatever it took to save someone else. She hadn't saved Veronica. She hadn't saved her mother. But she'd save Lauren if it was the last thing she did.

"You okay?" Brock whispered into the darkness.

It was almost as though he'd been able to hear the chaotic thoughts circling around her head. That seemed to be a trick he was getting better at.

"I'm okay," Olivia replied a little breathlessly, batting a tree branch out of her way. "I just want to get there."

"It's not much further. We're coming up on three miles from the road. Unless we somehow took a wrong turn…"

Olivia couldn't even consider the possibility that they'd somehow gotten it wrong and that they were further away from Lauren than when they'd started… She flicked her flashlight over the path ahead of her, but she saw nothing except more trees. She checked her phone to see if she could consult a map, but she had no signal. They really were alone out there.

"Do you think we should back up and reorient ourselves?" she asked.

"No. We'll only get lost if we try to change direction," Brock insisted. "We can press on. We'll get there. I know it."

There was a feeling inside her the further into the forest they delved. Olivia felt she could sense the truth reaching out to grab her, trying to reel her in and help her get to the bottom of it all. She continued even as her feet began to hurt, and her skin stung from the keen whip of the tree branches that lashed her. She pushed forward even as fear gripped her. The end had to be close. It had to be.

Another half-hour passed before Olivia heard the cry in the woods. It was a loud, desperate cry that could only belong to a human. Olivia stopped in her tracks, not wanting to make a single noise. She knew that if she did, she might lose the element of surprise. She didn't want to make herself known until it was absolutely necessary. Until they had the advantage. She turned and shined the flashlight on Brock, covering the beam with two fingers to shield it.

"We're close," Olivia whispered. "I have to go from here alone. If I run into trouble…"

She didn't even want to finish that sentence. She wished that she could ask for Brock to go with her, but she knew that would be the wrong choice. She had to appeal to Sandra, woman to woman.

She had to be alone. Having Brock there would only complicate the situation and could force it off the rails.

"Please be careful," Brock whispered to her. "I've got your back. I'll come running at the first sign of trouble, okay?"

Olivia nodded, even though she wasn't sure he could see her. She switched off her flashlight and allowed her eyes to adjust to the darkness. The last thing she wanted was for anyone to see her coming. It took a minute but as she pressed forward, she realized the trees cleared a little, as though someone had been maintaining the area. She noticed fewer brambles catching on her and fewer leaves crunching beneath her feet. It made it much easier for her to approach noiselessly, and she even caught a glimpse of the moon above her.

And in the moonlight, she saw the cabin ahead. It was really more of a shack made of old, dark wood, and it looked thrown together by someone who knew nothing about building. It didn't seem to have any windows, and the woodwork was shoddy. Through the gaps in the walls, she could see that there was some sort of light coming from within. Olivia swallowed. She knew she'd been right to abandon her flashlight.

She crept around the side of the cabin, doing her best to slow her racing heart. She walked carefully, sure that even the slightest misstep would give her away. After all, she knew what it was like to be a paranoid woman in the woods. She'd spent many nights lying awake, tuned into the noises of the forest. And now that she knew the horrors that the same forest held in its depths, she was sure that she was right to be scared.

She heard sobbing from inside the cabin. That was followed by someone talking. The voice was gentle and soothing, but garbled and quick. It was an odd juxtaposition, but Olivia was sure she understood. Sandra was a mother trying to make her terrified child feel better, but knew she was the cause of the fear inside her daughter. She was acting manically, losing her grip on what she was actually trying to achieve. She'd gotten ahold of her daughter, but where could she go from there?

Olivia had to stop her before she figured that out.

Olivia crept toward the jagged remains of the wooden door. There was no doorknob, but as she placed her palm on it, she felt it give easily. She pushed it open and it creaked a little, but she could still hear soft talking from the woman, along with the terrified sobs of her daughter. She hadn't been noticed.

Olivia braved putting the flashlight back into use, holding her gun in one hand, the flashlight in the other. The dim beam cut through the darkness in front of her and she saw several flies gathering in the air around them, their low buzz like a backing track to the voices of the women in the other room. It was then that she noticed the terrible smell of the cabin. It was as if every unpleasant smell she could think of had gathered in the small, cramped space. She could smell the damp wood and the faint smell of urine—and worse, the scent of someone who hadn't showered in some time. It was the smell of neglect and decay.

Olivia's flashlight flickered around her, searching for a route to the kidnapper and her prisoner who were in another room. Instead, her eyes fell upon something more sinister. On the wall across the room from them was a series of photographs. She saw that all the girls in the photographs looked similar, though they weren't all the same. She saw a photograph of a young girl laughing at the camera, her blonde hair blowing in the wind as she posed on a beach. She couldn't be more than fifteen. She wore a blue floral dress. When Olivia moved the flashlight, she saw a picture that disturbed her even more. It was a picture of Amelia, her face streaked with tears as she sat on the floor. Her wrists were bound with rope and her hair was a mess, but it was impossible not to note the similarities between her and the other girl. And then Olivia understood why.

She was wearing the same blue floral dress.

She shuddered. She couldn't imagine what Amelia had been

feeling at that moment, scared out of her wits and unable to communicate or understand what was happening. She imagined someone struggling to force her into the dress just to take the picture. And when she scanned the walls once again, she saw that there were too many pictures to count. She knew that she shouldn't be stopping to look at them, but it was impossible not to stare at the horrors in front of her. Some of the girls she could identify as the three victims she knew of, but many, she didn't recognize. How long had Sandra been doing this to young girls all over the country? And how many of them hadn't made it home?

Olivia had to end it. Right then. She held her gun with a steady hand and found the door with her flashlight. The cabin had become strangely silent and the floorboards creaking beneath her sounded louder than thunder. As she walked through the cabin, it was impossible for her to stay quiet, so she picked up her pace and stopped even trying to pretend to be stealthy.

As she swung the door open, she saw the room before her had been cast in the strange fluorescent light of the battery-powered lantern in the corner of the room. Olivia's mouth fell open in horror as she saw a young woman tied to the chair in front of her. Her mouth was gagged and rope bound her wrists and legs. She tried to scream, but the sound was muffled by her gag.

"Lauren?"

Her eyes widened and she managed to nod. Olivia couldn't see anyone else in the room, so she scanned her flashlight, looking for the person who'd tied Lauren up. Lauren writhed and strained against her bonds, desperately trying to break free. Seeing how hard she was trying free her wrists, Olivia suddenly understood how the girls' wrists had all ended up raw and bloody.

"FBI, Susan. Come out with your hands up," Olivia announced, her voice steady, her body taut and prepared for anything. "You don't need to hurt anyone else, please. I won't hurt you. I just want to talk. Please come out."

There was one corner of the room that wasn't cast into the light, still coated in shadow. And that narrow patch of darkness where the woman had taken shelter. She shuffled into the light, her head bowed, a gun in her hand, her entire body shaking. Olivia's eyes slowly widened in realization.

She knew this woman.

"Susan?"

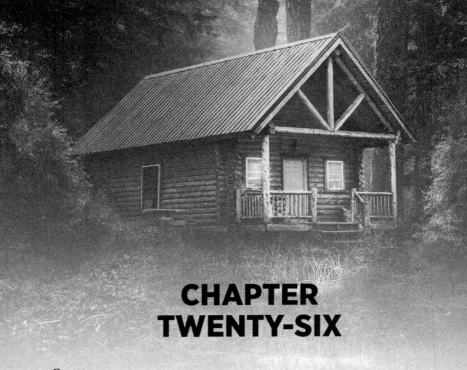

CHAPTER TWENTY-SIX

Susan…

OLIVIA COULDN'T BELIEVE IT. SHE HADN'T REALIZED THAT the person she was looking for was right under her nose the entire time. She never would've suspected Susan, but as she stared at her, unhinged and wild-eyed, it seemed to make more sense than any other explanation. Susan Combes was Sandra Best and vice versa. Lauren was the child Susan lost. Not to death. But to her own drinking.

"I never wanted you to see me this way, Agent Knight," Susan said, gesturing with her gun her head hung low.

She reached out and brushed her hand over Lauren's shoulder, not seeming to notice how the woman flinched away from her touch.

"I knew you wouldn't be able to understand," Susan finished. "Nobody can understand the pain of losing a child."

"You didn't lose me," Lauren hissed. "I was taken from you because you couldn't stop drinking. I was glad they took me from you."

Susan's face darkened and she looked like she was teetering on the edge of violence. Olivia was scared Susan was going to do something terrible if Lauren kept egging her on. She needed to talk her down. Needed to defuse the situation. Olivia tapped into her hostage negotiation training—something she hadn't used in a very long time. She swallowed hard.

"You can help me understand, Susan," Olivia said gently. "Let's put that gun down and talk about this. What are you doing here, Susan?"

Susan sighed, not looking Olivia in the eye. She looked at Lauren then stroked her cheek with her fingers. The woman's daughter recoiled like she'd burned her with acid. Susan frowned and her grip tightened on the gun. But then her expression softened, and she turned her face to Olivia. Susan stood behind Lauren. Olivia didn't have an angle to get a clean shot. She needed to get Susan away from her daughter or move to get a better angle. She didn't want to, but Olivia wouldn't hesitate to put Susan down if it meant saving Lauren's life.

"I used to go by that name. A long time ago. It was another life. I've had a lot of names over the years. I was born as Emily Crompton, but my mother abandoned me at an orphanage, so I abandoned that name, too. When I was old enough, I changed my name to Sandra Strickland," she said. "I liked that name. It gave me a chance to start again. And then when I got married, I became Sandra Best. The name you know me by, that's my most recent. I had to change it so that nobody would ever figure out who I was. How my past unfolded. I just wanted a fresh start."

Olivia nodded slowly, keeping a steady eye on Lauren. She could see the young woman was terrified, but Olivia didn't think Susan would hurt her. Lauren was the one thing she'd been fighting for, for so long. She wasn't about to let her slip away.

"What happened to you, Susan?" Olivia asked gently. "Taking children from their homes in the middle of the night—you know that's wrong. You're a smart woman. You know that hurting other people won't gain you anything."

Susan's eyes snapped up to meet Olivia's. "I'm not doing this to hurt anyone. I never wanted to hurt a single soul. I'm not a bad person, Olivia. I'm just lonely. So lonely…"

"But all those families you've taken children from. You hurt them," Olivia whispered. "You didn't just take Hayleigh, Sophia, and Amelia, did you? There were others."

A wry grin twisted Sandra's lips and she looked away for a moment, as if remembering the faces from the past. She finally turned back to Olivia who was edging to the side, looking for a clean line of sight. Susan raised the gun, pointing it at Lauren's head.

"Don't do that, Agent Knight."

Olivia stopped moving. "All right, all right," she said. "You're in control here, Susan. Just talk to me. What is this all about?"

Susan eyed her for a moment and let out a heavy sigh. She seemed exhausted. Like she was quickly running out of energy. Olivia was terrified of what would happen when her weariness got to be too much for her to bear.

"I didn't know what I was doing at the start. I just wanted company. I wanted the chance to be a mother again," Susan whispered. "I lost my baby girl. Her father took her away from me. He said I wasn't fit to be a parent. But I love Lauren more than anything in the entire world. That's why I had to bring her here today. Because all those little girls… none of them were good enough to replace my baby girl. I know that now. Can't you see how perfect she is, Olivia? Can't you see how a mother's love can drive her to do crazy things?"

Olivia didn't know what to say. "I don't have a daughter. I don't know what it's like."

"Then what about your own mother, Olivia?" Susan quickly tacked in another direction. "Did she love you in the way my mother never did? Did she do everything she could to protect you?"

The question transported Olivia back through the years. She had a sudden, sharp recollection of her mother snatching her out of the road, saving her from being hit by a car when she'd stepped before she should have. She thought of how her mother held her that day and cried as though her life had actually been taken from her. She thought of all the times her mom had done things for her.

And then she remembered that she'd disappeared. She'd left her when Olivia had needed her most. When she'd still been coming to terms with her sister's death, her mom was suddenly just gone without a trace. Had she simply abandoned her? At that moment, her heart ached as if her mother had indeed left her, the wound as fresh today as it was the day it happened. She looked up at Susan and she understood. She knew that being abandoned meant you'd never want to let the good things go away, ever again. No matter how destructive it became to keep them.

"But your daughter—she was safe," Olivia told Susan gently. "She was living with her father in Baltimore, wasn't she?"

"A girl's place is with her mother," Susan snarled, her hand clasping Lauren's shoulder once again. "I lost everything when she was taken from me."

"Why was she taken from you?" Olivia asked.

Susan didn't speak for a moment, wavering over her next choice of words. "I—I don't know. I wasn't unfit. I was her mother!"

Lauren let out a cry of rage and began struggling hard against her bonds.

"Because she's a drunk," Lauren snapped, looking Olivia dead in the eye. "All she had to do was look after me. All she had to do was stay at home and make sure I was okay. All she had to do was stop drinking. But she used to leave me, all the time. She'd go out drinking. She'd leave me alone, hungry and in dirty diapers. I've heard it all over the years. Love didn't take me away from you, Mom. You just didn't know how to take care of me!"

"That's not true!" Susan cried out, trying to reach for Lauren's bound hands, but Lauren screamed at her and flinched away from her mother as much as she could.

"It's true," Lauren explained to Olivia, not even looking at her mother. "It took me a long time to believe it, too, trust me. I used to love her regardless of everything she was doing. Even after the divorce, I used to look forward to seeing her on our visits. She swore she got sober. She swore she was better. And then she took me to the seaside."

Olivia's mind was cast back to the photograph she'd seen of Lauren in the blue floral dress, grinning on the beach. But now, it seemed the day in the photograph had had more sinister undertones.

"What happened?" Olivia asked softly.

"I didn't mean to," Susan sobbed. "I went into the arcade to get cotton candy while Lauren was on the beach. I—I stopped for a drink. Just one..."

"And then another, and then another," Lauren snapped. "She couldn't stop herself. She drank herself silly. Collapsed in the middle of the arcade. And the worst part was, I was left all alone on the beach, not knowing what had happened to her. It started to get dark. I didn't know what to do. I was just a kid. I was only fourteen."

Silent tears of anger slid down Lauren's cheeks and she glared up at her mother. "You ruined it all. You did, Mom. I tried to forgive you, but I can't. All my friends grew up with normal moms," she growled. "All you ever did was let me down. And now we're here. How the hell are we here? You have to let me go, Mom. I'm not yours anymore."

Olivia's heart ached for both of them. Susan's lip quivered and her face clouded over. Olivia could see the torment in her eyes. It was as stark and vibrant as the fear in Lauren's.

"I tried," Susan sobbed. "I tried so hard to do the things my mom couldn't. I never wanted you to feel abandoned the way I did. I never knew what love was. I tried to give all of mine to you. But everything got broken. Screwed up. It's all still broken..."

"So, stop trying to fix it! No one is asking you to!" Lauren screeched. "Let me go, Mom, I want to go home!"

"You don't understand everything I went through," Susan sniffed, seemingly unable to process that her daughter was talking to her. "I grew up alone. All I had was a doll to keep me company. She was my only friend in the world. Didn't I try to give you a bigger world than that, baby? Didn't I try to make you happy? That's all I ever wanted, to make you happy. To make you love me back. I thought I could do it. I thought me and your father would be happy. I thought he could help me get better. But all he did was watch me drown. I was depressed. I couldn't cope. He just told me to get over myself, but I kept going to a dark place. Wasn't it better to leave you alone for a little while than to drag you down into the dark place with me?"

Olivia tightened her grip on the gun in her hand. She didn't know what to do, except let the pair of them talk. She didn't want to make any sudden moves and put Lauren in danger. She just had to keep them in conversation to buy some time. She tried to take a subtle step to the side. As if she were reading Olivia's mind though, Susan shot her a withering glare.

"I fought for you when I got sober," Susan cried. "I just wanted you. My baby girl. The only thing in the world that was worth living for. But the world was against me. They wanted to keep us apart. This was the only way I could get us back together. No one else was enough to replace you. Don't you understand? Don't you see how much I love you? And I kept trying once you turned eighteen, didn't I? I kept trying to get you to talk to me, but you kept rejecting me. I had to try to find some way to survive without you. Those lovely young girls—I took them thinking I could replace you. That I could have that love in my life you'd never give me. But they couldn't fill the hole in my heart. Only you can do that, lollipop. My heart only beats for you."

Lauren stared at her mother in disgust, as if she couldn't believe what her mother had become. As if she didn't recognize the woman standing in front of her. When she looked at Susan, Olivia saw a woman broken by her past, trying to fix her future. But everything she'd tried to do was *wrong*. So wrong. She swallowed.

"Susan, I can see how upset you are. I can see that you feel betrayed and alone," Olivia said softly. "But this isn't the answer. You can't keep your daughter here. You say you love her but look how badly you're scaring her. Look at what you're doing to your daughter, Susan."

"I'll do better this time. I swear it," Susan said, her voice high and shrill. "I've learned so much from the other girls. I know how to stop them from crying now. I hiked to them every single week to feed them and make sure they were okay. I thought about them night and day, cared for them as though they were my own. I was good to them. They were helping me prepare for this day—the day I had my little girl back."

Something struck a chord in Olivia. She recalled the first time she'd met Susan. She remembered how Susan had been hiking through the woods that day. She'd misdirected them, told them that she'd never seen any buildings in the woods. She'd lied to their faces over and over—just as she had in her police interview. She'd inserted herself into the investigation, giving herself the perfect alibi for when she was actually stealing Hayleigh away in the middle of the night. And then there was the brick through her window—was that just another misdirection? Another way to throw Olivia off the scent? To get out of town that night and carry out her plans for the girls?

"I know how to take care of a child. I never learned that from my own mother. So, I had to practice, you see. I had to make sure everything was perfect before I brought my Lauren here," Susan insisted, raising her voice another level. "And everything turned out fine this time. The girls are home safe now. I figured out in time that I didn't need them. I needed my daughter. And I can't get in trouble for being with my daughter, can I? She's an adult and can make her own decisions now. So, you don't need to shoot me, Olivia. You

off

274

can just walk away and pretend I was never here. You can just leave me here to love my daughter. As I should have done from the start."

"I don't want to shoot you. Not at all," Olivia said quietly. "But I do need to take you out of here. Lauren, too. We need to go."

"No. This is my safe haven. I can't ever leave," Susan said. Her eyes were bloodshot, tears streaming down her pale cheeks. She was a mess. "I was doing so well here. You wouldn't have ever found me, would you, Olivia? Not if I kept being careful. You see, Lauren? I learned to *take care*. Even if I do still drink. It's just a little nip once in a while. Just to keep me balanced and even. Olivia had no idea who was taking those young girls. I did a good job. I didn't leave a single clue behind. It was so easy. All I had to do was find girls like you and figure out a way into their homes. My neighbor practically begged me to take a key from her so I could pop around and look after her child all the time. She couldn't be bothered to do it herself, so I brought Hayleigh here and I took care of her instead. And that Sophia girl? She couldn't go a day without arguing with her awful mom. She was better off with me. They both were. It was so easy to take them away to somewhere better. To try and love them like my own. To practice how to be a mother in preparation for you, baby. Don't you see, Lauren? I did this all for you."

"What about Amelia Barnes?" Olivia asked. She needed to know, to understand. "I know you used to live in that house. How did you get in? How did you get all the way across the country with her, undetected?"

Susan gritted her teeth. "That was my house, once upon a time. We were going to start a new life in Seattle. I lived there with my husband and my darling daughter. We only lasted a few months there before my husband decided to destroy our lives and file for divorce. He sold the house cheap, shipped Lauren off to Baltimore, and left me with nothing. I deserved the same chance at happiness that that family got to have. The chance my husband took from me. I kept going back to that house over the years, just to watch those people playing in my *home.* I'd tried it before, with other girls from different places across the country. But I could never get it right. Not until her. I just knew I was going to take her. She was in my house. It was like destiny. Like it was meant to be."

"So, you took Amelia Barnes and drove her back to Belle Grove."

"I had to take her somewhere far away. Somewhere she could only depend on me," she said. "I was her mother. She was my little girl. But it didn't work. She wasn't my Lauren."

"And when that didn't work, you had to find more girls locally," said Olivia.

"I did what I had to do! I needed *someone,*" she roared. "I need to practice. To get ready for my Lauren. I needed to make sure I was a good mother. A worthy mother. And guess what? I am."

"But you let them go," Olivia said desperately. "You let the girls go because you knew it was wrong, didn't you?"

"They were better off with me. For a little while," Susan repeated, looking off into the distance. "But they didn't understand that. They didn't want me. They wanted their real moms as they kept saying. And I realized I didn't want *them.* I wanted my baby girl. And now I'm here—we're here. I'm sorry, Olivia, but she's never leaving. She's going to be here with me forever—in whatever form that takes. You're going to have to make a decision soon."

Olivia's heart thundered as she watched Susan raise the pistol and point it at her. Susan's lip was trembling.

"I'm not a killer, Olivia. I don't want to have to kill you. But if you don't leave us in peace, then you'll have to leave in a bag. If you don't leave me with my baby girl, I will kill you," she said. "Or force you to kill me first. If you take Lauren from me, then my life isn't worth living anyway. But do you really want that blood on your hands?"

Olivia wavered. She already felt as though her hands were drenched in blood. The blood of her mother and sister, whom she couldn't save. How was she supposed to walk away from Lauren now? Lauren would wind up dead if Olivia left her. Olivia knew that Susan thought her heart was in the right place, thought she could go back to being the happy mother and daughter they maybe were once.

But when that didn't work—and it wouldn't—what was Susan going to do? Not making it work with girls she kidnapped was one thing, but not being able to make it work with her real daughter, the woman she'd done all this for, was something else entirely. Lauren's inevitable rejection was bound to throw Susan over the edge. And that was going to make her dangerous. The rejection would be so sharp and painful for Susan, there was no telling what she was going to do. What Olivia did know was that it wouldn't be good for Lauren.

Olivia slowly lowered her gun. "I'm not going to hurt you, Susan. I want you to know that you can trust me."

She put the gun back into the holster on her belt and put the flashlight on the floor. Susan eyed her suspiciously.

"What are you doing?" she asked.

"I meant it when I said I just want to talk to you," Olivia said patiently. She felt naked without her gun in her hand, but she knew it was the only way she could level with Susan. To get her to relax. "I know you're hurting inside. I know you want your daughter back more than anything. But there's something that you should know. You're a mother. No matter what happens, you'll always be a mother. No matter where Lauren is, you carry a piece of her around in your heart. That's why you hid those things in the woods, isn't it? The doll, the teeth, the hair?"

Susan nodded slowly. "They're all I have left of her. That doll—it got me through my childhood. I gave it to Lauren, but she abandoned it when she got too old for dolls. It felt like the closest thing I had to her, though."

"But that's not true," Olivia whispered. "Because Lauren is a part of you. You've messed up. You've upset her and now she's pushed you away. And I know that hurts, but it doesn't change that she's your daughter. Do you ever… do you wish your mother hadn't left you?"

Susan's face clouded over with emotion and her arm began to tremble, her finger still on the trigger of the gun.

"Of course, I do," she whispered. "All I ever did was love her. I don't know why she left me behind..."

"But you still love her, even though she left you? Even though she hurt you?"

Susan hesitated before she nodded. Olivia took a deep breath.

"Lauren will always love you. You're her mother. But sometimes, children have to go away. They have to live their own lives. You weren't well when she was younger. If you want Lauren back—if you want Lauren to love you—this isn't the answer. You need to get better. You need to go somewhere where someone can help you. You can get better and then be a better mom to Lauren. And maybe, just maybe, when you're well, Lauren will let you be a part of her life again. But you need to do the work on yourself first."

Olivia knew now that Susan wasn't in her right mind. She'd be able to get help in prison, so long as she was sent to the right facility. This was her last chance to get Susan to comply with her. But she thought it was working. She saw the fight leaving Susan's eyes. She saw the tears return. She looked down at Lauren, still tied to the chair.

"Is that true?" she whispered. "If I get help, will you love me again? Will you come and see me after she takes me away?"

Olivia saw Lauren waver. It was a promise she clearly didn't want to make, but it was the only thing she could say that would save her life. Olivia silently willed her to say the right thing. To go along with her and walk through the door she opened. Lauren cut a glance at Olivia then turned back to her mom. She swallowed nervously then nodded slowly.

"Yes, Mom. If you get help, I'll come to see you. And... and I never stopped loving you. You've done things I might never be able to forgive, but I'll always love you. I can't help it. Like she said, you're my mother."

Tears flowed freely down Susan's cheeks. Olivia could see in her eyes that it was all over for her. The fight and the anger had gone. Susan's gun hit the floor with a loud clatter, making Olivia flinch. She leaned down and pressed a hard kiss to the top of Lauren's head and stroked her hair for a long moment, looking at her daughter with the purest love Olivia had ever seen. Then she turned to Olivia.

"You can take me now," she whispered. "That's all I needed to hear. All I ever needed to hear."

CHAPTER TWENTY-SEVEN

OLIVIA WOKE THE FOLLOWING MORNING FEELING STRANGE. She'd finally solved the case and thought she'd wake up with a sense of satisfaction and accomplishment. But she couldn't really describe how she felt. It wasn't satisfied or accomplished though. She could finally start to move on from all of the complicated feelings it had brought to her life. She'd managed to stop something awful happening to Lauren and she'd seen the three girls get home to their families safely. She knew she should be celebrating.

But somehow, she didn't feel like celebrating at all. She wanted nothing more than to stay in bed all day and mope around. Because nothing about carting Susan away felt good to her. After everything she'd found out in the cabin in the woods, all she felt was pity for Susan. She had clearly been through a lot in her life. It would never justify her actions, but it cast them in a new, sympathetic light. She was a lost soul desperately searching for something she lost. Something that, on some level, she had to know she'd never be able to have again.

Susan was being brought up on several counts of felony kidnapping and child endangerment—which she deserved. She would probably spend the rest of her life behind bars. And she wasn't sure Susan deserved that. She deserved help. She needed help. Olivia didn't want to think about how many girls she'd mistreated and hurt over the years. She didn't want to linger on the number of families Susan had torn apart. In fact, she didn't want to think about Susan at all. She just wanted her gone from her mind.

But it was never that simple in her job. In her life. Although she wanted to mope around all day, Olivia knew she shouldn't. Wouldn't let herself. So, by eight that morning, she was up, dressed, and decided to walk into town. A little exercise might help clear her mind. She knew that Brock would be in bed for a while longer, not passing up the chance for a well-deserved sleep-in. Olivia grabbed coffee at the diner, which was much busier than she'd seen it since the disappearances had started. She guessed that people weren't so scared anymore now that Susan was behind bars. Her usual waitress served her black coffee and gave her a blueberry muffin, insisting it was on the house.

She noticed that people's attitude to her had changed almost overnight. People waved to her, gave her a smile, and said good morning. People who had usually walked by her quickly when they'd seen her on the street now offered her a greeting. She saw it as their acceptance of her as one of their own, and she didn't know how to feel about that. Sure, she'd helped the town by catching the kidnapper. But she'd never done anything wrong, anything to earn their distrust and aloofness in the first place.

Belle Grove was a strange little place, but Olivia knew that now they'd accepted her. She was one of them. And she was just glad that she didn't have to feel so alienated anymore. She finished up her coffee and went for a walk around the town. She no longer had to worry that a kidnapper was lurking around every corner, which should have been a relief to her, but it strangely wasn't. She still couldn't believe Susan had fooled them all for so long. She was smart and clever, but

Olivia couldn't believe she hadn't seen just how close to the edge of madness she'd been the whole time.

Olivia found the story of her life to be pretty depressing. A sad story that led to a worse outcome. Abandoned by her mother as a child, growing up alone with nothing but a doll to keep her company, bouncing around the foster care system, and likely being abused herself. And somehow, she made it all the way through that. She'd climbed out of her own personal darkness only to inadvertently perpetuate the cycle of tragedy by falling into addiction herself then mistreating her own daughter.

Olivia couldn't understand why she was getting so sentimental. Susan wasn't a good person. Maybe she wasn't bad through and through, but she certainly wasn't just someone who'd taken one wrong turn. She'd taken a wrong turn once and then continued down the wrong path for the rest of her life. Perhaps half of what Susan had said wasn't even true. Maybe she was still manipulating her and lying as she had the entire time. Maybe she was even so far gone that she believed her own lies.

Now that she was in custody though, had given a full and complete confession to the kidnappings of Amelia, Sophia, and Hayleigh, and was going to plead guilty to her crimes, Olivia couldn't shake the pity she felt for the woman. Couldn't stop wishing that her life had taken a different turn somewhere along that dark and twisted road. Olivia wished that someone had just taken the time to love Susan the way she'd so desperately wanted. Perhaps then, she would have managed to stay on the right track. Maybe then, there wouldn't be countless girls and entire families out there bearing the scars she'd inflicted on them.

Susan only confessed to the three kidnappings but wouldn't speak to any others. Olivia didn't know if there were other victims out there. Didn't know if there were bodies out there—girls who didn't live up to the ideal of Lauren that Susan carried around. It seemed clear that she'd been at it, trying to recapture that love with her daughter, for a long time. But she wouldn't give them the names of any other victims. Olivia was sure there were others though.

Olivia shook her head to herself and began walking back to the cabin. She knew she was being ridiculous. She shouldn't be trying to see the good side of someone who had wreaked havoc upon so many people for so long. But no matter how she tried, she couldn't get Susan to leave her mind—or the feeling of pity she felt for her. When she got back to the cabin, she found Brock sitting on the porch waiting for her. He smiled at her as he stood up.

"I thought I'd stop by for one of your famously crappy cups of coffee," he teased. "They've really grown on me."

Olivia smiled. Having Brock around made her feel a little better already. But her happiness was short-lived as she opened the door and let him inside. She knew why he was there.

He'd come to say goodbye.

She watched him head into the kitchen and sighed to herself. She'd always known that her time with him was going to be short. He was only in town to help with the case and couldn't live in the B&B forever, after all. But the thought of his leaving made her feel hollow inside. Maybe she understood how Susan felt, after all. She'd talked about having a hole in her heart that only her daughter could fill. Olivia was used to having a gaping hole in her chest from all the things she'd lost and knew she'd never be able to replace. That hole in her heart would linger for the rest of her life. But with Brock around, she felt at least a little more complete, that hole in her heart not so big.

"You want a cup?" Brock asked as he prepared his own coffee.

Olivia leaned against the counter, raising her eyebrows. "You feel pretty comfortable here, don't you? Barging in here and stealing all my coffee the way you do."

Brock grinned at her. "Pretty much. I've come to think of it as a home away from home."

Olivia forced her smile to stay on her face. "Are you looking forward to going back to DC?"

Brock shrugged. "I guess. I've missed being able to eat in more than one diner, that's for sure. There's more to do in the city, it's a little livelier. More vibrant. But I think I might miss this place. I've met some great people during my time here. Others? Not so great—meaning Susan, of course."

Olivia offered him a small chuckle. She didn't really feel like joking about what had happened, though. It still felt raw. Brock noticed her moment of quietness and cocked his head to the side, an inscrutable expression on his face.

"Penny for your thoughts," he said.

Olivia sighed. "Susan. Just everything that happened to her… I feel sorry for her."

"You're too nice for this job, Knight."

"I know, I know. I'm being sentimental about someone who doesn't deserve any sympathy. I know she's the villain here, but I truly believe that she would've been a good person if things had gone just a little bit differently for her."

"Wouldn't we all be better people if we didn't suffer," Brock said, arching an eyebrow. "It's the curse of being human. We let our pasts either destroy us or build us into better people. She didn't learn from her mistakes. In fact, she built all those mistakes and made them worse. That's the difference between her and us. Don't dwell on it too long, Olivia. It's not worth it."

Olivia nodded, saying nothing. But in the back of her mind, she was still comparing herself to Susan. She thought about how devastated she'd been when her sister had died, and how hollow she'd felt after her mother had disappeared. If she'd let that grief take over the way Susan had, what kind of person would she have become?

If she'd lost a child of her own, even if only in a legal sense, would she have tipped over the edge Susan had thrown herself over as well? She knew that people inherently liked to consider themselves as good, but most of them had demons of their own. After everything Susan had gone through, it made sense to Olivia that she'd crumbled. She'd been close to doing the same several times. But she hadn't.

It was what they did with their grief and the choices they made in spite of it that set them apart. Olivia had chosen to continue fighting through her agony, and Susan had succumbed to it. And seeing what had become of Susan, Olivia felt even more determined than ever that she wouldn't end up that way, no matter what happened in her life. She vowed to herself that no matter how dark the circumstances, she would never take the path Susan had. She would never give in to her grief and pain.

"What's next for you?" Brock asked Olivia, sipping his coffee. "Are you finally going to un-tense your shoulders? Maybe take a few days off? Maybe read Jane Eyre for the three thousandth time?"

"Maybe," Olivia grinned softly at his jibe and shrugged. "I don't know. I always get a weird feeling at the end of a case. Almost like Spring Break has arrived, but it's forecast to rain the whole time. Does that make sense?"

"Total sense," Brock nodded with a sad smile. "I know these cases tend to linger on your mind, but this is in the past now. It's not your responsibility anymore. You can lay that burden down, Olivia."

"I know. And I will eventually," she replied. "I guess I just tend to overthink."

"I know you do," Brock said.

His voice was gentle and Olivia noticed then how close together they were standing. Brock's eyes met hers for a split second, but then he averted his gaze as though he'd said something awkward.

"Brock?"

"Mmm?"

"You never told me—you never told me which case stuck with you the most," Olivia said.

She recalled how he'd closed himself off to her the day she'd asked him that same question. She had hoped he'd open up to her before he left her forever. Kind of like a parting gift. Brock chewed his lip.

"I think that's a tale for another day," he said.

"But we don't have another day," Olivia whispered.

A smile formed on Brock's face. "What are you talking about?"

"Well, you'll be going back to the city. We probably won't see each other again."

"Olivia, it's Washington, DC, not Mars," Brock laughed. "I'm only an hour away."

"But are you seriously going to want to trek all the way down here to see me in your spare time?" she asked. "Or invite me to see you? We're partners, but I'm sure you have plenty of friends who keep you occupied."

Brock nudged Olivia with his elbow. "You're going to miss me, aren't you?"

"I didn't say that."

"Didn't need to. It's written all over your face. Look at those puppy dog eyes!" Brock stuck out his bottom lip, pouting then crowed in a horrible falsetto, *"Please don't leave, Brock, I'll miss you so, so much…"*

She rolled her eyes and folded her arms over her chest, a familiar mix of irritation and affection washing over her.

"You never stop, do you?" she asked. "You're the most pompous man I've ever met."

"Pompous? What an honor," Brock cracked, winking at her as he sipped his coffee. "Pompous? You have gotta stop reading those dusty old British books. Who says pompous anymore?"

Olivia rolled her eyes again but finally offered him a smile. He set his cup to one side and placed his hands on Olivia's shoulders and let his eyes linger on hers for a long moment.

"Look, I know it's weird that I'm leaving and you're going to be on your own here again. But we are friends, Olivia," he said. "You don't need a reason to come to see me, and I definitely have a few reasons to come back here sometime. This isn't the end of us, Olivia. And someday, I'll tell you all my deepest, darkest secrets. How about that?"

Olivia couldn't help but smile. She had been so scared that Brock would go away that she'd never really considered the idea that it might be okay if he did. They didn't have to part ways forever just because he was leaving town. She was so used to the idea that everything good in her life left her life that the thought of Brock's being within an hour's drive of her—and that he wanted to see her again—seemed almost too good to be true. But she had to start believing that life wasn't all bad, that there were good things in her world, or she'd end up like Susan. She had to start looking for the bright side and the silver linings in life.

And Brock was a good place to start.

"I'm going to miss you, Agent Knight," Brock said with a smile, reaching out and ruffling her hair.

Olivia ducked away from his hand with a laugh, but unintentionally, she moved closer to him as she did. Their eyes locked for a moment and Olivia held her breath. Was his heart racing as hard as hers was? Was he thinking of kissing her as much as she was thinking of kissing him? She wanted to reach out, to pull him closer to her and feel his lips against hers. She'd been thinking about it for a long time, but now, they were closer than ever to its actually happening.

The moment seemed to last a lifetime, but when Brock smiled at her and took a step back, Olivia knew it wasn't going to happen. He skirted around the edge of the kitchen and walked toward the front door.

"Come on. Let's go," he said.

"Go where?"

"I'm sure I promised you and Maggie a round of drinks when we finished up with the case, didn't I?" he asked. "Well, the case is finished, so…"

"It's not even ten in the morning yet!"

"So? Time and tide wait for no one," Brock replied with a wolf-ish smile. "Let me get you a beer, Olivia. We deserve it."

Olivia tutted. "All right. I'm not much of a day drinker but today I'll make an exception."

As Brock let out a whoop and headed out the front door, Olivia allowed herself a second to let the heaviness of the moment sit on her chest. She felt as though she'd been rejected, and it sucked. But the sun outside was shining, she had someone new to call a friend, and she'd just solved the hardest case of her career. Life was good, and she had to remember that.

Life was better than it had been in a very long time.

EPILOGUE

I T WAS A QUIET SUNDAY MORNING AND OLIVIA WAS SITTING alone on her porch, reading *Wuthering Heights*. She'd had a lot more time to read since the kidnapping case had ended. It felt strange to be so relaxed, even two weeks later, but she had to admit, she could get used to long, warm mornings on her patio with her coffee and a good book.

She'd never read *Wuthering Heights* before, but it seemed the perfect book to follow up her case. The descriptions of the wild moors reminded her of her time in the forest, and she wasn't quite ready to leave the case behind yet. She'd learned a lot from it, and she wanted to remember the mistakes she'd made. She was glad it was over, but as more time passed, she felt herself itching for something new to sink her teeth into.

It didn't help that she'd spent the past two weeks mostly alone. She'd updated Paxton and Blake about the case on a video call, managed a phone call with her father, and visited some friends in DC. She'd posted about her visit on social media, hoping that perhaps

Brock would see it and try to get together with her while she was in the city. But if he'd seen it, he hadn't mentioned it or reached out.

Olivia hadn't heard from him since he'd left town. She was starting to think that maybe he hadn't meant it when he'd said they'd stay in touch. Maybe she and her small town were just more easily forgotten than he'd imagined. Perhaps he was already on a new case with a new partner. Perhaps he simply just wasn't interested in seeing her again.

She worried that maybe she'd messed it up during their moment in the kitchen when she'd been certain they were going to kiss. She'd known that trying to mix business with pleasure was a mistake from the start. Starting a romantic relationship with a co-worker was never a good idea. But then again, their case and partnership were in the past now. They weren't partners anymore, so what was stopping them?

Perhaps the fact that he isn't interested, Olivia thought.

She closed her book with a sigh and a stitch in her heart. Her thoughts always seemed to circle back to the things she couldn't have. Brock. Answers to her questions about her mother's disappearance and her sister's death. Peace and a quiet mind. She closed her eyes and tuned into the forest. At least it didn't scare her anymore. She'd faced the scariest thing the woods had to offer and had come out okay.

Susan was due to stand trial soon. Three families had been glued back together after the end of the case. Olivia often saw Hayleigh and Sophia walking around town, their arms linked as they giggled together, managing to return to something of a normal life. She envied them. At least they had each other. Most days, Olivia still felt she was on her own. She drank coffee each day at the diner without Brock to keep her company. She made small talk in the streets with the locals, and occasionally chatted with Maggie when she passed the police station. But she kept thinking about what Susan had told her.

"I'm not a bad person, Olivia. I'm just lonely. So lonely…"

Olivia shuddered at the memory. Was loneliness the thing that tipped so many people over the edge, onto the path toward chaos? Olivia didn't want to think about that. She didn't want to believe that this was her life now. That she'd simply wander alone, feeling useless, feeling as though everyone she came to care for was still at arm's length or just gone altogether.

The loneliness she felt was painful, like a constant stitch in her side. She wanted to feel that she had someone close by. Someone who cared about her. Someone who would always be there for her. But she had nobody like that. She scanned the forest, knowing there was nothing but wilderness out there. She never imagined that that would make her feel so isolated that she might as well have been the last person on Earth.

At least, she felt that way until she heard the sound of a car trundling up the road toward her cabin. Olivia stood and walked around to the front of the house to see who was arriving. She still didn't get many visitors, even after she'd been accepted by the town. Her first thought was that it might be Brock—it would be typical of him to just show up out of the blue—but it wasn't his car, it was Maggie's. She waved cheerily out of her open window as she approached the cabin. Olivia waved back, glad for a distraction from her own thoughts no matter what form it took.

"Hey!" Maggie called out. "How are you, Olivia?"

"Good! The weather helps," Olivia said a little stiffly. She'd never been good at small talk. "How are you?"

"Another lovely day in Belle Grove, thank you! Are you busy today? There's a new tenant moving into town. I tend to go and introduce myself when we get new people, just to make them feel at home! Make people feel they can trust their local police force and know they're safe, you know? Anyway, I thought you could come, too! Especially now that you're sort of a local celebrity and all."

Olivia blushed. It was true, she'd definitely gotten a lot more attention since she'd managed to catch Susan. She was probably the most exciting new addition to Belle Grove in years—which wasn't saying much, given that nothing ever happened in Belle Grove. But she shook her head slowly.

"Oh, I don't know," she said. "I doubt they'll want me to be disturbing them as they're getting settled in. But thanks for the invite."

"I insist, Olivia! It won't take longer'n two shakes!" Maggie said with a smile that told Olivia it was non-negotiable.

Olivia forced a smile in return. "All right. Give me just a minute to lock up."

A few minutes later, the pair of them were cruising through the town, the windows down and the wind in their hair. It did lift Olivia's spirits a little, she had to admit. When Maggie parked in the lot beside the diner, she nodded to the building.

"Our new resident moved into the apartment above the diner. It wasn't the hottest piece of real estate in town, but apparently, he knew what he was after. Come on. Let's go say hello."

Olivia followed Maggie around the back of the building and up the set of stairs to the private entrance, trying to prepare her best smile and small talk for the new neighbor. She knew that at least it wouldn't take long. Then she could head back to her book and self-pity on the patio.

Maggie knocked on the door. Loud music was playing inside the apartment, and Olivia wrinkled her nose at it. It reminded her of the day she met Brock and he'd had the loud music playing from his car radio. Then the door swung open and she felt like she'd been punched in the gut and had the air driven from her lungs.

"Glad you could make it, ladies," Brock said with a grin, opening his arms in a grand gesture. "Welcome to my humble abode!"

Olivia's jaw dropped. She couldn't believe he was there.

"Wh—what are you doing here?" she exclaimed.

He grinned back at her. "Couldn't stay away. I saw an opening on the market a week ago, and I couldn't resist. I packed up and hurried down here. Now you'll never get rid of me."

Olivia couldn't hold back her excitement. She rushed forward and threw her arms around Brock, feeling his chest rising and falling as he laughed at her. It was so unlike her to be that affectionate, but all the gloominess inside her had disappeared the moment she'd seen him. It felt like clouds parted and sunshine rained down upon the world.

"I'll leave you two to catch up," Maggie said with a knowing look in their direction. "And for this little stunt, I'll be expecting another drink, Tanner."

"You got it," Brock chuckled.

As she left, Olivia composed herself, pulling away from Brock. Her cheeks were flushed as she looked him up and down.

"I can't believe you're here," she said again.

Brock shrugged, his face split into a grin. "Well, I was driving back to the city two weeks ago and I don't know what happened. It felt like I was leaving a piece of my soul here. Even after everything that happened, even after the hardest case I've ever worked, I just wanted to be in Belle Grove. Don't ask me why; I couldn't tell you."

"You missed me," Olivia teased, pretending to punch his arm.

Brock rolled his eyes, but he was still smiling. "Well, I couldn't leave you here alone. You'd fall apart without me," he shot back. "But I'm here to stay. At least for a while. I've got nowhere else I want to be."

"You won't miss DC? You don't want to be in the thick of it all?"

"I guess I didn't love it as much as I'd thought I did. Maybe I'm getting old and am mellowing in that old age. Maybe I need the snoozy small-town feeling back. Although I've yet to have a dull day here, let's be honest," he said. "And I'll admit, I'll miss the city coffee. But it's free when I have it at your place. Oh, and that reminds me..."

He darted back to the kitchen and returned with a box that held coffee maker and a bag of coffee grounds in his hands. "This is for you. I can't believe someone who guzzles down a whole pot a day sticks to instant. Friends don't let friends drink bad coffee."

Olivia blushed at the thought of Brock's standing in her kitchen as he had so many times before, complaining about the standard of her coffee and teasing her endlessly about it. She imagined having that feeling indefinitely—but with better coffee, thanks to his wonderful thoughtfulness and it felt impossibly good. She took a deep breath, her cheeks hurting as she smiled at him.

"I'm glad you're back," she said.

Brock's eyes crinkled in the corner as his smile widened. "Me, too, Knight. And hey, I guess we'll be partners again, now that we're both living in this neck of the woods. Though it's all been pretty quiet on Jonathan's end. Almost seems like the criminals are on vacation or something."

As if on cue, Olivia's phone began to vibrate in her pocket and she looked up at him. "Thanks for jinxing it."

When she checked the screen, it was none other than SAC James. She hadn't heard much from him since she and Brock had solved the case, but she sensed that she was about to receive her next assignment. Brock's eyes glinted with excitement. He was obviously ready for anything.

"Well, you'd better get that," he said. "It's about time we got the team back together."

Olivia smiled and took a deep breath then answered the call.

AUTHOR'S NOTE

Thank you for reading *New Girl in Town*! We hope you enjoyed the first book in the Olivia Knight FBI Series. Our intention is to give you thrilling adventures and an entertaining escape with each and every book. However, we need your help to continue writing this new series.

Being new indie writers is tough. We don't have a large budget, huge following, or any of the cutting edge marketing techniques. So, all we kindly ask is that if you enjoyed this first book in the Olivia Knight series, please take a moment of your time and leave us a review and maybe recommend the book to a fellow book lover or two. This way we can continue to write all day and night and bring you more books in the Olivia Knight series. We cannot wait to share with you the upcoming sequel!

Your writer friends,
Elle Gray | K.S. Gray

P.S. Feel free to reach out to us at mailto:egray@ellegraybooks. com with any feedbacks, suggestions, typos or errors you find so that we can take care of it!

ALSO BY
ELLE GRAY | K.S. GRAY

Olivia Knight FBI Mystery Thrillers

Book One - New Girl in Town

Book Two - The Murders in Beacon Hill

Book Three - The Woman Behind the Door

ALSO BY
ELLE GRAY

Blake Wilder FBI Mystery Thrillers

Book One - The 7 She Saw

Book Two - A Perfect Wife

Book Three - Her Perfect Crime

Book Four - The Chosen Girls

Book Five - The Secret She Kept

Book Six - The Lost Girls

Book Seven - The Lost Sister

Book Eight - The Missing Woman

Book Nine - Night at the Asylum

A Pax Arrington Mystery

Free Prequel - Deadly Pursuit

Book One - I See You

Book Two - Her Last Call

Book Three - Woman In The Water

Book Four - A Wife's Secret

Printed in Great Britain
by Amazon